ALIEN CHILD

To Colleen Close,
Best wishes on your
life journey
Mona Lee

Alien Child

by Mona Lee

a **SNOW SHADOW** book
from *OPEN HAND PUBLISHING INC.*
Seattle, Washington

a **SNOW SHADOW** book
from *OPEN HAND PUBLISHING INC.*
P. O. Box 22048
Seattle, Washington 98122-0048
206-323-2187 • 206-323-2188 FAX
E-MAIL: openhand@jps.net
www.openhand.com

Design and production:
Deb Figen, ART & DESIGN SERVICE
Seattle, Washington • 206-725-2892
E-MAIL: artdesign@jps.net

Library of Congress
Cataloging-in-Publication Data
Lee, Mona, 1939-
   Alien Child / Mona Lee.
      p.   cm.
   ISBN 0-940880-62-8
   I. Title.
PS3562.E358A79   1999   98-54879
813'.54--dc21   CIP

FIRST EDITION
Printed in the United States of America
02 01 00 99   4 3 2 1

To my children, Dana and Erik

Glossary of Gallatan Words

cuerin	• An energy producing compound
diverra bone	• The metallic structure which forms the central portion of the Gallatan's brain and is capable of broadcasting thought waves
erely	• A Gornian animal used in genetic experiments, biologically similar to an earth sheep
Gallata	• A temperate planet with many islands and no large continental land masses
gla	• The eighth letter of the Gallatan alphabet designating a soft nasal sound
Gornia	• A small rural island on Gallata
grundgin	• A large land animal with spines and a thick exoskeleton
Jorka	• A Severelian computer
Korba-3	• The Intergalactic Federation's catalog number for planet Earth
kuda	• A fat, fluffy species of fowl
kuderein	• A clean compound used for heat and power-generation; burns only in combination with phoorea
krizzlut	• A biodegradable transparent wrapping material
luf	• The fortieth letter of the Gallatan alphabet, designating a gentle hum emitted through closed lips
madden fowl	• A domesticated bird, similar in habit and taste to chicken
mondathar	• A measure of distance comparable to two kilometers
Niso	• A cluster of galaxies with many planets inhabited by people cognizant of one another
neuta	• A small slippery animal with shiny skin
phoorea	• The chemical catalyst required to burn kuderein
Severelia	• One of Gallata's larger islands, site of a scientific research center
Shavinda	• A teacher of small children
Shiemacum	• The Gallatan space vessel with cryogenics, used for transgalactic scientific expeditions
skieron	• A sleeping pouch made of erely fleece
Sollia	• A small, rural Gallatan island
suncycle	• The Gallatan day
thoriemacum	• The transparent cylindrical conveyance used to board the Shiemacum
zajadc	• The customary Gallatan gesture of welcome and friendship; to grasp one another's forearms while touching foreheads together
yot	• third letter of the Gallatan alphabet designating a crisp, high-pitched tone

Part One: CONCEPTION & INFANCY

SAN JUAN ISLANDS ~ APRIL 13, 1967

She lay on her back in the cold, wet grass and gazed up through a cloud break into the infinite darkness. The *Shiemacum* had disappeared, but the ground still shook from its ascent. All her people were gone now. She was alone.

The spaceship's journey had been long, its stay on the planet brief. Everyone had worked to prepare Wella's home in a single Earth night.

The parting ceremony had been conducted with customary Gallatan intensity. The group meditation, which evoked a powerful collective trance, focused on the loneliness everyone would feel without Wella. Then the members of the crew zajaded by pressing their foreheads against hers, entered the thoreimacum to be elevated into the *Shiemacum*, and were gone. She might never see her own kind again. She might die before they could come to take her home. Wella questioned the Center's wisdom in selecting her for this experiment in a remote, barbaric world. She had always lived on a highly civilized planet, doted upon by loved ones, a member of a small island clan. How could she face an alien world alone?

Shulmina of Severelia had been last to go aboard. She had lingered barechested in the rain, her ample Severelian skirt rustling softly in the wind, her gray eyes glowing with their own mysterious light. "It will be difficult to overcome the pull of Gallatan mores and beliefs, but you must do so. Otherwise you won't remain long enough to bear a child and find it a home." Then she too had zajaded and disappeared into the thoreimacum.

The rain had stopped, but Wella's bare arms and chest were slightly chilled. Her damp skirt clung to her legs as she rose and walked to the top of the knoll where the erelies still grazed. Silhouetted there were the gables of the farm house and the large animal shelter, with a small, briar-choked stand of timber behind them. To think of owning this! Prior to her Earth training, she had never heard of "owning" land. She had always assumed that planetary surfaces belonged to the infinite universe.

She ran down to the farmhouse and walked all around it, checking the outer walls and windows for damage from the minor quake precipitated by the *Shiemacum*'s departure. One of the four pillars supporting the porch roof had loosened, so she pushed it back into place. Dry flakes of paint peeled off into her hands.

She sat down on the rickety wooden steps and looked across the inlet to the larger island. Several lights had come on in the village of Klahowya Cove. The Earth humans were very near.

Wella leaned against the railing and closed her eyes, focusing on her breathing until it came slowly, rhythmically. Then she rested her mind in a state of blue stillness, allowing the free flow of electrical charges into her brain by way of the diverra bone in the middle of her forehead. The fearful thoughts began to settle like grains of sand in a pool of water. Her eyes closed gently; her mind merged with the light and floated into the universe.

. . .

Emerging from trance, Wella thought the weather must have changed. She felt warm and was aware of a strange odor. She heard distant voices, tough and aggressive! She opened her eyes, but could not tell where the sounds were coming from. Then a small form appeared above the bank, just up from the beach. It was a human, shouting orders to someone below. Two long, serpentine strands of something crawled up the bank behind him.

Noticing that the dock was inhabited by a larger boat beside her own small one, Wella froze in fear and fascination as several other persons, small by Gallatan standards, appeared on the beach shouting frantically and struggling with something. Then they all began running up the lawn toward her with the two long strands still following.

In the dim light of dawn, Wella could not make out their features, but she could tell the humans wore almost identical clothing — heavy boots, and some kind of bulky robes trimmed in brilliant light. They seemed to have pointed heads from which wings, or perhaps ears, protruded on either side.

Suppressing the impulse to run and hide in the tunnel, Wella waited on the porch step, watching. Apparently no one had noticed her yet. Maybe it would be safer to know what these aliens were thinking; Shulmina had assured her it would be all right to use her telepathic abilities for survival. Still, she was reluctant to intrude upon unsuspecting minds. The humans were almost close enough to touch, when they turned abruptly and headed for the erely sheep grazing on the knoll. There they stopped simultaneously, as if guided by one collective thought, and their faces suddenly became visible, illuminated by an unknown light source at the back of the house. Their unstable shadows expanded, contracted, and danced to the erratic rhythm of moving light and sound — a crackling noise like crumpled krizzlut wrappings — coming from the same source as the light.

The Earth humans ran toward the sound and disappeared behind the house. Fear and morbid interest vied for possession of Wella as she stood, paused briefly, and then ran, not away from the invaders, but after them.

As soon as she rounded the corner of the house, Wella stopped short, frozen in wonder. There stood her magnificent animal house, engulfed by a great monster of leaping yellow flames. The inferno illuminated the surrounding meadow and belched black pungent clouds into the atmosphere. Great Mother Universe! This was a wood fire! In Earth training, she had learned about the primitive energy source and the dangers of it getting out of control. The snakelike things were hoses, which the Earth humans were using to spray water on the flames in hopes of suffocating them. White clouds of steam billowed into the sky, hissing and mingling with the smoke.

Suddenly, the fire-giant emitted a dreadful scream, and the barn's main support wall tumbled into the monster's belly. The flames were so hot, they would have soon spread to the main house if the uninvited humans had not arrived so quickly. Someone from the tiny village of Klahowya Cove, just across the inlet, must have noticed the fire and gathered the others together by a prearranged system of responding to poorly controlled fires.

The Earth humans were busy moving the hoses; no one seemed to have noticed Wella. She was considering whether she should speak out when she was startled by someone speaking to her from behind.

"You must be Miss De Gornia, the new owner," stated a clear male voice.

Turning, Wella saw a small person clothed — like all the others — in what she now took to be special garb for those controlling fires. The grotesque shape of the Earth humans' heads was an illusion created by the fire controllers' helmets. This man carried something under his arm, some kind of heavy, folded cloth.

Wella was surprised to find herself smiling at the joke her fear and ignorance had played on itself. Besides, it felt pleasantly odd to be greeted by name in such a bizarre situation by so alien a being.

"Yes, I am Wella De Gornia."

"We didn't know you were here yet. You must have come recently in your boat. Have you moved in permanently?"

Wella tried to make out the man's features, but the helmet still hid a lot of his face. He kept looking down at his feet.

"Yes, I've come to stay, but some of my things will arrive later from the mainland."

Still looking at his boots, the man shuffled uncomfortably. Then he made a throat clearing sound and offered the large piece of cloth to Wella. "I think you better borrow this blanket awhile to put over your shoulders, Miss De Gornia."

Wella regarded the cloth in bewilderment. It was heavy and cumbersome, like a primitive sleeping skieron. How could he ask her to wear such a thing? The heat from the fire was overwhelming. Maybe this was some local welcoming ritual. She took the blanket and draped it clumsily over her shoulders.

Brightening, the man looked at her face and smiled. Though small by Gallatan standards, his eyes were full of kindness. "Welcome to the Islands. Sorry about your barn. We thought it was the house at first, but we didn't know you were in it. Sure glad it wasn't the house, or you."

"I am also glad," agreed Wella.

The man nodded. "I'd better get to work." He pivoted on heavy boots and headed for the ruins of the barn where the others were systematically disassembling what was left of it. Wella carefully studied their use of Earth tools such as rakes, shovels, and axes. She had been introduced to these instruments in training. All the while, she listened intently, trying to make sense of seemingly random bits of conversation.

"I put in beans last week, but the crows ate them."

"You need to use some chicken wire."

"Ruth says business is picking up down at the docks."

"Tourist season's starting early this year in spite of the war."

"Weather's been good."

Wella shivered at the references they made to their institutionalized killing games.

"Harvey Rutherford's nephew, Mike, went down in a chopper last week. Did you hear about that?"

"Yeah, I read it in the Times. Nice kid, they say. Too bad."

"Yeah, my nephew, Billy, got his draft notice last week. Guess he'll be going soon."

Eventually, the group appeared to make a collective decision to stop working even though a rather large mess of smoking ashes still remained. Without a word, they gathered up the equipment and headed back down the lawn. Wella followed them to their boat and watched them wind the great hoses over a large spool. All the while, Wella had to tug, pull, and stumble over the blanket, wondering when it would be culturally acceptable to return it. The man had used the word "borrow" which certainly meant that, at some juncture, she would give it back.

Finally, the man came and stood in front of her again. "I'm glad we had the chance to meet you so soon, Miss De Gornia. I only wish it would have been under more fortunate circumstances. Sorry you lost your barn. Good thing it was insured. It's hard telling what causes a fire like that, but it probably had something to do with the earthquake. You know, we had a minor tremor this morning. Three point on the Richter Scale, the weatherman said. By the way, I'm Jim Krandle. All these folks are neighbors from Klahowya Cove."

Several of the others gathered around, peering curiously at Wella from under their visors.

One very small person with a soft voice said, "Welcome to the neighborhood. I'm Pamela Bradley. We'll be seeing you again." Smiling she removed an oversized glove and proffered a tiny hand. Wella had practiced the Earth custom in her training. But, now, trying it for the first time in real life, she realized how good it felt. A handshake was not as powerful or intimate as a zajade, but Wella sensed a brief fusion of spirits as she let go of the blanket to shake the stranger's hand. But the mood changed dramatically when the blanket dropped from her shoulders and fell to the ground. Instantly the smile faded from Pamela Bradley's face.

Her lower jaw dropped, and her mouth remained slightly ajar. For a painful moment everyone stared silently at Wella.

Jim Krandle opened his mouth as if to speak, but no words came out. In that instant Wella caught an accidental telepathic glimpse of her own appearance from Jim's viewpoint. He felt intimidated by her height and by the eyes which reminded him of huge dragonfly wings. Mostly, he was fascinated by her small, firm breasts. That was it! The bare chest, one of North America's strongest taboos for women. Wella quickly seized the blanket and wrapped it around her shoulders again, but it was too late. The damage was done.

One by one, the natives turned their embarrassed eyes from her and walked up the dock.

As their boat pulled away, Wella sat down on the dock to consider her blunder. Short term memory was one of Wella's weakest mental abilities, but she had assiduously memorized the list of North American taboos, arranged in the order of the Arabic alphabet. "A" — asking direct questions about the true feelings of others. "B" — boasting or speaking too openly about one's achievements. "N" — nudity, even in warm and moderate weather…. It had been of no use to memorize the list. She would not remember it in times of crisis.

Shulmina had warned her to maintain concentration and stay in the state of blue stillness at such times. Shulmina had stressed that Wella must dispel her own Gallatan taboo about invading the privacy of other people's thoughts. Telepathy was the one advantage she would have in this alien world where most people denied its existence. Wella recalled Shulmina explaining that when Earth humans accidentally transfer thoughts, they deny, even to themselves, what they have done. Wella must never admit to anyone that she was capable of mental telepathy in any form. Earth humans would assume she was afflicted with psychosis, a mental disorder in which electrochemical impulses of the Earth human brain become overstimulated and disconnected. Wella had practiced during training and could maintain the state of blue stillness even now, despite terrible distractions. In her next encounter with the Earth humans, she would make a concerted effort to spy on their thoughts.

THE SAME MORNING

Wella rose, ran up the lawn, and trudged around to the back of the house. Below the stone foundation was a small wooden door. She crouched low to reach the handle and open it.

At the back of the cellar was a tunnel which had been installed by the *Shiemacum* crew during the single night of its stay on the island. The passage, which could also be reached through a manhole cover in the woods, was filled with Gornish supplies, mostly functional manufactured goods and foodstuffs in insulated canisters.

Resting on the wooden table that the crew had brought down from the attic, Jorka looked like an ordinary globe lamp. Then Wella turned a knob at the base, and a display of purple flames flickered within, activating Jorka's self-regenerating energy source. It was comforting to view a safe cuerin flame after her recent experience with the terrifying wood fire.

She rotated the globe, locking Jorka's mind into the English speaking position. She might as well forget Gornish and the common speech. She wouldn't be using them for many sun cycles to come.

Wella sat down on a large canister and began fingering the letters at the base of the globe. Her words appeared in the transparent sphere as Jorka's pleasant voice spoke them aloud.

"Today is April 13, 1967 in Earth time. It is early morning on the planet Earth at longitude 48.5 degrees, latitude 123 degrees on Levin Island among the San Juan Islands of North America. A few clouds are crossing the sky from north to south. The large animal house was destroyed by flames which were extinguished by Earth humans." The phrase "animal house" disappeared and was replaced by "barn." Jorka was programmed to perfect her English usage.

"Acknowledged," answered Jorka. "Have you any questions?"

"Why was I chosen for this mission?"

There was a long pause. Jorka always needed more time to process "why" questions. Finally she said, "You tested higher than any other candidate on collective consciousness control, farseeing, and thought transference. The Anthropological Research Center desires to test the effect of your genetic strain upon Earth humans. You, yourself, are a test of the success of Gallata's most recent advances in genetic engineering. We are trying to determine whether, since your surgery, you will be able to mate and breed with an Earth human male, and transfer your Gallatan intuitive abilities to a logic and sensory-bound species."

Wella grinned. She could have predicted Jorka's response word for word, having heard it often enough during training. She wrinkled her brow trying to think of a way to word her objection in the form of a question. Jorka was programmed to give directives and answer questions, not to argue. Finally she asked, "What about memory, intelligence, endurance, and ability to withstand loneliness? Have I proven strong enough in those?"

This time Jorka's response was immediate and absolute. "Every Gallatan woman is strong enough for any mission the Center might assign."

Wella shrugged and smiled. She might have predicted that answer as well. She tapped in, "Is it all right to spy on Earth human thoughts?"

"You are advised to do so, if you sense danger to you or to your mission, or when you urgently need to communicate with someone who cannot hear your voice. You may use all your mental abilities on Earth in accordance with Gallatan standards of respect."

Wella shrugged again. Shulmina had once told her that she might as well forget all the points of her training and simply use good judgment in every situation. "Instructions, please. Include 'Daily Chores'."

"Daily Chores: Feed madden fowl, gather eggs, collect greens, make contact with erelies." The words remained in the globe a few minutes before they vanished and were replaced by, "Today's errands: Travel by boat to Orca Harbor on Merrick Island. Introduce yourself to a Mr. James Krandle at Island Realty, 310 Pine Street. Sign insurance documents requesting funds to replace the barn."

Wella stared at the instructions in awe. Since her first introduction to the Jorka at the Center, Wella had suspected the computer to be mischievously psychic, as were many of her programmers. Jorka always seemed to know what Wella felt most reluctant to do, and assigned that very task. Wella couldn't bear the thought of facing the Earth humans so soon after their first ill-fated encounter. She was tempted to disobey the computer. Who would know? Wella replaced the tunnel entrance carefully, so that it appeared to be a section of the stone cellar wall. Then she rubbed her fingers along the crevices between the real and simulated stones to make sure they still sealed properly after the quake. It was perfect. Beaming her appreciation of the clever *Shiemacum* technicians, she went outside to contact the erelies, who were grazing on the knoll.

She sat cross-legged on the lawn and returned her mind to the state of blue stillness. Within moments, her consciousness was merged with the collective mind of the flock. She could feel the electrochemical impulses from the diverra bone in her forehead creating a powerful fusion of all thought within the limits of its field. Thus was created the singular collective thought of erelies grazing contentedly, just as they had grazed — calmly, without comprehension — while watching the dramatic destruction of their barn. Erelies were simple animals. It was easy to merge with such uncomplicated minds.

Wella merged her mind with the contentedness of their grazing and then instilled in the mind of the lead ewe an image of the ewe walking over to Wella. Immediately acting upon that thought, the ewe trotted over and stood beside her. The rest of the flock quickly followed, forming a semicircle around the seated woman. Still maintaining the relaxed contemplation, Wella transferred to their collective consciousness the image of a fence around the lawn, clearly circumscribing their grazing area for the day. She kept the visual thought suspended long enough to assure its complete emulsification before she broke contact. Finally she opened her eyes and began patting their curly, yellow fleece lovingly. "Good erelies," she praised. "That was very good."

Wella left the erelies, completely confident they would stay on the lawn until she mind-spoke with them again. She had won many honors on Gallata for her skill in moving flocks by collective consciousness control. She was an expert at it, possibly better than any herdswoman Gallata had ever known. Persuading a few animals to stay in a small, grassy field was nothing compared with causing five hundred erelies to group in the formation of the Gallatan letter *yot* and then regroup in a *luf*. That feat had won Wella the interisland championship and had interested the Center in her as a possible subject for genetic experimentation in under-civilized worlds.

· · ·

There was very little furniture in the farmhouse, but one room upstairs contained a dingy wall mirror and a musty trunk left by former inhabitants. Wella's clothing, still in travel wrappings, was stored in the trunk. She carefully appraised her cloudy image to determine what would make it look more Earth human. After all, her mission was to mate and bear a child, so she must appear attractive by Earth standards. The long, flowing black hair should be contained, perhaps in a braid. The Gallatan woven skirt and sandals would pass. Wella had viewed many sight-scans of Earth women in similar attire. On Gallata, skirts of such length and fluidity were worn mostly by men. Wella thought she appeared rather masculine in the garment and wondered why she had never seen a scan of an Earth male wearing anything but those ugly leg-sleeves. The Center had provided Wella with a pair of stiff, blue leg-sleeves called "jeans," supposedly Earth's most popular garment for both sexes, but Wella found them miserable and planned never to wear them. Her favorite Earth garment was a soft, white blouse that buttoned in front. Wella watched her image in the mirror, as one long arm pulled a sleeve of the blouse over the other. She watched her face flush as she recalled how absurd she must have looked to the Earth humans as she stood upon the dock in a skirt with no blouse, typical attire most days on Gallata. There had been no time to put on Earth clothing. Surely the Earth humans would forgive her blunder in time. Shulmina had assured her that they had better memories than Gallatans but were equally forgiving. Shulmina had promised she would grow to love the people of the San Juan Islands and vice versa.

After carefully buttoning her blouse securely over her breasts, Wella appraised her mirror image as quite earthly. She was indeed taller than most local females but had been told that height was culturally valued in North America. Squinting, she tried to contain the wide sweep of her large green eyes even though she had been assured that Earth people approved of large eyes and would think them lovely.

Running down the lawn toward her boat, Wella recalled that she would have to walk in Orca Harbor. She could not understand the Earth custom of walking even to cover long distances.

LATER THAT DAY

Wella had been tacking into the wind against the tide without making much headway. This first sail in alien waters had proven more tedious than expected. A white sun sphere was half hidden behind a sheer layer of fog directly overhead.

It was getting late. Maybe Jorka wasn't so smart after all. It would have been much better to sail over to Klahowya Cove and run across the island along the road. Next time she would use the maps and plan her own route.

Since she had not encountered another boat the entire morning, Wella decided it might be safe to use *Terra*'s hidden advantages. Shulmina had encouraged her to use Gallatan technology whenever there was no chance of anyone observing. It was more convenient, less polluting, not as wasteful.

To activate *Terra*'s solar engine, Wella lifted an unobtrusive panel from her bow. The boat immediately lunged forward like a Sollian kuda fowl, clumsy but efficient. Soon *Terra* was moving swiftly, lightly into the wind. The only sound for several minutes was the sail flapping against the mast.

Wella became aware of a strange humming. Increasing in volume, the hum became a groan and then a rumble. The gray form of a vessel more than twice *Terra*'s size materialized out of the indefinite blend of fog and shiny water. Wella's nose quivered at her first scent of a gasoline-powered machine.

The boat pressed down upon her like a hungry sea grundgin after prey. Wella turned *Terra* slightly off the wind and replaced the panel to deactivate her solar engine. The grundgin drew nearer, its gray mass scarcely distinguishable from the water. Then it stopped a few feet away.

Two men were seated in the fore deck. One of them held a ledger and writing instrument as he squinted at *Terra*'s bow. They were dressed in identical stiff clothing of an almost colorless fabric. The man who was not writing stood up as if to speak to Wella. Frightened, Wella turned into the wind and luffed the sails. The man stared at her as if she were an indifferent object of the landscape. She thought his face quite ugly, though perhaps not by Earth standards. It was round and very red.

Wella closed her eyes and allowed the powerful impulses from her diverra bone to invade the surrounding energy field. Her mind began to merge with the stranger's thoughts:

/ *strange hippie woman* / *sailing alone* / *weird-acting sail boat* / *too fast for no engine* / *foreign looking* / His glance darted back and forth across Wella and the boat. / *maybe drugs from Canada?* / *no,*

Washington registration / "Terra" / keep under surveillance / maybe aiding draft dodgers /

The man spoke softly to the other who was seated. "Did you get the number?"

"Yes, sir. And the name."

"Something suspicious about this boat. Keep it under surveillance."

The man raised a cone-shaped object to his mouth and spoke to Wella in a voice amplified and distorted. "Thank you for stopping. We're looking for someone. Have you seen anything in the water?"

"No, I have seen no one," answered Wella, her voice trembling. At first she was confused because the words the man spoke did not match his thoughts. Then she recalled learning about the curious Earth custom of lying. Shulmina had assured her that a large portion of Earth human utterances were designed to mask rather than reveal the true thoughts in a person's mind. So many ideas were culturally unacceptable that it was often disastrous to reveal the true contents of a person's mind. Under such circumstances, lying was a natural form of self protection. Shulmina had insisted that Wella would soon learn to lie for politeness and expediency.

"Where have you come from?" demanded the amplified voice.

"Levin Island across from Klahowya Cove."

Oh, that's local, he thought, then asked, "Where ya' headed?"

"Orca Harbor."

As the boat pulled away, Wella noticed its inscription, "U.S. Navy Shore Patrol." She shuddered. That was a sanctioned mass killing service. What was it doing here? Shulmina had assured her that the killing games were happening far away from the San Juan Islands. Even so, many young men were being forced to leave their homes and travel halfway around the planet to participate. Some even went by choice.

Wella shuddered again and a surge of regret welled up in her. How could she be expected to mate with one of them and bear a child? She should have insisted upon artificial insemination.

Recalling the sad story, Wella began to weep softly. She used her soft woolen skirt to dry a tear from her eye. Then she pushed the tiller aside filling the sails with wind. If the Navy already had *Terra* under surveillance for whatever reason, that meant she was already noticed by the cruel earth humans who made the killing games.

. . .

Wella recognized the little man seated at the desk in the real estate office as the same one who had given her a blanket during the fire. He looked up in amazement, as though she were a vision of Maria of Sollia or some other Earth goddess. He said nothing at first, just stared wide-eyed and open-mouthed while Wella merged her mind with his thought sphere. She discovered that he was intimidated and impressed by her height and appearance. / *so tall* / *beautiful* / were the words suspended there. Then a visual image appeared of Wella as she had looked bare-bosomed that morning. Jim blushed and smiled tolerantly. Wella also blushed. It was humiliating to begin her new life as an object of ridicule and laughter, but Jim Krandle clearly liked her anyway.

He stood up and offered his hand for her to shake. Wella noted how pleasant he looked in lightly wrinkled business clothes, his head clearly visible without the fire fighter's helmet. Encircling the tan bald spot at the crown was a soft, transparent halo of blond, curly hair, at a height just right for Wella to rest her chin. Although she had never known a grown male so small, Wella judged him of average Earth height. Yet his physique was otherwise Gallatan, sinewy and angular. His handshake signaled acceptance, forgiveness. Wella wondered how so alien a creature could make such a favorable impression on her.

Maybe it wouldn't be so difficult to accomplish her mission after all.

"I've come to put in an insurance claim for the barn," she murmured, now captivated by his eyes which were so small, and yet so brilliantly blue,- that they eclipsed everything else in the room.

Suddenly, Jim Krandle startled Wella by running around the desk and offering a chair, holding onto it while she sat down. This again was some confusing hospitality rite they had neglected to teach her in training. She had been warned that there would be many such surprises. The Center believed in the ancient Gallatan precept that too much attention to detail would spoil the spontaneity of any endeavor.

After she was seated, Jim returned to his own chair and gazed at Wella with admiration. Her mind merged with his again / *alone in the world* / *family displaced during the war* / *traveled around two continents* / *no real home* / *might be of noble origin* / *wealthy at least* /

Wella smiled at the Center's clever system of diverting suspicion from the extraterrestrial origins of its subjects by telepathically implanting rumors — lies, so to speak — in the minds of local citizens. No one knew the source of the rumors. People had just started talking and no one was certain who said what. The result had been so much gossiping that no one would dare ask Wella where she really came from. Now the story of her shocking breach of custom would fuel their enthusiasm for tale bearing. Her blunder might actually enhance the diversion. Earth people's stereotype of extraterrestrials was nothing like their image of Wella standing on the dock looking awkward and out of place, half-clothed. Shulmina had always declared one of Earth humans' most charming characteristics to be their limited capacity for peripheral awareness.

"Everything will be fine," Jim was saying. "We received a voucher from your Seattle bank and a signed deed to the property from your agent months ago. All you have to do is fill out the application, sign it, and we'll come out to appraise the damage. A mere formality, of course, since we already know it was demolished. The barn was insured for $7,000, so you'll probably get the full amount."

Wella was impressed. In some ways the Center was more thorough than it purported to be. Using a primitive Earth communication system known as "the mail," they had assured that she would be able to maintain herself in this alien world. They had consigned Gallatan "hippy clothes" to shops in her name, bought her an island, made certain she would have plenty of "money," a substance integral to the capricious Earth system of goods and services distribution. It was incredible, really!

"I'll give you time to read the application while I get some coffee. Would you like some?"

Wella had been oriented to most Earth beverages, and her favorite was diet Cola although she didn't mind coffee with a little cream. She had been warned against alcohol, a deadly poison to Gallatan body chemistry. "Yes, thank you, with a little cream, please."

Jim showed Wella where to sign the documents and returned to his chair to gaze warmly at her while sipping his coffee contentedly. "Your agents did well for you in finding this place," he mused. "The Islands are a great place to live, nice people, beautiful scenery.... What more could you want?"

"I'm told it's a good place to raise sheep," she said, "because of the moderate climate and rich vegetation."

"Oh yes," agreed Jim between generous sips. "Many San Juan Islanders raise sheep, and there is a market for wool on the mainland. My father has a flock."

"I use the wool in my weaving."

"That's great," said Jim. "The tourists like to buy that kind of thing from the locals, and the shops in Seattle carry nice crafts too. This is one of the few places you can still make it with a craft, if you can produce a lot."

"I am very fast," Wella assured him.

It was obvious that Jim was purposefully, almost ceremoniously, making conversation with her. Then she recalled that this was often the way a mating relationship began between Earth people. They couldn't consciously do it the Gallatan way, by gradually reducing the percentage of spoken words while increasing the number of telepathic communications.

As she listened to Jim's chatter, she began to wonder what would

were going in. Then Wella saw Jim. He was seated on a bench talking with a woman, his head bent toward her, his eyes focusing on hers in rapt attention. The woman was wearing one of the Gallatan skirts the Center had consigned in Wella's name to the Orca Harbor Boutique. Her hair was the dark brown of Wella's erely ram and hung loosely about her shoulders. She was even shorter than Jim, too small and delicate to stand in a Gornish evening wind. Her blue eyes, though much smaller than Wella's were probably of average Earth size. They opened wide to stare at Wella when Jim stood up to welcome her.

"Wella, you came! I'm so glad you made it. This is Pamela Bradley. You met her the morning of the fire." If it had not been for the name, Wella wouldn't have recognized Pamela without the firefighter's garb.

Pamela nodded and took Wella's bowl of salad into the schoolhouse while Jim held Wella's arm and introduced her to others on the porch. Jim's father, Benjamin Krandle, a thick stump of a man, glowered at Wella. The others acknowledged her only briefly and went on talking, but Benjamin continued to frown at Wella through little nodules of eyes in the rough bark of his face.

Wella thought it might be safer to know what he was thinking, so she closed her eyes, and rested her mind in the blue stillness creating a flow of energy into the surrounding space, intercepting from Benjamin a vague fear of the islands being taken over by "hippies."

Wella was still not certain what a hippie was, but she was relieved to be taken for any kind of Earth human at all. This was the third Earth human she had spied upon, and not one of them had suspected her of being from an alien solar system. They didn't even seem concerned that she was foreign. Their major preoccupation was with her "hippieness" which was apparently something quite native, and yet vaguely unacceptable.

"Wella is into sheep raising," Jim was telling his father. "I promised to introduce her to somebody around here who knows sheep, and I guess you're the one."

"I have a small flock of Romneys," said Ben, but Wella, whose mind field was still merged with his, perceived the image of herself standing in front of him, barechested, and his face lit up with an amused smile.

Wella felt shaken and embarrassed. Her concentration broke and her mind fell out of the stillness losing touch with Krandle's. Her voice trembled slightly, but she steadfastly pursued the conversation as she had been taught to do in Earth training. "I have a few odd cross breeds with very fine multicolored fleece. I've been wanting to see what happens if I breed them with Romneys."

"My Romneys are well-bred sheep," snapped Ben. "I wouldn't

want to breed them with crossbreeds, but if you buy a sheep off me, it's your animal. I guess you can do what you want with it."

Wella brightened. "Do you have any colored ram lambs this year?" she asked hopefully. She had been told that most Romneys were white.

Apparently she had finally said the right thing because Benjamin flashed a broad, pleasurable smile. "You want to buy black sheep?"

"Well, one ram at least, and maybe one or two ewes."

"Black?"

"Yes, I use the fleece for my weaving."

"Black?"

"Yes, black, and gray, and brown, you know, colored. I have sheep of various colors and I like to interbreed them so I can use different colors."

Mr. Krandle was visibly impressed. "You mean you use it like it is? You don't dye it?"

"Oh, no," Wella assured him. "I would never dye it. You see my skirt, and Pamela is wearing another of the skirts I made. It's the real color of the sheep."

Benjamin raised his thick, gnarled hand to his head and scratched a couple of times, then shook his head slightly. He stooped over a little to examine Wella's skirt, reaching out to pinch a little of it between his fingers.

"These threads look sort of yellow. Are they the natural color?" he asked doubtfully.

"Oh, yes. That's from a very old ewe of mine."

Mr. Krandle shook his head a couple more times while continuing to investigate the garment closely. Finally, he straightened again and faced Wella. "That must take an awful lot of work," he pronounced gravely. A stout, square-cheeked woman came to Wella's rescue. "Ben, you know young people today are more adventuresome. They like to experiment. Wella is an artist. She spins and weaves some of the softest wool I've ever seen."

"This is my mother, Ruth Krandle," explained Jim, and Wella recognized the name. Ruth managed the Orca Harbor Boutique where most of the Gallatan skirts had been consigned. Ruth would, at some juncture, give Wella money which she could trade for things from other shops or for ferry rides to the mainland of North America. Ruth offered a hand, and Wella shook it vigorously.

Jim introduced Wella to several more people as they conversed their way into the building and across the dining hall. Most of them were relatives of his — aunts, uncles, cousins, and so forth. Obviously Jim belonged to one of Merrick Island's largest clans. Recalling that the most successful genetic experiments in the entire galaxy had taken place in large, extended family situations, Wella resolved to somehow make sure that it was Jim who fathered her child.

The hall was furnished with rows of long narrow tables. Perpendicular to the ends of the rows was another long table laden with many dishes of various types of food. People were lined up there taking turns piling food on plates. Wella watched the others carefully so that she could do everything strictly according to custom. After their plates were filled, Jim motioned for Wella to follow him. Thankfully, he clearly pointed out which chair she should sit in. Otherwise, she would not have known where to sit, having no designated place in any of the clans nor even any friends.

Jim sat across from her and introduced a very young man on his right as his brother, Marvin. Wella offered Marvin an awkward handshake across the plates of food, and between the glasses of lemonade and Coca Cola. Marvin responded with almost as much awkwardness, his face reddening around many little brown spots called freckles. The face was topped with close-cropped yellow hair that stood straight up, and Wella noted that Marvin's body had the curious gorilla shape of many Earth males. Benjamin was shaped that way too. She hoped that, if her child was born into this clan, he or she would be shaped more like Jim.

Despite his not-so-attractive appearance, Marvin spoke in a charming, friendly voice. "Pleased to meet you, Miss De Gornia. Sorry to hear about your barn burning down. Say, let us know if you need any help over there. That's what neighbors are for."

People began to eat the food on their plates even before everyone was seated. No one paused to wait for initial sharings or speeches such as inevitably preceded a Gallatan meal. In fact, conversation virtually ceased during the meal, so Wella had time to think about the cultural implications of various customs and groupings in the room.

Pamela sat down on the right side of Jim, and they leaned slightly together. Apparently Pamela and Jim were together in somewhat the same way as Jim's parents were. Almost every adult male, except for Marvin, was part of a mating pair. She had been warned of this Earth custom, but still found it shocking. On all Gallatan islands, people avoided pairing off in public. It was undignified for women to broadcast the identity of their current sexual partners.

Seated directly across from Jim and Pamela, Wella closed her eyes and rested in the stillness until her energy field joined with theirs. She wondered what it meant, their being paired together. Jim's parents and most of the other mating pairs were, in Earth terms, "married," which meant that there had been a ritual to publicly designate them as mating couples for an extended period of time, sometimes even for life. Yet this was not the case with Jim and Pamela. Therefore, Wella did not understand why they were together in this way. She couldn't recall anything in her study of Earth mating behavior which would account for a public mating couple where no ritual had taken place. Perhaps it meant they were publicly courting, which would seem even more absurd than undignified.

As her own energy field intercepted Jim's, Wella found him enjoying intense pleasure in the memory of the hug they had shared in the Real Estate Office, and of the sudden, startling involuntary thought of visiting her on Levin Island. Jim was so preoccupied with a sense of wonder about the sudden thought that Wella was tempted to send him another. She chose to wait for a more private moment.

Wella continued to sit with her eyes closed, maintaining concentration. Jim's thoughts came through clearly now. The image of her greeting him at the farmhouse gradually changed to that of Wella barechested on the dock in the early morning light. He smiled. Gradually Wella became aware that the same image was in Pamela's mind also, but she did not smile. Wella opened her eyes and looked directly into Pamela's judging eyes. The uncomfortable thought image of the barechested Wella was suspended in the energy space between them, a mental block forbidding Pamela to like this unusual stranger.

Still tuned into Pamela's thoughts, Wella realized that, although their feelings about the image of Wella barechested were quite different, Pamela and Jim were sharing the same thought, and what's more, they knew it. They didn't know they knew it, but they realized at some peripheral level that they were sharing a collective thought the way two erely sheep share the thought of following the lead ewe out to pasture.

Wella closed her eyes again, intensifying the energy from her diveira bone. Yes, it was really true, this entire community of rural Earth humans was sharing a collective thought image of her, Wella DeGornia, standing on the Levin Island dock barechested. Although each person felt differently about it, the visual thought was linked to some form of disapproval. Without knowing it, these Earth humans were partaking in a highly telepathic collective thought exercise, even while the soft gentle din of their conversation continued on about various neutral subjects like the weather and gardening. This was much like a Gallatan clan ceremonial dinner in that respect.

Shulmina had told her that this kind of phenomenon often occurred among Earth humans without them knowing it. The collective thought was sustained for at least twenty or thirty heartbeats before it began to disintegrate, and Wella felt someone tapping her on the hand. She opened her eyes to see Jim smiling at her. "My, you certainly are a sleepy one, Wella," he teased. "Imagine falling asleep at your first community potluck! I know we're dull country people, but you ought to try to stay awake."

Wella blushed. "Oh, I'm sorry."

Jim's grin broadened. "Oh, think nothing of it. I'm only kidding. You must be awfully tired, what with trying to farm all alone, getting your garden planted and so forth. We all understand. But try to stay awake a moment here, we have to do the formal introduction thing." He picked up his table knife and began striking his drinking glass repeatedly, creating a high-pitched ringing sound like a bell. "Your attention, please," he called out to the entire assembly.

All conversation abruptly ceased, and there was an awesome silence.

"I would like to introduce our new neighbor. Wella, will you please stand up?"

Ruth, who was sitting next to Wella, poked her arm. "Stand up, Wella."

Smiling, Wella pushed back her chair and rose. She felt very tall now and very much noticed. This potluck was feeling more and more like a Gallatan clan ceremony. "This is Wella DeGornia," announced Jim. "She has recently purchased Levin Island, just a few hundred yards from Klahowya Cove. Wella is planning to raise sheep there and to pursue her weaving craft. Let's give her a hearty welcome."

People began clapping their hands, a symbol of recognition by the collective consciousness.

Wella closed her eyes and felt an intense surge of energy expanding her awareness into the wider sphere of thought, absorbing the adjacent energy into her own mind. As she became aware of the collective thought, the entire community again shared the visual image of a tall, small-breasted woman clothed in a long skirt standing on the Levin Island dock. At that moment, Wella DeGornia, thinking very quickly, saw an opportunity to perform a wonderful act of collective consciousness control. Although she had attended many Gallatan clan ceremonies and had experienced much community thought-sharing, she was only a shepherd. She was not a Spiritual Leader or even a clan mother. This kind of ceremony had never been her role on Gallata, yet here was an opportunity to do something she had experienced others doing many times. In a way, it was similar to herding sheep.

Her eyes still closed, Wella merged her mind with the collective thought and saw herself on the dock barechested. Instead of reacting to the disjointed array of negative feelings, Wella projected her own, typically Gallatan, attitude of respect and admiration. This was, after all, a strong, vibrant woman filled with love and concern for her fellow creatures. This was an image of power, the image of a woman who is pleased with her body and bares her chest with pride. As Wella projected those feelings intensively into the collective thought, all negativity dissipated. Then she gradually caused the visual image to fade until it was forgotten.

When Wella opened her eyes, the Klahowya Cove Community Club was still applauding, and recognition had become real welcome. Wella's neighbors weren't sure what had happened to them, but they liked it.

LEVIN ISLAND ~ APRIL 20, 1967

During her morning meditation on the porch step, Wella noticed a small motorboat approaching the dock. Her mind, already in the state of blue stillness, merged almost automatically with the visitor's.

It was a tightly woven verbal train of associations that Wella identified immediately with Pamela. / *maybe still in bed* / *work to do* / *hope she's up* / *hope she's fully dressed* / *coming* / *fast* / *runs a lot* / *maybe jogger* / *marathon runner* /

"Good morning," greeted Wella, running up to shake Pamela's hand on the dock. She was delighted to have a visitor, her first after the fire crew.

Pamela shyly withdrew an envelope from her large, leather shoulder bag and handed it to Wella. "Jim asked me to drop off this check on my way to town. It's for your insurance claim."

"Thank you," said Wella politely. She was disappointed. She had wanted Jim to come himself; his visit was part of her plan for his fathering her child. Still, the wrong visitor was better than none. "Would you like to come up into the house and drink a cup of coffee or have some Coca Cola?"

Pamela smiled blandly and glanced at her wristwatch.

Wella noticed that she was wearing another Gallatan skirt. The skirts were selling well in Ruth's shop where Pamela worked also. Wella had already received a check in the mail which she picked up regularly at the Klahowya Cove store.

"I think I have time for a cup of coffee," said Pamela. "Anyway, I've been wanting to see your spinning and weaving equipment. I've thought of writing an article about it for the *Orca Harbor Weekly*."

• • •

There was still very little furniture in the farmhouse. The floor of the sitting room was made comfortable and inviting by a few cushions and erely fleeces arranged along the walls. Wella's spinning wheel and loom, both of real Earth cedar, stood by the stone fireplace. Like *Terra*, their Gallatan technology was disguised as ordinary Earth gadgetry.

"Your house is lovely," said Pamela. "Most houses are too cluttered." Wella was enough in tune with her visitor's mind to know that Pamela spoke the truth.

After they were seated comfortably, each on a fleece, holding a coffee mug, Pamela began to reel out questions rapidly, the way she did thoughts. She asked how much fabric Wella could make in a day, how she got ideas for designs, and so forth. But the image most prevalent in Pamela's mind was the thought of Jim.

Wella could not detect any obvious reasons for avoiding the subject, so she ventured, "I was hoping Jim would bring the insurance check himself. He promised to visit me."

During the awkward silence which followed, Wella closed her eyes and channeled all her available mental energy toward Pamela, straining to glimpse this Earth human's view of the world from within. Pamela's thoughts were like pieces of a torn page, shapeless and fragmented. Eventually, one clear idea emerged: / *he will surely come soon* / Pamela emitted a long, sad sigh of resignation.

"I would like very much for Jim to come and visit me," persisted Wella. She knew that idea was upsetting to Pamela. If she held it out there long enough in their shared mental space, the reason might eventually come clear, like the reflection of a face in settling water.

"Why don't you invite him?" snapped Pamela.

"I have invited him. He promised to come."

"Then he will come," stated Pamela. There was bitterness in her energy sphere. Then Wella recognized among the confusion of verbal thoughts / *in love with* / *Jim* / *in love with Wella* /

Wella smiled. Despite Jorka's long, painful efforts to help her understand the phrase "in love with," she had been unable to distinguish its subtle difference from "infatuated with." In the context of that phrase, "love," which meant a variety of things in any language, had something to do with sexual attraction. It was a nobler kind of attraction, but didn't necessarily last longer than infatuation, nor result in as pleasant or healthy a relationship. There was one certainty — it often resulted in mating. Wella couldn't understand why the thought seemed so terrifying to Pamela, so she asked very gently, "Pamela, would you be unhappy if Jim came to visit me?"

There was a strained pause. Then Pamela blurted out, "I'd be damned jealous!"

"You have probably noticed I have some trouble with English. I don't fully understand the word 'jealous'."

A smile of amusement broke through Pamela's sadness. "You feel it when someone has something you want."

Wella set her mug on the hearth and refilled it with the pot by the fireplace.

"You mean Jim is in love with me, but not with you?"

At first Pamela just stared at Wella in amazement. Then she smiled even greater amusement. "With Jim, it's possible he's in love with both of us. He's fickle."

"Fickle?"

"He falls in love with almost everyone."

"So, why are you jealous? Even if Jim is in love with me, he is in love with you as well."

Pamela's smile became laughter. "That isn't very consoling. I want to marry Jim."

"Why?" asked Wella ingenuously. Having gone this far, why not reveal the full extent of her ignorance?

Pamela bristled. She had somehow interpreted the "Why?" as an accusation of insincerity. "For lots of reasons. For one, I love him. We have been best friends all our lives, and for another, he's the only single man left on Merrick Island. The others are over in Vietnam, or else in the city, or else dead. Maybe you heard. Marvin got a draft notice. That's the latest."

Wella strained to imagine, or put together from captured fragments of Pamela's thoughts, the concept of "draft notice." Apparently it was some sort of death warrant that everyone took for granted, and to declare ignorance of "draft notice" would be equivalent to admitting she was alien. She resolved to ask Jorka for clarification, but fortunately, Pamela soon revealed the meaning in context by adding, "Lester wants him to join the Marines."

The shock of that thought broke Wella's concentration, and Pamela's energy sphere was lost. She recalled Marvin, the innocent young boy who sat near her at the potluck. Surely, he could not be in the killing games!

But Pamela was still going on about Jim and marriage as if there had been no mention of Marvin's impending doom. "Oh, Jim would make a lousy husband anyway."

Although it was too late to recreate the trance and tune into Pamela's thoughts again, Wella asked what seemed to be the most obvious question. "Why?"

"Well, for one reason, he's had an operation, because he doesn't want to have children, and for another, he'd probably sleep around."

Wella took a long, thoughtful swallow of coffee from her mug as she deciphered the meaning of "sleep around" from Pam's bitter words.

Her interest returned. If there were no single men, her only chance of fulfilling her mission would be with a married one, so she asked, "Do many married men on Merrick Island...well, do they sleep around?"

Pamela gasped, then burst into unrestrained laughter. "Well, I'm sure I don't know! I mean, I don't believe in gossiping, and if they do sleep around, they don't do it with me, of course." Her laughter trailed off in hollow embarrassment.

There must be cultural taboo against "sleeping around" also. Wella questioned more than ever the wisdom of the Anthropological Research Center. At that moment she even felt a surge of anger verging on hatred. How stupid of them to place her in a situation where all possible mates were either unavailable or being murdered, and assign her the task of conceiving a child! At the same moment she felt a surge of compassion for Pamela, in fact for all Earth women. No wonder their plight was considered one of the great injustices of the universe! She didn't care a whit about her mission anymore. She only wanted to make Pamela feel better.

"Maybe Jim isn't as fickle as you think, Pamela. I think you're wrong about him being in love with me. At any rate he hasn't come to visit me, even though I invited him to."

"He'll come. Invite him again."

"Even if he does come, I won't sleep around with him now that I know it would make you unhappy."

Pamela gasped and blushed profoundly. "All's fair in love and war," she laughed.

"In this culture, perhaps that's true, but I am a foreigner. In my culture a friend's concerns are more important to me than my own. You are the first to visit me or share your concerns, so you are my only friend in this world at the moment. I will not sleep around with Jim, not for anything."

After her generous promise, Wella felt some misgivings. She still wanted Jim to father her child, but that would be difficult after the vow she had just made. She wanted it even more now that she knew Jim was "fickle" as Pamela had defined it. Fickleness might not be an ideal trait for a husband, but to love easily was an excellent virtue for a father. But what had Pamela meant about Jim's "operation"? Wella decided to ask Jorka, rather than reveal her ignorance.

"You must be a very good person, Wella," said Pamela, as they walked together down to the dock. "I'm glad you moved here."

Wella didn't say she was glad also, because she wasn't. But at least she had made a friend. Before Pamela got into the boat, Wella grasped both her arms above the elbows. That gesture had won her a hug once. Maybe it would work again. It did.

After giving Wella a warm embrace, Pamela got into her boat. "When you're in town, stop by the store. We have one of your skirts on a manikin in the window. It's a beautiful display."

"Yes, I would like to see it," said Wella. "And please come back to visit me again."

Pamela pressed the button to start the engine. "Oh yes, I forgot to mention something. Jim told me to tell you to let us know if you want us to get a party of folks together to rebuild the barn. The insurance check will buy most of the materials, but not the labor."

"That would be wonderful! Imagine, a building ceremony."

Pamela wrinkled her nose. "Building ceremony?"

Wella blushed. "I mean party." But she wasn't really certain of the difference between a party and a ceremony. On Gallata, all parties were ceremonies and vice versa. Certainly the potluck had been both.

ORCA HARBOR ~ MAY 10, 1967

It was a warm spring morning and the mooring basin was filled to capacity with tourist boats, but Wella managed to squeeze *Terra* in between the boardwalk and a large yacht that was occupying a bit more than its share of space. As she lifted her skirt and stepped lightly over the gunwale onto the dock, Wella sensed someone concentrating upon her intently. Looking up, she saw a long, slender male resting in a canvas lounge chair on the foredeck. Beside him was a glass of iced liquid, and a radio, scratching out a piece of classical music. Barely clothed, the man's shimmering body reeked of artificially-scented oil. His angular face and firm body looked young, but the thick crop of neatly styled hair was frothy with middle age.

Wella closed her eyes momentarily and rested her mind in the blue stillness. Then she merged with the man's intense energy field. There she found a memory of herself sailing *Terra* into the harbor, recorded not as the difficult struggle it had been, but rather as a graceful, effortless dance performed in time with the music from his radio.

The man's mind seemed different, more erratic, than that of other Earth humans she had met. She opened her eyes again and met his gaze riveted upon her. She smiled and offered him a cheerful, "Good morning."

"You really know how to manipulate that sail," remarked the stranger, lifting the glass and raising it casually above his head. Wella recognized the gesture as a salutation known as a "toast." Ice cubes in the glass tinkled festively.

"Everyone else motored in this morning. It must have been quite a trick to catch the wind just right."

"It was challenging," agreed Wella, "But I'm getting used to it. My boat has no gasoline engine."

"Incredible!" he breathed, as his gaze turned toward *Terra*.

Leaving the man to contemplate his admiration and surprise, Wella hurried on to keep the business appointment she had made, at Jorka's command, with Ruth and Pamela.

. . .

It was early afternoon when she got back to the mooring basin. A soft haze delicately curtained the snow-covered peaks across the water, and a gentle breeze had come up from the north. The tourists were draped about the docks in various stages of dress and undress, still bathing their shiny, oiled bodies in luxurious sunlight. The long, tanned body was still lounging in his chair, smoking a cigarette and sipping his drink.

Passing in front of the yacht, Wella felt the intense energy of his gaze, and by the time she reached her own boat, she was certain he was following her. Turning to face him, Wella confronted for the first time an Earth human taller than herself. He removed his sunglasses and squinted into her face, as he reached past her to touch *Terra*'s gunwale. He was so close that the odors of oil, tobacco, and alcohol were almost overwhelming.

"I've been admiring your boat, and I was wondering whether you would let me come aboard and have a better look."

Wella's stomach tightened, but she faced him squarely, noting the quickening of his breath. She closed her eyes and searched in vain for the blue stillness, but the stranger's energy field was so strong that it interrupted the flow of electrochemical impulses from her diverra bone. She opened her eyes and looked again at the stranger. The yearning in his eyes spoke clearly his thoughts. Far more than "I want to see your boat," his expression said, "I want you."

Without the words, this man's invitation to mate was otherwise similar to a Gallatan's approach to a clan member she had known for at least a hundred sun cycles. It was shocking to be singled out in this manner by a stranger, but her mission was to produce offspring by an Earth male, and perhaps this was the answer. Maybe the Center, realizing their mistake in stationing her where there were so few opportunities for mating, had intervened to put the idea into the stranger's mind.

At the peak of her fertility cycle, a rush of intuition told Wella that conception was imminent. The thrill of this awareness heightened the excitement now growing out of her initial fear.

"Welcome aboard *Terra*," she said, bowing and gesturing with her palm toward the cabin as she had learned to do in training.

His long legs stepped lightly over the gunwale while he kept both eyes focused intently on hers. She watched from the dock as he examined the tiller, the rudders, the rigging, touching everything with his long brown fingers. "Would you like to sail her?" she invited as he climbed back onto the dock.

He grinned softly and looked down at his nearly nude body. It's chilly out on the Strait. "I'll need to dress warmer."

"Yes, I will wait for you here."

"Or maybe you would like to come aboard *Harriet* for a drink."

"*Harriet?*"

"My boat."

"Oh yes, of course," said Wella, noticing for the first time the name painted on the bow of the yacht. Before she had time to explain that she had meant to acknowledge the name, not necessarily the invitation, the stranger had climbed aboard and opened the cabin door for her to enter.

Wella stepped hesitantly onto *Harriet's* deck. If only there had been time to consult with Jorka. But what harm could come of this? The man intended only to mate. There was clearly little else on his mind.

The cabin below deck was paneled with shiny, black mahogany. There was a built-in red velvet couch on which Wella seated herself and ran her hand over it to feel the pattern of the weave. "This is fine cloth," she said

The man had looked away from her toward a counter near the wall where there were some beverage containers such as glasses, bottles, and a small sort of bucket.

While the man's attention was diverted, Wella closed her eyes and found the blue stillness expanding her energy field to include the stranger's. It was a powerful field concentrated intently upon mating with her even while somewhat diverted by the task of fixing drinks. The drink preparations themselves seemed a sort of mating ritual, his voice seductive as he spoke the words, "What do you want to drink?"

"Coca Cola. No alcohol, please."

"You don't drink?"

Wella had noted the Earth human tendency to use this type of beverage to overcome inhibitions, so she said, "Alcohol makes me very sick, but don't worry. I don't need it."

As in a Gallatan mating ritual, Wella spoke mischievously and touched the tip of her tongue to her upper lip. Then she projected into their shared energy field a visual thought of her thrusting her tongue gently into his mouth.

The man's hand jerked slightly as he poured the cola from a large plastic bottle into a glass of ice cubes. The involuntary thought had startled him and with his back to Wella, the man's energy field was now interrupted by other thoughts.

There was a woman, someone he feared would find out. There were time constraints, an appointment later in the day.

"No one will ever know," said Wella quietly. "We are alone. We have a short space of time to enjoy one another. It will not take long."

The ice tinkled in the glass as the man's slightly trembling hand lifted the glass of cola. He breathed deeply to regain his composure and turned to face Wella again, gazing at her now with even more admiration than before. He took a step toward her, proffering the glass.

As if at some level he was already familiar with the Gallatan thought transference mating ritual, the man interjected a clear verbal thought into their shared energy field: / on my one day of vacation / I should be so lucky as to meet a fast one like you! /

Feeling with pleasure the admiration in his eyes, Wella took the glass and maintained eye contact with him while she sipped the Coca Cola. He was certainly beautiful enough, and his genes would be strong.

"You have a lovely body," said Wella. At first the man blushed deeply as if embarrassed. Then he beamed profound appreciation and projected a visual thought of a passionate kiss into their shared energy field.

Wella stood up and handed the man back her empty glass.

Smiling gently and still maintaining eye contact, he took advantage of the signal to step closer. "Would you like another drink?"

"No, thank you."

While he replaced the glass on the counter, Wella intercepted a visual thought of the man carefully removing her blouse. The memory of her embarrassing first morning on Earth — when she learned how intense the local taboo against barechested women was — crossed Wella's mind. Yet it was clear that this man wanted to have as good a view of her as she had of him. It seemed only fair if they were soon to have intercourse. So she carefully and deliberately began unbuttoning her blouse while the man watched with wide-eyed approval. Wella felt the quickening of her own sexual desire.

After Wella dropped her blouse on the couch, the man reached forward and touched the tress of hair that had fallen down over her breast. His hand closed about the hair caressing it gently as his eyes still focused on hers. "You are a very exotic native," he said as his fingers began to move up and down through the hair finally stopping to curl themselves around her breast. Then he reached both arms about her waist and unloosened the tie of her long, brown Gallatan skirt. He gazed at her with intense desire for a brief moment before his mouth covered hers in a passionate kiss.

The first time, they mated while still standing, with Wella pressed against the smooth mahogany of the cabin. This seemed a bit barbaric, as did many Earth customs. She knew the boat was rocking. It crossed her mind to wonder if passersby could tell someone was having a mating ritual inside the cabin.

ORCA HARBOR ~ SAME DAY

Seated by the big picture window of the Harbor View Cafe, Mark's attention bounced from the harbor to the entrance and back to his watch. He was a little early for his five o'clock appointment with Krandle so he nodded when the waitress offered to refill his coffee cup. The mooring basin was still full now except for that small space beside his yacht.

The exotic woman with the incredible little sailing vessel had been gone less than an hour, and Mark wondered if she had been a dream. In fact, maybe this whole experience was a dream.

It had begun yesterday unexpectedly with a phone message, on the pile of little notes on his desk. "Krandle...Merrick Island...Orca Harbor School...639-8365...URGENT."

Mark had paused, flooded by memories of an eager kid in his political science class — summer of '65; didn't talk a lot, mild mannered. He would answer another student's long haranguing argument with a few pleasant words, and win every time. What was his name? A simple name. Jim. A crazy guy who liked kids but wasn't planning to have any; didn't want to overpopulate the world. Jim had organized an anti-war rally that summer and had asked Mark to speak. Once they went to a bar after class and talked about when the revolution would come. That was a fun summer. Mark once asked Jim if he intended to major in political science, maybe take up law.

Jim looked embarrassed and shook his head.

"What's your major?"

"Elementary education. I want to be a school teacher."

"No kidding. Why?"

"I like it. Besides, they don't get drafted."

"Yeah, but there's no money in it."

"I can go home at the end of senior year and never leave again."

"How many teaching jobs are there in the San Juan Islands?"

"One. With my name on it. Every member of the school board is a personal friend of mine. There are no unknowns."

Gradually Mark had learned that Jim planned to earn extra money working for an uncle who sold things like insurance and real estate to movie stars and European Royalty. A couple of his uncles were established businessmen in Orca Harbor.

Jim's allegiance to Merrick Island probably grew out of an excessive need for security. Who was Mark to fault anyone for that? Mark had married Harriet right out of law school because she was the only good looking woman in his class, and was the daughter of a prosperous Vancouver attorney. Every summer, amidst the stacks of mail on his desk, Mark had found a picture postcard or two from Merrick Island: the schoolhouse, the library, Mount Baker from Scenic Bay, the mooring basin. On the back of each card was the inevitable invitation to "stop by and visit sometime when you're boating around the islands." Had there ever been a phone message from Krandle before this? Certainly not one marked "URGENT."

He answered the phone, "Klahowya Cove School."

"Jim?"

"Yeah. Is this Mark Roberts?"

"Yeah. What's up?"

"I hear you work with draft dodgers."

"Thought you had a teaching deferment."

"I do. It's Marvin, my little brother. I think he's in big trouble."

"Is he a conscientious objector?"

"God, no. I don't know. He's an idiot."

"He's mentally retarded?"

A volley of laughter. "No, not that kind of idiot. A kid. No sense of responsibility. Stubborn. What can I tell you about Marvin? He does his own thing."

Jim told Mark quite a bit about this new client, a kid who had simply ignored his first draft notice, as well as Lord knows many subsequent orders to report for induction. His physical examination had been originally scheduled for March 23. It was now May 15, and Marvin had not so much as contacted the draft board. Whenever they phoned and left a message, Marvin was out framing houses, and he never returned their calls. He had not even told his parents about the draft notices. Jim found out when a Mr. Genzforth, from the F.B.I., came around asking questions. That was when Jim decided to phone Mark.

"You think you can help Marvin?" Jim had asked anxiously.

"I don't know. Maybe I can clarify his options."

"That might help," said Jim dubiously, but he had offered to pay Mark any price to keep his brother out of jail.

"What about out of the military?"

"I don't care about that. I just don't want him in jail. Keep him out of jail."

"What if he goes to Canada?"

"For the rest of his life?"

"Maybe."

"I don't care. But Mom and Dad would be upset."

"What about Marvin?"

"Who knows? He's hard to read."

The next morning Mark had taken off early from the Vancouver docks where he kept his boat. It was not unusual for him to spend the weekend cruising the San Juans alone, relaxing, looking for adventure, among other things. As usual, he had invited Harriet to come along, but as was often the case, she had to work. Harriet was a hard worker. She prepared each case meticulously. Every possible angle was thoroughly researched. Mark knew that when Harriet agreed to go boating with him, it was out of a sense of obligation. She wasn't into boats. She only liked it when the weather was warm enough for swimming so she could jump out of the boat. Harriet always needed to be doing something, whereas on a boat she felt obliged to do nothing. She was visibly relieved when Mark told her this was partially a business trip. That made her feel less obligated to go along.

Harriet never suspected Mark might have a little "fling" on his boating trips without her. He often wondered whether that knowledge would have made her come with him more often. He suspected otherwise. Harriet lived her life within carefully drawn boundaries. If she ever found out about his affairs, Mark would find himself promptly divorced.

Weather conditions had been great for motoring, and Mark had allowed plenty of time. He had arrived at the Merrick Island dock in the late morning hours with time to spare for relaxing before his appointment with the Krandles. He had just settled into a sunny lounge chair with his first drink when he saw the magnificent little sailboat tacking deftly into the harbor. Lifting his binoculars to look closer, he discovered that the sheets were tended by a woman whose long skirt and hair played on the wind as she worked. It was like watching a dance.

The whole thing had gone like clockwork. It was almost as if she had been sent from heaven. Maybe he had been living right for a change. After all, he had not had an affair, not even a one-night stand for over a year. He had been good to Harriet, sent her roses on their anniversary.

Seated in the window of the Harbor View Cafe and looking out at the scene of his earlier pleasures, Mark grinned appreciation of his own thoughts. Maybe God wasn't a prude like Harriet's church people made him out to be. Maybe he had sent an angel to have an affair with him.

Of course, he would have hell to pay if Harriet ever found out about his little fling, but she would never find out. The woman had not even asked his name. Recalling the scene, he could hardly believe his memory. After making love with her passionately for a couple of hours, Mark had begun to feel "all fucked out" as he would put it. That was when guilt feelings and fears about Harriet started to surface, and he also began thinking about his appointment with the Krandles. The woman was lying on her side on the couch at the time. Her eyes were closed, and she seemed asleep. He glanced at his watch, noting that it was after four. He still needed to take a shower and get ready to meet Jim at the Harbor View Cafe.

Instantly, as if she had read his mind, the woman opened her eyes and announced that she must leave. "The tide will change soon, and it will be difficult to sail home."

"Oh, that's too bad," said Mark. "I never got a chance to sail your boat."

"You must come another time. You must come to visit me."

Mark agreed that this would be an excellent idea, but pointed out that he didn't know where she lived. She showed him on his charts of the Georgian Strait — it was a tiny island, across a narrow inlet, just opposite Klahowya Cove. Mark figured that it must be near the schoolhouse where Jim Krandle taught his handful of kids. This was, after all, a very small world. The population of the whole island couldn't be more than two or three hundred at the most.

Mark had watched with his binoculars as the woman sailed her boat gracefully out of the harbor and disappeared around a point in the distance. It had not occurred to him until the moment she had disappeared from view, that he did not even know her name.

In the case of the other women with whom he'd had affairs, Mark had entertained varying degrees of anxiety about whether they might tell Harriet. As for this woman, who had not bothered to ask his name, there was no such worry. Far from feeling that she might want to exact a price for her services, she had seemed grateful. There were no strings attached.

Mark was still lost in recollections of his dreamlike afternoon when a hand touched his shoulder. It was Jim. He looked nearly the same, just a little older. There were tension lines in his forehead and between his cheeks and mouth.

They drove the inland road in an old, red pickup truck. Jim apologized for the appearance of the vehicle, explaining that Marvin used it to haul equipment for his construction business. Jim didn't own a land motor vehicle. He just used other people's or the company car or his bicycle.

Near Merrick Island's end, the road came out of a stretch of woods into a clearing that looked out over Klahowya Cove and the Strait beyond. Just a short distance from the shore, Mark could see a small island with a house and barn. That must be the island the woman had pointed to on the map. Surely she didn't live there alone. She must belong to a hippy commune. Mark had heard that there were several on the islands.

"Who lives over there on the little island?"

"A newcomer, a foreign woman, named Wella De Gornia. Real good sport. Folks like her."

Mark made mental note of the fittingly beautiful name as Jim pulled the pickup into a long, gravel drive way leading to a white, New England style farmhouse. There was another truck in the driveway, as well as an older Chrysler station wagon. The house was surrounded by several acres of fenced pasture dotted with fluffy white sheep, your typical scene by Grandma Moses. "Nice place you have here."

The Krandle living room was rendered cheerful by an airtight wood stove with a little glass window that revealed the fire, and a large Tiffany lamp. It was warm in the room, but the mood of the gathering was altogether chilling.

When Jim introduced Mark to Ruth Krandle, she stood up, shook his hand numbly, and spoke in a hushed monotone, as if a corpse had been laid out in the room. Her husband sat in a big, overstuffed chair and stared at the floor. He nodded and mumbled something when he was introduced. Marvin sat in the window seat looking out. He was obviously a younger version of his father in all respects, including the depressed body language. They both had thick arms folded like armor across their chests.

Mark sat down in the window seat opposite Marvin and addressed him pointedly. There was no reason to make a pretense of formalities. "Jim tells me you have a problem, Marvin."

"Guess so."

"Do you have a plan?"

"No."

"What would you like to see happen?"

"I'd like to see this cockeyed war end tomorrow."

"I mean, what do you want to do?"

"Jim said you'd help me figure this thing out."

"Marvin's going to enlist in the Marines tomorrow morning," pronounced Benjamin, without looking up from his targeted spot on the floor.

"That would be one option," said Mark. "The Army would then forget about the draft notice, and all would be forgotten."

Ruth stood up and took a step toward Mark. "Marvin has never been in a fist fight. How's he going to fight a war?"

"He would learn," said Benjamin, "the way I learned when I was his age. It's the way of men. You don't understand such things, Ruth."

"I understand what combat did to you." Ruth planted both fists on her hips and glared at him. "Please, God, don't let them have Marvin." She turned officiously away, as if to leave on that note, then paused, "Would you like some cobbler, Mr. Roberts?"

"I'd love some. I've heard you're famous for your blackberry cobbler."

Ruth waved away the compliment. "You've been talking to my sons. They could live on cobbler."

"Could you fight in a war, Marvin?" persisted Mark after Ruth left to get the cobbler.

"Why should I? It's a crock of shit. It makes no sense." Marvin turned toward Mark and faced him for the first time.

Benjamin too looked up, and his lip trembled slightly. "If everyone felt that way, the Commies would take over the world without battin' an eye."

"Bullshit!" said Marvin turning away toward the window again.

There was a heavy silence during which Ruth came back carrying a tray which she set carefully on a driftwood coffee table in the center of the room. She moved solemnly like a pallbearer at a wake. "Do you think you can help Marvin?" she asked earnestly, as she handed Mark a generous serving of cobbler. It was neatly arranged in a delicate china dish and topped with an ornate silver fork. Rich, dark red juice seeped from holes in the top of the pastry and around the sides. She also handed him a big linen napkin which he spread over his lap.

"Wow! This looks great!" said Mark. He found it distracting to try to counsel people while balancing a dish on his knees, but after the first taste, he stopped worrying about whether anything would be accomplished. He was here for the cobbler, nothing more. Then he felt awkward when both Jim and Benjamin turned it down. Ruth took a tiny piece, which she dabbed at a little with her fork, but didn't really eat. Marvin, on the other hand, ate heartily, as though it were his last meal on Earth.

Mark felt like a parent lecturing the kid while he was eating. "Marvin, Jim invited me to come here and help you decide what to do about your draft notices. Someone from the F.B.I. came and asked about you. That probably means you're on their list. They could arrest you and put you in jail. You could spend two or more years in prison."

"They'd have to find me," said Marvin with his mouth full.

"My God, you can't hide out all your life," said Jim.

Marvin choked out sentences between gulps of cobbler. "I could go to Canada. It's not far. I bet I could swim to Canada from here."

"Really?" said Mark replacing his fork in the dish.

"He probably could," agreed Jim.

"Marvin," continued Mark earnestly, "If you decide to go to Canada, you should have a plan. If you're on the list, you can't go through a border crossing. The officials on the U.S. side will put you under arrest."

"Why would I go to a border crossing? I know lots of places where you can row your boat up to the shore and just walk right into Canada, no questions asked." He finished off the first piece of cobbler, walked over to the coffee table, replaced it on the tray, and returned to the window seat with another large helping that had been meant for Jim.

"That sounds like a good first step," said Mark. "Then what would you do? Do you know anyone in Canada?"

Marvin finally looked up and smiled benignly, round cheeks stuffed with cobbler, teeth red with juice. "I know you. Jim says you live in Canada."

"Is that what you want to do, go to Canada?" asked Mark.

Marvin didn't answer, but the pace of his eating slowed a little. Perhaps he was thinking.

During the silence Mark became aware of soft, muffled sobs. Ruth was crying. "I don't want Marvin to go to Canada. He might never come back."

"He would be subject to arrest if he came back," said Mark.

Marvin finished off the last of his second helping and set the dish beside him on the window seat. Then he looked directly at Mark. "What do you think I should do? Jim says you know all about this stuff."

"You're the only one who can know what's best for you, Marvin. If you do decide to go to Canada, I can give you some names of good people to contact. My wife has some Quaker friends who like to help draft resisters. They would get you a work permit."

"My son isn't a draft resister," said Benjamin emphatically. "He's going to sign up for the Marines in the morning."

"No!" gasped Ruth, "He would be killed."

"Well, Marvin, you have to make up your mind what you're going to do. But I guess it's important for you to know what others want, too. Jim, what do you think Marvin should do?"

"I think he should have gotten a girl pregnant and gotten married, but I guess it's too late for that. Or maybe he could break his leg or something, and get reclassified as physically unfit."

"Maybe he should tell them he's a conscientious objector," suggested Ruth. "You're a lawyer, maybe you could help him with that."

"That's another option," agreed Mark.

"Why don't we do that?" Ruth persisted. "That's the real reason Marvin didn't report for induction. He couldn't stomach war. He couldn't kill anybody. Could you help Marvin get conscientious objector status?"

"I'd be willing to try," said Mark, "But my track record isn't real good on that. Nobody's is yet, but we're starting to get the hang of it. Are you churchgoing people?"

"Once in a while, not often," admitted Ruth.

"It would be a little easier to make a case if you were into going to church a lot, especially if you were Quakers."

"Maybe we would be Quakers if there was a church like that here. We have only two churches."

Mark turned to his client again. "Are you a conscientious objector, Marvin?"

Marvin made direct eye contact with Mark momentarily, blushed, then looked away out the window. "I'm not even sure what it is."

"It's someone who sincerely believes that war is evil, immoral."

"Doesn't everybody?" asked Marvin.

Mark was impressed with the lack of hesitancy in that response, spoken in an ingenuous tone, but with an edge of sarcasm. Maybe the kid really was a conscientious objector. He launched into his lawyer routine about how if Marvin wanted to request Conscientious Objector status he'd have to write a statement that must be convincing to the draft board. He finished with a promise to help write the statement. All the while, Marvin continued to stare out the window, as if he weren't listening.

At some point, Ruth took the tray and dishes to the kitchen and returned with another tray of coffee, which she served in silence while Mark droned on over the same material at least three or four times. Mark felt uncomfortable doing most of the talking, but the rest of them were more than economical with words. Jim stared silently at the road ahead when he drove Mark back to town. He looked even more worried now than before.

"Do you think our meeting was beneficial?" asked Mark.

Jim shrugged. "There's no predicting Marvin, but I think he may take some definite action soon. Lord knows what he will do, but I don't think he'll choose jail. He'd be a caged bird."

"I kind of think he'll go to Canada," observed Mark. "That's the only option he's seriously considered, if any."

Jim shook his head. "I can't really see Marvin doing that either. He has so little sense of adventure. And what with Mom being so dead set against it.... If you ask me, the conscious objector idea is too ludicrous. Marvin's a philosophical type in his own way, but not like that. The kid isn't dumb, mind you. He's just not the type to sit around and verbalize his rationale. Marvin just does whatever he does, if you know what I mean."

KLAHOWYA COVE ~ MAY 11, 1967

Marvin woke up thinking about the one piece of berry cobbler left from the lawyer meeting last night — the one Ben didn't eat. That delicious piece of cobbler might be waiting for him in the kitchen. It would make a fine breakfast along with a couple of fried eggs.

Then he remembered about the F.B.I. man, Mr. Genzforth. Maybe he would come back today, maybe on the 10:45 interisland ferry. Better be gone by then. He would go help Wella nail the aluminum roofing sheets on her new barn. She would pay him, give him some rice pilaf and salad for lunch. He got up happy to find the house quiet and deserted. As usual, everyone else had gone to work before him. They were all in the wrong businesses, couldn't make their own hours.

Luckily they had not eaten the cobbler. There was nothing like Mom's blackberry cobbler. Marvin had spent about half of August helping her wrestle those beastly briars to make sure there would be plenty of berries to last in the freezer until next year. He deserved his share of the cobbler.

Outside, there was a haze over everything, and Marvin could barely see down to the schoolhouse. It didn't look like much of a day for putting up a roof. Maybe the fog would burn off.

Marvin went into the shed and rummaged around for his large coffee can of roofing nails. He put the can in the back of the pickup with the two dozen sheets of aluminum roofing and his carpenter belt for the short drive down to the dock where Jim's motorboat was moored. By the time he had all the supplies loaded into the boat, it was starting to look a little low in the water, but Marvin wasn't worried. He had loaded it fuller than that a time or two. He got in bravely, started the engine, and cast off toward Wella's place across the inlet.

About a quarter of a mile down and halfway across, Marvin spotted a large boat riding at anchor. He could barely make it out in the fog, and might not have noticed it, if not for its lights peering at him like little possum eyes through the haze. Marvin had never seen a boat like that in this inlet. He wasn't sure, but it looked like one of those Shore Patrol boats that came through the Strait from time to time.

People said they were looking for drug smugglers, but Marvin didn't believe that, because he knew the Coast Guard took care of that kind of thing. He figured the military boats must have something to do with making sure there were no spies about, what with a war going on and all, but he couldn't figure out what the thing would be doing here. Despite his curiosity, something told Marvin not to go over and investigate.

When he got to Wella's, she was already standing on the dock waiting. She always did that whenever anyone came to see her. Must be awful lonely over here by herself. Why did she want to live on an island all alone? And why did she always have to wear those long skirts? How was she going to climb around on the roof in that getup? Nice lady, but kind of weird. Never saw a harder worker though.

"Hi, Wella," said Marvin cheerfully. "Ready to go to work?" He handed her up a six foot slab of aluminum. She apprehended the big awkward thing gracefully, as if it were a playing card, deposited it lightly on the dock, and reached for another. It was going to be a chore for the two of them to cart all this stuff up the lawn, let alone get the job done today. It had taken the whole community club a couple of hours just to get the poles and trusses up there for the main bearing walls.

Marvin could feel Wella staring silently at him while they unloaded the boat. A couple of times he thought she said something, but then realized it must have been his imagination. Once when Wella's skirt got snagged by a dent in a piece of aluminum, Marvin seized the opportunity to try and talk some sense into her. "Better change to some jeans, Wella. You can't lay roof in a dress."

Wella finished adding a piece of aluminum to the stack and looked at him. "We can't do the roof today," she said.

"Yeah? Don't you remember? We talked about it at the potluck Saturday before last. I said a week from Monday I'd show you how to put on roofing. Tomorrow I have to build a deck for the Luethy's. This is the only day I can do it."

But Wella continued to stare at him coldly. "You must go to Canada today, Marvin." She spoke like a judge pronouncing a death sentence.

Despite the fact that Marvin had been quite warm from physical exertion, he suddenly felt every drop of his blood turning cold. His eyes met hers for a long steady moment while he tried to make sense of it. How did she knew about Canada? Who might have told her he was thinking about Canada?

Then a wave of anger swept over him. Even though he had grown up on Merrick Island and should take it all for granted by now, it still bugged him that everyone, even newcomers, knew more about his own business than he did. Outwardly he passed off her comment with a nonchalant wave of his hand. "I ain't goin' nowhere. Where'd you hear that rumor?"

Still Wella kept staring at him with that cold, determined expression. "If you don't go to Canada today, Mr. Genzforth will come and take you to a cruel place and lock you up."

There was the cold sweat again and a wave of mild nausea. "Who told you that?"

"It doesn't matter who told me. It only matters that it's true." Her expression softened, and her face was lined with concern. "I wouldn't tell you to go to Canada if it wasn't necessary. I know it will hurt your mother, but it would hurt her much more to see you in a cage. You have to go now, Marvin. He's coming for you now."

"Now? This very minute? I'm not ready."

"You can go now in Jim's boat. I'll go and tell your mother and ask for your things and bring them to you later."

"Oh, come on, Wella. I can't go to Canada now. At least I have to go home and get my stuff."

Aside from being scared and confused, Marvin thought the whole scene ridiculous. Anyway, his plan to put up roofing and have lunch with Wella was clearly off for now, so he got back in the boat and cast off toward Klahowya Cove again.

As he crossed back over the inlet Marvin noticed that the large boat was still anchored in the middle, glaring at him through the fog with its piercing eyes. He wasn't sure why, but something about it gave him the creeps, like monster movies when he was a little kid.

After he docked and got out of Jim's boat, Marvin looked out again at the large silhouette of a boat and noticed that it was moving now slowly toward him, growing ever so slightly larger in the fog. It was close enough now that Marvin knew for sure it was the Shore Patrol from Whidbey Island. What was it doing here? A wave of panic swept over him and he wanted to run like a little kid from some unknown imagined something. But he got control of himself and started to walk slowly back up the road toward the house. He would come back down and get the pickup later. Now he needed to be on foot, just in case he needed to run and hide. Marvin swallowed hard. He could hardly believe his thoughts as he continued to walk up the road toward his house.

After rounding the bend past the schoolhouse, Marvin stopped to peer up the hill through the mist. There was a car in the driveway in front of his house, and a strange man standing on the porch. Then there was a voice inside his head, repeating something weird Wella had said earlier, "Mr. Genzforth will come to take you to a cruel place and lock you up."

Marvin heard his own voice in his head repeating something weird he had said himself last night, "I could swim to Canada from here." Then suddenly, as if by a fear reflex, Marvin turned without another thought and ran back to the dock. The large, gray silhouette was closer now, but it had stopped still several hundred yards out. Maybe he couldn't swim to Canada, but he could swim across the inlet. He had done it many times in childhood, and something told him that was the only thing to do right now. If he went back to the road, the strange man, probably from the F.B.I., would be there. If he got back in the boat and cast off, the Shore Patrol would see him, and maybe they couldn't care less about him, but maybe they were looking for him.

He paused a brief moment, looking at the lead-gray water. Marvin knew well how cold it would be. He and lots of other kids from the Klahowya Cove School used to have swim races across the inlet during the summer vacations, and Marvin had been the undisputed champ. He quickly peeled off his parka and trousers and tossed them into Jim's boat. Next he crouched down among the docked boats and made a careful, shallow dive into the water. The cold shocked him at first, but soon faded away as Marvin began to swim with powerful, rapid strokes in full concentration upon winning the race.

Marvin peered out at the patrol boat each time his face rotated out of the water for a breath of air. The craft remained still the entire time, its prow pointed toward Klahowya Cove. Probably no one in the boat had the slightest inkling that a human was swimming across its path through such frigid waters. As he approached the dock on the other side, Marvin could see Wella standing there watching him swim toward her.

When he pulled himself up onto the dock, Wella handed Marvin a robe of soft, yellow wool. Marvin accepted the garment gratefully and put it on because he was shivering intensely. The robe was much too long, but it was warm, and Marvin stopped shaking almost the moment he put it on.

"I am glad you're going to Canada," said Wella even before Marvin had said anything, let alone anything about Canada. He couldn't believe what was happening to him.

"We must go quickly now," she said, as she crossed the dock, climbed into her own boat, and began raising the main sail. He thought he heard her telling him to follow her, but she couldn't have said anything — she was too busy rigging the boat.

Feeling completely miserable and awkward, Marvin stepped off the dock into the boat, steadying himself with his hand on the gunwale. Once safely in the boat, he crouched down on the deck all curled up in the robe. He started to shiver again even though the robe was quite warm. "What will I wear in Canada? I have no clothes. I don't have my stuff."

"While you were swimming back across, I phoned Jim. We have planned everything. Jim will bring your clothes."

"But where am I going?"

"You are going to Victoria, to a kind family. The clan of the Dunhams will take care of you, and help you find work building houses to earn money for your food and lodging. You will like it in Canada."

The boat was fully rigged now and Wella had cast off, confidently running with a gentle wind. Her hand was steady on the tiller as she spoke. A large chart was spread out on the deck, but her gaze was fixed upon the water ahead. "The village where the Dunham family lives is a small suburb of Victoria. Jim says it won't be hard to find. He gave me the address."

Marvin curled up into a tighter ball and pulled the bathrobe protectively around his thighs. "You mean to say I have to walk through a suburb of Victoria in this bathrobe?"

Wella shrugged away this objection nonchalantly. "I keep extra dry clothes in the storage bin in the galley with the food stuffs. In fact there is a pair of jeans. I do hope they fit you, Marvin. I never wear them. You can keep them to remember our adventure."

Marvin groaned. He wasn't much into adventures. He just wanted to go home and forget this whole thing. Maybe it was all Wella's imagination. Maybe there was no F.B.I. man. If only that were true! But it wasn't. Jim had talked to the F.B.I. man, too, and Wella wasn't the type to pass on idle gossip or get hyped over nothing. From the little Marvin knew about Wella, one thing was for sure. She didn't talk much, but when she said something, she meant it.

Marvin was surprised to find he could actually squeeze himself into Wella's brand new jeans. He knew they were new, because they were still in a sealed cellophane wrapper from the store. They were a lousy fit, tight across the hips and too high-waisted. After rolling them up to make big cuffs at the ankles, Marvin thought they looked almost normal — more presentable than the yellow bathrobe. Still, it was too cold to sit around in the wind in his wet T-shirt, so Marvin put the robe back on over his jeans.

As for the food Wella had mentioned, Marvin found some hard, grainy-looking cakes sealed in the same sort of plastic wrap. It was wholly unappetizing. He'd have to be pretty hungry to eat that stuff. He should have signed up for the Marines right away, when he first got the draft notice. But it had made him so goddamn mad. What kind of a free country was this anyway?

The hours dragged by slowly for Marvin, with nothing to do but shiver and worry and wonder whether he should have joined the Marines and whether he should still try to join the Marines. It was beginning to look like the only way he'd ever see home again.

To take his mind off his problems, Marvin offered to man the tiller but Wella said it was easier for her to concentrate while steering the boat. So Marvin remained huddled on the deck watching vague forms of islands float by like big hairy monsters in the fog. Several times he asked her anxiously if she was sure she knew the way, for he had lost track of it long ago. "As long as I can concentrate," she answered confidently.

Around noon, the fog lifted somewhat and the sun started to break through. That was when Marvin first saw the approaching military patrol boat, probably the same one he had observed in the inlet. It was maybe a quarter of a mile back, about the same distance it had been from the Klahowya Cove dock the first time he saw it. The fear that had been hanging over Marvin tightened into a grip around his heart. "That fucking patrol boat's following us!" he moaned.

"It follows me sometimes," Wella answered soothingly.

"The patrol boat follows you? Why does it do that?"

Wella shrugged. "The man in the boat doesn't know why. Someone he calls 'The Chief' told him to follow boats with certain numbers. Mine is one of them."

"That's stupid. Do they think you're a spy or something?"

Wella laughed. "Sometimes they think I'm a spy. Sometimes they think maybe I'm a drug smuggler. The man in the boat thinks it's boring to follow me. I never do any of the things they think I might be doing, so it gets very tedious for him to follow me. He just does it because it's his assigned duty."

"Doesn't it make you nervous? Why don't you complain to the authorities, tell them you're a law abiding citizen, and you want to be left alone. You shouldn't have to be harassed by the fucking Navy when you're minding your own business! They're probably just suspicious because you're a foreigner."

Marvin felt sorry after he said that. He was afraid it might hurt Wella's feelings, but she only laughed.

"After it becomes very boring they will stop following me," she answered soothingly.

They sailed on in silence while Marvin let his mind drift idly with the flow of its own thoughts until one surfaced. "Wonder what they'll make of you crossing over onto the Canadian side?"

"Is that against the laws of this planet?"

"Oh, no. You can even go ashore in Canada without a passport."

"Then they can make what they want of it. It will be another boring item for the man to write in his book."

Marvin felt considerably relieved now that Wella had reassured him that the military patrol boat was after her and not him. He even felt hungry enough to unwrap one of Wella's little grain bricks and try to eat it. After a couple of bites he felt completely full, and decided to lie down on the bunk and take a nap.

When Marvin woke up and peered out through the tiny cabin window, the sun was lowering toward the mountains. The boat was anchored dead in the water a half-mile out from a large land mass, maybe Vancouver Island.

Strangely enough, Wella sat in the stern with a fishing pole in hand, the line dangling over the side. Her eyes were closed, as if she were asleep, but her forehead was wrinkled in worry, or perhaps concentration.

As he came out of the cabin onto the deck, Marvin noticed that the military boat was still out there and coming closer now. In fact, he thought he could make out the figure of a man standing on the deck. "What's going on, Wella?" he demanded.

The woman opened her large, strange eyes and looked at him as if from some distant world, "Quiet!" she commanded. "Go back inside and stay there. Keep down!"

Feeling helpless and confused, Marvin darted back into the cabin and crouched down near the entrance. "What the hell's going on, Wella? You nuts or something? What's with the fish?"

Still holding her fishing pole, Wella let out more line and crossed the deck until she was within whispering distance of the cabin entrance. "I'm trying to make the patrol boat think our only reason to be here is to catch some small animals to eat. Now that we're in Canadian waters, they can stop us and ask us our names and numbers. They will ask your name, too, if they see you. If you tell them your name, they will find it on their list, and they will take you to the cruel place and lock you up."

Marvin thought about that for a moment. Then he thought about his trousers still in Jim's boat docked in Klahowya Cove. That's where he had left his driver's license.

"Oh, come on Wella. I think your imagination has got the better of you. Besides, I'll give them a phoney name."

"They won't believe you. They'll ask to see your identification."

"I don't have it with me. It's in Jim's boat."

"Then they'll take you away and lock you up anyway."

"My God, Wella, where do you get such notions? I've been living here all my life. I read the local papers every day. So far that's never happened to anyone around here. I don't know where you're from, but here they have to have a damned good reason to lock a guy up."

"Marvin, please believe me, they will lock you up if they find out or even suspect who you are. It has happened before. It was only last week when they locked up a stranger who was trying to run away from the killing games just like you."

Marvin was exasperated. This woman was so naive and yet so sure of herself. How could he explain anything to someone so stubborn. "Wella, thousands of draft dodgers have gone to Canada. Most of them walk right in, no questions asked."

"Not all," insisted Wella stubbornly. "And I promise you they are on their way here to ask questions right now."

Wella was standing in front of him, with her back to the patrol boat, and as she spoke, the boat moved slowly toward them. Despite the fact that Wella was a little touched in the head, he had a faint gnawing feeling that maybe she was right.

Terror gripped Marvin with the realization that this woman knew very well what she was talking about. Even though he had not spoken his thought aloud, she was nodding, "Yes, Marvin, you must swim to Canada. You must crawl over the prow. Keep low so they won't see you. Then jump into the water. On the shore, straight ahead of the prow, is a yellow cliff. Below the cliff is a narrow, steep-roofed house. An elderly woman with white hair is standing on the beach waiting for you. Her name is Cynthia Dunham."

Marvin looked at Wella in disbelief. She wasn't kidding. "How the hell do you know that?" he demanded.

"You said you could swim to Canada. Do it, Marvin," she urged.

Still crouched in the cabin doorway Marvin stared up at this strange woman who had brought him away from the safety of the only life he had ever known. How did she know he said anything about swimming to Canada? The only time he had ever spoken it aloud was last night to his family and the lawyer. Good Lord, the grapevine was fast!

But Marvin had a chilling feeling that something more than the grapevine was at work here, something a lot spookier, though he really couldn't put his finger on it. He should have taken Ben's advice and joined the Marines. Life would be hell in the Marines, but there would be no decisions. Now he was facing a strange new world with no family or friends to turn to or give him advice. What ever made him think he wanted to go to Canada instead of joining the Marines? Now he was trapped. At this moment there appeared to be no choice. He was, in fact, already in Canada, and therefore subject to arrest, unless he could get away before the patrol boat arrived. And it was coming, looming ever larger as it came.

Automatically, almost as if he had been hypnotized, Marvin felt his body taking actions that left his spirit behind. Still crouched in the doorway so as not to be spotted by the patrol boat, he reached up with both big hands and grabbed hold of the edge of the cabin roof. Then he pulled himself up until he could throw his right leg over the top. Quickly he slithered on his stomach under the boom and across the roof of the cabin. He didn't have to look back to see whether the patrol boat was still coming. He knew it was, because the hum of the its engine had increased to a soft growl. Reaching the prow of the boat, he dove head first into the frigid water. It wasn't until he tried to launch into his famous frog kick that Marvin realized he was still wearing those damned tight jeans.

Wella remained bent over the small animal lure in deep meditation for a long time. She must stay in contact with Marvin's thought sphere to make sure he reached the woman waiting for him on the shore, but she must not stand up and watch him swim away. It was difficult to concentrate because Marvin's thoughts were so confused and difficult to understand. His mind was racing with thoughts of not wanting to go to Canada. His mind was also spinning with thoughts of wanting to join the killing games instead. The thoughts battled one another and canceled each other out. At the same time, Marvin was feeling angry with his father, and ashamed of hurting his mother. He felt fear of the unknown shore ahead. Perhaps the person waiting for him on the shore was not there to help him. Maybe that person will turn him over to the authorities and have him arrested.

Wella's eyes remained closed and her concentration was deep, though she knew, at the periphery of her awareness, that the patrol boat was approaching. Suddenly, a large hand gripped her shoulder and gave her a rough shake. She looked up into the face of a stranger... well, not entirely a stranger. It was the same man Wella had seen on her first day on this planet. He was the man who sometimes followed her boat to read the numbers. But this time the man had left the patrol boat and come aboard *Terra*. He was standing on *Terra*'s deck beside her. This was confusing, because Wella had been taught that it was not the custom on this planet to board someone's boat without their permission. Then she remembered that when they wanted to arrest someone it would be different, and Wella knew that this man wanted to arrest Marvin, and probably thought he was still on board.

"Wake up!" the man commanded sharply.

Wella smiled in amusement. This man was apparently confused, too. First of all, he was mistaken, because Marvin was already on the shore of Canada. He was also mistaken in his assumption that she was asleep.

toward her in the water. At first she thought it was a seal, but then something told her it was Marvin.

Jim couldn't identify exactly what it was, but at that moment he knew that there was something very different about Wella De Gornia. Here was this strange woman who had never set foot, or in this case set sail, in this country before, and she managed to find a particular house and a particular person on a particular beach miles away with very scant directions. Jim had told Wella roughly where Morris Cove was and had given her the address, but he had anticipated poor Marvin wandering about for hours trying to find the place after Wella left him off on some deserted beach. What kind of woman was this anyway? She seemed so straightforward, even naive, yet she was such an unspeakable enigma.

When Jim had promised himself to keep this love thing under control for Pam's sake and his own, he had never expected to encounter a woman like this. He had decided a long time ago that he was stuck with Pamela. Sure, Pam was as jealous as anyone, but she was the only one who understood. She was the only one who would still love him despite his love-vulnerability neurosis. At that moment in his reverie, Jim happened to glance out the window just in time to see Wella jogging up the road; she was probably going to pay Ruth an evening call.

Fear squelched his urge to run out and call to Wella as she ran by. Was he going nuts? At times, he really believed Wella was reading his mind and sending him thoughts. People with those kinds of fantasies were labeled schizophrenic.

Jim sat at his desk frozen in fear of his own thoughts. He wasn't sure how long he sat, but the room was quite dark when he finally decided to give it up for the day.

After he had locked up the schoolhouse and started to walk up the road, he saw her tall, slender silhouette moving swiftly down the hill toward him. The fear and love rose to a crescendo as she approached, and the craziness told him that he had been somehow influenced by Wella's mind to walk out onto the road at that very moment so she could stop and talk with him.

"Jim! I was just coming to see you! I wanted to invite you to my new barn ceremony — I mean barn-warming party. It will be Friday at seven-thirty."

"This Friday? Uh, well, of course." Jim could scarcely contain himself. Wella's cheerful invitation had disarmed his fear, but now he wanted to take her in his arms and kiss her tenderly, and that thought frightened him a lot. There would not have been time, however, because Wella had hurried off down toward the dock calling back.

"That's wonderful! I have to go now. It's getting dark." But after she had left a wide safe space between them, she stopped suddenly and turned to look at him again. "Don't forget to bring Pam, of course."

"Uh, yes, of course. Anything else?"

"Like what?"

"Do you want me to bring anything? You know, like beer?"

"Oh yes, that would be good. Many people seem to like beer. How about Coca Cola? Can you bring some Coke?"

"Sure. I'll bring a case of each."

Wella turned again and jogged on down the hill calling back. "Thank you, Jim. Thank you. My new barn will be very warm."

THE LAST FRIDAY IN AUGUST, 1967

By the end of the summer, Friday night parties at Wella's beach had become a tradition. On the last Friday of August, it rained all day and was too cold for a beach party, but Jim took Pam over to visit Wella anyway. They sat in Wella's big, bare living room by the fire. The room was beginning to feel like home to Jim by now. He liked to converse with Wella and delight in her naive comments. He found sitting on the floor in what appeared to be as much a workshop as a sitting room, to be more relaxing than the upholstered comfort of other living rooms.

That day he felt more need for comfort than usual. The long dreaded letter had finally arrived. After so many years of carefully planned evasion, of cleverly keeping one step ahead of them, the Army had finally trapped him. He stared silently into the fire, drawing faint comfort from its gentle dance while Wella hung their wet jackets over the spinning wheel and brewed them cups of hot tea.

Pam began talking about the latest fashions and making fun of the tourists. Every so often, he nodded or smiled at something that was said just to make it seem like he was listening. Wella interrupted, "Jim isn't listening. He is worrying."

Pamela stopped short in the middle of her description of an elaborate sun hat a woman from one of the tourist boats had worn into Ruth's shop. The attentions of both women were now upon him.

"What's wrong, Jim?" demanded Pam. "Has something happened to Marvin?"

Jim shrugged. "I can't tell you much about Marvin. He hardly ever writes. Mom's pretty worried, but I guess they tell the family if a kid gets killed. So, no news is good news."

"You have bad news about yourself," persisted Wella. She was reading his mind again.

Pam looked puzzled, "Has there been a quarrel?"

Jim felt a grimace reshaping his face. By tomorrow noon everyone in Island County would know he was being abducted into the Army. It didn't matter whether he told anyone or not. Information like that somehow seeped through the cracks of peoples' minds. It had always been that way, but it seemed even more so lately, since Wella moved there. "No, no quarrel," he said, "just the inevitable friendly letter from the Army."

Pam slammed her cup down so hard on the hearth that Jim was surprised it didn't break. Some of the tea splashed out on the bricks. "Oh, no, not again! Aren't you too old to be forced into the Army?"

If only Pam could absorb pain quietly, rather than splashing it back at him. "I'm twenty-five. That's the maximum age."

"You got a letter the other year," argued Pam. "Remember, you just had to get a letter from the school superintendent."

"This time it won't work. They aren't exempting teachers anymore."

At the periphery of Jim's awareness, he saw Wella thoughtfully sipping her tea and gazing calmly into at the fire. "What does the letter say?" she asked almost in a whisper.

"It says a lot of gobbledygook that means I have to take the physical next Tuesday."

Wella continued to sip her tea. "What does it mean — 'take the physical'?"

"It means if I'm strong and healthy, I can go and get killed."

She took another long sip. "Doesn't going to war mean you have to try to kill people yourself?" she asked so softly that Jim could barely hear her.

"Of course. You have to kill in order to not be killed."

"You couldn't do that." She spoke now with firm conviction in a clearly audible tone.

The comment had come so swiftly that it startled Jim. He had to sip tea a moment searching for the next response. "No, I guess I couldn't do that."

"If you couldn't kill anyone you won't be much help to them. Maybe you should just tell them you couldn't kill anyone."

Jim felt his heart warmed by Wella's naivete. He smiled and looked across into her eyes now gazing at him with soft concern. "They have no deferment category for the inability to kill. If you can't kill, you get killed instead."

"They must be cruel." Wella returned her thoughtful gaze to the fire. "What deferment categories are there?"

"Damned few," said Jim. Then he fell back into brooding silence. After awhile, Wella's clear, quiet voice broke in again. "What few?"

Jim wanted to ignore the question. It was elementary and made little difference. To be polite, he summarized. "They used to defer students and married guys. Now about all that's left is fatherhood."

"Fatherhood?"

"Yeah. You have to have a kid."

"You can't have a kid. You're a man."

Jim looked at Wella's face for a sign that she was kidding. "Your wife has to have a kid or at least be pregnant."

Wella shook her head sadly. "I'm pregnant. Too bad for you, I'm not your wife."

Jim looked hard at Wella now. A touch of something that felt a little like shock, but even more like jealousy, welled up in him before he had time to rationalize them away with more enlightened attitudes. He didn't have to expose his feelings by asking for an explanation. Pam did that for him.

"Pregnant? How?" she demanded.

Wella bowed her head and looked away. Then she spoke in the tone of a school girl accused by the teacher. "I'm afraid I ran around with a married man. I know you warned me against that, Pamela, but no one saw us."

Jim felt a touch of humor emerging again despite his effort to fight back that little gnawing imp of jealousy.

"Why didn't you take the pill?" persisted Pam.

"I wanted to get pregnant," said Wella. "You told me there was some kind of law against running around with married men, and all the unmarried ones are gone on account of war, but surely there's no law against being pregnant."

"There is. Your baby will be illegitimate," insisted Pam.

"Illegitimate?"

"Yes, Wella. Please don't tell me you don't know what that means? You can't be that out of it." The pitch of Pam's voice was gradually rising, and Jim felt humor lifting his mood slightly.

Wella stood up and busied herself with feeding the fire. She fed it from a stack of driftwood arranged along the wall. Meanwhile, Pam was almost shrieking. "It means your baby has no father, no name."

"She will have a name. I will call her Dana."

"What if it's a boy?" grinned Jim.

Wella sighed and sat back down. Jim detected a note of deep satisfaction in the sigh. "She isn't a boy. She's a girl," she asserted confidently, and relaxed into the cushioned seat.

Still smiling, Jim got on his knees and crawled over to Wella. He took her hand, pressed it against his lips, and kissed it. "Will you marry me?" he begged melodramatically. He was finally having fun, and by this gesture hoped to include the two women in his feeling. But it didn't work. Wella jerked her hand away angrily, glanced at Pam, and then glared back at Jim. "No! Of course not! Pamela is my friend — that would be very bad."

Jim was a bit taken aback by that reaction. But Pamela declared dramatically, "Wella, it's the only solution. You need a husband and Jim needs a pregnant wife." Jim felt his chin drop in amazement and rejection.

Wella was mumbling something in what must have been her native tongue, a language Jim didn't recognize. It sounded something like "Ipths wirdyeth se zenfumeth." She stood up, walked over to the fire, and rubbed her finger tips together as if to warm them. Finally she turned and faced them with her back to the fire. "There are always many solutions to every problem. I think we should form a new clan. The child will be yours in name, but really ours."

Pamela looked really bewildered now, but Wella continued with her inscrutable line of reasoning. Apparently thrilled with her idea, she rushed over, knelt down beside Pamela and took hold of her hand. "We could form a new clan," she repeated. "Dana could be the child of Jim and Pamela Krandle, but in spirit she would be our child, the child of the clan. No one would have to be told outright."

Jim felt amusement, horror, and confusion all mixed together. "Good Lord, Wella, you mean, to get out of marrying me, you would go to such an extent as to give away your own wanted baby?"

Pamela chimed in, "Give away your child! That's unnatural."

Wella shook her head emphatically. "This must be understood. I will not give you Dana. We will all live together as one clan. The child will be ours."

There was a long silence while Jim let Wella's words sink into his mind then filter down into his heart. When they finally settled there, his mixture of confused feelings was gone. In its place was a simple, profound sense of awe. This woman who seemed so naive was simply operating out of a sense of values none of them could imagine or comprehend. He glanced over at Pamela who had also fallen into a thoughtful silence. Pam had a pretty provincial mind, but maybe even she was beginning to catch on. He crawled over to Wella and took hold of her hand again. "You're a damned good sport, Wella." It was, after all, worth a try, what with the Army hot on his trail.

. . .

Slumped into her cushion, Pam tried to make sense of what was going on. Wella was very odd, but Pam couldn't help but like her anyway. For all her weird notions, Wella could be trusted to keep her feelings under control, and to keep her promises. Obviously, Wella knew Jim's feelings got out of control now and then. But even though she liked Jim in return, Wella could be counted on to keep her distance. Actually, it was kind of nice having Wella around. She was a good safe outlet for Jim's — what did he call it? — "love-vulnerability syndrome."

But this stuff Wella was talking about now was a bit far out. Apparently, Wella wanted all three of them to live together under one roof, kind of like in a hippy commune. Then Wella would have the baby, and everyone would be told it was Pam's.

How was she going to convince people she was pregnant? Wouldn't it be obvious that Wella was the one who was pregnant?

The amazing part was that it involved an imminent wedding ceremony between Jim and herself, and Jim was up for it. Pam had always hoped that they would get around to marriage sooner or later; now Jim really seemed to go for the idea. He must be crazy. Maybe he had started smoking marijuana again. Of course, he wasn't the one who had to pretend to be pregnant and go through a big nine-month charade. The hard part would be between herself and Wella. Jim had the easy part. He just had to get married and then lie to the Army about his wife being pregnant.

"Doesn't the Army want to see a doctor's certificate that your wife is pregnant?" asked Pam, breaking a long moment of silence.

Jim shrugged. "I don't think so. At least not here in Island County. They just want to see the baby and the birth certificate."

Pamela could hardly believe her ears. She would try to reason with him. "Jim, you can't be serious. How would I convince people I'm pregnant? How would Wella convince people she wasn't?"

"Why would people think I was pregnant if I didn't tell them?" asked Wella in her incredibly innocent manner.

She had to be kidding.

"Well, obviously you'd look pregnant. I mean your stomach would grow. You'd walk funny. Maybe you'd have morning sickness, stuff like that."

Amazingly enough, Wella looked astonished like this was news to her. Then she shrugged her shoulders and smiled.

"No one will know. I will always wear a loose woolen robe. I will run fast as I always do. I will continue my work, and I won't have any sickness. I promise."

Pam searched Wella's smile. "How do you know, Wella? Have you ever been pregnant before?"

Wella gazed at Pam with complete sincerity. "No, I've never been pregnant before, but I promise no one will suspect from my appearance or behavior."

Pam could hardly contain her astonishment. These people, her closest friends, must be crazy. A part of her felt like getting up and walking out. But where would she go? Pam imagined herself walking the beach around Wella's little island. It wouldn't take more than fifteen minutes to make the full circle even stumbling over logs and rocks as the tide came in. She wouldn't get very far. In fact, she would end up right back where she started. Pam had often felt trapped like that growing up on a small island. Whenever she felt the need to put distance between herself and others, she was always faced with the surrounding expanse of frigid waters. "All right. That's fine, Wella," she said, hearing the sarcasm in her own voice, "You seem so sure you can put on a convincing act for nine months of not being pregnant, but what about me? What am I supposed to do, wear a pillow in front like Santa Claus?"

For answer, Wella merely looked at Pam as if she was speaking a foreign language.

Jim had been listening with the slightest trace of smile at the corners of his lips, but now he rose to his haunches and began to crow with excitement. "Yes, Pam, don't you remember? A couple years ago, we went over to Seattle and saw my cousin Theresa in a play. I don't remember much about the play, but Theresa played the part of a pregnant woman. She looked really pregnant. It was a costuming trick. She rented something from a costume shop."

That did it. Now Pam really felt like getting up and walking out. Why stay here with crazy people? But she was trapped on this tiny little island, and these crazy people happened to be her closest friends. She pictured herself getting up and running down to the dock, starting the engine of Jim's boat and driving away. But where would she go? She knew no other life but the one on this narrow, confined, island world. She had always hoped one day that life would involve her marriage to Jim, but she had never thought it would be under such bizarre circumstances.

ORCA HARBOR ~ AUGUST 9, 1967

Before she left for the church, Pam took one last look at herself in the full length mirror. After all, from the point of view of beauty, fashion, and wish fulfillment, this was probably the high point of her life. Theresa had helped her select the antique, white taffeta gown in Seattle. Her long, dark brown hair had never been complemented by so fitting a garment, especially when offset with her mother's pearl earrings. This was all Pam needed to look and feel like a princess.

Pam wondered how long she had looked forward to this moment. She had probably started fantasizing about it the first time Jim had smiled at her in the Klahowya Cove School yard. She was six years old at the time. All through school Jim Krandle's warm personality had made him popular with all the girls, and Jim had loved all of them in return.

When they were alone, Jim always assured Pam that she was the prettiest girl on the island, and Pam knew she was his favorite. Over the years, they had grown closer. They had exchanged stories of family quarrels and other private troubles. The first sexual encounter for either of them was together in the meadow overlooking Hidden Cove. They had a huge audience of Mr. Overby's dairy herd staring at them from across the fence.

Although Jim had dated many other girls during high school and college, he had always come back to Pam. After he moved back to the island and started to teach in the school, Jim had stopped dating other women, even though he still liked to meet them and talk with them. He was smart enough to know that the island school teacher must not have a loose reputation. He had to stick to one woman, and the natural choice was Pam, with whom he had the strongest ties and who was indeed, in his stated opinion, "the prettiest girl on the island."

But there was a slight imperfection in Pam's image of herself as the princess bride that morning. In the fairy tale, you married the guy because he was madly in love and needed you at his side. With Jim, this was clearly not the case. Maybe he would never have gotten around to marriage if it weren't for this threat of being forced into the Army. As Pam walked down the aisle of the First Presbyterian Church, she figured everyone in the church was probably thinking the same thing. Worst of all, as the perfect picture of the fairy tale bride, she wasn't supposed to be pregnant, which, of course, she wasn't, but everyone had been led to believe she was. Such is life.

During the recitation of the vows, Pam looked out at the gathering of her family and friends. Her mother, Cynthia Bradley, was seated in the front pew on the left side alone. As usual, if you didn't know she was the church secretary, you might have mistaken her for Queen Elizabeth II, sitting there so regal and perfect. As far as the general public knew, Cynthia Bradley was not subject to the normal range of messy human emotions. But Pam knew better. At least she knew her mother had feelings. Over the years, Pam alone had been privy to many demonstrations of the feelings her mother expressed only within the walls of their cottage. But even to Pamela, Cynthia's feelings were seldom revealed at face value. Pam hoped her mother was pleased about the wedding, but she would never know for sure. Although

Pam had resolved to be an open person, unlike Cynthia, she could not help but admire this woman who, having lost her husband in the Korean war, had brought her daughter up quite respectably.

The front left pew was packed with Krandles. In fact, the church was about half-filled with Krandles or half-Krandles. They tended to be a close knit clan. In front, beside Ruth and Ben, sat Cousin Theresa, who was bulging a little. Theresa had learned she was pregnant after her boyfriend, Charles Redtree, joined the Air Force to avoid being drafted into the Army. No one in the family had ever met the guy, but Theresa said he had grown up on the Summamish reservation and was extremely handsome and polite. That was all the family knew of him. It occurred to Pam that, if all went according to plan, Wella's child and Theresa's would grow up as cousins close in age. Maybe they would be friends, as Theresa and Jim had always been.

Another face that singled itself out was Wella's. She was sitting way in the back, and it looked like she was asleep because her eyes were closed and she seemed to be off some place. That was one of the eerie things about Wella. Often at a gathering like a potluck supper, she would seem to go to sleep. She wouldn't slump down or nod or anything, but her eyes would close like that. But if someone teased her about going to sleep, it always came out in the conversation that Wella had been keenly aware the whole time. In fact, she seemed to know more than anyone else about the feelings and interactions of people present.

As she recited the marriage vows, a strange feeling came over Pamela. It was a feeling that she was being watched. Well, of course she was being watched. About two hundred people were sitting out there focusing their rapt attention on her and Jim and the Reverend Powell.

"Do you take Jim Krandle as your lawful wedded husband from this day forward...?"

Pamela heard the words as if from a distance in a dream, but the reality she experienced at that moment was not the presence of so many people watching her get married. Maybe the excitement of the wedding had taken hold of her imagination, but she felt as if she were being watched inside her soul. It was like a powerful energy field filled the church and encompassed the minds of everyone there. It wasn't an unpleasant feeling. In fact, it was quite nice, a feeling of great love intensifying with each additional second.

As the marriage vows ended, Wella opened her eyes, looked straight at Pam, and smiled. At that moment Pam felt all warm and glowing inside, and she smiled back. Then she noticed that everyone in the church was smiling that same glowing smile. It was a delightful experience, but positively eerie.

After the reception, Jim and Pamela left for their honeymoon. They didn't go far. Jim said the closest place as beautiful as the San Juan Islands was probably southern France, and they couldn't afford to go there. So he borrowed Wella's fancy sailboat for a cruise around the islands. They had reservations to stay a night each at Rosario and Roche Harbor, and Jim wanted to tie up here and there in little picturesque coves and harbors that weren't so well known by the tourists. Jim and Pam knew lots of places like that after so many years of being friends and lovers. Jim planned one day to write a book entitled, "One Hundred and One Places to Make Love in the San Juan Islands." He hoped to self-publish it and sell it to the tourists.

ROCHE HARBOR ~ TWO DAYS LATER

It wasn't the choice of location that dampened her spirits on that lazy August afternoon as she sat on the Roche Harbor Hotel veranda with Jim. The place was, after all, as much like the Riviera as anything Pam's imagination could conjure up. Even if they had gone to France, Pam would be haunted by the same nagging feeling. She was now officially and legally a Krandle, but the satisfaction she should have felt was negated by her conviction that Jim had married her — not because he was in love with her — but to avoid being abducted into the Army. Sure, Jim had been in love with her once, but that was when he was a kid. Now she was more like an old shoe that fit well. Far from being like newlyweds, they were more like a couple who had been married half their lives. There wasn't much excitement in their relationship. Besides, Jim was currently under the influence of his neurosis, and his mind had been on Wella for the past several weeks. In fact, he would have married Wella if she hadn't turned him down.

Besides her anxiety about her relationship with Jim, Pam worried about the pact they had made with Wella. She was such a dear person, but there was something very strange about her. At that moment, while seated with Jim under an umbrella in the restaurant veranda of the Roche Harbor Inn overlooking a festive array of yachts and sail boats, she felt as though Wella was watching her. It was scary. Wella was supposed to be back on her own little island some forty miles away, sheering sheep, weaving and minding her own business. Why did it feel like she was watching? Pam knew it was impossible, of course. Maybe she was going nuts.

Jim was saying, "Why don't we rent bicycles and go for a ride over to British Camp. My bones are cramped from sitting in that boat all morning."

At that moment a biplane buzzed the harbor, its passengers waving invitingly at the tourists below. "I'd rather take a plane ride instead," said Pam. "It only costs fifteen dollars for half an hour."

"We could rent bikes all day for half that," commented Jim. Then he looked sorry and hastened to add, "Maybe we could go for a half-hour biplane ride and then rent bikes. I mean it isn't like you take a honeymoon trip every day."

"That would be okay," said Pam, but she didn't feel very enthused. Anxiety had gotten the better of her.

There was a long silence while Pam looked down at her hands, wanting to tell Jim what was bothering her, but not knowing where to begin. She could feel his eyes on her.

Finally he said, "For years, you've wanted to spend the night in Roche Harbor. So now we're here, but you don't seem to be having much fun."

The biplane buzzed the harbor again, so Pam could not have been heard even if she had tried to answer. How could she tell Jim she felt like Wella was here spying on them?

After the noise faded away, Jim said, "I hope you're not worried about the Army finding out you aren't really pregnant. They've already stuck my file way in the back of the drawer. I'll be forgotten for at least another year. Besides, you're going to do an Academy Award performance at this pregnancy act. I just know it."

"I'm not worried about the pregnancy act, at least not at this moment." Pam was about to break down and try to share her complex of feelings with Jim when she was interrupted by a young waiter imperiously demanding their order. He looked like something out of a slick magazine ad, with his white tuxedo jacket and a little serving towel over his arm. Although Pam had been holding the menu in her hand for several minutes, she hadn't really looked at it. To avoid embarrassment she ordered a chef's salad and some Rhein wine.

Jim ordered the same thing to get rid of the waiter. "I'm glad you aren't worried about the pregnancy act," he said. "You'll do great. So what's the problem?"

"I'm worried about Wella."

"Why worry about Wella? She's going to be fine no matter what."

"But we have to live with her on her island, unless we can dig up a kid from some place else real fast."

"You don't want to live with Wella? I thought you liked her."

At that moment the waiter came back with the wine. He must have heard Jim's question. Maybe he was listening curiously for her answer. Pam shrugged and took a sip of wine, waiting until the waiter left. It felt weird to be talking about Wella and at the same time to have this feeling that she was listening in on their conversation along with the waiter. Finally she responded, "Of course I like Wella. You can't help but like her. She'd give you the shirt off her back."

"Does that make you feel uncomfortable?" asked Jim. "I mean, does it make you feel obligated or something?"

Pam shook her head. "No, I don't feel obligated to Wella." She paused and then wrenched her true feeling out of that tight place in her chest. "I feel scared of Wella."

"No kidding!" exclaimed Jim. Then he reached suddenly across the table, took hold of her hand, and looked into her eyes. "So do I!"

"Really?"

"Yes, really."

"Why?"

Jim hesitated as if he didn't want to answer.

"Really, Jim, please tell me why you feel frightened of Wella," persisted Pam. "It's important."

"Well," returned Jim, "I'll tell you if you first tell me why you're afraid of her."

Pam paused to gather her thoughts. "I can't put it in words exactly, but Wella does things to my mind."

Jim's eyes lit up as if in recognition of his own unspoken feeling. He paused, groping for the right words. "Pam, does it feel like Wella is sometimes, well, sort of, reading your mind?"

"Yes, and sometimes putting in thoughts. Jim, you know, sometimes I even hear Wella's voice in my head."

Jim responded with a recognition reflex that sent a chill through Pam. It wasn't her imagination after all. Jim had experienced it too. "Me too," he admitted.

There was a awkward silence. Finally, Pam said, "We better not tell anyone we think Wella is a mind reader." She laughed nervously.

"No, of course not," agreed Jim. "It wouldn't help to spread it around. Even though it's scary, I'm pretty sure Wella wouldn't do any harm with it."

"Is that why you're in love with her?"

"Who said I was in love with Wella?" Jim laughed a hearty but nervous laugh. Then he said, "Sure, Pam. No need to lie to you. You'd guess my feelings anyway. I've had some pretty strong feelings about Wella in the past few weeks. But I couldn't marry Wella De Gornia, no matter what. She's too scary for one thing, and for another, I decided years ago that if I ever got married it would be to you. I mean, I never really wanted to get married. The only kind of guys who want to get married are the ones who feel incomplete without a wife. I don't feel that way. I could make it on my own."

Feeling rejected, Pam pulled her hand away and reached for her glass to take another sip of wine. "So, next year you'll be too old to get drafted, and we can get a divorce," she remarked sarcastically.

At that moment, the waiter returned and served them tiny salads in silver bowls. Pam thought she saw his eyebrow twitch slightly in response to her remark.

Jim didn't seem to notice the waiter. Dodging the salad, he reached for Pam's other hand and looked sincerely into her eyes again. "Come on, Pam, I feel like the luckiest guy in the world to have a woman like you, a woman I can talk to, one who will love me even with my weaknesses. I really love you, Pamela. I love you in a way that I could never love Wella or anyone else. You're my friend."

After the waiter had made a hasty retreat, Pam leaned toward Jim, and squeezed his hand in a maternal gesture. She would try to make him understand. "Jim, if I really am the prettiest girl on Merrick Island, like you always said, don't you think I should be married to someone who really wants me for a wife?" She took a bite of the salad, but found it rather tasteless. She was glad it was small.

Meanwhile, Jim had been staring at her with a look of concerned bewilderment. Then something seemed to dawn on him. He got down on one knee, still holding on to her hand as he slid it off the table. He pressed Pamela's hand to his lips and looked soulfully up into her eyes. His lips felt warm and she could feel them trembling a little. "Oh, I'm so sorry, Pam. I had no idea you thought I wasn't in love with you. My God! I've been hopelessly in love with you as long as I remember. Why, I worship the ground you walk on!" He kissed her hand again.

"Please, Jim, get up," she pleaded "Everyone in the restaurant is watching."

Still holding her hand tenderly, Jim returned to his seat at the table. "Anything you say, my love. I'd do anything for you. Name it!"

"That was embarrassing, but it was awfully sweet of you. Do you really mean it?"

"Pam, I beg of you, don't ever entertain the slightest notion that I would prefer to be married to anyone but you. Not Wella, not the Goddess Venus, not anybody. You are far more beautiful, more lovely, sweeter, more understanding than any woman in the world. I love you. I'm so glad you married me. You've made me the happiest man on Earth."

At the periphery of her awareness, Pam saw the waiter return almost on tiptoe, and place the check ever so gently on the table. But he wasn't important anymore. Her attention was on Jim. He was laying it on awfully thick, but she knew Jim well enough to know he would never fake such an outburst of feeling. She was so touched that she began to cry softly, but now everyone in the restaurant really was watching, so she forced back the tears. "That's awfully sweet, Jim. I guess I'm really lucky to have such a lover for a husband, even if you are a bit fickle. Most guys these days are such hard-nosed jerks."

Suddenly Jim's face lit up with that worshipful smile that used to kill the girls when he was a kid. "Pam, what do you say we put the plane ride off until tomorrow. It's still warm and sunny, and I want to get over to the San Juan County Park. There's a wide expanse of meadow there overlooking the water. It's a lot like Mr. Overby's pasture." With that, he stood up and grabbed the check, as if he meant to leave at that very moment.

Pam stood and reached for Jim's arm. "Jim, you haven't finished your salad, and we've already paid $20 for a room in this fancy hotel. Why would we want to make love in a County Park?"

Jim stood there looking as if his feelings were hurt. Gradually, his expression changed to thoughtfulness, and finally to immense delight. "Good Lord," he breathed, "I nearly forgot. After all these years. We don't have to make love in Mr. Overby's field anymore. And we can make love whenever we feel like it. That's great! I'm so glad I married you, Pam."

Before she realized what was happening, Jim's arms were around her waist and his lips were pressed to her's in a kiss that could only mean he was in love with her. It made her so happy, she didn't much mind that they were still in the restaurant in front of all those people.

LEVIN ISLAND ~ WINTER, 1968

Wella was pleased that Jim and Pam were coming to live with her, but at Jorka's advice, she tried not to appear overly enthused. Jorka explained that North American peoples would not understand the Gallatan need for a clan since they tended not to live in large groups. In fact, they would expect her to be somewhat reluctant to relinquish something called "privacy." Jorka explained that "privacy" was to many Earth humans, especially North Americans, "a valued sense of being without companions."

Although she understood the concept, it left Wella confused. She typed in, "Please define 'loneliness'."

Some time elapsed while Jorka processed the comparison. "Loneliness is an unwanted sense of lacking companionship."

"I have been very lonely living here," typed in Wella. "Perhaps I should just tell them I am lonely."

"Yes, it would be wise to admit your loneliness, but you must at the same time learn to value privacy if you are to live with Earth humans."

Wella consulted with Jorka about every action and decision during the days before and just after the arrival of her new clan. Jorka agreed that the arrival of Pam and Jim meant her mission was going well. The child would have a clan. Dana would even have a traditional Earth human family unit in the event that Wella should die or leave Korba-3, Earth. That was all the more reason to manage every detail prudently, and not offend the Earth humans.

At Jorka's advice, Wella got Bill McNaulty, a friend of Marvin's from the construction business, to help her build a small apartment in half of the barn. Wella would then live in the barn and "rent" her house to the Krandles. Jorka said the new barn was unnecessarily large anyway. Erely sheep spent most of their time in the meadow and would come into the barn only rarely during the winter rains for lambing. Jorka even displayed plans for the apartment in her globe, and Wella carefully copied them on graph paper purchased in Orca Harbor.

Jorka's plan worked extremely well. The house rental idea created a strong public motive for Pam and Jim to move to Levin Island. Where else could they rent so fine a home so near the Klahowya Cove Schoolhouse? It was Jorka's idea to — in a sense — lie to the public and spread it about that Wella wanted to rent out the house for both "security and financial considerations." It would provide income to help pay taxes and would mean more people about. After all, it was not entirely safe for a woman to live alone on an island these days. None of this made much sense to Wella, but she noticed many nods of agreement when she told people about it at potlucks and in the shops of Orca Harbor.

Wella liked her new apartment because it was more like a Gallatan dwelling, all in one room, rather than divided up into little rooms like Earth dwellings. But she was disappointed that she wouldn't be living in the same house with Pam and Jim. She had looked forward to the presence of other intelligent beings. Jorka assured her that Pam and Jim would gradually warm up to the idea and include her more and more at their hearth until it would seem as though they all lived under one roof. Jorka pointed out that after the birth of the child, Pam and Jim would need Wella to feed and take care of the baby.

By early December, the Krandles had moved themselves and their belongings from their temporary residence, a small room called "the teacherage" behind the schoolhouse. Each morning they would motor over to Klahowya Cove in Jim's boat. Jim would walk up to the schoolhouse, and Pam would ride with Ruth in her station wagon, or in Marvin's old truck, across the island. They would spend most of the day in Ruth's shop, as they had always done. After Jim and Pam left in the morning, Wella would go down to the tunnel to consult with Jorka. She had so many questions these days with Earth humans living so close.

In the evening, when Jim and Pam came back, Wella, at Jorka's suggestion, would invite them to her apartment for dinner. Jorka would even prescribe the menu and give careful instructions for the preparations. It was amazing how much Jorka knew. She even knew what kind of food different people on Merrick Island liked to eat. For Jim and Pam, she suggested spaghetti with berry cobbler for dessert.

Wella noticed that Pam was beginning to look different. She wore dresses and blouses that were loose in front. Jorka suggested that Wella not ask how Pam managed to look a little larger in the abdomen with each successive sun cycle. Pam had made several trips by large boat to the city, where she must have learned about the "costuming trick" Jim had mentioned.

In December, Jorka gave Wella many instructions about an important Earth ceremonial series called "Christmas." Wella was glad that it occurred before lambing time because there was a lot of work to it. In addition to her usual spinning and weaving, Wella had to make special gifts for all the Krandles and for several other people in the community club. She had to cut down a small tree and bring it inside and drape it with strings of popcorn, little red berries and other things Jorka told her to buy at the shops in Orca Harbor. She had to learn several new recipes. There were many parties on Merrick Island, and Jim and Pam hosted a party, too. They put little colored lights all over the front of the farmhouse and the barn. Wella found that delightful. Even on Gornia, the most ceremonious of Gallatan islands, there were no ceremonies more lovely than Christmas. It was plain to see why the Earth humans needed this custom. Those were otherwise incredibly dark days with hardly any sunshine. Wella thought she might not have survived them had it not been for Christmas.

• • •

Wella was very happy when the Earth month of February arrived. The days were clearly getting longer and new lambs were being born every few days. Best of all, Pam started what she called "maternity leave." By this time her costuming trick was quite noticeable. Having never seen a real pregnant Earth human, Wella asked Jorka to show her a view scan of a pregnant Earth human woman, and was amazed at its likeness to Pamela's figure.

"You're doing very well at looking pregnant," she told Pam.

Pam laughed. "You're doing pretty well yourself at not looking pregnant. Are you sure you're pregnant?"

"Oh, yes," Wella assured her. "I am pregnant."

· · ·

One chilly morning, Wella went out to tend the sheep and found everything outdoors covered with a wet, white substance — the Earth phenomenon known as "snow." She was careful to remain under the barn roof while feeding the sheep, to avoid getting her feet wet. Jorka had advised that in snow she should wear the same boots she wore for digging clams, but they were stored in the cellar and she didn't want to take the time to fetch them. The sheep were already very hungry.

As the sheep rushed about excitedly, jostling her for the grain, Wella filled the trough. Then she stepped back to watch them greedily munching their breakfast. As usual, the soft crunching was a relief after the bleating of their earlier anxious hunger. As she listened to the sheep munching, Wella noticed another sound. She recognized it immediately as the faint, high cry of a lamb in trouble.

Bravely, Wella stepped out into the snow and trudged around the barn in the direction of the sound. Her movements were awkward; her feet tended to give way and slide in all directions as the cold wetness crept in over the tops of her shoes.

As she had expected, there was a newborn lamb trapped behind a row of fencing at the edge of the barn lot. It looked drenched and pathetic, like the tiny drowned sea neuta Wella had once found on the coast of Gornia. But this poor creature was not dead. Shaking with fear and cold, the thing was gray in color like the Romney she had bought from Ben. It hardly looked like a sheep at all, but there appeared to be no erely traits.

Wella stooped down close to the fence. Then she took hold of the hem of her skirt with both hands and tenderly wrapped the soft woolen fabric around the lamb, careful not to touch it with her skin. Jorka had warned that a Romney ewe would reject any lamb with a foreign scent.

After she got back to the barn with the lamb, Wella tried to get each of the Romneys to claim it, but none of the Romneys would have anything to do with the poor, abandoned creature. Fortunately, after several tries and a little telepathic encouragement, Wella was able to convince her lead erely ewe to adopt the strange orphan, even though she already had a pretty large lamb of her own to feed.

Wella sat for a long time on the hay-covered barn floor cradling the wooly lump in her lap while it nursed the ewe. A deep sense of satisfaction came over Wella. In a few weeks she would be nursing a baby of her own. It would be her own biological child; it already lived and moved within her. She probably would have been denied this privilege if she had not volunteered for a mission of genetic experimentation; population was so carefully controlled on Gallata. Maybe the experience of motherhood would be worth all the sacrifices she had made.

Wella closed her eyes and watched the blue stillness within, as her psyche merged with the separate energy field inside her body. Wella felt that she already knew Dana. Even in its trancelike state within the womb, the child's mind questioned and sorted, trying to classify sounds and movements, thoughts and dreams from the surrounding world. Wella knew her daughter, Dana, had inherited psychic potential unknown to the culture in which she would live. What a fascinating experience it would be, to watch her grow up in this alien world. Would her abilities survive in a society that could not recognize them, let alone nurture them?

Gradually Wella became aware of Pam's voice calling. "Wella, where are you? What's going on?"

"I'm out here in the barn," Wella called back, pitching her voice just loud enough to be heard outside and yet not disturb the lamb or ewe. Jorka had strictly forbidden her from using any telepathic practices or ceremonies among the Earth humans ever since the wedding, when Pam and Jim had started feeling so uncomfortable about such things.

"What's happening?" demanded Pam as she came into view at the open doorway.

"This lamb got lost from its mother during birth. Now the ewe won't take her."

"Oh, that's too bad," said Pam. "Guess we'll have to bottle feed the poor thing or it'll die."

"No, my lead ewe is nursing him. She's adopted him."

"Wow! That's great!" Pam came closer to get a better look. "I've heard some cows will do that. But Ben says sheep will never adopt an orphan lamb like that."

"Some do," remarked Wella nonchalantly. "My lead ewe is good about that."

Pam knelt down beside Wella and watched in silence, apparently calmed by the nursing scene. Finally she uttered a soft quiet sentence, barely ruffling the stillness. "Guess you'll be having your baby pretty soon, too, Wella."

Wella didn't answer at first. She always felt a little hurt and confused when either Jim or Pam referred to Dana as her baby and not theirs. It wasn't surprising that they still didn't understand the clan concept. After all, Gallatan-style clan civilizations were unknown on Earth.

A chill passed through Wella as it crossed her mind that some Earth humans might be like so many Earth sheep, unable to mother children not biologically connected to them. Then she recalled that adopting children was a common Earth custom. In fact, one of the children in the Klahowya Cove School was adopted from strangers in the city. She would try to talk with Pam about her feelings. "Dana is not only my child. She is our child," she said.

"Yes," said Pam. But her voice was not entirely convincing.

At that moment, the lamb stopped nursing, writhed about a little, and then flopped off of Wella's lap into the hay. He stood up uncertainly and took one step, and then another. The ewe walked away and the lamb followed. Within a few short minutes, the newborn lamb was bounding about the barn in joyful play.

Pam laughed. "Too bad human babies don't develop that fast after they're born."

As if in response to Pam's remark or in imitation of the lamb, Dana began to move about in the womb, and it occurred to Wella that Pam had not been introduced to her yet. "Dana is developing too," said Wella. "Would you like to feel her move?"

Pam looked surprised at first. Then her eyes lit up with excitement. "Yes, that would be great!"

Wella took Pam's hand and placed it on her abdomen where she felt the movement. Then she closed her eyes and began to meditate. Jorka had forbidden it, but surely she would understand the importance of cherishing and enhancing this ceremonial moment when Dana and the clan mother would meet for the first time.

In the quiet darkness behind her closed eyes, Wella saw and felt the blue stillness again, encompassing within her awareness all three energy spheres. All that attention was concentrated upon the sensory experiences of the moment, the soft pressure of Pamela's palm against the warmth of Wella's abdomen, the quick rippling movements of the tiny body within. The mood of this collective energy sphere was one of togetherness, of enjoying the same precious moment. There in the quiet blue stillness Wella's mind merged with the unifying mood. Then she took a deep, strong breath, and in one great effort of will, raised the feeling to a crescendo of ceremonial clan unity, much like the feeling Earth humans call familial love. When Wella opened her eyes Pam was smiling at her with an expression of closeness and love greater than any Wella had known since Shulmina of Severelia had left her in this alien world alone. Maybe with enough patience and careful planning, clan life was possible anywhere in the universe.

* * *

Wella was concentrating fully on the psychic process of quieting an erely sheep for sheering, when her body — separated as it was at that moment from her mind — felt the initial stirrings of childbirth. Wella was afraid that if she broke the trance, the sheep would jump or bolt, and the sheers would slip, causing an injury to one or both of them, so she calmly dismissed the physical sensation until the job was done.

By the time she had finished the sheering, the sensations had stopped, but Wella had been taught to give full credence to such feelings. It would be better to prepare for Dana's birth and not have her come than to have her arrive in an unprepared home. She released the lamb from its harness and watched it dart out of the barn and hurry to join its mother.

Wella was disappointed that Pam had gone to Orca Harbor that morning to buy food. It would be better to have someone available in case of unexpected emergencies. Besides, it seemed almost unnatural to be giving birth without the presence of a clan and a ceremonial collective.

Pam had been studying about Earth childbearing practices called midwifery. She had been concerned that the secrecy of their unofficial adoptive plans would preclude the use of a physician. Wella fully understood Pam's concern. For just as Pam felt the need for the conventional birth trappings of her culture, Wella longed for the presence of her Gornian clan mothers — experienced as they were at officiating at her own birth and ever so many others.

Wella was also glad to be alone. As a Gallatan woman, she would have to give birth in the Gallatan way, and Earth humans would find it strange. It was enough of a challenge just to give birth, let alone feel obliged to live up to alien expectations the whole time. It was enough just to try and live up to their expectations for simpler things like eating, planting a vegetable garden, or sheering sheep, let alone to have to give birth in their way. Still, she should let Jim know. He would want to try to get in touch with Pam and tell her to hurry home.

Wella gathered up the sunny yellow fleece she had taken from the ram lamb, carefully folded it into a large woven sack, and carried it into her apartment. On the way she felt another series of rippling contractions, and she began to feel excited. Dana would surely be born today.

After brewing herself a cup of tea, Wella went to the phone in her kitchen area and called Jim at the schoolhouse. "Hello, Jim, this is Wella."

"Hi, Wella. What's up?"

"Dana is coming out."

"Oh, wow! Is Pam around?" Wella was pleased at the excitement in his voice.

"No, she went to town."

"Oh, dear. Maybe I should come over." Jim's voice sounded frightened now, and although Wella couldn't understand this reaction, it felt good to know his feelings were deeply connected to Dana's birth. In that way, he was acting like a true clan father.

"No, Jim, you must stay at the school. There are many children who need you at the school. Dana is only one child. She doesn't need you yet. She will need you later, but not yet."

"Oh, uh, okay, Wella. But are you sure you'll be all right? I mean, having a baby is pretty serious business. Maybe I should phone Ruth and find out if Pam stopped by the shop."

"Yes, that would be good," said Wella. "I would like to have Pam come soon to help with birthing Dana."

"Good," said Jim. "Yes, I'll do that. If I can't reach her, I'll call you back in a little while. You're at the main house now, aren't you?"

"I'm going there now to get things ready."

At Jorka's advice, Wella had suggested to Pam and Jim that the baby ought to be born in the main house, and they had agreed without hesitation. It had not been so easy, however, to convince them that the event should take place in the sitting room, but Wella had insisted, stressing that the warmth of the fire would be good for the baby. Wella also thought the child should not be placed off in an upstairs bedroom as the Earth humans expected, but should be born in the clan's central living area. As she hung up the phone, Wella felt another rippling sensation in her abdomen. This one lasted longer and was much stronger than the others. She had better hurry now. Better not even take time for a last minute conference with Jorka. At any rate, Jorka had already given her a list of simple instructions. She had written it out and had stored it in the drawer with the towels, flashlight and matches.

After locating the list, Wella left the barn apartment and crossed the barnyard toward the farmhouse. The sun was breaking through a space in what seemed a great herd of clouds passing over. Wella appreciated its cheerfulness, for the Earth sun had been entirely hidden by clouds for many cycles. It had occurred to Wella to wonder whether she would ever know its warmth again. It was fitting that the sun would make an appearance on the day of Dana's birth.

The instructions were simple enough, as were most of Jorka's lessons. "You should be clothed in a loose robe of erely fleece. The child should be born in a warm room, preferably near the fireplace. Cover the floor area with a large sheet of cloth such as Earth humans use to cover a sleeping platform. Arrange four cushions on the sheet in the form of the letter yot, as shown in the diagram. Have on hand a sterile basin of warm water, some mild soap, a surgical kit, some towels, a camera, and an infant skieron which in English is called a bunting. Sit down on the cushion which forms the trunk of the yot, and place both your legs on its alternate branches. Now begin to meditate. Move slowly into a deep trance. Find the blue stillness. When the contractions grow strong and powerful, stay in the stillness watching from within. If you lose concentration, the contractions may take over and control your mind. This would be very painful. But if you stay in the blue stillness, giving birth will be a good experience, always to be remembered."

Wella had rehearsed most of these procedures many times. Shulmina had stressed the importance of learning the rituals, since Wella would not have her Gornian clan mother and friends to help with the birth. Shulmina had assured her that most Earth humans were not trained adequately in child birth rituals and practices. Therefore, Jorka had been programmed to describe the purpose and use of most of the ceremonial items.

Jorka did not include an explanation for use of the camera, which was not part of the Gornian birthing ceremony. But Wella had taken part in enough Earth ceremonies to understand that the camera was a most important Earth ritual object. She wasn't sure at what point in the ceremony the camera should be introduced. She would leave that up to Pamela, who had most often performed that function at other ceremonies, such as the barn warming and Christmas.

Wella was grateful for Jorka's instructions. They gave her something to think about besides how excited she was. The instructions continued for several pages, including what to do in case of various alternative circumstances, but Wella decided to focus on getting the first paragraph right, for it contained the most essential step, the blue stillness. She might not have survived a day on this planet, had it not been for a quiet meditation at just the right time.

But first she had to build up the fire. Pam had left quite awhile ago and it had nearly gone out. And she must hurry. The contractions were growing stronger and more frequent.

•••

Seated on her cushion in a deep meditative trance, Wella drifted into a memory dream state, recalling the birth of her clan cousin, Cardugan. His mother, Miryamnita, had insisted that Wella have the honor of participating. Miryamnita had been especially fond of Wella. The older woman had wanted to reassure Wella that their relationship would not be neglected after the birth of her own biological offspring.

Wella could see the clan hall as clearly in her dream as she had during the real event. Now she saw it from Miryamnita's viewpoint, seated in her place on the same cushion arrangement with many of her clan gathered around for comfort and companionship.

Everyone was concentrating on merging with the psychic sphere of the mother and child. Together they experienced the almost violent sensations of pulling, pushing, separating. There were no visual sensations, only body sensations, darkness, feeling and physical activity. The group was in awe at the powerful, involuntary contractions, and they also felt excitement, wonder, and pride.

Wella's mind drifted in and out of the vision of herself as a Gallatan mother giving birth in the clan hall. At times the vision became the simple memory sequence of Cardugan's birth. She had been a small child when Cardugan was thrust from Miryamnita's body onto the soft skieron spread before her. Three clan fathers had helped to gather him up and bathe him. He had looked rather pathetic and had wailed the whole time. Wella recalled feeling sorry for him. He was, after all, a male and could never hope to be the clan mother. If he could tread and speak softly enough, he might aspire to be a teacher or a member of the council. Wella smiled at this recollection, for Cardugan had wished only to be left alone to live as a mountain herdsman. He had grown into a mild, thoughtful young man, and Wella had made love with him, once when they met at a herdsman's ceremonial festival, and again when they were together in the mountains. Jim was a little like Cardugan in personality. Wella felt a twinge of regret that she might never see Cardugan again. Her friendship with Jim might have to forever replace the one she had enjoyed with Cardugan since childhood. But Jim was a fine intelligent being, and Wella liked him very much.

Gradually, Wella drifted back to her place as birth giver, seated on a skieron in the center of the clan hall. The clan mother, Rhama, was seated opposite Wella, gazing at her with pride and gentle concern. Rhama's psychic energy merged into Wella's.

As Wella sat enjoying the feeling of closeness to the clan mother, the oneness with Miryamnita, it began to feel like this was not entirely a dream, but rather a psychic transference defying the vast reaches of space. Somehow the clan mother knew she was giving birth at that moment, and was psychically communicating the love and concern of her family and friends. She realized that she had never really been alone on Korba-3. If she needed her clan, they were accessible by way of the psychic rituals for which they were famous throughout the universe.

The contractions were growing stronger now, and more frequent. She could feel Dana moving. She was being pushed out of Wella's body by forceful movements that Wella would never have intentionally inflicted upon her. It was incredible that her body could do this of its own accord with no help from the controlling mind. Wella had heard Earth women talking about the pain of childbirth. Surely it must be frightening for them. There was apparently no psychic unity with the child, no blue stillness. But surely they must feel the awesome power of birth. Even an erely ewe could experience that.

Wella was pulled momentarily out of the dream state by a particularly powerful contraction, although her eyes remained closed and the meditative trance endured. During a respite between contractions, she became aware again of the strong psychic presence of her Gornian clan, though their dream presence was gone. The feeling was so powerful that Wella felt compelled to open her eyes to make certain there were no Gornians physically there in the room with her.

When Wella opened her eyes, she was pleased to find Jim and Pamela standing in the doorway watching her. Maybe it was not the presence of her Gornian clan that Wella had sensed, but rather that of her small Earth family, the two fellow inhabitants of her new island home.

Pam looked extremely tense and worried. She held in her hand one of the books she had been studying on midwifery. "Are you all right, Wella?" she asked anxiously.

"Yes, very good. Just a little tired. Dana will be out soon."

While Pam remained standing in the doorway looking frightened and holding the book, Jim rushed over, knelt beside Wella and took her hold of her hand. He looked very concerned. "What can we do to help?" he asked.

Wella felt a warm smile well up in her, but that was interrupted by a terribly powerful contraction, and Wella knew then that her concentration had been interrupted enough by the couple's arrival to weaken the trance. She moaned in automatic response, and Pam's expression grew more frightened. "Are you sure we can do without a doctor?"

"No, no, Pam..." Wella was frightened now. If someone came from the larger island, everyone would know she was the biological mother, and the plan would be ruined. No one would accept Pam as the clan mother. Their customs were too different.

Apparently misinterpreting the fear in Wella's response, Jim said, "Maybe we should phone Dr. Blackston."

Pam nodded and opened her mouth, as if to agree with Jim, but no words came out. Instead her mouth remained open and her eyes fixed on the space on the sheet between the cushions supporting Wella's legs. At the same time Wella's body and mind were gripped with a dramatic feeling like a great fist opening, closing tightly, and then opening again in complete relaxation, as Dana slipped softly from Wella's body onto the sheet between the cushions.

Jim uttered a low whistling sound of wonder and appreciation, "Wow, that was great! Congratulations, Wella! You were right. It's a girl!" He picked up a towel and wiped the amniotic fluid from the baby's face and nostrils as the umbilical cord wrapped itself once around his wrist.

Pam dropped her book and rushed over to have a better look. "We need to cut the cord," she announced, picking up the scissors from atop the stack of towels Wella had prepared.

Jim lifted the baby carefully with one hand and stretched the cord a little taut with the other. Pam stared wide-eyed for an instant, taking aim with the scissors, then deftly snipped it without actually touching anything with her hand. Jim wrapped the towel around Dana absorbing the rest of the fluids. Then he cradled her against his chest, gazing tenderly at the face.

"God, this is a pretty baby. I've never seen such a beautiful one, I mean, new born like that."

Pam leaned over to get a better look. "She has green eyes and black hair like Wella. Won't people suspect she's Wella's baby and not ours?"

Jim continued to gaze fondly at the child. "Good Lord, no, Pam. She doesn't look at all like Wella. She looks exactly like you."

"Does she really?" asked Pam doubtfully.

"Yes, exactly. Don't you think so, Wella?" Still cradling the baby Jim leaned over so Wella could have a better look.

Wella smiled, and a warm feeling such as she had never known before filled her heart. This was apparently part of the Earth birthing ritual, and the correct ceremonial response was obviously, "Yes, exactly. Dana looks a lot like Pam." And, in fact, it was not a lie. The baby really did resemble her clan mother more than she did her biological one. Her eyes were more like Pam's, and she had a sweet, oval face, not a long angular one like Wella's.

Wella had never before seen a clan mother smile with so much joy. Pam said, "I must get the camera. Where's the camera, Jim?"

"Here," said Wella. She reached over behind the basin and the big stack of towels she had made ready, in accordance with Jorka's instruction.

"Oh, great!" beamed Pam peering through the little box at Jim and Dana. She clicked the shutter again and again. There were lots of smiles and expressions of approval. The little light bulb on top of the box flashed on festively each time she clicked.

Wella recalled Jorka's instructions about pouring warm water in the kettle to wash the baby and all the rest of it; but there would be plenty of time. She did not want to interrupt this beautiful camera ritual.

LEVIN ISLAND ~ MARCH 20, 1968

Through the fog in his brain, Jim tried to recall the dream. He could only remember the last few moments, even though it must have gone on for hours. Dana was sitting up all by herself in the big, fancy highchair Pam had bought for her in Seattle. Only instead of sitting idly in the kitchen where it wouldn't be used for weeks, perhaps months, the chair was in front of his classroom over in the school-house. Dana was talking to his class, giving a report on religion in ancient Egypt or something. Jim reached out from under the covers and rubbed his eyes. Then he opened them to the dark stillness.

He smiled, recalling the dream again, trying to etch it into his memory so he could tell Pam about it in the morning. This one must be wish fulfillment. Here was this month-old, helpless creature who had to be waited on, carried about, and couldn't give you the satisfaction of a decent conversation. He was anxious for her to grow up so they could all get on with other things.

It was dark in the room; all Jim could see was the lighted electric alarm clock. It was 3:15 am, about the same time he had found him-self waking up each night for the last couple of weeks. The first few days after Dana's birth, he had awakened at various odd times, but now it was falling into a pattern. Jim rolled over on his right side and buried his head in the covers. He knew what would inevitably hap-pen next in the pattern, but he hoped it wouldn't. It couldn't be real. It had to be his imagination.

What was it really? It was something like textbook descriptions of an aura before a seizure. First he felt ravenously hungry. Then he felt a kind of burning or itching sensation in his lower abdomen. Then there was this feeling that Dana was with him somehow, right there inside his head.

Of course, Dana wasn't really inside his head. She was down the hall in her crib. But one thing was for sure — she wasn't sleeping. Reluctantly, Jim pried his nude body out from under the cozy electric blanket and braced himself against the edge of the bed. His feet recoiled with shock as they touched the cold wood floor. Then they patted frantically about for his slippers. His hand found the fuzzy bathrobe on the night stand.

By the time he turned on the light in Dana's room, which Pam referred to as "the nursery," Jim was starting to wake up. The light was soft and low in the room which Pam had decorated in yellow gingham ruffles. A big yellow sun was painted on the pastel blue wall and below it several white lambs frolicked in a meadow. They had pink and blue bows around their necks. It was all Pam's doing, but Wella had praised it lavishly.

Jim was still amazed at how smoothly all this had gone. He had been anxious about this baby business, what with two mothers and all. But Pam had orchestrated everything, apparently to Wella's delight. Everything Pam said was gospel, whether the subject be diaper sterilization, feeding schedules, you name it. Pam had apparently read up on all this stuff, and Wella had no opinions of her own, except for a strange quirk or two now and then, like her insistence on giving birth in the living room.

When he looked down into her crib, Dana was gazing softly up at him. Jim had known lots of kids in his day, but none so sweet and loving. Of course, he didn't confide this opinion in anyone, because everyone said babies don't have personalities yet when they're only one month old. Dana gave him a broad, happy smile of recognition, although everyone claimed babies don't really smile that early. Pam said maybe she was grimacing from gas on her stomach.

If people thought he only imagined that Dana smiled and had a personality, what would they think if he told anyone what he really noticed about her. For instance, from the moment she was born and he picked her up, Jim had this feeling that Dana had bonded with him somehow, identifying him as her special person. Each time he looked at her, he felt it more intensely. In fact, she was looking at him at this very moment, and the feeling was so powerful, it made his index finger tremble slightly as he reached into her crib to tap her playfully on the tip of her nose.

"Hi, Dana. Bet you need a change." Jim slid the same finger inside the diaper. Fortunately, it was only wet and warm this time, no gunk.

As he deftly changed the diaper, fitting the clean one snugly into place, Jim recalled the first time they had tried it. What a joke that was! None of them, not even Pam, really knew how. Pam knew the theory, of course, but doing it was something else.

After changing the diaper, Jim picked up Dana and carried her gently downstairs and into the living room, which was dimly lit by some coals left in the fireplace. Wella was sound asleep in her big, homemade sleeping bag in front of the fire. Her long, dark hulk resembled an Egyptian mummy case in a museum.

Still cradling Dana in his arms, Jim knelt down beside Wella and slipped the baby in beside her. "Wake up, Wella, it's mealtime," he said softly and tapped her shoulder.

Wella opened her large eyes, and Jim could see the fireplace embers reflected in them. There were dark shadows of smile lines between her mouth and cheeks. Like all beautiful things, she was improved by darkness. "Thank you, Jim," she whispered, and snuggled close to the baby. Before leaving the room, Jim sat for a moment on the rocking chair Pam had installed in front of the bay window. It was the only real furniture in the room now which seemed bare without Wella's spinning wheel and loom. Maybe they should ask Wella to bring it back in here. It would be easier for her to care for Dana in here after Pam goes back to work.

Listening intently, Jim could hear a faint suckling sound from the baby. If only he could watch — it would have been even more fun than watching the lambs nursing the ewes, but Wella was disappointingly discreet about the whole thing. She often nursed when he was present, but Jim never once got the slightest glimpse of a breast, let alone its nipple.

There had been a lot of discussion about how Dana should be fed. Pam had insisted that breastfeeding was the way to go. Jim had agreed but wondered whether it would work. For instance, what if Pam and Jim had to go out with Dana and leave Wella at home? It was particularly important that Wella didn't nurse the baby in public because that would mean the end of their charade which was otherwise going quite well. Everyone thought, though no one had explicitly said, that Pam was the biological mother and Wella the sort of baby-sitter or nanny.

Pam had gone to great length to solve, at least in her own mind, this breastfeeding problem. She had ordered a special breast pump from a surgical supply house in Seattle so that once in a while Dana could get used to a bottle. To use the pump, Wella had to hook herself up to a tap of running water which created pressure to somehow operate the gadget. To his amazement, Wella never complained. Instead, she commended Pam on the excellent idea and assured them that it worked very well.

When Jim had asked her to demonstrate, Wella had become inordinately anxious, and he thought she might bolt for the door. She had looked mightily relieved when he assured her he had only been joking.

Before he left to go back up to bed, Jim stoked up the fire. He couldn't hear Dana nursing anymore. She and Wella were both asleep.

...

A chain of brass bells clanged annoyingly as Jim entered the Klahowya Cove Store. Bob Smith was seated on his stool behind the counter sipping coffee and reading the morning paper.

"We got some school mail back here for you, Jim," said Bob. "You must've forgot to pick it up yesterday."

"Oh sure, uh, guess I've been a little out of it lately. Been up every night with the baby and all."

Bob beamed appreciation as though it pleased him to witness the universality of human misery. "So it goes with babies," he crowed. "They have to wake up crying in the middle of the night. It could go on for weeks. Better get used to it."

"Crying? Uh, yes. The baby wakes up and wants to be fed...wakes up crying."

Crying, that was it! He had known something was wrong, but he hadn't put his finger on it until now. This kid practically never cried. Let's see, when did she cry? The only instance he could recall was when Wella accidently cut the tip off the poor kid's wiggly little finger while trying to trim a tiny nail. Poor Wella was beside herself with remorse. She and Pam were both trying so hard to be perfect mothers. Maybe that's why the kid didn't cry. She had two perfect mothers doting over her every minute. Maybe the child wasn't allowed the normal amount of frustration.

Having explained the lack of crying as the consequence of too much solicitation, Jim tried not to concern himself with it as he went about his duties at the schoolhouse. But it was hard to get it out of his mind. That afternoon Sharon Streely started bawling at recess when Jerry Markson stole her Brownie hat. All kids cry, especially when they're only a month old.

As he rang the bell to end the recess, Jim recalled the eerie feeling he experienced each night upon waking. Most babies cry in the middle of the night. That's how they let their parents know they're hungry and need changing. Dana didn't cry at night, yet he had been waking up at around 3:00 am to find her awake, wet and hungry. After recess he gave the kids a study period to work on book reports, which really meant a pleasure reading time. That way they would be quiet. Jim needed some time to mull over this strange feeling that was coming over him. It was like the feeling he had about Wella when she first came to the islands. He had even talked with Pam about it on their wedding trip. It felt like Wella was messing around with his mind. Pam said she felt it, too. But that feeling had been gone for a long time. He had almost forgotten about it. Surely he wasn't imagining that a tiny, one-month old baby could mess with his mind. That was utterly ridiculous.

•••

Pam was sitting up with the bed light on as Jim slipped in between the sheets. She was reading Baby and Child Care by Benjamin Spock. It was her bible. She was always quoting from the work and giving him and Wella advice. Jim propped his head up with a pillow and peered over Pam's arm at the book. "What does Dr. Spock say about crying?"

"Crying?"

"Yes, what does he say about babies crying?"

Pam shrugged. "Nothing. Well, lots of things. It's normal for babies to cry. If they cry a lot, you have a problem. But babies who are well cared for don't cry a lot. When they cry, you figure out what's wrong, or you just pick them up and rock them." Pam's tone was a little impatient, as though she thought his question too elementary.

"What if they don't cry?"

Pam looked at him like she thought he was crazy.

"Most babies cry," he said.

"So?" Pam shrugged again.

"Dana doesn't cry."

There was a long silence. She was obviously thinking about what he had said. "No, you're right. Dana doesn't cry much."

Jim sat all the way up in bed so he was eye-to-eye with Pam. "That's putting it mildly. Compared to the average baby, she doesn't cry at all."

Pam's brow wrinkled slightly. Jim could tell he had touched off an alarm in her. "You think something's wrong with Dana because she doesn't cry?"

Jim slid down under the covers again. "No, I doubt it, but it makes you wonder. Why doesn't she cry?"

"She has no reason to cry. We take good care of Dana. She does cry when she gets hurt, like when Wella accidently stabbed her with a safety pin, but most of the time there's nothing to cry about."

Jim closed his eyes and felt himself drifting off to sleep. Pam worried about everything worth worrying about. If the champion worrier wouldn't take it on, there was no need for concern.

LEVIN ISLAND ~ MARCH 4, 1971

It was way up there, soaring in and out of the clouds, a tiny flyspeck of a thing. Then it grew larger, falling now, plunging with powerful force upon him. His little legs were already in motion, scampering over clumps of earth, charging recklessly through tangles of weeds and grasses for the safe dark place. It was too late. Jim thought he could feel the bone-crunching grip of a great beak piercing his flesh even as he awoke. Worst of all, he could still hear the piercing cry of the eagle after he knew it was only a dream. No, it wasn't an eagle. It was the baby crying.

Pam was already out of bed and racing down the hall. Jim could hear Wella hurrying up the stairs. They would meet in Dana's room and Wella would look on helplessly while Pam comforted the child until she was quiet.

Soon the crying stopped, and Jim could hear them going another round with the same argument they had already had a dozen times. Actually, there weren't many subjects they disagreed on regarding Dana, but this thing about the nightmares was sure to precipitate controversy every time.

Apparently, Wella's mother had cured her and other siblings or cousins or something of nightmares by a strange system of playing with the babies and drawing pictures for several minutes afterwards and talking to the poor sleepy creatures in the wee hours about things they couldn't understand. Pam even claimed that once or twice Wella had gone so far as to bundle the poor kid up in the middle of the night and take her outside to play. They had gone out and rescued lambs trapped under fences or found little, half-drowned rodents down on the beach. Jim thought it pretty ridiculous and harmless but preferred to humor Wella so long as she didn't keep anyone else awake. She and the kid could sleep in, but he and Pam had to get up and go to work.

"I don't think your system is working," Pam was saying. "She's still having the nightmares."

"It will work," Wella insisted. "It may take more sessions."

"Why don't we try just putting her back in bed?"

"Oh, no. We must not do that. Dana will have nightmares throughout her life."

"But how are you helping her, Wella? You aren't making sense."

Jim groaned. He would have to get into it again. Otherwise, he might have to listen to them arguing for quite awhile. He couldn't recall exactly how long this had been going on. Dana had started sleeping through the night when she was around five or six months old. Then she had left him in peace until about two months ago around the time of her third birthday. That was when the nightmares had started.

Jim had begun to notice some pretty strange things about Dana long before that. Her development patterns were all screwed up. So far, she didn't seem to know how to talk. At least she didn't talk even though it was obvious she understood everything that was said, and a good bit that wasn't. If it hadn't been for the crying at night, Jim would have been afraid Dana had no vocal mechanism. He might have even thought she was retarded if it weren't for the way she could draw. At the age of three, Dana would sit there with her crayons and draw these amazing little cartoon representations of people and animals and things. You could even recognize some of the people by little features she'd put in. Grandma Ruth had a small pointed nose and was always depicted in slacks and an apron. Then, with the gray curly hair, there was no mistaking who it was. At the age of three this kid could draw a lot better than any first or second grader over at the schoolhouse.

The really strange thing about the kid was the way she played. Jim had never seen a child so oblivious to dirt. In fact, the place she most enjoyed playing was in the chicken yard. She would sit there in the middle of the chicken shit, and if Pam scolded her about getting dirty, this weird kid, who seemed to comprehend everything else, would just give Pam a blank innocent look and go right on crawling around in the crap.

Jim's memory of one chicken yard incident relaxed his mind with momentary amusement, but then he recalled a stranger one he had witnessed when no one else was around. In fact, it had given him such an eerie feeling that he had never mentioned it to anyone. Anyway, they would have said his imagination worked overtime, and maybe it did. The way Jim distinctly remembered it was that Dana was sitting in the middle of the chicken yard with a rooster and about fifteen hens marching around her in a perfect circle. Jim thought it looked strangely like a routine the Island County drill team had performed in a parade that morning in Orca Harbor. The chickens had kept marching around Dana in a circle like that for several minutes, and Jim had gone over for a better look. Dana was kind of curled up in a ball with her head between her legs. She seemed to be asleep.

"Hi, Dana, you okay?" he had asked gently.

Dana had just looked up casually in her sweet, innocent way, and the chickens had dispersed as if frightened by a fox and scurried off in all directions. Then there was the way Dana played with really young lambs. That was really weird. Jim had grown up on a sheep farm. He had even raised a lamb once or twice for a 4-H project. If he knew anything about anything, Jim knew that lambs acted totally wild until you got them to their first sheep showing contest at the fair. No matter how often you practiced with them, they were totally spastic until the final day when they walked out there in the show ring and somehow managed to do everything just right by the book. That's why he knew the things Dana did with lambs at the age of three were impossible. For one thing, they would come right up to her even if she didn't have a bucket of grain or anything to feed them, and then they would follow her around like dogs. Jim had seen older kids do that kind of thing with bottle-fed lambs, but Dana's power over those critters had nothing to do with food or them getting used to her or any explicable thing like that. One minute a lamb would be darting around the field acting like the wild creature it was, and the next minute there it would be following this baby around the barnyard.

Jim was relieved when Pam finally gave up the fight and came back to bed. After Pam went back to sleep, he lay there in the dark thinking about Dana. He could hear Pam breathing steadily close beside him, and he could just barely hear Wella talking softly to Dana downstairs in the living room. He recognized the familiar rhythm of her precise English spoken with that strange, European-sounding accent, but he couldn't quite make out what she was saying. She was speaking in that annoying limbo volume at which Pam always played the radio down there in the morning, just loud enough so he could hear, quiet enough so he couldn't.

Part of him wanted more than anything to know what they were saying. The other part wanted to go to sleep because it had to be pretty close to morning already, and before very long the alarm would ring, and it would be time to get up and go over to the schoolhouse. So he tried to stifle his curiosity, but the harder he tried the more curious he became.

Maybe it wasn't just curiosity calling him down to the living room. For one thing, it would be nice to be with them, nice to have their company. Pam had gone back to sleep, but he was wide awake now. Might as well put on his bathrobe, go on downstairs, and find out what Wella was up to with Dana. Heaven knows it had to be a pretty strong urge of whatever sort to pry him out from under the covers on a cold, dark morning.

Even as he descended the stairs, Jim began to catch little snatches of Wella's monologue, and just after he passed through the living room door Jim stopped frozen in wonder and dismay. "Eagles have to eat little animals. That is the order of the universe. Eagles kill by instinct. It is their nature. They cannot be civilized and learn to eat plants or flowers like sheep. That is something we cannot change or improve." It was too strange! Wella was talking either about his dream or something very similar. Perhaps this was a mere coincidence. At least he hoped so.

Recovering his composure without a word, Jim walked over to the wood pile, selected a large piece from Wella's tidy driftwood collection and placed it on the fire. Out of the corner of his eye, he could see that Dana appeared to be asleep and apparently not even listening to Wella's lecture. She was slumped against Wella's arm, her eyes closed. On Wella's lap was the large pad of drawing paper and in her hand a fat, brown crayon. It was by means of these middle of the night play therapy sessions that the family had learned that Wella was also good at drawing. She could draw an amazing likeness of almost anything she had ever seen once. Normally Wella just casually tossed her amazing works into the fire, but one night she had neglected to tidy up after herself, and Pam had found the drawings in the morning. Wella had seemed genuinely astounded when Pam had raved about them. It was as if she thought everyone could draw like that.

After he finished feeding the fire, Jim crept over and peered over Wella's shoulder at the picture. Then he immediately felt faint and slumped down onto a cushion on the floor. "Let me see that drawing, Wella," he demanded, rudely snatching one from her lap. It was a perfect rendition of an eagle grasping a mouse by the nape of the neck, the mouse dangling limp and lifeless from the eagle's beak.

"You can have all these if you want," offered Wella proudly, like one of his students wanting to please the teacher. She handed him two more drawings of an eagle in different stages of descent toward its prey. Jim stared at them, his amazement verging upon horror. Looking at the drawings was like reliving his dream. He didn't know what to say, but he knew he had to talk to Wella about this. He had let a lot of strange things go by since knowing her, but that was because there was no documentation, nothing to pin on her. Here was hard evidence — the woman was psychic as hell. There was no question about it.

Meanwhile Wella had picked up Dana and was on her way toward the door.

"Please don't go, Wella. I need to talk to you."

"Yes, Jim, but I think I should put Dana back in her bed first. She is asleep."

Jim stared numbly at the drawings until Wella came back and sat down in her former place. He was glad she looked at him, made eye contact. It always made him nervous when she closed her eyes. When she closed her eyes and seemed almost to be asleep, that was when she was scariest. Sure, he wanted to communicate with her now, but on his own terms, at his own pace, in words. The normal way.

"Wella," Jim began hesitantly, "These pictures are of a dream I had a little while ago, earlier this morning."

He had barely gotten out the words before Wella's face relaxed in an unrestrained smile. "This is a happy night then, Jim. You and Dana and I have all been together of one mind."

"Wella, that's weird. I mean it's downright scary."

"Why so, Jim?"

"Wella, stuff like that isn't supposed to happen. Several people don't all think together as if they had one mind."

Wella just continued to smile in that confident way. "You are wrong, Jim. It often happens. It even says so in your book." With that she crawled over to the bookcase under the bay window where he kept his old textbooks from college. "I read about it in one of these," she said peering eagerly at the spines of several large volumes. "Here. It was this one." She pulled out a black, hardbound volume with such force that two others fell to the floor in its wake. "It's called The Study of Dreams." She sat back on her haunches and began leafing rapidly through the pages. "It says in here that psychic phenomena occur often in dreams. Have you not read this book, Jim? It says that people who record their dreams often dream the same dream as other members of their family at the same time."

Helplessly Jim watched Wella maneuver. She was getting away again, wriggling out of his trap. Of course, he recalled reading that, but it just wasn't the same. It left room for doubt, room to question. It wasn't as graphic or explicit as this. "Wella, I need to talk to you. I need to have you be as honest with me as I am with you. I can't read your mind like you can mine. It isn't fair. None of this is fair!"

Wella's innocent smile vanished. Without losing eye contact with Jim, she dropped the book and crawled back over to her cushion. She never once closed her eyes but sat in her favorite sort of sloppy lotus position. All the while she kept looking into his eyes with deep concern, waiting to hear him speak. This was his moment. There was no one around but him and Wella. He had better have his say.

"I've been wanting to talk with you about this for a long time, Wella. You know I have. That's why you've avoided me."

Wella said nothing. She just kept gazing into his eyes, obviously listening.

"I know there's something very different about you, Wella, and I know Dana has inherited a lot of that. It's in the structure of your brain. I don't know where you came from, but there's no one else like you anywhere around here." He felt a shudder go through him. "It's a big load for a little kid, such a nice little kid. I never thought it possible to love anyone the way I love that kid."

Wella smiled her broad happy smile momentarily and then her intent, listening look returned.

"But Dana is no normal child. There's no fooling me on that. I studied child development. It's all in that green book over there on the floor, the big one you dropped when you were trying to find the one on dreams. There's nothing normal about Dana. She's a magnificent, wonderful child, but she isn't normal." He could hear his voice cracking as a heretofore unrecognized wellspring of emotions bubbled to the surface. "Can you tell me why that is, Wella? Why are you and Dana so different from all of us?"

"Different? How?"

"In lots of ways. Sometimes you read minds. I'm sure of it."

Wella blushed profoundly. Then she grinned sheepishly. "I cannot lie to you Jim. You are my friend. Sometimes if I really relax and concentrate, my mind can intercept brain waves from other minds. It is a talent and a skill like any other, like drawing."

Jim could feel his jaw drop involuntarily. He was sure Wella was perfectly sane. She was so practical and down-to-earth. If she would claim such a thing, it must be true. It was too scary. It made them too special. It made him too vulnerable because he loved them.

"Wella, I want more than anything in the world to be Dana's dad. I want to watch her grow up and change and become the incredibly unique person she will be one day. But, I'm so afraid that someday you and Dana will disappear in the same mysterious way you've come to us. We are ordinary, rural people here. We aren't into exotic things. I'm so afraid you'll leave us, and I won't be Dana's dad anymore." Jim stopped speaking and rested his head in his hand. For a long moment, he listened to the silence and the occasional popping in the fireplace.

Finally, Wella said, "Dana is your child. I cannot take her away. You and Pam put your names on the government documents when she was born. My name is not on the documents. Besides, I don't want to take her away. I want you to be her father. I want Pam to be her mother."

"That's a promise? You won't take her away?"

"I will never take Dana from you, Jim." So saying, Wella's face broke into a smile as if she had suddenly remembered something. She jumped up. "Wait here, Jim, I have made another document. I was planning to take it to the real estate office so Mrs. Phillips can put her stamp on it to — how do you say — notarize it. Wait I'll be right back. This document, it is called a will. It will make you feel safer. Please wait here, Jim, until I come back."

Jim gazed up at Wella now towering above him, her face shining down like a rice paper lantern hung from the ceiling, the two strange, big eyes like butterfly wings painted on its surface.

"You have made a will, Wella? Why? You are so young. You don't need a will yet."

Wella blushed the way she often did when asked a question that might reveal that naive side of her weird brain. "I was advised to make this document," she said. "I was told everyone here must have a will."

This time, Jim blushed at his own naivete. "Well, yes, of course, I forgot. It's really essential for you to have a will, Wella. I mean being a poor man with not much to my name, I just didn't think of it. You have property and all."

While Jim rambled his apologies, Wella disappeared through the door calling back, "Wait here, Jim, I will be right back!"

While Wella was gone over to her apartment in the barn, Jim got up and went into the kitchen. Through the window he could see the gray light of dawn bringing the surrounding island world slowly to life. A layer of fog was starting to lift off the silver gray waters of the inlet below. At the first sight of Wella, the sheep had begun to gather near the fence and beg in soft, plaintiff tones.

For something to do, and because he needed a pickup, Jim began puttering about the kitchen to brew a pot of coffee. It was perking enthusiastically and getting pretty done by the time Wella came back. Jim took the pot into the living room and set it down on the hearth where Wella was already seated on her favorite cushion by the fire. A big brown envelope rested in her lap. Jim poured them each a mug of coffee while Wella plunged one long, thin hand into the envelope and pulled out what looked like a lengthy, handwritten manuscript. "Be careful not to spill on this, Jim," Wella warned. "This is very important." When he had settled down opposite her, Wella carefully placed the document on his lap.

"Is this your will, Wella?" Jim glanced at it dubiously. "It isn't even typed."

"If it needs to be typed, we will ask Pam or Ruth or Mrs. Phillips. I don't know how to type the right way. I would make too many mistakes."

Jim took a sip of coffee, and then began carefully studying the document. After reading the first couple of paragraphs, he realized that it didn't much matter about the type. The handwriting was quite legible, with lettering as formal and uniform as — and considerably more attractive than — a typewriter's. The most remarkable characteristic of Wella's will was the legal jargon. It sounded perfect, better than Mark Roberts could have done. After thoroughly digesting the first page, which was mostly introductory legalities, Jim looked up and took another sip of coffee. "This is pretty good, Wella. How did you learn to write this stuff?"

Wella blushed, as if trapped by the question. "I was instructed to do this."

Jim nodded. She must've been instructed by one of various European lawyers who had handled the purchase of Levin Island. He continued to study the document carefully, taking a sip of coffee after every two or three paragraphs and growing more and more astounded. Jim knew a little about wills from his work with real estate. This was certainly an authentic one, and it effectively bequeathed everything upon Wella's death to his wife, Pamela Krandle. If Pam should happen to die before Wella, everything would be left to Dana.

As he read, Jim felt his throat and chest clogging with too much feeling and that old love of Wella taking over again. Before he could finish reading the will, Jim had to rub a tear from his eye with the sleeve of his bathrobe. He was too choked up to say much, so he just handed the will back to Wella and said, "That's great. You did a good job on that. We'll get it notarized right away."

After Wella had gone out to feed the sheep and Jim had gone on about the business of getting ready for work, he found himself still thinking about the will and wondering how he really felt. He should be relieved. Wella had obviously showed it to him in order to alleviate his fears. She meant to demonstrate her commitment, to show that, no matter what anyone else thought, the Krandles were her family, adopted forever and always. So why was he still worrying?

The answer dawned on Jim while he was cruising in his boat across the inlet. There was a cool mist in the air blowing lightly against his cheeks, clearing the confusion from his mind. That was it. The will made it obvious that Wella had no intention of going away and taking Dana with her. Another possibility seemed even more likely now. Maybe Wella intended to go away and leave the child behind. That was ridiculous. Why would anyone go away and leave her entire earthly fortune, and her child, to boot? It wouldn't make sense, unless — and the thought was entirely absurd — she had another fortune, another life somewhere else. For instance, maybe she was extremely wealthy, and had come here just to have the baby and have it adopted so her own people wouldn't know she was pregnant. That idea was as implausible as every other theory he had come up with.

Jim was approaching the dock now, so he turned the throttle to slow the boat and drift on in. He was thinking hard, but things still didn't add up. He tried to recall some of first rumors about Wella. There were several different stories about who she was and where she came from. The most popular one was that she had come from gypsies. That might explain some, though not all, of Wella's strangeness. Gypsies were notorious for a lot of things, not the least of which was an inability to settle down. He had even heard that gypsies had been known to sell their children. Lots of things were said of gypsies. It was hard to know what to believe. Wella had always managed to manipulate situations to avoid questions about her origins. Jim had wanted to respect her wish for privacy, but this morning she had opened up to him a little by showing him her will. That had barely whetted his curiosity, like snatching a momentary glimpse of the universe through a five-cent peek into a telescope. He would have to find more opportunities to talk to Wella alone. It was high time — they had been close friends and neighbors for nearly four years.

LEVIN ISLAND ~ ONE YEAR LATER, MARCH 15, 1972

Jim woke up suddenly from another dream, most of which he had already forgotten. He knew it had been frightening, and it seemed to be about Marvin. Mom and the neighbors had been talking a lot about Marvin lately. Mom said Marvin was supposed to be stationed temporarily somewhere nearby, maybe even on Whidbey Island, on some sort of secret training mission. He wouldn't be allowed to come for a visit until after the training.

Jim had never received a letter from his brother, but once in awhile Marvin had written to Mom. She claimed his mind had been completely overhauled during his four years in the military, and that he had been a smashing success. She said he had escaped from a prison camp and had won some fancy medals for bravery. Dad said he planned to reenlist.

In the dream, Marvin was curled up in a dark place, kind of like a mouse hole or cage. He couldn't stand up. Then later on in the dream, he was swimming in dark and frigid water.

Jim strained to recall as much of the dream as possible so he could tell Wella about it. Maybe she and Dana had the same dream.

As the dream faded, Jim gradually became aware of his surroundings. On his left, Pam was still sleeping. He could hear her breathing. But there was something on his right, a sound so soft it could have been the breath of an elf or fairy, disturbing the air scarcely more than a falling leaf. It was Dana breathing as she stood beside the bed. Her face was only a few inches away. He reached over, touched her cheek and whispered, "Hi, Dana," very quietly so as not to wake Pam.

For the past several nights, instead of crying, Dana had come in to see Jim. That was better because it didn't wake Pam. The rest of them could do play therapy or whatever all night long, and Pam didn't mind. In fact, she didn't know.

Jim still wasn't sure why the midnight play therapy should cure Dana's nightmares, but he had to admit it was pretty fascinating, especially what with practically the whole household having the same dreams. In fact, he had developed the habit of going to bed early just in case he might want to get up in the middle of the night.

Jim reached for his bathrobe on the night stand. Rising up in the cold darkness was getting easier all the time. After wrapping the robe around himself and loosely tying the belt, Jim took Dana by the hand and they tiptoed down the stairs.

Wella was already sitting by the hearth. She had a big drawing pad and a large black crayon on her lap. Dana knelt down in front of Wella and eagerly took the crayon. She was getting good at the game.

Intrigued, Jim watched as Dana began her picture. At first, it seemed that she had lost her talent. Instead of drawing, she began to scribble all over the paper very fast and hard. Pretty soon, however, he realized that she was trying to color the entire page black. When there was hardly a speck of white showing anywhere, she handed the crayon back to Wella and looked up at Jim as if to ask for his approval.

Jim felt on the spot. He wanted to praise Dana's efforts, but he didn't quite know what it meant. Still, there was something uncannily familiar about her creation. Indeed, it reminded him of something but he didn't know what made him feel uncomfortable, and he wasn't sure why. "Is that all, Dana?" he asked.

After a thoughtful pause, the child took the pad of paper back from Wella. She studied the black page for several seconds and suddenly began scratching away some of the crayon with her tiny fingernail. It was an art education technique Jim had taught her. The recommended media was construction paper of one color and crayon of another so that the result would be a duo-chromatic picture, but this one would be black and white. Dana was bent over so close to her drawing now that Jim couldn't tell what she was doing.

After finishing a tiny scratch drawing in the corner of the page, she began scratching something larger in the center. Dana had finished her picture and handed it to Jim.

Amazed, he recognized the subject immediately. It was his dream. The tiny drawing in the corner was a small human-like figure curled up inside what looked like a bird cage. The cage was represented by a little square with stripes up and down for bars. A man was behind the bars. The scratch drawing in the center was a larger rendition of apparently the same man with arms outstretched as if he were floating in a black abyss. Although it was a rather generic human, there seemed to be something vaguely Marvinish about it. For one thing, the head was slightly square, and the figure had a barrel shaped chest. Jim shook his head in utter disbelief. He swallowed hard. Then he looked helplessly at Wella. "I had this dream, too," he choked.

He expected Wella to break into a big smile as she always did when she learned that anyone dreamed in unison, but instead, she looked frightened.

"What's wrong, Wella? It was only a dream."

Wella shook her head emphatically. "It was more than a dream."

"What more? What do you mean, Wella?"

"It was not just a dream."

"Well, what was it then?"

"There is no word in your language for it. It was like your dream of the eagle and the mouse. That very event or something much like it really happened, if not at that moment, perhaps earlier that day. A dream comes from within your mind. This comes from the surrounding world."

"Oh come on, Wella! How could it come from the surrounding world?"

"Easily. In the same way our dreams are shared. By brain waves transmitted through the air, like sound waves or radio waves. You know about sound and radio waves, Jim. They are described in those books upstairs, the ones you bought for Dana. You know, the many books that look alike, the ones with the beautiful name. They are called *World Books.*"

"Wella, sound waves and radio waves travel through the air. It says that in the *World Books.* But nowhere in the entire encyclopedia, or in any other reputable scientific literature, will you find anything about brain waves moving through the air."

"If brain waves did not move, we could not dream alike. Yet several times you and Dana and I have dreamt the same dream at the same time. If brain waves were trapped inside your head as you believe, this would not be, Jim. You must try to be reasonable. In fact, you must listen to me now and do as I say. Someone nearby is in danger. He may drown or be killed by the cold. We must try to find him."

Jim felt numb. He stared dumbfounded at Wella. She was serious.

• • •

Jim sat in the cockpit, holding Dana on his lap while Wella tended the tiller. He had wrapped himself and the child first in life jackets and then in one of Wella's big woolen sleeping bags. He hugged Dana close, and her small body was like a heating pad keeping him warm. Only their stocking-capped heads protruded out into the wind. He felt like a turtle or a mother kangaroo being hoisted away by poachers. He couldn't turn back now if he wanted to, which he did. For one thing, if they didn't turn back soon, they wouldn't get back before morning.

Luckily it wasn't a school day, but Pam would be frantic, wondering what happened to them. She had raised quite a fuss about their traipsing out at night with the little one. But Wella insisted they must search as a group because they had all participated in the dream.

They were making good time now running down wind, but going back would be a lot harder. If only they had taken his motorboat. It was insane to be out at night in a sailboat. Jim had suggested they motor, but Wella said they must have a quiet boat in order to concentrate.

"How do you know which way to go, Wella?" he asked. His voice trailed off in the wind, and she didn't answer. But something told him Wella knew exactly where she was going. Oddly enough, he seemed to know himself. They had started out with no discussion of the directions or plans, but with an unspoken solidarity about their destination.

"Aren't you afraid of getting lost, Wella?" he persisted.

"No. I know these waters well. I have studied the charts carefully."

Jim had lit two safety lanterns and hung them over the sides so they would be visible to other craft, not that he expected anyone else to be prowling about at this hour.

"Shouldn't we use the searchlight?" They were surrounded by a thick, waxy darkness like the crayon drawing Dana had made.

"No, we can see farther without them."

Of course, she was right. A searchlight would limit their range of vision to within its sphere. Still, all he could see were a few flickering lights from Cross and Hanford Islands on either side of the Channel, but when they were about half way through the passage, a pair of yellow eyes appeared from around the east end of Cross Island.

To his amazement, Wella responded by immediately extinguishing both safety lights. "Why did you do that, Wella?" he demanded.

"What?"

"Why did you turn out the safety lights?"

"I don't want them to see us."

"Why not? It's illegal to go about at night with no safety lights."

"That was a Navy patrol boat."

"So?"

"We might have to enter the restricted waters."

"I don't think we should do that. We could get in trouble."

"We probably won't find the person in the water if we don't go there. And if we talk too much we won't be able to concentrate, and they might hear us."

For what seemed a painfully long time, they listened to the waves licking the sides of the boat. Every so often the pair of yellow eyes would appear again, although Jim couldn't see well enough to tell where the lights were going to or coming from.

Despite the little heater on his lap, Jim could feel the stinging dampness of night starting to penetrate his body, especially the toes. He also felt Dana shivering a little. Several times he fought off momentary temptations to insist they turn back.

He was just about to break the mandated silence when Dana did it for him. "The man is there!" she whispered in precise English. It was the first full sentence Jim had ever heard from her.

"Man? Where?" Jim spoke in hushed tones matching Dana's.

Dana poked her arm out from under the blanket and pointed straight ahead. Jim peered into the liquid blackness of blended water and air. Now he was glad Wella had extinguished the lights because they would have interfered with his ability to perceive nuances of light reflected by uncertain shapes floating in the water. "That isn't a man over there, Dana. It's only a log," he whispered uncertainly.

Wella steered toward a dark, solid mass tossing about on the waves. Meanwhile the yellow lights appeared, vanished, and reappeared. They were larger this time.

"The man is on the log," whispered Dana with solemn finality. She wriggled off Jim's lap and knelt on the deck to lean over the gunwale.

Peering dubiously at the thing, Jim detected a glimmer of glass reflecting light, perhaps from the patrol boat drawing ever closer. When they were almost on top of the object, Jim made out what seemed to be a thick arm clutching the log. The reflective glass was from a crystal watch strapped to its brawny wrist. Another arm was dangling in the water, and a rubber-clad head was pressed against the log, scarcely discernible from it. The only evidence of consciousness in the limp body was its death grip on the log. "Whew!" murmured Jim. "Looks like we found that guy in the nick of time."

Wella turned off the wind and luffed the sails. She pulled the boat up alongside the log, and tossed the anchor overboard. Jim reached out and grasped the arm with both clumsily gloved hands. Pulling with all his strength, Jim was able to raise the body far enough out of the water for Wella to wind a rope under the arm and across the upper portion of the back and chest. The victim groaned, but did not struggle. The yellow lights appeared again, very close.

Together, Wella and Jim pulled on the rope, heaving the shoulder up alongside of the boat, listing her starboard. The left arm was now above water, and the abdomen was resting on top of the log. Wella grabbed the left arm and pulled while Jim tugged on the right. It was a maneuver from the water safety class he had taken as a kid. Wella must have taken the same class. She had the routine down pat. Soon, the body, clad in shiny black rubber, shone like a freshly caught tuna on the deck.

Wella dropped the sail and without a word helped Jim drag the hulk into the cabin. Grunting and breathing hard, they shoved the heavy body into a storage space below one of the bunks. Wella stuffed several blankets and sleeping bags in around it. Then she picked up Dana, who had begun to cry, and returned to the cockpit. Jim could barely see her out there holding the child on her lap while fumbling awkwardly with the lines.

He should go and help Wella, but the compulsion was too strong. He had to get a better look. He fumbled in his pocket to retrieve his flashlight, then carefully uncovered the face. When he had fully confirmed that the face was Marvin's, Jim's mind went numb. It was not surprise he felt, nor shock. It was horror at the full realization that he had known all along, ever since waking from his dream, that it wasn't just a dream. He had not found Marvin just now. He had found him nearly an hour ago when, true to form, his incorrigible brother had for some inexplicable reason fallen or perhaps plunged into the Strait in the middle of the night, thus psychically waking his family from fitful sleep.

Marvin's face was white and rubbery, like a dime store Halloween mask. Jim pulled off his glove and reached under Marvin's chin to feel the pulse. He thought he felt something ever so slight, but hadn't really decided for sure, when the ghostly face was suddenly illuminated by a brilliant light. In fact, the whole cabin was bathed in light. Jim felt exposed as if the eye of God had found him unexpectedly. He quickly replaced the blanket over Marvin's face, realizing that a searchlight was shining on him from the patrol boat now just a few feet away.

When Jim came out on deck, Wella was conversing across the wind with someone silhouetted against the light. "You are in restricted waters and there are no safety lights on your vessel," accused the voice of God.

"We are sorry," Wella called back in her usual tone of complete credibility. "The wind is very strong. Our boat has no gasoline engine. We want to go to Levin Island across from Klahowya Cove."

"We could give you a tow, but we're searching for someone. Have you seen anyone in the water?"

Almost without thinking, Jim blurted out, "We haven't seen anyone. It's too dark. We're lost. We have to get home."

"What are you doing out sailing at this hour anyway?"

"Oh, we've been at it a long time, several hours. It was still light when we left. Went to a friend's for dinner on Ludsby Island. Got too far downwind trying to get back."

"Okay, we'll radio for help. There are two other patrols out tonight. One of them can relieve us while we tow you back."

This couldn't be happening. It must be another dream. A big guy in a yellow tent of a raincoat threw Jim a line. Jim threaded it through a cleat in the prow, and they were soon bounding away like a chariot behind a giant steed. Jim wasn't sure what Marvin had been about, but from all outward appearances the military were, with great power and gusto, helping him go AWOL.

. . .

It was still dark when the patrol boat pulled *Terra* into the inlet between Klahowya Cove and Levin Island. The military patrols knew the neighboring waters pretty well and had good charts. They hadn't even asked directions.

When they came within a few feet of the shore, Wella untied the rope and their boat drifted ashore. The patrol boat backed off a little, illuminating the dock with its searchlight. Jim assumed they were shining the light to help them see their way, but he was worried about Marvin stashed under the bunk. Just in case he was AWOL, they better not pull him out with the patrol boat looking on. On the other hand, they needed to get him into the house and warm him up. They weren't finished saving him yet.

The light was so bright that Jim could see all the fine natural colors of Wella's long skirt as she climbed out and tied the boat to the pier. When he handed Dana up to her, the child's small shadow, darkened Wella's face. Jim stopped to wave a friendly farewell to the patrol boat before they trudged up the lawn. Their shadows rose up, changing shapes before them like genies from a lamp.

When they stepped into the living room, Wella placed her finger over her lips and looked straight into Jim's eyes. Clearly the gesture meant to be quiet. Jim was aware that the patrol boat was still down there shining its light on the pier, but surely no one down in the inlet could hear them inside the house. Wella was sure acting strangely. In fact, come to think of it, she hadn't said anything all the way back from the naval base. Jim had whispered to her that it was his brother they had rescued, and Wella had nodded knowingly.

Otherwise, no one had said a word all the way home. Jim had just sat there in the cold, weighted heavily with worry about Marvin. During the years while Marvin was away, Jim had trained himself not to worry about him, but now that the kid was back in his care, the responsibility was on him again.

Wella carried Dana into the bathroom, plugged the tub drain, and turned on the warm water. Jim followed. "What's wrong, Wella? Why are you acting like this?"

Then something weird happened that Jim couldn't explain. It was as if he heard Wella speak without opening her mouth. It was like he heard her voice inside his head. *"They are listening,"* were the words he either heard or thought he heard her say.

"How?"

"By waves that travel through the air," was the reply, and it seemed to come directly into his head in Wella's voice. He thought about it a minute and then realized the words meant they were listening electronically like in some kind of spy movie. At first Jim thought she must be delusional. But then he thought about it a little longer and realized that if anyone was delusional, it had to be him because Wella hadn't really said anything. She was calmly taking off Dana's clothes and putting her in the bathtub. No, Wella wasn't delusional and neither was he. It was about time he started believing in Wella, in the way she was different. Anyone who could put thoughts in his head without speaking had to be right about a fairly plausible thing like a military boat spying on them electronically.

Jim took Dana's rubber ducky from the shelf and placed it in the water beside her. "We've got to get my brother in this tub," he whispered softly enough for his voice to be muffled by the running water.

"They'll leave soon," consoled Wella's voice inside his head.

EARLY MORNING FERRY FROM ANACORTES ~ MARCH 16, 1972

Aaron glanced over his shoulder again to make sure no one was looking. The ferry coffee shop wasn't the best place for a file review, but there hadn't been time before he left. Lieutenant Peters' call had awakened him scarcely an hour before departure time. Then Gloria had called while he was in the tub. His mother had a way of phoning at the most inopportune times, such as while he was having intercourse. She seemed to know.

It had been awkward to beg off from her invitation to dinner. "I haven't seen you for over a month," she had protested. "I'm so sorry Mom, but I'm on an assignment. Have to go to the islands. It's on that case I mentioned."

Aaron liked to feed his mother little crumbs of his job so she could brag to her friends about the secrecy if nothing else. He had dropped little hints that his island discoveries could mean a lot to his career.

To the untrained eye, the island files might look like just another boring scrap book on another nest of subversives. But Aaron had seen enough files to know the difference.

The others spoke at worst of rebellious entertainment: newspaper reports of rally speeches, inflammatory poetry, folk songs. There was scarcely a pen name, let alone an alias. There were birth certificates, articles in the school newspaper from Small Town, U.S.A., never a whiff of a Soviet spy ring or even a drug smuggling operation among them. But the island files were different. Sure, they contained the usual network of trails leading nowhere, but nowhere, in this case, was positively intriguing. There were plans for a boat put together at Garland Shipyard in Ballard. The company had received the drawings in the mail, but the envelope and return address had been lost. There was a copy of the payment check, however. It came from a bank in Switzerland.

Aaron had the plans analyzed by an expert who had been unable to identify their origins but had determined them superb. In fact, Garland had taken it upon itself to abscond with certain features of the plan and had come up with a design that had won the Puget Sound annual yacht race two years in a row. The result was that Garland had recently emerged from near bankruptcy, and was now doing quite well.

The original craft was now owned by a coven of hippies who lived on a small family-owned island. The file contained copies of all titles, deeds, etc. obtained from the Island County Court House. It was stuffed with medical records, marriage certificates, birth certificates, wills, etc., often revealing dubious connections.

Most interesting was a woman's passport indicating dual citizenship, France and Yugoslavia. Expert analysis had determined that she was probably of Gypsy origins. But while Gypsies in her part of the world were generally poor, this woman had somehow amassed a minimal fortune. Most of the money had been laundered through several banks, so it was impossible to pin down its origins. Aaron was a long way from figuring out what it all meant, but it had to be some kind of spy front, unique in its particulars, but classic in its basic structure.

As for the school teacher, he was your classic subversive who might get sucked into something out of zealous stupidity and blind Marxist idealism. His file contained several papers he had written for political science. It was appalling to think of how many commies were allowed to teach school in this naive, unsuspecting country of ours.

In the case of the young Marine, his role was bound to be important if, at this moment, inscrutable. The file contained copies of the kid's military personnel records and intelligence dossier. In addition to evading his draft notice before enlisting, this young man had done some fascinating things. The intelligence file made a pretty strong case that the kid had intentionally surrendered to the enemy, and had possibly been released under the cover of a mock escape.

In fact, young Marvin Krandle had been the key to all this. Aaron had stumbled onto the whole thing while working on a completely different assignment. He was supposed to arrest one of the many young men trying to sneak into Canada rather than being abducted into the Army. That had sounded pretty easy because it didn't matter who he nabbed. Any draft dodger would do. The unlucky fellow was to be used as a test case to gain publicity, hopefully to stem the tide of thousands of young Americans immigrating to Canada. Just when Aaron had thought the thing was nearly done, he learned that Marvin Krandle had joined the Marines. Mr. Krandle had disappeared one night only to show up the next morning in a Seattle recruiting station. Aaron had gone back to square one and found another victim for that assignment. Meanwhile, the Marvin Krandle file had been the spore from which a thick fungal mass of documents had grown. As the ferry pulled into the dock, Aaron tossed a last quick glance over his shoulder and tucked the files into his briefcase with a sigh of satisfaction. Surely, he had uncovered an imminent threat to U.S. security and the American way of life.

· · ·

Aaron hated to admit it, but his stomach went slightly queasy as he approached the base. He had gotten a little sick the first time he was there, because he hadn't been adequately briefed on the place. Right out in plain view, two guards had been holding a group of maybe half dozen naked men at bayonet point along the wall of a brick building. Meanwhile a guard had shoved one of the naked men's heads back against the wall, pried his mouth open and searched inside with a flashlight. Aaron had been told it was a mock prisoner of war camp so he should have expected that sort of thing, but he really hadn't thought about the implications. He felt annoyed at his lack of grit. After all, these trainers were doing their valiant duty to strengthen men for what they would endure in the defense of their country.

Aaron stopped his Oldsmobile sedan at the barricade and handed his identification papers to the guard. The guards who normally wore dress green were now in camouflage fatigues. That meant the base was in a state of alert. The guard took Aaron's papers inside the phone booth-sized guard house. Aaron could see him through the window talking into a phone receiver. Soon the guard came out, handed Aaron the papers and flagged him on.

The training camp was at the far end of the base several miles from the first guard station. His papers had to be checked again at the inner gate and yet again as he entered the security building. Inside, a camouflage-clad youth was seated at a desk beside the coffee urn looking very intense. "Good morning, Mr. Genzforth," he saluted. Aaron was pleased to be recognized. Feeling right at home, he stopped and poured himself a cup of coffee before entering the briefing room.

Aaron was a little late and the conference table was nearly full of Marines in tan, spotted camouflage. Aaron felt the power of his contrasting image in a gray silk flannel suit.

At the end of the conference table was a podium backed by a wall chart of the entire Strait of Juan de Fuca. Lieutenant Peters stood up and motioned for Aaron to take the empty seat beside him. "This is Aaron Genzforth from the U.S. Investigative Service. As some of you know, Mr. Genzforth and his agency have been working with us to help control these local waters so important to United States security. We're going to share with him all reports of last night's search for Krandle. Mr. Genzforth knows a lot about these waters and the neighboring islands. We hope that he can shed some light on what happened last night during your patrols."

Aaron listened carefully to all the reports as several successive patrol leaders stood at the podium. Nearly all had been involved in adventures or made interesting observations. One member of a land search patrol had fallen into a bear trap laid by the base gamekeeper. The young man had injured his knee and was now laid up in the infirmary. Several boats had been spotted in or near the restricted waters. All had been searched at short range by thousand watt searchlights, although none were boarded. Audio-surveillance equipment had recorded virtually every stray conversation held by anyone in the vicinity. Several illustrative tapes played mundane interchanges between what seemed to be local sport fishermen. Aaron sensed that the tapes were more for the Shore Patrol's entertainment than anything else.

"You fellas about through for the night?" croaked an elderly male voice through the speaker. "I'm about stiff myself."

"Yeah, hope the old lady's ready with a stiff shot."

"Yer lucky y'got an old lady. I ain't got nothin' but a cold beer and a cold bed waitin.'"

As was the custom, no names or identification were required of civilians, although the names and descriptions of all boats and identifying registration numbers were carefully noted and reported in the briefings. Aaron's meticulous note-taking and occasional probing questions seemed to encourage the speakers to expound in great detail. Frequently, he would search through the file to cross-reference a name or registration number.

After all patrols were debriefed, Lieutenant Peters took the stand again, "Does anyone have further questions? Mr. Genzforth?"

Aaron felt under a lot of pressure at that moment. He knew he wanted to elicit their cooperation to continue the search more productively, but he wasn't sure how to approach the subject. "I need a few moments to go over my notes and...."

"Fine, sir, take your time," crooned Lieutenant Peters. "Meanwhile, would anyone like to offer an opinion on Krandle's current position?"

One youth across the table stood up. "Krandle was spotted at least once in the water. We searched every inch of land on the base and neighboring islands. He could not have stolen away unnoticed. He's dead of hypothermia by now. Maybe it's time to notify the family he's missing at least."

Aaron felt a shock go through his system. How could these guys be so naive? "Nonsense!" he snapped. "Marvin Krandle is no more dead than you or I!"

All faces turned on him like spotlights. "In fact," continued Aaron, "Krandle was in his brother's home probably sleeping peacefully in a warm bed for much of the time you fellows were out in the cold looking for him."

Everyone gaped at Aaron in various stages of amazement, confusion, and suspicion. No one said anything for quite awhile, but soon everyone began mumbling in sarcastic tones to one another. Nothing like a little healthy controversy to wake people up.

"Would you mind telling us how you know that, Mr. Genzforth?" The man who spoke up was one of the patrol leaders whose name tag identified him simply as Anderson. He was a big, football player kind of fellow, the very guy who had apparently towed Krandle home in the tall woman's boat. No wonder these guys were losing the war.

Aaron felt tempted to be blatantly rude. But he had better contain himself while in their territory. He might need their help. "Well actually, it was your report that gave me all the clues."

"I told you? How could I...?"

"Maybe you didn't have all the information. Did you know that the boat you towed home last night basically belongs to Marvin's brother?"

"The hell it does. That boat belongs to a woman. She's well-known to the Shore Patrol. Minds her own business."

"Maybe so, but she has written a will, leaving the boat to one Pamela Krandle, Marvin's brother's wife. They all live together in a sort of hippie commune."

By this time, even Peters' expression had changed from suspicion to disbelief. "It seems to me like a pretty big coincidence that Marvin's brother would just happen to be out there looking for him last night. How did he know where to look?"

"Obviously, someone must have told him," reasoned Aaron.

"Who could have told him? The camp has no phone access. All

mail was censored." Peters' eyes darted around the room as if they meant to take aim and fire at someone for breaching security.

"I really have no idea who told him," admitted Aaron humbly, "But I think this matter should be investigated further."

LEVIN ISLAND ~ LATE MORNING, MARCH 19, 1972

Waking up from his dream, Marvin realized that the machine-gun fire shattering his throat and lungs was really a violent cough, convulsions so powerful that they heaved his body up and down like a jack hammer. Even before the fit subsided, the fear returned. He was wrapped in something very hot; he couldn't escape. His eyes were almost open, but he couldn't identify the dimly lit room, which was familiar, somehow. Maybe the Shore Patrol had found him. He wasn't dead. At least he didn't seem to be.

A fire nearby cast long moving shadows on cream-colored walls and ceilings. There was a stone hearth, also familiar.

Someone or something was seated on the hearth, large eyes peering through a long curtain of dark hair. No, it wasn't an animal. It was a small child looking at him with deep concern and wonder.

Marvin closed his eyes again and clenched his fists. "The enemy can appear in any form!" shrieked Sgt. Callahan's voice inside his head. Would he ever look into the face of a stranger without reliving that nightmare? In the darkness before his mind's eye there appeared another unwelcome memory of another young girl, maybe four or five years younger than himself. A crazy impulse, perhaps morbid curiosity, had brought him to the edge of the rice paddy to have a better look. She had fallen in when he had shot her, she who he had thought was a man armed with a rifle. About all he could see of her was the face, the eyes frozen open in fear. Most of her body was submerged in a murky green soup of blood and muddy water. What he had mistaken for a rifle was really one of those long poles the people used to carry water. But this one had no buckets on the ends. The pole lay on the mud walkway between the rice paddies.

He didn't have to watch the ugly film again. But he always let the memory play itself out, looking on with morbid curiosity as he had done the first time.

He felt his arm yank the leather strap from his shoulder and drop his machine gun into the disgusting mixture. He watched the stuff splash on his shoes and trousers.

Marvin wasn't sure how long he had stood staring at the butt of his gun, barely visible below the surface of the water. At some point it had vaguely crossed his mind that he was in the enemy line of fire and could be gunned down or taken prisoner. Worse yet, some gung ho officer might have him court-martialed for dropping his guard. But he didn't care. He had stopped caring. Absently, Marvin had raised both hands above his head and marched, deliberate and unfeeling as a robot, into the village where he had known the Viet Cong would be waiting.

He opened his eyes again to find the little girl still staring at him. There was something familiar about all of this, even the child. "Ko sten gee?" he mumbled, then remembered it was the wrong language. "What's your name?"

"Dana Krandle. I am almost four years old."

"Krandle, Your name is Kran...."

Another fit of coughing forced his eyes to shut and a more recent memory surfaced. He was swimming with several other guys in frigid waters. They were on a so-called training maneuver. But everyone knew it was punishment for outspoken remarks. In the real P.O.W. camp, Marvin had observed such tortures, reprisals for escape attempts. This was different. It was to break them into complete hatred of the "Enemy."

He had been thinking about how close home must be and almost wishing he was back in Vietnam where the water would be warm. He had been eyeing the horizon, trying to recognize some familiar landmark, like a mountain or a madrona tree hanging from a cliff. Everywhere black islands poked furry heads out of gray water into the eerie light of winter.

Although he had not been told the precise location, this had to be the San Juans. Presently he had noticed a gnarly log tossing about on the waves just a few feet away. The tide was going out. If he could grab hold, he might go out with it. He glanced over at the bank. The guard just happened to be looking the other way. Almost before he knew what he had done, Marvin found himself clutching the log and floating out toward the middle of the Strait. In fact, the log had been caught in the tide pool and had turned him around so that he could no longer see the guard. All he could see was cold gray water and a big nameless island way across on the other side. He thought he heard men shouting but he couldn't hear what they were saying. He was already too far away. Silently, Marvin clung to the log with all his might. Pretty soon his body would be numb, and he would die of hypothermia which was more peaceful than drowning.

When Marvin's eyes blinked open again, the figure on the hearth had at least doubled in size. Marvin felt his eyes automatically bolt open wider to have another look. This person was definitely familiar. It was his brother or perhaps a dream of his brother. "How do you feel, little brother?" is what Marvin thought he heard the vision say.

"Not s'good," he mumbled back. "Where am I? How'd I get here?"

"Levin Island. We pulled you out of the drink."

Marvin closed his eyes again. He had to think about that one. How the hell did Jim find him out there in the vast expanses of water? He should have died of hypothermia long before that could have happened.

"You called to me in a dream, little brother," Jim answered his thought.

Since when did Jim start reading people's minds? Been living with Wella too long. Maybe she gave him lessons. Stranger things have happened. He heard people say they had some kind of hippy commune going here. Maybe they had a religious cult of some kind. He closed his eyes again trying to understand. Maybe he was suffering from what the Navy doc had called — what was it again? — paranoia. The Doc had warned him he might succumb to that again even after he got clean.

From the dark space behind his closed eyes, Marvin heard Jim's voice still talking to him. "I know you're pretty sick, Marvin, but it would help if you could recall what you were doing out there in the water last night."

"S'posed t' be dying of hypothermia," mumbled Marvin.

"I know. But why were you there? Did you fall in the water? Surely you weren't trying to swim to Canada again."

"S'posed t' be dying," repeated Marvin.

In the darkness behind his closed eyes, Marvin felt Jim's hand rest gently on his forehead. He felt Jim's long, cautious pause. Then he heard him ask, "You mean you were trying to commit suicide?"

Marvin opened his eyes again and looked at Jim. His brother's face looked a lot older now. There were deep lines between his mouth and cheeks. Jim had always worried about him too much.

Marvin closed his eyes again. Maybe he should tell Jim everything. The guy was no prude, he had even done a little marijuana himself. Maybe he should tell about the drugs and how he and a lot of other guys had taken them to make their world bearable. Maybe he should tell Jim how the officers knew the guys were on the drugs and looked the other way, because it made a lot of them really get into it, feel like big warriors able to gun down anything that moved. But there was no use trying to explain all that crap. So he just said, "Yeah, suicide. Guess you'd call it that."

Jim looked even more tormented now. At first he didn't say anything about the suicide. Instead, he just stroked Marvin's forehead lightly and said, "We've got to get you to a doctor. You're burning up with fever." But that didn't last long before Jim fell into his old pattern of trying to talk some sense into Marvin. "I heard you enlisted again. If the war was so hard on you, Marvin, why didn't you just come on home while you had the chance? Why'd you join up in the first place? Wella had you all the way to Canada, and then you turned round and joined up. You could have made it in Canada. You could have worked in construction, maybe eventually started your own business. And what's this about suicide? How could you think of suicide? It would kill Mom if you did a thing like that."

"Everyone would have thought it was an accident. No one would have known if you hadn't pulled me out. Now, she'll know I tried to kill myself. Everyone will know."

"Not unless you tell them. Knowing you, they'll think you've gone off your rocker and were trying to swim to Canada again." An edge of anger in Jim's voice told Marvin he had pushed his brother's button. Five minutes back together after five years, and they were already into the old routine. The difference was, now Marvin knew that it was a game, two rams butting heads. Back across the world of those few short years, Marvin didn't know anything then. God, he was stupid! But he didn't have time for remorse because Wella suddenly appeared, towering over him like some big cartoon genie in a Cinerama theater. She was an incredible sight draped in her long, homespun skirt and matching cape. Bossy as an umpire, she interrupted his thought. "We must find a safer place for Marvin. They're coming back!"

Marvin felt the hardened smile lines of his face crack a little. It was good to see Wella again, even under such abrasive circumstances. The last time he had seen her, she was commanding him to jump out off the boat and swim to Canada. "Hi, Wella. It's been a long time," he said.

"Oh, Marvin, did I awaken you? I am pleased that you look healthier today. Can you stand up? I must take you to my special place."

"Who's coming back, Wella?" asked Jim. He too seemed confused.

"The Shore Patrol. This time they have a special document that gives them permission from the government to search everywhere."

Wella crouched down beside Marvin and thrust her arm under his back to lift him up. Marvin tried with all his might to cooperate, but he was suddenly seized again by a fit of coughing. Anyway, Wella seemed to manage pretty well on her own. Deftly as a medic rescuing the wounded, she draped his arm across her shoulder and grasped it with the opposite hand. Using Marvin's arm for leverage, she pulled him off the floor. At that moment, the big sleeping bag fell off Marvin onto the floor. Jim tried to help by pulling it out from around his feet as Wella stumbled him forward. That was when Marvin noticed he was wearing the same too-long bathrobe she had lent him the day she took him to Canada. He hoped her "special place" wasn't far. His legs felt like they'd been through a milling machine.

"What special place?" asked Jim, who still looked as confused as Marvin felt.

"Maybe it would be better if we just let Marvin go back to Whidbey. We shouldn't have brought him here. We could all be in hot water."

"Do you want to go back, Marvin?" Wella asked ingenuously.

"Well, no, of course not. I'd be court-martialed and put in jail. But, I don't want to get anyone else in trouble either."

"If we are all quiet and discipline our minds, they will not know you are here," Wella assured him.

"What special place?" insisted Jim. "Where are you taking Marvin?"

"I must not tell you. It is better that no one knows. A man who is coming with the Shore Patrol is very good at intercepting thoughts from other people's minds. He does it unconsciously without knowing what he's doing. You must close your eyes, Marvin, while I lead you to the special place. No one, not even you, must know where you are while the men are searching." Marvin felt the smile lines crack again. Speaking of old games, this seemed much like the one he had played before with Wella. He was in the dark, and she was carting him off into the unknown. "I'm sorry, Wella, I don't get the point of all this. But, one thing for sure, I can't walk in this getup with my eyes shut, not even with you leading me."

"All right, Marvin. You can keep your eyes open for now, but when we get near the place, I will cover them with a cloth." So saying, Wella started pulling Marvin toward the door.

As he stumbled out onto the lawn, Marvin felt his lungs automatically inflate with a large breath of fresh air. It hurt a lot, but, to his relief, no coughing ensued. He was also pleased to see that the sky had cleared a little. The weak winter sun peered at them through a grove of trees across the inlet. There were a lot of sheep grazing on the lawn in front of the house. Wella's herd must have nearly doubled since he saw them last. Away across the inlet, he could see the Klahowya Cove School House and even part of his parents' house. He was home.

Wella led him around back of her house and down a stone stairway into the cellar. He had to stoop to get through the entrance and Wella had to fold herself nearly in half. She couldn't even straighten all the way after they got inside. It was dark and cold in the cellar. He hoped he wouldn't have to stay down there long. The only light came from the open doorway through which they had just passed. The makeshift walls were of stone, with cement stuffed unskillfully in here and there. He had been down there once or twice long ago, looking for tools to help Wella with the barn. In fact, he had hoped one day to contract with Wella to put in a whole new foundation, as he had done with a several old houses in Orca Harbor. There was a lot more stuff down here now. In fact, he thought he even recognized a cultivator, a chain saw, and some old tools that used to be kept in the shed behind his parents' house. Also new, was a stack of large metal canisters along one wall. He wondered what was in them. He also recognized an old trunk that had been left behind by the Levin family before they sold the place to Wella. Marvin hoped Wella didn't intend to make him hide in there. He recalled with a shudder the cage he had been placed in at the training camp. He had been in there several hours, unable to stand up or straighten out his body. Supposedly such cages were standard equipment in P.O.W. camps, but Marvin had never seen one over there.

"You don't have to get into the trunk, Marvin," Wella was saying, "But I must ask you to sit on it while I cover your eyes. I must not let you see the way in."

Relieved somewhat, but still dubious, Marvin sat down on the trunk. Wella took off her cape and tied it around his head. He hoped she wouldn't leave it there long. He could barely breath.

He felt deserted and a little insecure when Wella let go of him and moved away. He could hear her walking about the cellar shoving things around. After a few minutes, she came back and took hold of his arm again. "Come, Marvin. I'm ready to take you to my special place now." Marvin stood up with difficulty and, amidst another fit of coughing, walked with Wella for what seemed a fairly short distance, perhaps no more than ten or fifteen feet into a space very different from the cold, damp cellar. He felt warm, and there was a soft, purple glow visible even through the woolen garment draped over his eyes.

After Wella removed his blindfold, Marvin thought he must be in a dream again. For the scene was so changed that he might have been transported by spaceship to another world. The musty cellar had disappeared and instead, occupying what must have been almost the same space, was what seemed to be a giant piece of white sewer pipe, maybe twenty feet long and seven or eight feet in diameter. There was a white wall at either end of the pipe with a closed door in each. Near the front door was a table displaying what appeared to be a strange lamp or heater. Purple flames danced in a transparent globe that rested on what appeared to be a solid metal base. Otherwise the place was nearly empty except that Wella had made him a bed by positioning another of her warm hand-woven sleeping pouches near the lamp. This sleeping pouch was spread out with a queen-sized pillow, and Marvin found it inviting, despite the strangeness of the setting. Wella was giving him instructions in a monotonous tone, as though she had him under hypnosis. "You will lie down here now, Marvin, and be very quiet. If you feel like coughing, look at the purple flames. They will quiet you. In fact, if you gaze at the flames all the time, they will help you to be quiet and calm."

Marvin felt his body obey Wella's instructions with very little help from his mind. After all, he had little energy to resist, and his choices were limited.

SAME AFTERNOON

Bundled in her favorite gray woolen sweater, Dana stood on the front porch watching Wella with an expression of deep concern. The child knew a lot about what was happening but was too young to understand any of it.

Dana held in her hand the metal scoop Wella always used to feed the sheep. She knew it was time for the afternoon feeding, an event she never missed. She wanted life to go on as usual.

"We'll have visitors soon," said Wella.

"I can do the chores myself." That sentence was longer than average for Dana. She was starting to act more grown up now, probably because, at some level, she knew that she would soon be on her own in an alien world.

"Thank you, Dana. Be careful of the ram when you go into the pen. He may charge and knock you down to get the grain."

After Dana went round toward the barn, Wella sat down on the porch step gazing up the inlet. The patrol boat would arrive soon, and Wella needed time to understand the heaviness in her heart. She needed to reflect upon the many errors she had made. She had always conferred with Jorka on most decisions relating to the child or to diplomacy and human customs, but she had never told Jorka about her dealings with Marvin. She knew that Jorka would not approve. In fact, Wella vaguely feared that this kind of activity challenged more than custom and mores, and would hasten the day when she would have to leave Korba-3.

That morning, Wella had intercepted thoughts during her meditation that told her patrol boats would come back to look for Marvin. With that, she had gone directly to Jorka and tapped in the entire story, beginning with the first episode when she had taken Marvin to Canada, and ending with his rescue from the Strait early that morning.

Wella recalled her shock at Jorka's simple, unfeeling response. "Your mission is ended. You must mind-blend with Shulmina of Severelia, and prepare for return to Gallata."

Wella shrank back as though the computer had assaulted her

physically. After recovering, she tapped in, "I am not ready to go. The child is too young. She needs my help and nurturing."

"Your mission is finished. You have provided well for the child. Now you must return to Gallata."

Nothing would come of arguing with Jorka. Wella could disobey Jorka. She could even lie to Jorka, but a quarrel would achieve nothing. Besides, Jorka's advice had always proven wise, and she dreaded the consequences of disobedience. For instance, if she refused to return to Gallata, her recent adventures might lead to imprisonment and possibly to government knowledge of her true origins. Someone from the government knew a lot about her already.

A faint droning interrupted Wella's thoughts and, as she surveyed the distance, a gray speck materialized, growing larger with the increasing sound. Alongside other conflicting feelings, there emerged a strange exhilaration about the proximity of this Earth human, probably male, who knew so much. But fear dominated all other sensations. Unfortunately, there would not be time to take Jorka's advice and leave the planet Earth before he arrived.

Wella wasn't sure how to entertain visitors from Earth's government and there wasn't time to consult Jorka again, so she did as she had done for other visitors. She went into the kitchen and placed a kettle of water on the stove for tea. On such a cold, damp afternoon they would not want Coca Cola.

· · ·

Fascinated, Dana stood frozen on the lawn as the large gray boat arrived at the dock. Unable to run away, she watched three men in black ponchos trudge past her like giant ravens scouting their way up the lawn. Behind them came another figure, looking out of place in a long, tan raincoat with wide lapels, like city people wore. The man in the raincoat stopped in front of her, his tiny blue eyes fixed intently on hers, his long, thin nose quivering slightly, like a hungry ewe's.

"What is your name?" he asked.

Dana did not answer. She felt uncomfortable talking to Grandpa, let alone a stranger from the city.

"Can't you talk, little girl?"

Dana shook her head.

The man kept looking into her eyes, trying to see into her mind. "Why don't you talk?" he demanded.

Dana shrugged her shoulders and tried to smile. She wanted to show her friendly self, but the frightened one had taken over. She must not think about Uncle Marvin. Wella had told her not to think about him while the men were here from the patrol boat.

"We are looking for someone," persisted the man. "Have you seen a man who was sick and nearly drowned?"

Dana shook her head. Wella had told her to lie about Uncle Marvin. Wella said sometimes one had to lie.

"Are your parents home?"

Dana shook her head.

"Are you home alone?"

She shook her head again and pointed toward the house. Wella had come out onto the porch where she now stood talking quietly to the other men. But the man in the raincoat would not be distracted. He remained focused on Dana. "Is that your mother?" he inquired.

Dana shook her head again.

"Who is it then?"

"Wella."

The man threw back his head and laughed. "So, you can talk. I'm so glad. I was worried about you."

Dana laughed too, but she still feared the man as he moved on up the lawn toward the house.

Dana followed from a safe distance. She heard the man in the long raincoat introducing himself to Wella. He squinted up at her as she towered over everyone from the top step. But the name sounded strange to Dana, and she couldn't quite make it out. She heard the man say they were looking for someone, and they had a warrant to search Wella's land.

"Go right ahead. Search all you want," said Wella. "Would you like to come in for a cup of tea first?"

The men in the black rubber ponchos cleared their throats and looked at one another. They looked bewildered at first, then finally began shaking their heads. The other man said, "Yes, thank you. I would like some tea. Perhaps I'll take a look around inside too." He cleared his throat very heavily. "I suppose you'd know if someone were hiding inside your house, but stranger things have happened."

Wella and the man in the long raincoat went into the house for tea, but Dana stayed to follow the other men around and watch the outdoor part of the search. She knew a lot about searching because she played hide-and-seek a lot with her cousin Charlie when he was visiting from the city. She often searched for lambs hiding among the blackberry briars surrounding the woods.

The men were good at searching. They started way out on the beach and walked all the way around the island, even wading in the surf to look behind boulders and logs. They circled the island several times, drawing gradually inward toward the house. They found all the good hiding places on the meadows and beaches. They even found all the good hiding places in the cellar. They took a pitchfork and sifted through the hay in the barn, then went in Wella's apartment and looked in the closet and under the bed. They saved the woods and blackberries for last.

The men didn't seem to know the special way Dana searched for Charlie among the briars. She would sit down on the big rock at the edge of the patch, close her eyes and think of nothing. She would just watch the patterns of light on the backs of her eyelids for awhile until, soon, a soft blue light appeared inside her head. After she had watched the light for awhile, thoughts would appear of things Charlie liked. It could be anything — knights fighting dragons, baseball cards, or Aunt Theresa. Most of the thoughts didn't make a lot of sense, but if she kept letting them come, there would be a clue. Usually it was a flashing picture of something lost among the briars, or the bark of a certain tree, the holly bush, the old well pump. Then Dana would call out, "One, two, three on Charlie beside the well pump!" Sometimes, Charlie proved her wrong by appearing from somewhere else, but not very often. The men could have found Uncle Marvin a long time ago if they had known that way of searching. But she had promised Wella she wouldn't think of Uncle Marvin while the men were on the island.

By this time Dana no longer feared the men as much. They had not spoken to her, but had simply accepted her watching almost as if they enjoyed her company. One of them had a young, dark face and thick layer of fuzz on his head like a freshly sheared lamb. He smiled at Dana a lot.

Dana followed closely as they approached the fortress of blackberries surrounding the woods. They walked all the way around it looking for an entrance, but of course, there were none large enough for them.

One of the men said, "Someone could be hiding among the trees over there."

The dark, friendly one said, "How would anybody get in there?" Then he turned to Dana. "Is there a way in?" he asked.

Dana nodded.

"Show us, then," dared the dark-faced man.

Dana led the search party around to the opposite side of the woods. When she came to a place the lambs used a lot, Dana got down on her hands and knees and began crawling through a small, twisted tunnel of briars. The briars scratched her face and snagged her skirt and sweater, but it was worth it to get to a good hiding place. Finally she came to a tree trunk and curled up like a possum huddled against its damp bark. It was her favorite hiding place. Charlie never found her there.

After a long silence, she heard the men talking quietly among themselves. Then she heard them grumbling and swearing as they struggled with the briars. Finally one of them called, "Are you in there, little girl?"

"Yes, I'm hiding," called Dana. "If you can't find me, you have to yell, 'Ally ally oxen free'!"

The men all laughed. Then they called in unison, "Ally ally oxen free!"

When Dana crawled out from under the briars, she felt damp and cold, so she decided to go on in by the fire. Besides she didn't want to miss *Sesame Street* and *Mr. Rogers*.

The men in the black ponchos had gone around to the opposite side of the woods. She could still hear them complaining as they hacked away at the briars. How silly of them to think they could clear away all those briars. If they could do it, Mom would be pleased. She wanted to put a picnic table out under the trees.

The man in the long raincoat stood by the bay window looking out. Wella sat at her loom, her hands sweeping rhythmically back and forth. Without speaking to either of them, Dana walked over and sat down on her fleece in front of the portable television set. Wella had already turned it on. Blocks, balloons, and frogs bounced, vanished, and bounced again to a lively counting tune. *Sesame Street* was nearly over, and Mr. Rogers would soon appear. It would be hard to watch Mr. Rogers with the strange man standing there.

Why didn't he go back to his boat? There had been plenty of time for him to drink tea and to find every good hiding place inside the house. The *Sesame Street* theme song began, with children playing in sunny city parks on a summer day.

The man sat down on the rocking chair in front of the window and fixed his gaze on Wella. Above the din of the music, Dana could hear them trying to talk.

"Your little girl doesn't talk much. Is she shy?"

"She has no playmates here. She'll talk more after she starts school next year. Her father teaches at the school."

"What's her name?"

"Dana."

"Is she your daughter?"

Dana felt the tenseness of Wella's hesitancy to answer.

The *Sesame Street* song trailed off into a silent screen, gray like the winter weather outside.

"Dana and I are very close, Mr. Genzforth," answered Wella. "I have always taken care of her, because her mother works in Orca Harbor, and I work here at home."

A room with a door appeared on the tv's screen, and Mr. Rogers entered through the door, singing.

Dana could see Mr. Genzforth out of the corner of her eye. He leaned forward in his chair, until his face was very close to Wella's. "The child resembles you. You mean to say you aren't related?"

Wella blushed. She didn't seem to know the answer at first. Finally she said, "I've heard it said that people who spend a lot of time together grow to look alike." Then she laughed. "Some people have told me the lead ewe of our flock resembles me. But no one has ever said that about poor Dana. Most people say she looks like her mother, Pamela Krandle. Pam is a beautiful woman."

Mr. Genzforth started laughing too. But then he did a strange thing. He suddenly reached forward and touched the middle of Wella's forehead almost as if he wanted to make sure it was real. It reminded Dana of the way she and some of the other children had touched Santa's whiskers during the Christmas party at the school house.

Wella stopped laughing immediately. She dropped her loom and stood up, glaring at Mr. Genzforth who also stood up and faced her. Dana had never seen Wella looking so upset or frightened. As for Mr. Genzforth, he had stopped laughing, but he still smiled the way Mr. Rogers did, like he had to because he was on television, not because he felt it from inside.

At that moment a lot of banging and stomping could be heard from the porch. The men had stopped looking for Uncle Marvin among the blackberries and had come back to look for Mr. Genzforth.

"Well, it seems our search has ended for now," said Mr. Genzforth with forced cheerfulness. "We didn't find what we were looking for." He shrugged, and flashed another Mr. Rogers smile. "You can't search forever. Of course, the same is true of hiding. You can't hide forever, either." He bent ever so slightly at the waist, almost as if he meant to bow the way people sometimes did on television. "Thank you for the tea, Miss De Gornia."

Wella didn't follow Mr. Genzforth to the door or down to the dock like she did with most visitors. She just stood staring blankly at nothing for a long time. Dana knew that Wella was thinking very hard, and she hated to interrupt, but she finally decided it best to remind her that Uncle Marvin, wherever he was hiding, would need to use the bathroom again.

LEVIN ISLAND ~ EVENING, MARCH 17, 1972

Pam and Jim praised and congratulated Wella when they came home and found Marvin installed comfortably again in front of the fireplace. Wella had wrapped him in one of her big sleeping pouches, so he looked cozy and relaxed.

The family gathered around Marvin in a festive mood, to eat Pam's special chili and help plan Marvin's second escape to Canada. No one asked about the secret hiding place that had fooled the Navy Shore Patrol. They probably thought there would be plenty of time for that.

Wella sat on the hearth watching the scene as if from a distant, sadder place. She wanted to tell them she would soon be gone. She longed to part with them in the Gallatan way, by collective consciousness sharing and eulogizing. She felt sadder than she had at the loss of her clan on Gallata. If only she could at least utter a few simple, repetitious "goodbyes" as was the Earth custom that had become so sweet and familiar now. But she understood Jorka's insistence that all Earth humans must believe she had drowned in the Georgian Strait. It would be too great a burden for anyone, no matter how trustworthy, to know the full story. In fact, she should not even allow herself to ponder this now. Someone might inadvertently intercept some of her thoughts.

Presently, Wella became aware of someone small and quiet watching her from the corner of the room. Those eyes had been on her off and on all day as the sadness deepened in them. The child was old enough now to begin intercepting thoughts in times of accidental day trance. She undoubtedly knew. She also knew that Wella loved her very deeply and would not leave her willingly.

Pam perched on the edge of the rocking chair, balancing a bowl of chili on her knee and discussing the plan. "The wind is so strong tonight. I think we should wait for better weather," she urged. "Besides, Marvin should have more time to rest and get well."

Jim sat cross-legged on the floor, a large chart spread out before him like a picnic cloth set with his beer can and bowl of chili. Wella couldn't see his face, but a small, shiny bald spot peered like a fresh-laid egg in his nest of soft, blonde hair. He laughed away Pam's characteristic caution without looking up and pointed to a spot on the map. "Mark Roberts may have already left to meet us. He's planning to anchor here. We have to get Marvin there sometime tonight."

Wella felt tense and miserable. Jorka had made it clear that the thoriemacum would come for her somewhere in the darkness that night, out on the Georgian Strait. Because of Mr. Genzforth's interest and probing, all traces of Gallatan materials and sources, including herself, must be removed from this place. Jorka had stressed the importance of using conversation rather than thought transference to communicate with the Earth humans during her last few hours. Jorka had also advised Wella to remind them of important imperatives in raising the child, such as the need to avoid alcohol, poisonous to the Gallatan system, and to raise her in the Gallatan way, with close ties to their large circle of family and friends. It would have been easy to communicate these ideas through collective meditation, but even after so much practice, Wella was still not confident of her ability to convey complicated thoughts conversationally, throwing in subtle sentence formations at opportune times, hoping to be understood.

She leaned toward them, groping for the words, straining for cues. It felt as awkward as the time she had tried to play volleyball at the community club picnic. Suddenly she blurted out, "If something happens, if there's a storm and I don't come back from Canada this time, you must remember Dana can't drink beer or any kind of alcohol. It would make her sick." Everyone looked at Wella. Dana picked up Jim's beer can and sniffed down into the hole.

"Yuck!" she shuddered. "I would never drink beer. It smells awful!"

"That's good, Dana. You must never drink alcohol of any kind and you must always stay close within the family."

"What's the matter, Wella?" said Jim. "The weather isn't that bad tonight. I've seen you out sailing in higher winds than this, just for the fun of it."

"If you're worried about sailing tonight, I think you should all stay here," said Pam. "Marvin could go to Canada another time."

"Do you think the wind is too strong, Wella?" asked Jim. He had not taken his eyes from her face since she had spoken.

Wella folded her hands in her lap and looked down at them. "No, Jim's right. The weather is not that bad." She forced a smile.

. . .

Wella sat on the porch looking up at the stars. She knew one of them was not a star but rather the *Shiemacum* reflecting the sunlight from the other side of the Earth as the Earth moon did at night. Jorka had assured her that the *Shiemacum* would enter into orbit around the Earth that afternoon. Within a few hours, it would descend to a distance traversable by the thoriemacum, which would come to get her later in the evening. The thoriemacum, transparent as glass, but much stronger, would not be visible at night, but Wella would feel the suction of its powerful whirlwind force, and would enter through the eye of its storm. It would be difficult to board the thoriemacum at night from a boat. Wella had rehearsed it many times, but that was long ago; the thought of it frightened her now.

She closed her eyes and entered into the quiet blue stillness that gradually expanded until it seemed to fill the entire universe. After a long silence, she heard the mind voice of Shulmina of Severelia speaking as if she were very near.

"Wella of Gornia, we thank you for the good work you have done on the planet Korba-3. The experimental subject, Dana Krandle, is a fine, sensitive child with many Gornian traits. We understand your sorrow at leaving her. But she will not be forgotten. Our studies of Dana and her progeny will contribute immeasurably to the vast Gallatan knowledge of genetics, and of how barbaric life forms evolve to higher civilizations."

Even as Shulmina spoke, a visual image of the ancient woman appeared within the blue light. She wore a long robe with many interwoven patterns of natural color. A cataract of white hair fell across her shoulders, blending imperceptibly with the grays and tans of her garment. Shulmina smiled warmly at Wella from her distant place. As Wella basked in the feeling of love, another image emerged. She, Wella, stood beside Shulmina holding Dana in her arms and the feeling was of great pride and love shared among them.

Wella did not know how long she sat enjoying the visions in her meditation, but she came out of the trance to find Dana seated on her lap. They shared a long, loving embrace, perhaps Wella's last Earth hug. She recalled her first awkward hug with Jim in the real estate office in Orca Harbor and many others she had shared with the members of her adopted clan. The most psychic of Gallatan intimacies would never replace this form of communication. Having once experienced hugging, she could not live without it. She would introduce the custom during her returning ceremony on Gallata.

• • •

Following the Krandle custom, Wella sat on the bed beside Dana and told her stories until she drifted off to sleep. Jorka had suggested many of Wella's bedtime stories — Gallatan tales vaguely disguised as Earth folklore.

The tale she told during their last moments together was one of Dana's favorites about a woman who embarks upon a journey to find the magic maker, but in the process of searching, learns that she has the power to do magic within herself. Wella liked the story and thought it the best choice for the occasion. Taking the story's lesson, Dana would use the strength within herself to go on without Wella. Dana drifted off to sleep even before the story ended.

After gently touching Dana's forehead with hers, Wella went down to the tunnel which was now empty, except for Jorka and the small wooden table on which she had been installed by the *Shiemacum* crew so long ago. According to plan, both Jim's and Wella's boats would participate in Marvin's escape. Jim would leave early and travel for awhile southeast in the direction of Ludsby Island before heading north toward Canada. Jim hoped this would attract the attention of any patrol boats that may not have given up the search for Marvin. Then when Marvin actually did leave with Wella, the Navy would hopefully be long gone after the wrong boat.

Wella lifted Jorka from the table, and with arms outstretched, twisted her globe until a small opening appeared in the base. Next, Wella carefully tilted Jorka sideways, allowing a tiny drop of flaming, *kuderein* liquid to trickle out onto the floor. Returning Jorka to her upright position, Wella twisted the base back into its closed position and stepped out of reach of the tall, dancing, purple flames. Shrinking in size as they rapidly multiplied, tiny lavender tongues scurried about in an ever-widening circle, lapping up white walls and floors as if they were milk.

Wella stood at the entrance watching with sad fascination as the tunnel casement gave way to layers of root systems, animal burrows, crumbling dark Earth, and rock. It was as though a skin rash had exposed an unsightly array of internal anatomy not meant for view. A pair of reddish, purple eyes peered at Wella from one of the burrows and then vanished into the darkness.

Awestruck, Wella watched the flames devour the floor beneath Jorka's table. Because it was crafted entirely of Earth material, the table remained intact on the sodden Earth. Containing no phoorea, it, of course, did not react with kuderein. An unperturbed stream of water trickled through its legs and disappeared under the stone foundation of the house, just short of the tunnel entrance where Wella stood. Unlike the Earth fire that had destroyed her barn, kuderein combustion left no smoke or residue. Reacting with phoorea, kuderein would reproduce itself indefinitely, until everything containing that substance was gone, leaving a dark, empty cavern sealed off from the rest of the universe, perhaps never to be found, unless someone decided to remodel or destroy the house.

Wella stepped out of the tunnel into the musty cellar and set Jorka carefully on the trunk while she replaced the camouflaged door and ran her finger along the seal. The seam was still solid as ever, its edges not discernible from other lines and crevices in the stone foundation. She shoved the trunk in front of the entrance to reinforce the deception. Then she tucked Jorka carefully under her arm and emerged from the cellar into the damp, cool night. The wind was stronger than usual, and Wella shuddered to think of the undertaking she must accomplish that night. She longed to return to the comfort of her small living quarters inside the barn, light a wood fire in the stove, and enjoy privacy, a now familiar and valued concept.

Instead, Wella began, robot-like, to recall Jorka's instructions and to perform the tasks at hand. First, she surveyed the inlet to identify all craft in the area. It was very dark, however, and the boats in Klahowya Cove were not discernible. The only lighted vessel was a familiar one anchored across the inlet just below Klahowya Cove. It was a fishing guide service reputed to know many special places in the local waters. Wella had once tried following the guide around with her sailboat, meditating for several hours in hopes of intercepting his secrets, but that method had not succeeded even as well as some of her other attempts at fishing. Even though she had never really understood the "money" system, Wella knew that hiring the guide would have been an expensive way to obtain food. Jim had explained that tourists employed the guide, not because they wanted food, but because they liked to boast about catching large fish. There was some mysterious cultural symbolism associated with large fish.

Using the lavender glow from Jorka, still tucked under her arm, Wella strode resolutely down the lawn and across the dock to board *Terra*. A rush of excitement made her hands tremble a little as she knelt down on the floor of the cabin where she had already spread out Jim's map, now bathed in the lavender glow of Jorka's light. She pulled aside a movable panel revealing a hollow place inside of the keel where there was a built-in circular repository exactly Jorka's size and shape. The repository had been there all along and had been interpreted by Pam as a storage area for the thermos bottle and lunch for summer outings. Carefully, almost lovingly, Wella placed Jorka into the space that would serve as her final work station and eventually, so to speak, her tomb.

Using Jorka's light, Wella peered at the map until she found the place Jim had marked. Because Jorka was now installed in *Terra*'s control panel, Wella didn't even have to obtain directions from the computer. Instead, she merely reached down into the keel and typed in the name of their destination, "Winston's May Cove, British Columbia."

Before replacing the panel over the keel, Wella used Jorka's light to inspect the cabin's readiness for the trip. She spread a thick, woolen skieron on the bunk for Marvin. He was still very ill and would fortunately sleep most of the way, oblivious of *Terra*'s transformation from wind to a mysterious equally silent energy source.

It would soon be time to get Marvin, but first, recalling Jorka's instruction, Wella must spend time in deep meditation and hopefully blend with any consciousness spheres that may influence the journey.

For instance, the military Shore Patrol might still be looking for Marvin, or perhaps Mr. Genzforth, from the U.S. Investigative Service, might still be about.

Wella wrapped her hooded cloak around her for warmth as she settled out on the deck for her meditation. Immediately the perplexing image of Mr. Genzforth came to mind. Why had he touched her forehead? Surely he did not know about the diverra bone. Yet he had placed his finger directly upon it. Certainly, he had not intercepted any thoughts about it from Wella. She had not considered it in a very long time. Maybe Mr. Genzforth had that strange mental ability Earth humans called "intuition."

When Wella had asked Jorka to define "intuition," her response had been vague. Either Earth humans had the ability to know things in a way that Gallatans could not or else they could intercept thoughts without knowing what had happened, and call that "intuition." In any case, intuition was an ability that even Earth humans did not understand. Some of them, probably the least intuitive ones, didn't even believe it existed and attributed intuition to excessive imagination.

Mr. Genzforth's mind was different from the other Earth humans Wella had known. Whereas the others tended to be trusting and not judgmental, Genzforth was suspicious and reproachful. It terrified Wella to think of leaving the child on the same planet with him.

The last of Jorka's instructions was the most peculiar. During her meditation, Wella called the sheep out to the lawn and set them to grazing in an intermittent pattern evenly dispersed between the house and dock. Her final and most distasteful chore before fetching Marvin was to go back to the apartment and change to the jeans that Wella had worn at Jorka's insistence, not more than two or three times previously. On the other occasions, Jorka's insistence on the jeans had been purely cultural. Wella would have been too socially conspicuous on those occasions in a Gallatan skirt. This time, however, there was a practical reason.

Jorka's plan was that Wella and Marvin, under the cover of darkness, would leave the farmhouse and crawl down to the dock by weaving in and out among the sheep. Jorka had insisted that the maneuver would seem quite natural to Marvin who, after all, was trained as a Marine.

• • •

Wella woke Marvin by gently tapping his cheek. He looked at her dully through a fog of fever and antihistamine.

"You're wearing pants, Wella. You never wear pants."

"It's time to leave," she said softly. "You have to put this on." She handed Marvin the wet suit Jim had taken off him the night before. It had been carefully stashed in the tunnel.

"Are you going to help me walk again?"

"No, we're going to crawl, in case someone is watching."

"Back to the secret hiding place?" he asked hopefully.

"No, to Canada. Jim and Mark are waiting for you in Winston's May Cove."

"Do I have to go?"

Wella nodded.

"Why?"

She shrugged. "Jim doesn't want you to go to jail. He says jail is bad for you. It makes you mentally ill."

To Wella's delight, Marvin smiled. Then he nodded. "You bet! Jail's for th' birds," he slurred.

Wella would never forget the experience of crawling down the lawn with Marvin. He didn't actually crawl, but rather pulled himself along by his elbows. Wella had seen Earth human males do this on television as part of the killing games. Wella tried the elbow walking, but it didn't work very well so she resorted to crawling as planned and for the first time realized the value of jeans which protected her knees and, despite their stiffness, gave her legs the necessary freedom of movement. Even though the grass was wet, and the jeans were soaked at the knees, they didn't feel particularly wet or cold.

Marvin took the lead even in his weakened condition. Deftly, he wove his body in and out among the sheep. When they reached the dock, Marvin hesitated only a moment before his silhouette hunched over the dock stealthily as a sea otter, and slipped into the boat. Wella watched with amazement and then imitated the maneuver. It was unlikely that anyone watching the house and lawn in the darkness would detect their departure.

Once inside the cabin, Marvin and Wella both remained low and silent while Wella helped Marvin wrap up, soggy suit and all, in the skieron. Cooperating automatically as if he had been hypnotized, the young man closed his eyes and, as if the bizarre maneuver had scarcely disturbed his slumber, went back to sleep.

Quietly, Wella cast off from the pier and let *Terra* drift on the current out into the channel. The tide was going out so they floated soundlessly downwind and were swept like a piece of flotsam around the west end of Levin Island.

After they were beyond sight of Klahowya Cove, Wella crouched down on the cabin floor and stealthily removed the panel masking Jorka. True to the splendor of her programmers, Jorka had already registered their location in small, purple letters on the surface of her globe. Activated by the movement of the current, Jorka's power source had taken over control of *Terra*, and the boat was picking up speed, moving faster than ever before under sail power.

Wella crept out onto the deck and peered over the gunnel into the darkness. Islands floated by like giant sea monsters in the night. Here and there, lonely sparkles of light revealed the presence of Earth human dwellings along the dark cliffs and shores. As she watched, an uneasy feeling gradually became a full realization that, despite their stealthy departure, they were being followed. One distant light was moving toward *Terra* very fast. It was the large, white light of a fishing guide boat, and would have seemed harmless enough, had it not been in steady pursuit and gaining on them.

Wella returned to the keel, opened access to Jorka, and typed, "Lighted craft approaching rapidly from behind."

Gently, certainly, *Terra* accelerated, but when Wella looked out again, the lights were still drawing closer, so she typed, "Much faster, please."

Terra lunged forward with such force that Marvin opened his eyes briefly.

"What's going on, Wella?" he grumbled.

"I think someone is following us," answered Wella, placing a hand on the tiller, so it would appear that she was in control of the boat.

"Not this again!" Marvin groaned. "Haven't we been through this before?"

"Try to rest, Marvin," urged Wella. "You must conserve your strength for when we get there. You might have to swim a little. Can you manage that?"

"How far?" moaned Marvin.

"I don't know. I'll get as close as possible, but we don't want whoever is following to know we're meeting another boat. We must make a good lie out of this, so that the boat continues to chase me and leaves you alone. That was Jim's plan."

"Sure, I can swim a little ways," agreed Marvin. "I might die of pneumonia tomorrow, but I can swim a hundred yards tonight." He ducked his head under the skieron, coughed several times. To Wella's relief, Marvin fell asleep again without noticing they were traveling many times faster than any sailboat on Earth. Wella was also relieved that the pursuing craft appeared to be a lot farther away now.

Unfortunately, however, as *Terra* rounded the end of a large land mass, another boat approached from the east, and Wella recognized its ominous pair of yellow eyes. It was the military Shore Patrol, probably the same boat that had towed them home after they found Marvin.

She crouched lower, reached into the keel and typed, "Faster please. Military boat approaching from the east."

Terra lunged forward like a competitive runner at the sound of the starting bell. Marvin stirred a little, but his eyes remained closed.

Terra's incredible speed soon left both pursuers far behind. The distant twinkle of their lights seemed to express confusion and frustration. Eventually they faded into darkness.

Wella watched *Terra*'s globe carefully now. The computer had begun to register their proximity to Winston's May Cove. When *Terra* approached to within a Gallatan mondathar of their destination, it would be time to replace the panel and awaken Marvin for his swim. *Terra* had slowed down again to within believable sailing speed, and Jorka's controls automatically raised *Terra*'s sails for the sake of appearance, even though they flapped uselessly most of the time.

When Wella spotted Jim's boat near the distant shore, she touched Marvin's cheek to wake him up. The pursuing boats were within view again, advancing more swiftly, now that *Terra* had slowed her speed.

Marvin struggled awkwardly out of the skieron and stood uncertainly, leaning over the bunk. He looked miserable.

Wella wanted to hug Marvin as she had Dana earlier. She felt close to this young, Earth male. She had been with him during a difficult period of his life. She hated to see him go into the water again. He would not get well until he could remain warm and dry for a long time.

Keeping her left hand on the tiller to maintain the appearance of controlling the boat, Wella reached forth her right hand to shake Marvin's in the traditional Earth human friendship gesture. "You only have to swim a little more now, Marvin," she urged gently. "The Shore Patrol will be here soon. They'll follow *Terra*, so you must leave now."

Marvin returned Wella's handshake energetically. Then he let go of her hand and reached his arm across her shoulder in a sort of half hug. "You have to come and visit me when I get settled in Canada. I promise to stay this time if I get there all right." He started coughing again.

"You'll get there," Wella assured him. "But you must leave now." She glanced over her shoulder at the advancing lights.

Marvin squinted at the lights. Then he crouched down and slunk out of the cabin. His rubber wet suit reflected the advancing lights as he slid like a seal over the side. *Terra* listed slightly starboard and then righted herself again as Marvin silently entered the water.

As Marvin swam away, *Terra* made a sharp, portside turn and sped off toward the middle of the strait. Wella went aft and stood on the deck where she closed her eyes and began to meditate. She entered the clear blue light, her mind looking on calmly while her body trembled with fear and anticipation.

Presently, she felt *Terra* begin to spin round and round like a top. As the rotations increased in velocity, Wella opened her eyes. Her mind remained in the state of blue stillness as her eyes watched the dark blend of water and land whirling about her.

An expanse of black water lay in all directions as the boat spun round in what seemed to be the center of a whirlpool. *Terra's* sails were now wrapped clumsily about the mast. The lights from both pursuing craft were closer now, approaching cautiously. The smaller one was close enough to recognize by dress and manner the figure standing on deck. It was Mr. Genzforth. He held something up to his face, perhaps a small pair of binoculars.

Despite her fear, Wella felt a twinge of amusement. She smiled. Even with binoculars, Genzforth could not see the transparent cylinder descending from what to him would be the heavens. In fact, the thoriemacum now occupied the small space with Wella on *Terra's* deck, coming to rest on its on own mass of swirling air. *Terra* was spinning very fast now, and Wella had begun to feel dizzy, even faint. Might as well get this over with, as the Earth humans would say. It would only take a minute.

Bravely, Wella turned and stepped backward into the powerful suction, a maneuver she had practiced often. Like a piece of wool swept up in Pamela's vacuum cleaner, Wella felt her body pulled flush against the thoriemacum's outer wall. From there, an even stronger force directed her through a narrow passage until it seemed as though she were a pickled fish looking out from inside one of Pamela's canning jars. The gap closed, and Wella knew of no way to open it other than to wait for the thoriemacum to be sucked through the base of the *Shiemacum*, now orbiting Earth.

As the thoriemacum ascended, Wella could see Aaron Genzforth peering intently into the darkness. Wella smiled again. Genzforth could not see the thoriemacum. Even in daylight, it was nearly invisible. To human eyes, it might appear that Wella was flying, or being "assumed into heaven," as in the Earth human legend of Jesus. Genzforth would be wise to keep such a story to himself, for fear of being labeled, in Earth human terms, "stark raving mad." In fact, it might already appear to others that Genzforth had been chasing an apparition that night.

The force that lifted the thoriemacum into the sky exerted an equally powerful downward force on *Terra's* deck, and the fine sailboat that had so long been Wella's charge, had already sunk several hundred feet to a cold, wet resting place. Genzforth would have nothing to show the Earth humans he had either persuaded or paid to join his fruitless chase. A small whirlpool or disturbance in the surface of the water was all that remained for them to see.

As the thoriemacum transported her above the Earth, Wella gazed at the litter of islands following the great mass of its mother continent. Wella faintly regretted that there had not been time to see more of this planet, so unlike the one from which she had come. Most of Gallata's small islands could be visited by sailboat. It would be far more difficult to tour all of North America as well as the wide expanses of ocean and land beyond. Perhaps one day Dana would explore the Earth.

Thinking of Dana, Wella closed her eyes. As the thoriemacum ferried her body swiftly above the Earth, Wella's mind entered the clear blue light to find the child was with her now in dreaming. In fact, their minds were fused, suspended there in the light, sharing and intensifying the love and respect they felt for one another.

ORCA HARBOR FIRST CONGREGATIONAL CHURCH ~
MARCH 25, 1972

Dana never liked to sit still for a long time. But church was okay if she had drawing pencils. She liked to copy the designs in the colored glass windows. Sometimes strange thought pictures would come to mind, and she would weave the pictures into the designs the way Wella laced grass and vines into her weaving. Dad would rave about the drawings after church, and Mom would praise her for staying quiet and clean for such a long time.

This time it wasn't quite as hard to sit still. She didn't feel like playing. She missed Wella. Besides, this was a special service. Reverend Barra said they had gathered to say "goodbye" to Wella because she had gone up to heaven. Lots of people told stories about Wella and about favors she had done for them. Even Grandpa Ben got up and said Wella was the best one he ever knew to think up excuses for a party. He said he would never forget Wella's "sunset viewing ceremonies," as she called them, on the beach. Then Reverend Barra reminded everyone that Wella never drank alcohol at parties, and that was proof you didn't have to drink to enjoy a party. Sometimes the people smiled at the stories, but mostly they just cried. Mom and Grandma Ruth cried nearly the whole time.

Finally, Dad got up. He was real choked up and could hardly speak, but he thanked everyone for coming. He said Wella would have liked them to tell funny stories and enjoy themselves at her memorial service. But then he sat down crying.

They came out of church to find the clouds gone away and the wet world shining with signs of spring. Dana felt the sadness lifting a little, but she still didn't feel like joining the group of bigger kids playing tag on the lawn. As usual, the grown-ups stood around talking nearly forever, with the kids dodging in and out among them and the great oak trees. Dana sat down on a stone step, intending to draw a daffodil. The air felt a little cold, despite the sunlight, so she gathered her soft sweater around and carefully fastened every one of its mother-of-pearl buttons. It was good to be wearing one of the skirts Wella had woven for her. Besides being pretty, it kept her legs warm.

Dana was intent upon matching the different shades of yellow petals as closely as possible with her limited choice of drawing pencils, when a shadow fell across the page. Startled, Dana looked up into a face she recognized but did not like. It was the man who had come to look for Uncle Marvin, the one who dressed like he was from the city and smiled like Mr. Rogers. Only this time, he was wearing a black overcoat and a tie with designs akin to something on church windows. This was the man who had said something to Wella that frightened her. Maybe that was why she went up to heaven. Dana frowned at the man to let him know he was not welcome, then began intently coloring the petals.

The man did not take the hint and go away. Instead, he sat down uncomfortably close to Dana on the step and looked over her shoulder at the drawing, his shadow still interfering with the light. Dana wanted to tell him she needed the full sunlight to match the colors, but she couldn't explain. Like most grown-ups, he would probably go away when he realized she could not explain things very well.

"You draw very well for a little girl not yet old enough to go to school," observed the man.

"Yes," agreed Dana.

"Who taught you to draw like that?"

"I did."

"You taught yourself to draw?"

"Yes."

"How?"

Dana had to think about that. Finally she said, "I look close at things."

The man was silent for a moment. Then he said, "Oh, yes. Observation is a good skill. Maybe one day you will be an agent like me."

Dana shook her head. "I will not be like you," she assured him.

The man started to make a laugh but chopped it off in the middle. What came out was a kind of snort.

"It's all right to laugh today," said Dana. "Dad says Wella wants us to have fun at her memory party."

The man snorted again. "Don't you feel sad? Don't you miss Wella?"

Dana looked up from her drawing into the man's face. The sadness that had settled like a dull weight in her chest now rose to her eyes in the form of tears.

"Yes, I miss Wella," she said.

Still holding her color pencil, Dana dabbed her eyes with the sleeve of her sweater until they felt hot and itchy.

She felt trapped by the man's eyes searching her intently as if to squeeze out some unknown secret. It was as though he was watching her suffocate inside a jar the way her cousin Charlie did once with a large black beetle. When the man spoke again, his voice was soft, but the words were not soothing. "Is it true that Wella died?" he asked. "Do you believe she won't come back?"

Dana swallowed hard and nodded emphatically.

"Where did Wella go?" the man persisted.

Dana gazed through her tears at the liquid yellow of the daffodil, "Up to heaven."

"Where is heaven?"

Dana did not answer. She did not know where heaven was, but she had wondered about it ever since Mom told her Wella went there. Dad had said, "Wella died. She can't come back." Dana remembered when a lamb had died. Wella had built a large fire on the beach and burned it. The smoke went up the way Wella had gone up in her dream that night. But Dad said Wella's body was in the bottom of the strait. Dana shook her head. The man had asked her about something she could not understand, let alone explain.

"How do you know Wella went up to heaven?" persisted the man.

Between sniffs and sobs, Dana managed to look at the man again and to say "Mom said so, and I saw it in a dream."

The man looked hard at Dana, capturing her gaze. His face twisted up and his eyes opened wide as though she had startled him. "You saw it in a dream?"

"Yes, a dream. I dream a lot."

"When you were asleep?"

"Yes. I only dream when I sleep."

"Tell me about your dream."

Dana strained for words, but they would not come. Then, recalling a game she used to play with Dad and Wella, she turned over her picture of the daffodil and began to draw on the other side. Across the top of the paper she drew some heavy, black cloud-monsters sucking up a drinking glass-like thing with Wella trapped inside. Along the bottom, she drew a black water monster with a big mouth sucking up Wella's boat. The man peered over her shoulder intently at the drawing. At first he looked puzzled, then shocked. A high-pitched breath, almost like a whistle, came out of his mouth. "My God, that's remarkable," he said. "I had a dream like this too!"

Dana nodded. "Sometimes people dream the same dreams." Somehow she felt better now about the man because he had dreamt with her the way Dad often did. She handed him the picture. He held it with both hands, continuing to examine it with an astonished look on his face.

"You can keep it," Dana said. She gathered up her pad and drawing pencils.

Then she stood up and walked over to Mom, who stood in a circle with several other women. Mom bent over and gave Dana a hug. Then they joined hands and walked off together toward Grandpa's car. "You were very good and brave in church this morning. I was so proud of you, Dana," said Mom. Her praise helped more of the sadness go away. Before they got in the car, Dana glanced back at the church step. The man was gone.

Part Two: CHILDHOOD & ADOLESCENCE

SEATTLE MENTAL HEALTH CLINIC ~ OCTOBER 30, 1980

While she waited for the shrink to come in, Dana checked out the office cluttered with books and papers. A big touring bicycle was parked under the window and a helmet rested on top of a stack of journals. Mom said Dr. Diana Holt was pretty old, but she rode in on the Burke Gilman Trail every day, all the way from Bothell to the University District, even in pouring rain. It was a great bicycle, reminiscent of a huge insect, a wasp or praying mantis. Its sleek, black frame was rigged with lots of gear cables and wires. A pair of lights bulged out from under the handlebars like a couple of weevily eyes. The window commanded a grand view of Mount Rainier, sitting up there like an ancient goddess, draped in her great white shawl. This grandmotherly idol gazed down from the pink glow of her heaven on an array of urban ugliness — telephone wires, used car lots, traffic congestion.

Dana didn't know what she would say to the shrink. It was Mom's idea that she should see Dr. Holt. Mom was alarmed by how homesick Dana was for the Islands, even though they had been living in Seattle for two years. Mom was also worried about the drop in Dana's grades since the island school had closed. They had moved to Seattle for Dad's new job, and to live near Charlie and Aunt Theresa. Mom also thought Dana was going crazy because she spent so much time thinking about the accident, blaming herself for Charlie's head injury.

Maybe Mom was right. Nearly two years had passed since Charlie fell from the viaduct, but Dana relived the whole scenario in minute detail a dozen or more times every day. She would close her eyes at any given moment and could still feel the soft wind of that October afternoon tugging at her heavy, dark hair...

• • •

A trace of summer lingered; the late afternoon sun filtered through gray clouds that hung low over the houses and trees. The store windows and pavement along the avenue radiated the soft solar heat they had absorbed all day.

The breeze seemed to emanate from the park ahead, beckoning Dana, so she stretched forth her long, denim-clad legs and pummeled the pavement harder with the rubber soles of her sneakers. She could hardly wait. The park was her island now. At least it looked something like an island, so separate from the unfriendly sea of her new city life — the school with tidy rows of desks in which you were expected to remain virtually motionless throughout the long hours of daylight; the teacher who didn't seem to like her; the traffic lights; the choking smell of exhaust, the incessant roar of traffic. The park wasn't as beautiful as a real island, and there were no sheep, but there were kids to play with.

"Don't you think we should go home first?" her cousin Charlie nagged, as he followed a stride or two behind. "Your dad said to finish your math homework right after school. Then you can go to the park. You're behind in all the subjects. You never do your homework." Charlie liked to act like Dana's self-appointed conscience.

Dana stopped at the corner to wait for a traffic light. "You should go home first if you want to, Charlie. But I just couldn't possibly sit for another minute. I have to run."

Running would make the blue light come. That was the only way Dana saw the light in the city. She would start running and fall into a trance. Pretty soon other kids would follow and get on a collective imagination trip. They would chase a giant woolly mammoth or something.

"Mom says I should stay with you when you're in the park," said Charlie, still doggedly following. "The grown-ups are afraid you might get raped or somethin'."

While they waited for the light to change, an old woman approached. Her face looked like a large pomegranate tied slightly askew to her swollen body with a plaid wool bandana. Her tiny azure eyes were barely large enough to peer out over the bulges of her cheeks.

Dana nodded and smiled. "I've no money today," she apologized. "Spent it on Twinkies."

As the light changed and they started across the street, Charlie said, "Mom says you shouldn't give money to bag ladies and bums. They spend it on drink. It's their downfall."

"Mom gives them money," said Dana. Charlie got tedious at times, although he meant well.

After they reached the opposite side of the street and turned the corner, Dana could see the tops of the trees in the park, and she started to run again. She could hear the pads of Charlie's sneakers bouncing on the pavement behind. Glancing over her shoulder, Dana observed that the red-faced boy called Patrick had joined them and was gaining on Charlie. Kim Lui rounded the corner, followed by his younger sister. The group was growing. They were all running. If Dana could just concentrate fully on the running without allowing a single distraction, the blue light would come.

By the time the group of about ten young runners passed under the stone arch way at the park entrance, Dana's mind was afloat in the light, and the group was with her.

Gradually, there emerged before their collective mind's eye the image of a great dragon, its golden scales aglow from the light of its own fiery breath. The great beast hovered over them, then pumped the air, eagle-like, with the broad span of its wings and darted away, disappearing beyond the farthest trees on the other side of the park. "After the dragon!" shouted Kim Lui. The dragon image, born of Kim's imagination, entered the collective thought through the medium of Dana's concentration. The group of runners had become mounted warriors in plate mail, mighty and fearless.

Dana continued to run, fully mindful of the running that created and sustained the trance.

"Charge!" yelled Charlie, as he dashed past Dana. Her cousin's mind, usually resistant to trance, had also succumbed.

He was now running faster than Dana. She was so startled to see Charlie involved, that it nearly broke her trance, but weeks of practice had taught Dana to maintain concentration despite severe distraction. Back on Levin Island with the sheep, there had been few interruptions. Here in the city among the children, the game was harder, but Dana was learning, teaching herself an art she could explain to no one.

After entering the park, the group ran along the blacktopped path that led up and over a grassy knoll, and down the opposite side where the woods began. Approaching the woods, they switched to a soft, gravelly side trail that lead past the playground, through the woods, alongside one leg of the viaduct, and down into the ravine.

When the viaduct came into view, the children's collective imagination saw it as a huge castle, home of the dragon. By this time the group had its second wind, and the power in their pounding hearts and racing legs was limitless. Dana concentrated on the energy, feeling it increase within her soul, and thereby swell accordingly within the collective spirit.

By the time they reached the viaduct, images of plate mail and horses had vanished. The only remaining thought was the joy of running, feeling that power for its own sake transforming itself into the urge and the collective intent to ascend. As they started to climb, another image entered their collective mind, generated by one of the individual minds, but spreading to all through the collective. Medieval warriors again, they stormed the castle walls, climbing swiftly with practiced limbs. Most of the group had done it many times by now, their long pulls and stretches swift, flowing, and without hesitation.

While they worked steadily at the climb, the collective imagery changed yet another time. A feeling of excitement had arisen with rushes of adrenaline as it crossed the collective mind that they might be pursued by police. With that thought, there emerged the image of a daring burglary assault upon an opulent villa to heist precious jewels that were under guard in an upper chamber. Dana had to concentrate most intently now upon the skillful movements of her climb, careful not to be distracted by the fascinating fluctuations of collective imagery.

The danger of police was real, but experience assured the group that they would spot the arrival of patrol cars in plenty of time to escape arrest. A more real danger was the possibility of someone falling. Complete mindfulness of the act of climbing within the steady, unbroken trance was the only way Dana could facilitate the return of all players safely to Earth.

Eventually all nine climbers clung to the highest rungs, their arms wrapped about the steel girders in deadlocked embrace. The youngsters exchanged peevish glances that reflected awe and triumph in the collective awareness of their own courage. They were so close now to the cars whooshing by overhead, that the surges of wind thus created pulled at their nylon jackets, tugged at their hair, even threatened their balance.

Dana remained focused through this brief pause. Nothing less than a bomb could distract her now, although she noted that Charlie was nearly as high as the rest of them. Resistant for many days, and often threatening to tattle, Charlie had only recently begun to join them in the climbs. Even so, no one had teased or coaxed him. His legs were shorter after all, and he lacked faith in his athletic ability.

From high above the city, the collective awareness panned the view like a television camera. Beginning with the steady stream of miniature cars on the distant boulevard, their gaze passed on to the pink and green painted Victorian school building where they had spent the long tedious day. They watched throngs of tiny pedestrians, then scanned the rolling green hill near the park entrance where a patrol car was now stopped. Together, their collective mind's eye watched the toy car door open and a police kewpie doll emerge.

"Fuck! It's the fuzz," groaned Patrick.

"Jiggers, the cops!" yelled Kim Lui, drawing them back into the jewel heist. Like a gang of seasoned cat burglars, they simultaneously began their descent.

Dana found it easier to concentrate and hold the trance during the climb down. You had to be so meticulous about it. With the right arm encircling a girder like a lasso, you lowered the body as the left hand grasped the rung on which you stood to steady yourself while the left foot was lowered to the next rung. You didn't let go of the upper girder with your right arm until the left arm had fully encircled the lower rung and both feet were planted firmly on the one below. Dana was good at this and could do it swiftly, but every movement required complete concentration. One slip would be the last.

Cat burglars, of course, did not slip.

When her feet finally rested among the ragweed, Dana closed her eyes briefly, focusing on the blue light. Keeping the light in view of her mind's eye to maintain the trance, she opened her eyes and looked around. Patrick and Kim Lui were nowhere in sight; several others were running into the woods.

Looking up, Dana saw Charlie and Kim Lui's sister still suspended above her. The girl was just a short way up, coming down fast. In fact, by the time Dana had breathed deeply and slowly, in and out, the girl was also down, and off she went crashing into the woods.

As for Charlie, he looked like a great parrot on its perch. He was still climbing down, but slowly, much too slowly.

Dana strode over to the path and sat down cross-legged in the short grass beside it. She closed her eyes and kept her mind suspended in blue light. It would not help to watch Charlie climb down. If she allowed herself to be distracted — even for a moment — the light would disappear, and with it, the collective thought that gave Charlie the confidence to overcome his fear of heights.

Dana didn't know how long she sat looking into the light. Probably it was a matter of seconds, but it might just as well have been hours, for there was no awareness of time in this pure light that had sustained her through countless boring lessons at school. It would get her through Charlie's down-climb so long as there were no interrup.... Dana felt her arm wrenched veritably out of her socket as she was jerked discourteously to her feet.

The blue light vanished as Dana looked into the angry eyes of a police officer. His policeman's hat was pushed back, and his chest heaved in and out as though he was trying to catch his breath, or else he was angry enough to kill. Dana could smell his sour breath and acrid body odor.

"No!" screamed Dana in horror. "I was concentrating!"

Behind her, from somewhere above, came a paralyzing shriek, then a slight jostling of the Earth beneath her feet, and a sickening, crunching sound, like Mom breaking chicken bones. The policeman relaxed his rude grip on her arm, and she swirled around to find Charlie lying motionless on the ground a few feet away, his eyes closed, his face buried in dry ragweed. His scraggly, dark hair was soaked with something that might have been sweat — or blood. Blood trickled out from beneath Charlie's hair, ran down his cheek, and disappeared into the weeds.

. . .

The ancient therapist had settled down directly across from Dana, her pale, wrinkled face and white head not more than a few feet away. Right away, Dana had noted a strange resemblance between the woman and the mountain, even though Dr. Holt was not wearing a white shawl, but was dressed casually in gray wool slacks and a white cable knit sweater. She wore comfortable walking shoes of brown leather. She spoke in a friendly informal tone. "Well, Dana, do you know what to do in therapy?"

"Yes, I think so."

"What?"

"Talk..."

The doctor's face exploded in a mass of smile line wrinkles. "You've got it!" she declared and then sat just smiling at Dana for an uncomfortably long time.

Dana smiled, too, at first, but then began to feel uneasy. Finally, she added, "...about my problems."

Dr. Holt's agreement was registered with another explosion of smile wrinkles.

"That's it!" she agreed. "Your parents' medical insurance pays me to listen while you talk about your problems, or anything you want to talk about, and I'm supposed to help you clarify things and figure things out. If you don't have any problems or don't want to talk, I'll just be here with you. That's all there is to therapy." With that explanation, Dr. Holt stopped talking and just looked at Dana again in a kindly way.

Dana still felt anxious. She was supposed to talk and didn't know what to say. Finally, she said, "Is that your bicycle?"

Dr. Holt nodded and kept looking at her kindly.

"Did you ride here?"

"Yes."

"Far?"

"Several miles. I live out near Bothell."

After a pause, Dana observed, "That must be good exercise."

Dr. Holt nodded gravely and just looked at Dana some more.

With all this silence and quiet staring, Dana feared the blue light would come so she created a distraction by tossing her gaze about the room and letting it fall on the view outside the window. "You have a nice view of Mount Rainier." Dana rattled the words out quickly, like machine gun fire, to sustain the distraction.

The doctor swiveled her chair slightly so she could see the mountain, "Yes, it looks lovely today." Then she turned back and faced Dana who was now looking at Mt. Rainier and Diana Holt at the same time, and again noticing the resemblance to Diana's face, old and majestic like the mountain.

Dana felt strangely embarrassed now as if maybe Dr. Holt was looking at her from within the blue light and could tell what she was thinking. Then, to Dana's astonishment, the therapist said in a casual offhanded tone, "I climbed it last summer."

Dana felt as if the lower half of her face had dropped off, as her eyes popped out of her head. "No kidding? All the way to the top?"

"All the way."

Dana didn't know what to say. First of all, she had never met anyone who had climbed Mount Rainier, although she had heard that lots of people did it. Once she and Charlie had walked up a long steep trail through a dense rain forest all the way to the top of Mount Constitution on Orcas Island. Then they had walked all the way down again and jogged back to the mooring basin. They were nearly dead when they got back. But Constitution was an anthill compared to Rainier. Dana had always assumed that people who climb Mount Rainier must be supermen, young supermen. But Dr. Holt was a tiny old lady, older than Grandma Ruth. "Last summer?"

Dr. Holt nodded.

"You must be pretty strong."

The doctor shrugged slightly and sat looking pleasantly at Dana in silence.

Eventually, Dana remembered that she wasn't supposed to be talking about Dr. Holt. "I'm supposed to be talking about my problems," she said.

"Are there problems you'd like to talk about?"

Dana thought about that question. Then she shook her head. "I don't like to talk about my problems. People think I'm crazy. I told Dr. Phillips a lot. That's because he asked. I told Mom. It just worried her. She couldn't help. I haven't even told Charlie, much."

Dr. Holt leaned forward until her face was very close to Dana's, and took a deep breath. Then she exhaled a waft of onion-scented air. "I don't think you're crazy," she said very sincerely. "Dr. Phillips wrote down everything you told him. I read it all, and I don't think you're crazy."

Dana felt tempted to let the blue light come now. That way she might be able to find out whether Dr. Holt was really as sincere as she seemed. But something told her to trust this elderly person. Older people weren't trying to do anything but just live. Besides, it would be a waste of Dad's insurance money to spend the therapy session off in a trance when she was supposed to be talking. Also, it was pretty special to sit in the company of someone who really wanted to listen to her, didn't have any other agenda, and didn't think she was crazy.

"All right, then," said Dana, "Maybe I should tell you the big problem, the one I haven't told even Dr. Phillips." She looked testily at Dr. Holt who just sat gazing at her calmly, waiting apparently to hear all, part, or nothing of whatever she wanted to share. But the sincerity of that steady gaze was too much. Dana looked down at her hands, which were fidgeting awkwardly. Then suddenly, without warning, Dana began to cry. She wasn't sad, exactly. She cried to let go of the feelings welled up inside, the strongest of which was relief that she planned to tell the big one and not be thought crazy.

Without diverting her gaze, Dr. Holt snatched a tissue from a box on her desk and placed it gently into Dana's trembling hands. The long, fingers dabbed awkwardly at the tears running down her cheeks. Then she looked directly into Dr. Holt's gentle old eyes and said, "I don't belong on this planet. I think I'm an alien."

Dr. Holt's eyes blinked ever so slightly, and Dana was sure her left jaw twitched just a hair, but the old woman's kindly gaze was otherwise uninterrupted. She made no voluntary response other than to wait.

"So, now do you think I'm crazy?" asked Dana.

The therapist shook her head emphatically. "I know you are not crazy." She leaned toward Dana even closer. "I don't even believe you are situationally psychotic or whatever it is Dr. Phillips suggested. If you say you don't belong on this planet, I know that is the way you feel, and I accept that. It must be a painful feeling."

Dana thought about that. "Well, yes, it is painful. First of all, if I tell anybody, except for you, they'll think I'm crazy. Second of all, I wish I knew who I am, how I got here."

After waiting a few moments, as if to make sure Dana was finished, Dr. Holt said, "Can you tell what makes you feel like you don't belong here?"

Dana thought about that a moment, and then shook her head. "I know it's crazy. If you don't think it's crazy, you must be crazy too. But, well, it's the way I think. Nobody else thinks the way I do, or so it seems. Other people's minds don't work the way mine does."

"You mean about the blue light and all?"

Dana nodded, letting her gaze drop hopelessly.

"But, you enjoy the blue light. It's pleasant for you at times. Sometimes it helps you. That's what you told Dr. Phillips."

Dana breathed a deep sigh of relief. No one had ever acknowledged that before, but it was true. The blue light was magnificent. Other people believed it evil because they thought it meant she was crazy. Dr. Holt, who knew she was not crazy, could therefore accept that it was good, or that it could be good if properly developed and controlled. At some level, Dana had been training this talent, this gift, all her life, learning to control it and use it wisely. But the blue light was a powerful talent and had not been easy to work with. It wasn't like with drawing. All you had to do was draw. And, besides, other people knew how to draw and could help. Other people believed in drawing.

While Dana pondered these thoughts, the therapist looked at her in that kindly way, saying nothing. Finally she said, "Maybe you should let the blue light come while you are here with me sometime. Maybe we could work on it together."

Dana gasped partly from surprise and partly from relief. "Yes, that would be worth trying."

"Maybe we should do it next time we meet," suggested Dr. Holt.

Dana thought about that a moment. The blue light had been trying to come ever since she sat down in this comfortable chair looking out at the mountain. It was capricious. Some other time, it might not be in the mood. "Why don't we try right now?"

Dr. Holt shrugged. "As long as you're so eager, we might as well get right to work."

Dr. Holt lit a tall taper candle that emitted a soft spicy scent as it burned. She turned on some Asian-sounding music and turned off the electric light. It was as though she already knew all about trances and did this sort of thing all the time.

Dana could still see well enough to make out everything in the room, even the Raleigh label on Dr. Holt's bicycle, but the light was soft and natural. The shiny, black bicycle frame reflected the candlelight in several different places. Dana leaned back in her own pillow chair and began to relax. Dr. Holt's pale loose eyelids closed slowly, and Dana thought the old woman had probably fallen asleep. Dana focused her attention on the candle flame. Maybe she would fall asleep herself.

When the blue light came, Dana noticed that it felt better than it had ever felt before. She had an intuitive feeling that the light was intended for just such occasions. It wasn't supposed to be experienced in isolation with only one person knowing about it. It should be enjoyed in togetherness with friends as a way of tuning into one another and getting close. As Dana's mind sailed into the light, she found herself experiencing images of a cold and dangerous world made of snow and ice, perhaps hundreds of feet deep. Supporting herself with a sort of walking stick or cane, she walked gingerly along behind other people who seemed to be friends, although Dana didn't really recognize any of them. They had to walk carefully because there were large cracks in the ice, and the snow was wet and slippery. Suddenly, without warning, Dana felt herself slip and fall. Now she dangled from a rope several feet below the others. Looking up, she could see the faces of several companions peering over the edge. They shouted orders, tried to reassure her, but they too, were panicked. Suddenly, the light vanished and Dana was back in the small therapy room with the candlelight and an old woman who seemed to be asleep.

She reached over and touched Dr. Holt's wrist.

Dr. Holt opened her eyes and yawned. "Did the blue light come?" she asked.

"Yes, and I had sort of a dream."

"A dream?"

"A scary dream."

"Tell me about it."

"I was walking in a strange world where there was nothing but ice and snow. I fell over a cliff of ice."

Dr. Holt's old white face exploded again in her map of smile lines. "You remarkable child!" she exclaimed. "You read my mind! I was recalling a climbing accident like that just before you distracted me."

UNIVERSITY HOSPITAL MEDICAL RECORDS DEPARTMENT ~
SAME TIME

Pam stepped aside to let someone pass through the turnstile before she entered. As she made eye contact briefly with the gentleman, it crossed her mind that he seemed to recognize her in a cool, distant way. He was tall and slender, very nicely dressed in a gray tweed business suit. His eyes were small and fluid. Pam nodded, felt her cheeks blush slightly, and hurried on through the turnstile wondering why she felt ill at ease.

She had to pay fifteen dollars to get a copy of Dana's records and had to show her driver's license to prove her identity. Then she took the records to the cafeteria to read while drinking a cup of coffee and waiting for Dana. There were several typewritten pages, so Pam flipped first to the diagnosis and conclusions.

"Axis I: Atypical Childhood Psychosis; Axis II: no diagnosis."

Pam wasn't sure what that meant, but she figured it must be what they said when they couldn't tell what was really wrong. Maybe they never could tell what was wrong. At least Dana wasn't schizophrenic. In fact, the conclusions were, on the whole, encouraging. The doctor didn't think Dana needed psychotropic medication, and she figured Dana would outgrow her problems. The child had already managed to control her symptoms to an unusual degree. She could tell when the hallucinations were about to begin and could, to some extent, prevent them. What's more, Dana showed very few signs of chronic depression. Her current depression was situational because the child felt like a failure and a disappointment to her parents and she still felt responsible for her cousin's accident.

The Wechsler Intelligence Scale had been administered, and Dana's I.Q. measured in the high average to superior range. There was some evidence, however, of developmental delay in both verbal and numerical abilities, but the doctor did not recommend Dana for any special education services. Dana's academic underachievement

appeared to be due to concentration problems resulting from hallucinations and anxiety. Dr. Phillips' only treatment recommendation was
several months of psychotherapy with Dr. Holt.

Pam flipped back to the section entitled "FAMILY HISTORY."
She had read it before in the session with Dr. Phillips but now wanted
to review it more thoroughly. Mostly it said good things about the
family, such as that Dana had positive relationships with everyone in
her stable extended family, although she felt closest to her father.
It said Dana had described her mother as kind of aloof and a perfec-
tionist, but that she felt loved by both parents. Toward the end of the
section, Dr. Phillips pointed out that Dana's marginal school performance perhaps had to do with fear generated by the strong emphasis
both parents placed on education. He said that prior to the family's
move from the San Juan Islands to Seattle, the child had learned everything first hand from her parents and her childcare providers.
Under those circumstances, her developmental pattern had not been
a problem, because Dana had been spoon-fed information whenever
she was ready for it. The move had changed that too abruptly. The
majority of children with whom she now attended school were ahead
of Dana in many of the skills required for school success. Dana had
reacted with shock. In fear of displeasing her parents, she had turned
her attention toward her developmentally advanced spatial perception and imagination. According to Dr. Phillips, that was the breed-
ing ground of Dana's delusional system.

Pam had felt anxious before and during the session because she
had feared being asked whether she was Dana's biological mother.
Amazingly enough, no one had ever questioned that before. Everyone
had seemed to take "yes" for granted for so long, it hardly seemed a
lie anymore. Still, it might have been difficult to be asked by a professional psychologist who was probably trained to smell out such fabri-
cations. But Dr. Phillips didn't ask. Pam smiled at the thought that, by
now, her maternal bonding with Dana was so complete it would be
impossible to disclaim the child.

Pam glanced up from the report, and her gaze crossed to the next
table. She gasped. There was the man she had met at the entrance. He
was making eye contact with her again and surely recognized her
from somewhere.

"Hi Mom," a cheerful, adolescent voice interrupted.

Pam drew a deep breath and smiled up at Dana. "Oh, hi, Love.
Want to get a pop before we go home?"

"No, thanks. I had one already. We should hurry, I have lots of
homework."

It was reassuring to hear Dana speak voluntarily of homework.

On the way out, Pam stole another anxious glance at the man who was still staring at her. As they walked through the maze of hospital corridors, Pam held his face in mind, trying to recall where she had seen him before.

"Do you remember where you parked this time, Mom?" Last time it had taken them several minutes to find the car.

"Yeah, sure. It's down at the end." The face was vaguely familiar.

While Pam inched her way through the rush hour traffic, she glanced over at Dana. She had a pencil and workbook out, and seemed to be doing a math problem. Maybe the therapy was helping. Who was that man?

Without looking up from her homework, Dana said, "If I pass my algebra exam, can Charlie and I go visit Uncle Marvin during spring break?"

Marvin. The man was someone who knew Marvin. Yes, that was it, the investigator who tried to find Marvin when he was AWOL. Pam smiled. What a good memory she had! It was so long ago. Wonder what the poor fellow's doing now that there's no war and no draft dodgers or anything to worry about. Maybe he's doing something useful, like trying to keep drugs away from kids. Let's hope.

LEVIN ISLAND ~ JULY 12, 1982

Charlie's sweaty, brown forearms glistened like polished leather as he lifted the heavy iron cylinder and let it fall with four, five, six deafening clangs, driving the metal fence post farther into the hard ground with each mighty blow.

"Good play!" sang his cheering section.

"Your turn!" Charlie handed Dana the post pounder.

Dana and Uncle Marvin had to make a game of the work to keep Charlie going. After all, it wasn't his idea to spend summer vacation building fences. Left to his own devices, he would be snorting coke with Patrick and Kim Lui in the Park. Having never lived there year round, Levin Island didn't feel like home to Charlie. He seemed to view it as a prison, a sort of rural Alcatraz.

At first Charlie had grooved on Dana's idea of traveling all the way by bicycle and ferry. It was their first time to go that far without help from any adults. But it had been hard to keep him going over the long stretches of country road. He had been even more restless during the ferry rides, not being content as he once was, to sit hour after hour, reading books about wizards and dragons. It was sad, but Charlie didn't seem to enjoy reading that much, since his accident.

One thing that had actually improved for Charlie was his enjoyment of games, no matter whether it was soccer, baseball, even mathematics, so long as he could beat Dana, and usually he could. Although he was inexplicably changed, many of Charlie's talents had returned in full force.

"Okay, Let me at 'em!," sang Dana, playing out the game theme for all it was worth.

Uncle Marvin pried the tape measure out of his jeans pocket. Then he bent over and walked gorilla-like along the twine marker, his hairy back facing the sun. He placed a small rock where the next post should be. Charlie reached in the wheelbarrow for another post and held it up for Dana. Standing erect and barechested, Charlie might have resembled one of his Native American ancestors displaying a newly crafted spear.

Dana lifted the heavy pounder and placed it over the top of the post. Uncle Marvin bawled, "Let 'er rip!"

Dana lifted the cylinder again and brought it down over the shaft with all the force she could muster, but the stubborn sod gave way barely an inch or two, burying only the tip of Charlie's spear. She lifted the pounder again and brought it down hard. This time, enough progress was made that Charlie could remove his hand, allowing the post to stand on its own, but there was a long way to go before Uncle Marvin would give her a point.

Charlie said, "Marvin and I'll go have a beer while you finish driving this one in, Dana. Looks like it'll take awhile."

Uncle Marvin tugged at his stump of blonde ponytail.

"No, Charlie. We have to finish up to that marker by the house. Then it'll be time for a break. I've got some cold pop for you in the fridge."

Dana lifted the pounder again to give it her all, fully prepared for the post to barely budge. She could never have anticipated the result that left her stunned. Instead of doggedly resisting, the earth gave way, swallowing the entire post in one gulp. Dana jumped back to avoid being wounded by the pounder as it thudded to the ground at her feet. She crouched down to pick up the pounder and to look for the post, but there was no trace of it. Her slender, bare fingers poked around in the hole the post had made, but there was only rock, dry dirt, and gravel. It was as if the fence post had never really existed.

She looked up into Charlie's bewildered eyes. "What did you do with the post, Dana?" It was as if he expected her to shout, "April Fools!"

But apparently it was Uncle Marvin's joke. He began laughing, hooting, slapping his thighs. Tears rolled down his cheeks. "Wow! Good job, Dana! Guess you don't know your own strength."

Dana stood up and glared at Uncle Marvin. "So, what happened to the fence post?" she demanded.

There followed a renewed convulsion of uncontrolled merriment. "Looks like you buried it in one blow," he managed to croak.

Charlie now turned his judgment upon the real culprit. "Dana isn't strong enough for that, Uncle Marvin. What did you do with the post?"

Uncle Marvin collapsed in a limp pile on the ground, allowing his composure to gradually return while Dana and Charlie fixed him with accusing stares. Finally he said, "We're over the septic tank and the area where Wella used to have a cellar. There was a lot of hollow space down there once upon a time. It's mostly all filled in now by erosion, but once in awhile you find some empty space. I found some last year when I dug up the septic tank to pump it out."

Uncle Marvin reached for another fence post and stood it up a few inches from where the other had been. "Try again," he directed, "But this time not quite so hard."

Dana lifted the fence post pounder and started in again halfheart-edly. Her mind still pondered the discovery of a mysterious hollow space under the back pasture. So did Charlie's, because he said, "Is there a tunnel under here?" He stomped his foot as if expecting the earth to cave in or emit a hollow sound.

"Well, I guess you might call it a tunnel. It's the remains of an old cellar." As if determined to maintain the pulse of their labor, Uncle Marvin rolled out the tape-measure again. "Bring the wheelbarrow on up," he ordered.

Mechanically, Dana pushed the wheelbarrow up the line and held up another metal shaft. "Aren't we going to try to retrieve the other post? Dig it up or something?"

This time, it was Uncle Marvin's turn to pound. He dispatched the job with one brief but terrible clangor, and moved on. "No, that would be more trouble than it's worth."

While she held up the next post for Charlie, Dana mused, "I don't remember Wella having a cellar."

"It was a secret. Only Wella and I knew about it."

Charlie exclaimed between pounds, "Wow, a secret tunnel!"

Dana was skeptical. "If Wella had a secret cellar, how come only you knew about it?" After all, Dana had lived on the island for years with Wella, but Uncle Marvin never lived here in those days.

"She hid me in there while you were out showing the Shore Patrol around."

Ah, yes. That was the secret hiding place the Shore Patrol never found. Dana recalled the story. So did Charlie. They all laughed. But

Dana would not be distracted from the image of a dark empty space under the pasture. It seemed to be calling to her as if it were the womb that had given birth to her.

She was still thinking about it when they stopped to rest under the shade of the house. Uncle Marvin brought out a six-pack of Diet Pepsi, apologizing that it was the only kind of pop he kept on hand.

"It's one of my favorites," Dana assured him.

"Mine too," agreed Charlie. They were thirsty from all that work.

"Where was the entrance, Uncle Marvin?" Dana asked between gulps.

"Entrance? Oh, you mean to the cellar. No one knows."

"If no one knows where the entrance is, how did you get in there?" Dana was beginning to wonder if he had made the whole thing up.

"I was a pretty sick puppy. Don't remember rightly. Seems like she made me wear a blindfold."

Charlie's eyes lit up. "Maybe there's treasure down there. Mom said Wella was loaded."

"Baloney!" said Uncle Marvin. "There wasn't a damned thing in there except for some old lamp or stove or something."

Dana asked, "What was it like in there? Did she make you wear the blindfold the whole time?"

"Well, you know the way I remember it was real nice and cozy down there with this kind of purplish light from the lamp. Seems like it had clean, white walls, round like the inside of a big plastic pipe, but the pipe's gone now. Figure one of the renters must have dug it up and took it away while no Krandles lived here. Come to think of it, that big pipe would have been a treasure, worth quite a bit of money, I'd guess." Charlie's eyes lit up again. "Maybe it's still down there."

Uncle Marvin shook his head. "I snooped around under there pretty thoroughly while I was working on the septic tank. There ain't nothin' down there anymore but a lot of old dirt and worms and stuff like that."

That description apparently dampened Charlie's enthusiasm for the subject, because he never brought it up again. But Dana's thoughts kept returning to the dark, hollow space which seemed symbolic of her efforts to discover her own identity in the dark, hollow spaces of her mind and heart. She had promised Dr. Holt to ask Uncle Marvin what he could remember about her early years, but it was so hard to talk with grown-ups. Anyway, the alien feelings pretty well dissipated on Levin Island. Here, she felt connected to whatever or wherever it was she did belong. That feeling was constantly enforced by memory associations as her glance fell by chance upon an old pump, a large rock down by the beach, a sheep with some peculiar resemblance to one of its ancestors. Those memories wrapped themselves around her like a warm, soft fleece, and the alien hostilities of planet Earth seemed far away.

• • •

Uncle Marvin ran a pretty good galley. His idea of dinner was a wiener roast down on the beach every night of the week, weather permitting. He had a special spot on the farthest side of the island away from Klahowya Cove. As they sat there through the evening, the darkness would descend and they couldn't see the lights of a single house. All you could see besides water and Mount Baker with its alpine glow in the distance, were some islands away off in Canada and an entire universe of stars overhead.

Uncle Marvin wouldn't allow their boom box anywhere near the place, so the only sounds were their own voices and the gentle sucking of wavelets at the shore.

A sheep path led almost all the way there, because the watering trough was filled automatically by a small stream oozing out of the embankment above. Three bright orange madrona trees hung out over the spot, which the winter tides had furnished with a big driftwood log for sitting.

Uncle Marvin transported the invariable menu down there in the wheelbarrow. It consisted of hot dogs, buns, marshmallows, corn-on-the-cob wrapped in tin foil, a large can of fruit cocktail, and Diet Pepsi. There were three twelve-ounce bottles of beer, but those were not for sharing.

Uncle Marvin kept the bottle opener which he called the "church key" zipped into the pocket of his parka. Charlie would try to talk him out of some beer, but Uncle Marvin had his instructions. Aunt Theresa really worried about Charlie's problems being compounded by alcohol. The doctor had warned of a high incidence of that in head injury patients. With Dana, there was no contest because, given her allergies, the slightest whiff of the stuff could put her in the hospital.

Uncle Marvin squatted down near the fire so he could feed it with driftwood and nurse his first bottle of beer. Dana spread her parka out on the ground and leaned against the log where it was easy to reach the coals and roast things slow and brown. Charlie sat on top of the log, thrusting his wiener boldly into the flames to let it get crusty black all over. He said hot dogs tasted better that way, but he also appreciated the speed with which that system could dispatch a whole pack of wieners. "I wanna get done by eight so I can go in and watch *Star Trek*." He reached for the bag of marshmallows and began processing the first one in the same manner. The marshmallow burned even better. It looked like a miniature torch, and Charlie waved it gleefully in the air.

Dana said, "I'm going to stay out here all night and listen to Uncle Marvin tell stories about the war, and Wella, and going to Canada."

Charlie said, "I've already heard all those stories."

Uncle Marvin looked sheepish. "Not all. Some are banned."

"Tell the banned ones," said Charlie.

Uncle Marvin took a big sip of beer and leaned back on his haunches looking dreamily up at the sky. He closed his eyes. "Let's see stories. Banned stories." Suddenly his face blushed crimson in the firelight. Then he shook his head. "No, that didn't really happen. Must have been a dream."

"Tell us your dream," said Dana.

Uncle Marvin said, "I don't know. Maybe it really happened, and maybe it was a dream, but I have this vague recollection of Wella running out half-naked to watch her barn burn down, and there was the whole Klahowya Cove Volunteer Fire Department which, in those days, was nearly everybody, trying to put it out." He burst out laughing at his story. So did Dana and Charlie. "Poor Wella, she must have been so upset about the barn that she forgot her blouse. Boy, was she humiliated when she realized what she'd done."

When she managed to stop laughing, Dana said, "I could see Wella doing something like that. She always seemed so spontaneous. But the way I remember her, she always wore yards of clothing. She and Mom always dressed me in those long hippie skirts they liked to wear. I liked them pretty well in those days, but I wouldn't be caught dead in one now."

"Know any more banned stories?" asked Charlie.

"Sure, lots. You'll just have to give me time to remember, and you have to promise not to tell anyone, especially your parents. I could get in big trouble."

"We tell grown-ups as little as possible," said Charlie.

"Yeah, what they don't know won't hurt them," agreed Dana. "But some grown-ups are cool, like Uncle Marvin."

"If Wella was alive, would she be cool, Uncle Marvin?" asked Charlie.

"I guess so. She was sure different. In fact, there was nobody quite like Wella, except..." Uncle Marvin blushed crimson again and hid his face in his hands.

"Uncle Marvin just remembered another banned story," laughed Dana.

"Tell us," urged Charlie. "Don't be shy. We won't tell."

"I was going to say 'except Dana'."

"There's no one like Wella except Dana?" Charlie looked disappointed. "That's your banned story?"

Uncle Marvin didn't answer at first. He looked at Dana, making full eye contact, checking the effect of his remark on her. Then he looked away. "I guess it's more of a theory than a story."

Dana was astounded. Something told her Uncle Marvin meant that as more than a casual observation, and, despite the closeness of the fire, a chill went through her. But outwardly, she maintained her complete composure. "What do you mean when you say I'm like Wella?" she asked coolly, almost indignantly.

"Well, you've always reminded me of her."

"In what way?"

"You look like her for one thing. And you're, as you said, 'spontaneous, uninhibited' like Wella. You just bomb right in there and maybe worry about the consequences later. And you're, well, good-hearted, like she was."

Although she felt spastic inside, Dana continued to maintain her cool. "Well thank you, Uncle Marvin. That's a compliment," she said.

But Charlie said, "What d'ya mean Dana looks like Wella? I've seen pictures. Wella must've been nine feet tall."

"Dana is no shrimp," observed Uncle Marvin.

"I'm only five feet nine," said Dana.

Charlie asked, "Wella was no blood relation to us, was she? Why would Dana look like her?"

Marvin shrugged, but he kept looking at Dana for a long while. Then he looked at Charlie and said, as if only for his benefit, "Dana spent a lot of time with Wella during her most formative years. It's amazing how much you can learn to be like someone..."

"How would that affect her height?" Charlie objected.

Marvin shrugged again, and drained off the rest of his second bottle of beer. "Maybe it's only a coincidence, but maybe who you're influenced by can effect your growth hormones."

Charlie looked skeptical. "Guess I'll start hanging out with the Harlem Globe Trotters. No offense, Uncle Marvin, but I think your theory's a little strange, and *Star Trek* must be started already."

Uncle Marvin said, "Suit yourself, Charlie. Want to go in and watch tv, Dana?"

Dana reached into the cellophane bag. There were a few soggy marshmallows stuck together at the bottom. She pulled one out and stabbed it with her stick. "Think I'll stay out awhile," she said.

After Charlie disappeared over the embankment, Uncle Marvin opened his beer. Then he sat down in Charlie's place on the log and began to gently suckle the bottle.

Dana felt a gap left by Charlie's departure. It had been Charlie's job to pump Marvin with questions.

She continued to ruminate about what Uncle Marvin meant by her likeness to Wella. Meanwhile, Uncle Marvin seemed to take her silence as a cue to change the subject, because he said, "I don't have much use for *Star Trek* and that kind of stuff myself. Oh, I guess it's all right, but that *Star Wars* nonsense really fries my brain."

"Why?"

Marvin leaned back and gazed upwards. "Folks that are civilized enough to figure out how to cross those distances would never stoop to anything so infantile as war."

"Maybe not," agreed Dana.

Marvin continued his monologue as if talking to himself. "But anyway, it's good to see Charlie still likes creatures from outer space and stuff like that. At least that's one part of his brain that didn't kick the bucket."

Dana lifted the marshmallow from the coals and blew at it frantically. Uncle Marvin meant no harm in the statement. He probably didn't know she felt to blame for Charlie's accident. Her heart was all but exploding by now. She had to seize the moment, awkward though it may be, so she said, "Well, he's in good company then. I feel like an alien myself. I don't even think I belong on this planet."

Uncle Marvin looked at her in shock at first. Then his expression softened. "That's a tough way to feel," he said.

"Yes, I've been seeing a shrink."

"Does it help?"

"Maybe. But, Uncle Marvin, I thought perhaps you could help. I've been trying to remember things from when I was really little that might have made me feel that alienated as a child."

"Yeah, that's what they make you do in therapy. What have you remembered?"

Dana shook her head. "Nothing much. I was pretty happy. I know one thing. I always felt angry about the way Mom and Dad always talked about Wella and did things the way she would have wanted. Who cared what she would have wanted? She was dead!"

Uncle Marvin chuckled. "You've got a point. Why do you think she's so important to them?"

"She left Levin Island to Mom in her will. Big deal!"

"That is a pretty big deal," said Marvin, "But I doubt if that has anything to do with anything."

Dana took a deep breath and looked into Marvin's eyes. They were clear and honest despite his intoxication. He knew something that he was going to share. "What then? You mentioned you had some theories and they're all banned. Please tell me them, Uncle Marvin."

"They'll skin me alive and hang me from a tree if they ever hear my theories. Besides, there's probably nothing to them."

Dana smiled in spite of herself. He was going to open up. A grown-up was going to give it to her as straight as he knew how. It didn't matter how mixed up his perceptions might be, just so long as they were really what he believed. "Please tell me, Uncle Marvin."

"Okay, well first off, I'll tell you why you feel like an alien. You were awfully attached to that Wella, and you thought she'd always be there for you, but all of a sudden one day you woke up and she was gone. No wonder you've always bristled at the mention of her name."

"But she died. She couldn't help dying."

"Explain that to a four-year old. Besides, you're psychic, aren't you?"

Dana was astounded but dramatically relieved. He knew! He admitted it just like that, straight and open. "Yes. How did you know?"

"Oh, I didn't know. I think your Dad hinted as much to me once, and I guessed the rest. You know things kids ain't supposed to know. But that's beside the point."

"Go on."

"Maybe it'll blow your mind."

"No, please tell me."

"Okay, well, you see I always thought your dad had a thing for Wella. And, well to make a long story short, my theory is that the reason you're so mad at Wella is because she was your real mom, and she abandoned you at the age of four, not to death, but to go off, God knows where. But she faked the death, and you knew it. You knew better than all the lies you had been told, but you didn't want to admit it because here were these nice people that loved you and doted on your every gesture, and they lied to you right and left."

Dana took a deep breath, gasping for air. Uncle Marvin was serious. He must be crazy. Where did he get such notions? It was a long moment before she could look at him again.

He wasn't joking. She leaned back against the log and closed her eyes. There was a trembling inside her, but there was something else, something new and different, a sigh, a sense of relief. Maybe Uncle Marvin was right. Maybe she had known it all along at some deep unconscious level. When she opened her eyes again, Uncle Marvin was still gazing at her with that same clear expression of concern.

"But where did Wella...? Where did my mother go if she didn't die?"

Marvin leaned his head back and looked up at the sky. "This is the part of my theory that'll really blow your mind." Dana followed his gaze heavenward. Then she looked skeptically at him and burst out laughing. "Oh, come on, Uncle Marvin, you're the one who needs a shrink."

Her uncle laughed too. "Sure. Everyone says that. Besides there's a part of my theory that's all full of holes."

"What's that?"

"It's the part about your mom, not Wella, the other one, Pam."

"What about her?"

"She's jealous as sin. There's no way she'd be living happily on a deserted island with some exotic alien that was screwin' around with her man."

"You can bet your life on that!" agreed Dana. And they filled the empty universe with the echoes of their cleansing laughter.

LEVIN ISLAND ~ JULY 15, 1982

The big shovel handle clattered against the side of the wheelbarrow which Dana propelled clumsily along the fence row. She paused at each post to carefully examine its position and surroundings. Once, as she bent down, a bulky flashlight dropped out of her pocket, and Dana retrieved it awkwardly, her slender hand swimming in an oversized male work glove. The rain had finally stopped, but the grass was still wet, and its cold dampness seeped through her sneakers.

The correct post had to be up near the house, but which one? Knowing it would be slightly out of line from the others didn't help. The fence resembled an assembly of new recruits outside an army barracks; not a professional job to say the least. Too bad she hadn't paid closer attention at the time. She had been so preoccupied with the realization that there was a tunnel, that she had not attended to its exact location. But she would have to dig in the right place on the first and only try. It would take some doing to disguise the digging in one spot, let alone two or more. Besides, there wouldn't be time to try again before Charlie and Uncle Marvin returned from Orca Harbor with the groceries.

In the end, Dana chose the spot by pure intuition. When she stepped on the place, a feeling told her this was it, and she set about methodically breaking the sod in the "woman's way" Pam had taught her, by straddling the shovel with both feet like a pogo stick. To keep her balance, she held onto a fence post with one hand and to the handle with the other. Fortunately, the moist earth gave way as easily as pudding. She stepped off the shovel and scooped out a gigantic bite of rock and black soil garnished with a tuft of grass. An earthworm, fat and juicy as Grandpa's liver sausage, disappeared into it with lightning speed.

Dana lay the clump of earth aside gently, hoping that it would remain intact like a piece of the jigsaw puzzle to be reassembled later. In the same manner, she took another bite and then another, carving out a brown, earthen bowl large enough to sit in. She stood at the edge of the bowl, hollowing it out bite by bite with the shovel and tossing large helpings of mud and rock into the wheelbarrow. Almost every shovelful contained some small curio; a sow bug, a silver gum wrapper, a tarnished silver spoon.

If the wheelbarrow got too full, she planned to empty it over onto the dirt barn lot to avoid a telltale mess on the grass. But that point was never reached. For, after fewer than a score of tries, she felt what she was searching for, lack of resistance, empty space. When she pulled the shovel out, the bowl had become a funnel with a small hole at the bottom. Several rocks rolled into it and disappeared. With the next bite, the hole became a mouth large enough to swallow a watermelon.

Dropping the shovel, Dana knelt down and carefully peered in to investigate. It smelled musty down there, damp, and earthy, but there was something strange and unexpected about it. For where she had anticipated total darkness, there was light. In fact, she could clearly see some four or five feet down a silver gray surface awash in mysterious glowing liquid. Dana yanked the flashlight from her pocket and aimed it down into the hole, but found its faint glow of little consequence in confronting the blunt incandescence already there. It seemed as if there might be a subterranean world below, where the day was bright and sunny. Pushing back her initial fear, Dana jumped up and, with trembling hands, retrieved the shovel to enlarge the opening. When she thrust her head in again, the view was better. What had seemed a mysterious glowing liquid was actually water reflecting light. What light? There was no way to tell without going in.

Carefully, Dana sat on the muddy edge of the hole, dangling both feet down, and ever so gingerly, lowered her body until her sneakered feet were standing in cold running water.

This end of the tunnel was so shallow from erosion that Dana had to crouch fairly low to get her full body into it. Once inside, she viewed a world so strange and unexpected that it took time to interpret the input from her senses. It was like a brightly lit cave or an animal burrow, with a stream running across a gray, clay floor strewn with rocks. One metal fence post lay in the stream along with bits of long abandoned things, a squashed tin can, and an old rubber boot. A narrow pipe ran along the twenty-some odd feet of ceiling from the stone foundation of the house to the opposite end, where a ladder led to a manhole cover bolted with a lock.

Between the ladder and the spot where Dana now crouched, was a most unexpected sight. A small forest grew there. Little trees sprouted from coffee cans, spreading their intricate leafy branches out in all directions. The musty smell of earth blended with a pungent herbal scent. Two grow-lamps hung from the pipe and filled the tunnel with white ethereal light. Overlapping splays of leaf shadow were daubed like primitive art over gray-brown layers of earthen wall. Uncle Marvin's marijuana plants!

Better get out of here. Uncle Marvin would be furious if he found out she knew his hiding place!

While planning her escape, Dana noticed something red and glossy peering out from the shadows of the miniature forest. At first, it seemed to be a sort of Gypsy chest adorned with fancy gold letters, Charlie's treasure perhaps. Stepping closer, Dana made out the "Heineken" label, upside down. It was the old beer box that had been kept in the barn for years, and carried down to the beach, or wherever it was needed, to serve as almost anything — coffee table, stepping stool, sheering bench, or sturdy carrying basket. Dana and Charlie had used the thing as a table for playing house when they were small. Now she would stand on it to climb back out of this hole the way she had come.

But if the beer box was moved from where Uncle Marvin had left it, he would know someone had been down in the tunnel. In fact, he would figure out who had been there. With luck, Dana would be back in the city by then and, so long as she didn't rat on him about the marijuana plants, Uncle Marvin would not be the one to bring it up.

As she stepped into the forest space, Dana noted that the ceiling on that end of the tunnel was supported by creosote-covered pilings, much like the ones Uncle Marvin had used to repair the boat dock. Here, she could straighten somewhat, but still not to full height. Her back was beginning to hurt from bending over. For relief she sat down on the beer box whose present life was clearly being lived as the stool upon which Uncle Marvin sat to prune and care for his plants. Perhaps he would even sit there and smoke a joint.

Dana's imagination could all but materialize an image of Uncle Marvin sitting there with that expression of sublime contentment he always wore when he had managed to forget that the universe beyond the San Juan Islands was not entirely empty. But in the next moment, Dana experienced a phenomenon that she could hardly believe, let alone understand. Without having made a conscious effort in that direction, Dana found that it was she, not Uncle Marvin, sitting on the beer box. It was as though, in conjuring up the image of her uncle sitting there, Dana had projected herself there in his place. White light surrounded her now as did the scent of damp earth and marijuana. Scores of tiny leaf-fingered hands gently tickled her cheeks and patted her forehead. Uncle Marvin's expression of contentment became her own, and his feeling pervaded her soul. She was warm now except for her feet which still rested in the shallow stream running along the tunnel floor, a perpetual automatic watering system for Uncle Marvin's plants. Dana picked up her feet and propped them on the edge of one of the coffee can pots, and soon even they were warm. What was happening to her? Could it be the lights? Maybe it was fumes from the marijuana plants. Incredibly, at some distant historic moment she had been anxious to get out of the tunnel because her uncle would be back from town soon. How trivial such concerns seemed now.

Dana was not certain when the white light became blue or when the walls of the tunnel faded into the infinite universe, but this was no ordinary dream. Her eyes were open and gazing into apparently infinite space. It wasn't even an ordinary hallucination. Something real was happening that defied Dr. Holt's or anyone's diagnosis. She was really warm now. In fact, even her socks and sneakers felt dry as if she had been toasting them by the fireplace for a long time.

Dana closed her eyes to enjoy the warmth and sleepy peacefulness. The sense of surrounding infinite space remained, but now there was sound. At first it seemed to drift in from far away, a kind of wailing, like Native American songs wafting in from last summer at the Suquammish Pot Latch with Grandma Redtree, only sweeter and gentler. Gradually, the wailing began to weave in and out among undulating sounds, like kettledrums and booming pipe-organs, that harmonized with powerful stringed instruments, none of which she recognized. It took some time to decide conclusively that what she was hearing was really music, and that there were human-like voices singing or chanting a message in a foreign tongue that spoke directly to her heart.

In her mind's eye, Dana could see a large group of people seated in a circle all around her, singing just for her. The song was a message of love and warmth, welcoming Dana into their circle. The instruments still played, but now the sound came from inside Dana's head — more like a dream — and a voice spoke from within the confines of her own skull. *"We have reached you at last."*

"At last...at last...at last." The voice trailed off, echoing joyfully and blending with the music. Then it came back full and clear inside Dana's head. *"I am Wella of Gornia, your loving mother. I have tried so long to speak with you. I have missed you and longed for you.*

Thank you, Dana, for coming to the one Earth place with which I am connected, so that we could reach you. Mother and the Council have long since convinced the Research Center that it was not good to leave you on the distant planet called, by its inhabitants, Earth. If you choose, you may come and live on the island of Gornia on the planet of Gallata where you rightfully belong. Our spaceship, the "Shiemacum," hovers ever near you, with our mother, Shulmina of Severelia. She would send the thoriemacum, a conveyance to bring you there. By that means you could leave the planet Earth. You have only to contact us in a deep trance, as you have done today, and the thoriemacum will be on its way to you."

At first, Dana felt nothing but confusion. She didn't know how to communicate with the voice in her head, let alone what to say to it. She knew it was Wella. She knew Wella was her biological mother. At a deep unconscious level, she had known that all her life, but her conscious mind had always denied the notion. It was all so strange, so weird. Only readers of cheap tabloids believed stuff like that.

"You know you are not nuts, Dana. You have always known that," came the response in Wella's voice from inside her head. Wella and this "council" were listening to her thoughts.

"Mother and the Council can only read your feeling thoughts and pre-verbalized concepts. They don't speak English." came the amused reply.

This was entirely too weird. She wanted to go back and be a Seattle kid playing in the park. It was almost better to be nuts than to be a real alien.

"It is good that you love your adopted home and want to belong there. It is also good to be who you are. Gallata is a beautiful civilization where everyone is treated with respect. We work hard and always express our creativity in our work. There is no war. Crime is rare. There are no secrets, not for long. We sit together and meditate until our thoughts blend and become one."

"You meditate together?"

"Yes, we have ceremonies for that. Everyone at the ceremony goes into the light and knows the thoughts of the other. Everyone experiences the collective consciousness. So, dear Dana, let me tell you what to do if you ever wish to come permanently to Gallata. You must return to the tunnel or to the tree grove in the meadow just above it. You must sit there and meditate until you are within the blue light and call to us from your trance. Shulmina of Severelia will come for you within a few days or weeks. When you arrive on Gallata you will have aged but a few Earth years, and you will be greeted as a hero.

"Hero? Why?"

"In a successful genetic experiment, you are the blending of two worlds. If you stay on the planet Earth and have children in a safe environment, you will blend the strengths of Gallatans with those of the Earth humans. That will increase their creativity, their spatial perception, their ability to meditate and blend in thought."

"Wouldn't it be more heroic to stay here and do that?"

"Yes. And that life will not be easy for you, Dana. It is a choice you need to make without pressure from a mother. I must warn you that there can be danger for you if you stay. In your case, the government already has some knowledge of your differences, and that is one reason the Center has agreed to let you come to Gallata. They think the study is doomed in any case."

"The government doesn't know I'm alive."

"They know many things. Most Earth humans, I'm told, are very naive about things that their governments know and keep records on. For your safety, my daughter, you should come to Gallata."

"I have another mother. She would die if I suddenly disappeared. But she wants me to be something I'm not. Wouldn't it be the same in your world? I'd be an oddball there for sure."

"Perhaps in some ways, but we have ceremonies that blend thoughts, and, in that way, all would eventually understand and accept you."

Dana's mind stopped reeling while a profound realization settled over her. Everyone on Gallata was like her. They would not think her crazy or strange. They all sat around in the blue light together sensing and realizing their collective spirit. It would be heaven.

"It isn't a perfect world, of course," Wella corrected. *"There is no perfect world. Most Earth humans wouldn't like it here. Our life styles are agrarian, almost primitive, on islands such as Gornia. If you want to do scientific or learned work, you have to live at the Research Centers, and life can be stoical there. My life on Levin Island was more exciting in many ways."*

"But the ceremonies — they must be wonderful."

"Yes, we are having one now. We contacted you through the power of the collective consciousness."

Dana basked for a moment in the realization that there were people in the universe who not only believed in collective consciousness, but made developing it the centerpiece of their culture. It was as though she had wandered for many years in a desert and finally found her home, a group of kindred spirits who knew how to communicate, not with words, but directly through waves of mental energy shared among them. *"Why can't Earth people do that?"*

"They can, but it is much harder for them. They have no diverra bone."

"They have no what?"
*"Diverra bone. That is an organic metallic structure, an integral
part of the Gallatan brain system. The brain is attached to the diverra
bone which can be taught to broadcast and intercept thoughts."*
"Do I have a diverra bone?"
*"Most definitely. I felt it when you were an infant, while your
skull was still soft. It is located in the forehead above and between
the eyes..."*

Wella's mind-voice trailed off and the warmth vanished. A hand
on her shoulder shook Dana's body which had turned suddenly damp
and cold again. A dark human silhouette was bent over her, blocking
the light.

"What the hell you doin' here, Dana? You scared me to death. I
didn't know what happened to you." It was Uncle Marvin. Dana was
relieved to sense more concern than anger in his voice.

"I was having a vision. Wella was here. She talked to me."

"Good God, Dana! Have you been nibbling on these damned
leaves? I gotta get rid of these plants. Sure as hell they're gonna get
me in trouble one of these days."

BAINBRIDGE ISLAND FERRY ~ MORNING, FEBRUARY 5, 1985

Aaron first noticed Dana through the window of the ferry coffee
shop. She stood on deck wearing the popular, basic Mafia black of
Seattle youth. In Europe she would have been taken for a very young
widow in mourning, with her long black stockings, ankle-length skirt,
and oversized black rain parka. The only touches of color were a red
canvas daypack and bright red lipstick. She was competing with several other kids in a game of tormenting sea gulls. The object was to
hold up popcorn and taunt the birds into swooping down and grabbing the food while in flight. Dana was doing quite well on account
of an obvious height advantage, even over the boys.

The moment before he spotted Dana, Aaron had set his tiny watch
camera and steadied it to snap a well-known Peace Activist, Sister
Mary Theresa, whose feminine rotundity had filled the window frame.
By the time Aaron looked back again, Sister Theresa had disappeared,
and Dana was in her place, so he took her picture instead. Dana was
more attractive anyway. It would be a great portrait, black and white
on colored film, with big gray birds taking shape out of the winter
morning fog. Too bad the negative would sit unseen in a file folder
for the next dozen or so years collecting dust.

The sight of Dana Krandle there gave Aaron pause. She was supposed to be in school. What was she doing hanging around with a

bunch of kids headed for a rally protesting the arrival of a nuclear weapons train? One thing for sure, she would not be here with parental blessing. The kid was getting pretty defiant lately, not that she had ever been especially compliant. She was bound to get into an unequivocal jam sooner or later, and by that time, her file would be substantial.

Aaron sat sipping his coffee and studying Dana for several minutes just outside the window, not an arm's length away. Her proximity was both electrifying and disturbing. He had watched her from a distance off and on, or perhaps constantly, over the years, without ever having the opportunity to speak with her face to face, to test his theories, or fantasies, whatever they were.

How often had his memory replayed the events of that night in the Strait of Juan De Fuca? How often had he been tempted to try and meet with Dana, maybe even open up about what he saw — thought he saw — that night, a woman shooting up into the sky like a rocket. Impossible! Only a kid would believe him. But as Dana Krandle's file swelled with juvenile court records, school papers, psychiatric progress notes, it all fit together, feeding the fires of his imagination. To all outward appearances, she was just another kid feeding sea gulls, a sweet slender profile with long, black, over-permed hair and too much dark red lipstick. In her attitude and outward behavior, there was little evidence that she knew any better herself, but the barely legible scrawl of her therapist's progress notes told an intriguing story. Of course, there was no hard evidence anywhere, nothing more than dreams, hallucinations; marijuana's effects, perhaps.

As for that dark winter night in 1972, Aaron had been sane and sober, if a little tired and stressed. Regardless of the circumstances, he had never been given to hallucinations. In fact, he had been shocked to learn about the sleep researchers' discovery that all people dream nightly, himself included. Until then, Aaron had believed that he could not dream. He had no recollection of his dreams, let alone hallucinations, except that one time.

His memory of the incident had grown a little fainter over the years, and he had derived several inventive theories about how an optical illusion might have been perpetrated by the rapid movement of the boats in a nighttime accident, but there always remained that vivid mental picture of a woman rising swiftly into the sky until her form dissolved in mist and darkness.

At one point Dana turned and almost made eye contact with Aaron, but her attention was distracted by a tall blonde youth, also in funeral attire. He spoke to her and flashed an insolent smile. She responded with a few surly lip movements and a mischievous grin. Their mouths emitted little puffs of steam into the damp February morning. It was like watching a silent film without subscript, leaving conversation to the imagination, and Aaron was disturbed to find himself filling in a bit of flirtation, and feeling a twinge of jealousy. He wasn't above a little trifling now and then, but he had never been foolish enough to take that sort of thing seriously, especially not to get involved with children. He prided himself on his youthful appearance but tended to prefer older women who had been divorced two or three times and didn't expect much commitment.

As he drove off the ferry, Aaron spotted Dana again. She was stood at an intersection with a different group of kids. One of them held up a sign that read, "Bangor." Dana stood in front with her thumb thrust out into the lane of traffic.

Aaron pulled over and stopped, whereupon a waif of a youth with Gandhi glasses ran over, opened the door, and started to scramble in. "Fancy rig you got here," he said.

"Sure," said Aaron. "And you get to ride with me, provided you invite the young ladies there to come along."

"No problem!" Leaving the door ajar, the boy ran back to the others. Aaron watched through the rear view mirror as he nodded and gestured enthusiastically. Soon Dana crowded into the back seat with two other girls while the Gandhi fellow settled himself sedately in front.

As they started down the highway, Aaron glanced into the mirror at the girls squirming in the back. The agency should have provided him with an old VW bus or something for field trips. The car was even more out of place in this crowd than he was.

To invite conversation, Aaron said, "I suspect you're all headed for the big demonstration."

Dana responded without hesitation. "Yes, I'm attending for my research project."

"Did they let you out of school all day for that?" inquired Aaron.

The boy in the front seat interrupted, "Not me. I'm playing hookey. I'm Rick. This is Jenny and Hope, and Dana." Some young people were still being brought up with a few social graces.

"Pleased to meet you. I'm Aaron Genzforth. I'm going to the rally too. So I can take you all the way."

"I'm in Contemporary World Problems," persisted Dana.

"Ms. Watson got us excused for the day, but my mother doesn't know about the rally. She wouldn't approve."

"Is your mom conservative?" asked Rick.

After an awkward pause Dana stammered an uncertain reply. "I don't think so. I think she just doesn't believe in protesting and stuff like that. She's what you would call apolitical."

"Most people are apathetic," said Rick.

"Mom isn't apathetic. She's adamantly opposed to anything that smacks of politics. She doesn't even like Dad being in the teacher's union. She thinks we should just tend to our own backyard."

"Your Dad's a teacher?" asked Rick. "What does he teach?"

"Fifth grade at Richmond Elementary."

Rick said, "Oh, I see," with an air of condescension. He had probably thought Dana meant he was a university professor.

"You in Lucinda Watson's class?" another girlish voice chimed in from the back seat.

"Sure," said Dana. "It's a good class."

"I'm surprised your Mom doesn't pull you out of there if she hates politics," said Rick. "That's what it's all about from what I hear."

"Mom doesn't keep up with what's going on at the high school. She's pretty busy working and going to school herself. Anyway, my doctor recommended Ms. Watson for a teacher."

"I heard Ms. Watson's kind of strange," insisted the other girl. "I heard she tore the text books apart before she gave 'em to the students."

"No, that's not true! She just got some old discarded texts from last year's European History class and whited out the page numbers. Then she took them apart and shuffled the pages. We formed teams to see who could put them in order quickest. Afterwards each group had to summarize what they learned from the experience. It was fun! I always hated history before I had Ms. Watson."

Lucinda Watson. That name was familiar. Of course. Aaron had been working on her file just the other day. There had been complaints about her from some of the parents and school board members. Watson was still fairly young, but her file was pretty substantial already: Big black woman, lots of leftist causes, not confined to the usual local civil rights stuff, liked to travel around in summer picking coffee in Nicaragua, cheering at rallies supporting Third World insurrections, on file with the C.I.A., as well. It was frightening that young minds were being entrusted to the likes of Lucinda Watson.

"I've heard Ms. Watson lets kids play around and do whatever they want," said the other girl.

"Oh, no. I've done a lot of work for that class. I've learned a lot. We have to pick our own projects. The subjects can be almost anything, but they have to employ our talents and be connected with something we discussed in class."

Aaron felt his mouth curling in a smirk. That would leave a fairly broad range of choices. From what he had heard, nearly everything was discussed in Lucinda Watson's classes — from sexually transmitted diseases to the ingredients of hamburger wrappings.

"What's your project about?" asked Rick.

"Nonviolence. I'm drawing pictures about it," answered Dana nonchalantly.

"How can you draw pictures about an abstract subject like that?"

"I've got some here in my backpack." There was a lot of shuffling about behind, and then a large sketchbook was thrust over Rick's shoulder and into his lap.

As Rick slowly turned the pages, Aaron tried to steal a glance at them out of the corner of his eye, but with four kids in the car, he needed to pay attention to the road.

Rick studied the drawings carefully. Then he handed the sketchbook back over the seat. "Pretty good, but some of those pictures aren't very nonviolent if you ask me."

"You didn't get the point," Dana objected.

"What's the point?"

"The pictures are about strong nonviolent acts of civil disobedience confronting violence," explained Dana. "When Ms. Watson talked about Martin Luther King, I got pretty interested in some of his ideas."

More shuffling was heard from behind, and then another maidenly voice pronounced even harsher judgment. "Some of these pictures are nightmares, Dana! Did you really draw them yourself? You have a lot of talent, but some of these pictures are ghastly."

The third girlish voice offered a dissenting view. "Some of them are very beautiful."

Aaron felt so overwhelmed with curiosity about Dana's drawings that he offered to buy them all hamburgers for lunch as they passed through the town of Poulsbo. While they stopped at the drive-through, he snatched a glance at one of the drawings. It was a sort of cartoon depicting people in various prison settings interwoven with profiles of Gandhi and someone Aaron didn't recognize. "That's Thoreau," Dana explained when one of the other girls inquired.

Aaron recognized Dana's style. He had viewed other samples of her art. It was striking, but there was an almost irritating naivete about the stuff. She persisted in drawing the same way she had always done through childhood, stubbornly refusing to benefit from the many art classes she had taken in school. Dana had better learn other skills if she hoped to earn a living. She should be learning to write, not draw, term papers on something a little more realistic than nonviolence. How absurd!

...

Aaron lost track of most of his passengers during the rally. If they wanted a ride back they would have to find him. He wouldn't even recognize them if he saw them again, except for Dana.

The crowd gradually swelled to four or five thousand, filling a mile of railroad right-of-way that ran down through woods and entered the Submarine Base by a high-security gate. The gate, and miles of equally forbidding fence, were heavily guarded by Marines. Helicopters circled constantly overhead.

Once a newspaper reporter interrupted him to ask questions, but Aaron shrugged impatiently, without losing sight of Dana. Several times she spun around and looked straight at him as though she had eyes in the back of her head and knew he was watching her. The first time it had happened was right after they got out of the car. Aaron had been walking directly behind her, and Dana had made an about face as if she knew exactly where he was and said, "Thanks for the ride, Mr. Genzforth." It had taken him by surprise, and it was disconcerting to find himself flattered that she recalled his name.

Every so often Aaron would remind himself that he had not come to watch Dana. He was here to take pictures of specified subversives and record their anti-democratic statements, but he couldn't find anybody he was looking for. Maybe the rally organizers had asked certain members of the United Peoples' Party and other visible individuals not to come. The rowdier element of city rabble rousers had not cooperated with the "strict nonviolent discipline" at the last train vigil.

These Bangor radicals were really into their discipline thing. There was hardly any suspense here even though reports were being rumored around about excitement elsewhere along the tracks all the way to Texas. Dozens of arrest scenarios had occurred in other cities. In California, the train had actually run over a protestor sitting on the tracks. It was mayhem.

This demonstration was very different, more like a church service. Everyone, even the local sheriff and railroad officials, were playing carefully choreographed roles and reciting scripted lines. Even the dismal February weather conspired to set a scene of austerity and sacrifice. It would have been a nauseating spectacle had it not been so boring. Besides, the train was late, and by mid-afternoon, the cold had seeped through to Aaron's bone marrow.

As for Dana, her role was as clear as anyone's. She had not come to have fun or enjoy a day off from school or even to participate in the demonstration. Her purpose was to take pictures, not the easy way with the cameras or video equipment so common in the place, but with pen and drawing pad. She worked tirelessly all afternoon without the advantage of so much as an easel. Most of the time she stood with her sketchpad resting on her left arm while drawing with the right gloved hand. She sat down a couple of times, once on a railroad tie and once on the open tailgate of a pickup truck. She seldom spoke to anyone.

Even when people walked up and peered over her sketchpad, as Aaron had done a few times, Dana just kept right on working. She seemed totally engrossed in her endeavor. At times, Aaron suspected the youngster to be in some sort of trance. In fact, a surrealistic quality about the drawings tended to support that theory. One sketch Dana worked on for over an hour consisted of a variety of objects blended together like a collage. It was difficult to determine where one image ended and the next began. The central focus was a huge sea gull, the feathers of which faded in and out of a mushroom cloud. Woven into the drawing were faces of several rally speakers and a train with human body parts strewn about before it. Aaron wasn't sure what, if anything, the drawing meant.

At about sunset, Aaron's attention was drawn momentarily away from Dana to the long awaited arrival of the nuclear weapons train. He wasn't sure how everyone, including himself, came to know the train was near. There was no announcement from the microphone. In fact, the whole group, all of several thousand people, started singing at the time.

Their song seemed to echo back at them from the surrounding woods. The helicopters growling overhead were scarcely audible as the crowd chanted, "Love, love, love. People, we are made for love. Love each other as yourself, for we are one." They intoned this artless verse over and over so monotonously that Aaron thought he would become ill. Was he being hypnotized? He felt strangely drawn in, as if he too were a participant. Suddenly, he knew.

In fact everyone knew. The train was near, very near, not in view yet, but it would be arriving at any moment. Then suddenly, as if by magic, the train appeared over the horizon growing larger and more ominous as it approached. It was like a long, white fortress. You could almost see the eyes and machine gun barrels peering out through slit turrets. Uniformed guards were spaced along the outsides of the cars, each supporting a machine gun over one arm and clutching a handrail with the other. It was an impressive display of power in bold contrast with the procession of about two dozen demonstrators who filed out onto the tracks. This was a special group who planned to sit on the tracks in front of the train. The majority were women, and their average age was well past forty. Their manner was solemn and resolute as pallbearers at a funeral. Most of them wore wool caps and sported cold, red noses. Aaron wasn't sure whether they were more reminiscent of a church women's auxiliary or bag ladies in a soup line. They each stepped upon a separate railroad tie and then sat down simultaneously on the track as if somehow invisibly cued. All of their eyes closed together, as they calmly faced the oncoming train.

At the moment when their eyes closed, it occurred to Aaron that something weird was happening, something even stranger than a bunch of people sitting down in front of a train. That was when Aaron began to suspect that this whole crowd of several thousand people were all in a sort of trance, a kind of group hypnosis. Maybe Aaron had partially succumbed to it himself. To test his theory, Aaron turned to an elderly man standing next to him. The man had a sharp beak of a nose that protruded way out from under a heavy, crooked brimmed hat. Tears were running down his pale, sagging cheeks as his voice croaked out the song. Aaron touched the man gently on the arm and asked, "Is one of those women your wife?"

The man did not answer. In fact, he didn't seem to know anyone was speaking to him. Aaron shook the man's arm harder, but the man continued to sing, oblivious of everything but whatever was happening inside his head.

Fascinated, Aaron tried in a similar manner to get the attention of another demonstrator. It was a young woman with a baby in a backpack. Even the baby seemed to be in the trance.

On the third try Aaron did manage to get someone's attention. It was Rick, the boy with the Gandhi glasses. Aaron touched Rick's arm roughly and said, "Some train, eh, Rick?" The boy's eyes opened wide in a startled expression, as though he had been rudely awakened from a dream. Then he glared accusingly at Aaron as if he had committed some grievous breach of protocol.

Mumbling an apology, Aaron backed off into the crowd, and that was when he caught sight of Dana again. Now she was standing on the bed of the same pickup truck that she had been sitting on earlier. Her eyes were closed, and it almost looked as though she slept standing up. Aaron moved closer, wending his way through a crowd that gave way like soft earth before a plough. Aaron halted before the tailgate of the pickup truck and gazed up at Dana. She looked like a piece of sculpture or a priestess in a pulpit, hugging her big sketchbook to her chest as though it were a Bible. Unlike the thousands of other people standing around at ground level, Dana was not singing. Her lips were still. One slender hand still held the black fountain pen with which she had been working, but Dana was neither drawing nor singing. She seemed somehow transfixed. Probably his imagination was getting the better of him, but Aaron thought he saw a strange light, a sort of aura, emanating from Dana's forehead.

At that moment Aaron felt an inclination, an inner wisdom, bidding him to leave this place, a warning that he had stumbled upon something he had not the wherewithal to understand; any attempt to investigate further would confound, rather than elucidate, the mystery. It was not Aaron's nature to back off from his suspicions, especially not when his concept of the order of things was being threatened.

Aaron touched Dana's wrist with a trembling hand. "Hello, Dana!" He shouted loudly enough to be heard above the singing and, perhaps, to awaken someone who might be asleep. "I was wondering if you wanted a ride back to the ferry afterwards."

Aaron had not known what reaction to expect, but he was astonished by what did happen. The singing stopped instantly, even as he spoke. It did not trail off gradually. It stopped suddenly, somewhere in the middle of the refrain, "Love, love, love, love. People we are made..." It stopped.

In that same instant, Dana opened her eyes and smiled down at Aaron. So simultaneous were the two events, the smile and the cessation of singing, that there seemed to be a causal relationship between them. It was a radiant, infectious smile that disarmed Aaron, mitigating his astonishment. Then someone pressed a lighted candle into his hand.

A motley crew of so-called "Peace Keepers" wearing green arm bands mulled through the crowd passing out candles as the train slowed to a snail's pace and came to a complete stop just a few feet short of the demonstrators seated on the tracks. The sheriff's deputies and the railroad security officers set to work removing limp, compliant bodies and arresting people, putting them on buses while the Peace Keepers finished passing out candles.

By the time the train passed on into the base, the crowd was singing again. It was like a dream. Maybe it was a dream. For a moment Aaron felt himself strangely drawn in again.

After the tracks were cleared of people, the gates opened and the train moved on into the base. The performance was over.

Aaron looked around for Dana. She wasn't standing on the flatbed of the pickup any longer. He maneuvered through the crowd, searching. People were starting to leave. The spell was broken. There was no longer a train. There was no longer a Dana. Maybe he was going crazy. Otherwise, he wouldn't be harboring this strange feeling that the spell on the whole crowd had been broken, not so much by the departure of the train as by the absence of Dana Krandle, an unknown sideline observer who had expressed little more than an academic interest in the proceedings, a kid reporting on the rally for a school project.

Aaron had given up his crazy hope of driving Dana back to the ferry, of spending one hour alone with her, talking to her, feeling her out, asking questions, but there she was again. There she was alone in the darkness, jogging along the side of the road. She would hardly have been visible in her dark attire, were it not for the red backpack that bounced along behind.

Aaron pulled up and stopped about a hundred yards ahead of her, got out, walked around and opened the front passenger door. He held open the door as she slowed to a cautious lope, squinting at him in the darkness. "Dana, wait. It's me, Aaron Genzforth. Do you want a ride back to the ferry?"

She stopped just a few feet away, leering at him suspiciously.

"It would take you all night to run back to the ferry," he observed.

Dana continued to stare at him for another tense moment. Finally she said, "Sure, thanks, Mr. Genzforth," and got in the car.

Aaron's hour alone with Dana in the close confines of the front seat of his car fell short of his expectations. For the first few miles, she sat speechless and tense as a deer who had just caught the scent of a human and was ready to bolt. Aaron tried to make conversation. He asked her how her school project had progressed and when it was supposed to be turned in to Ms. Watson. He assured her the sketches he had seen were great and that she would get an A.

He asked her whether she had enjoyed the rally.

"Yes, of course, it was wonderful. And you?"

"Sure, sure, it was very nice!"

"Why were you there?" The question seemed to come from the Spanish Inquisition. No point in being phoney. She knew he was not in sympathy with the demonstration.

"To take pictures."

"You didn't take any pictures." She had been watching him all afternoon as carefully as he had been watching her.

Perhaps she had taken up his offer for a ride because she had been almost as curious about him as he was about her.

"The people I came to photograph didn't show up. Then I got interested in watching you draw."

"Are you a newspaper reporter?"

"No." Something told him not to lie to her, to be as sincere as possible. Despite an ingenuous quality about this young woman, she would not be easy to fool.

"So, what, are you an agent or something?"

Despite himself, Aaron began to laugh. He laughed so hard he nearly lost control of the car. The right front tire felt some gravel. "Be careful, Mr. Genzforth. It wasn't that funny." But she was laughing too. She had taken his laughter to mean that the idea of his being an agent was absurd. The sincerity of his laughter had disarmed her.

Dana seemed to be relaxing more, so Aaron turned on the tape deck which had been stopped halfway into a soft classical piece. Maybe it wasn't the sort of thing a teenager would fancy, but it would help Aaron relax. It was unlike him to feel shy and speechless. He needed to size up the situation, and come up with a game plan. Time, after all, was limited. He had waited many years for a moment like this, but he had never imagined that he would feel so out of control. He had rather expected to be his cold and calculating self, ready to reap as much benefit as possible from the opportunity, benefit in terms of "information," pure and simple.

But something strange had happened to him that afternoon as he watched Dana standing on the bed of that pickup truck. She resembled a priestess casting a spell upon the masses of her followers. Had he fallen for this child? Now the benefit he wanted was quite different. Instead, Aaron felt a frightening need to be noticed by this child, to be wanted by her. He even felt the uncanny desire to make some sort of pass at her, something very subtle, of course, that he could easily back out of if it didn't go over well, which it probably wouldn't, given the age difference.

He stole a sideways glance in her direction. Her eyes were closed, and her head bobbed ever so lightly as he slowed with the traffic. Was she dozing? He spoke her name softly.

"Dana?" She did not answer. She must be very tired after the long day. She had worked hard on her drawings, braving the weather and the crowds, among other things. Had she done something to the crowd? Cast some sort of spell? He must be insane to imagine such things.

Now he was with her, and she was asleep. He needed a plan. If Dana was still asleep when they arrived on Bainbridge Island, he would stop by his mother's house. The place would be deserted, of course, but he would pretend that he had expected his mother to be home and that he had just stopped by to check on her. No matter that the plan wasn't very subtle or convincing. This was a rare opportunity. He had to take some advantage of it. As Aaron pulled off the main road, Dana emitted a soft moan. She was waking up. "Where are we?" she asked with more composure than Aaron would have anticipated. He was ready, of course, with a full explanation. "I want to stop by my mother's house out on Harbor Road. The ferry doesn't leave for another hour and a half, so we have time."

"You can drop me off here. I'll jog the rest of the way."

"No, please. I wouldn't think of it. You shouldn't be out jogging on the road alone at night. It's dangerous. Hasn't your mother told you that?"

"Yes. She also said not to get in cars with strange men."

Aaron wanted to tell her that he was no stranger, that he had known her most of her life. Instead he said, "Of course, I'll let you out if you insist, but it's still pretty far to the ferry. You would probably miss the next crossing, and there won't be another until late tonight."

For reply, Dana sat stiff and motionless, staring at the taillights of the vehicle ahead. So much for making a pass. She would probably gouge out his eyes.

As they pulled into the driveway, Aaron tried to conceive of the effect his mother's house might have on someone like Dana. She would undoubtedly be impressed, even as she tried to maintain her teenage "cool." His mother was not home, but she had left several lights on for security. A floodlamp lit the front facade, with its carved cedar doorway and stained-glass rose window. If Mother were here, she'd brag for the millionth time about how the window was salvaged from the ruins of some French cathedral destroyed during World War II. Another floodlamp lit the swimming pool alongside the house, and beyond lay the dark waters of the Puget Sound. The bejeweled Seattle skyline could be glimpsed through the branches of the tall fir trees that had been pruned to enhance the view. Aaron got out of the car, walked around and opened the door on Dana's side.

He gestured invitingly. "Wouldn't you like to come in?"

She continued to sit very erect, looking straight ahead as if the same taillight were there to stare at.

"No, thank you. I'll wait here."

"All right, as you wish." But he left her door open.

Even though he had anticipated that no one would be home, Aaron made a great show of ringing the door bell several times before he fumbled about for the key and entered, leaving the door ajar behind him. Before going on into the kitchen, he turned on the chandelier to illuminate the sitting room which was furnished with more than a dozen brocaded French Provincial settees and chairs. He also lit the gas fire that simulated logs burning on the hearth. He hoped the brightness would tempt Dana in from the cold.

Next Aaron went on into the kitchen and turned on the tea kettle. He rummaged about, opening and closing cupboard doors until he found a box of chocolate-frosted biscotti sealed in separate cellophane wrappers. He unwrapped several, arranged them on a china plate, and carried them into the sitting room. He might not have noticed the black-garbed figure leaning against the French doors to the veranda, had he not been anxiously looking for her. But Aaron felt his heart skip a beat as the light flickered across her face.

"Oh, hello, Dana. Uh, apparently my mother isn't home, but she won't mind us warming up with a cup of tea at her expense. Would you like some?" He set the plate of cookies on the mantle piece.

Although Aaron couldn't quite make out Dana's mumbled reply, he took it for consent, and hurried back into the kitchen to fetch the tea. The kettle had begun to emit little sounds of life but was not yet steaming. Very methodically, he set about trying to locate china cups, saucers, and tea pot. At one point he opened the liquor cabinet by mistake and it crossed his mind to have a shot of cognac, but that was decidedly off limits. Dana was known to be allergic even to the scent of alcohol.

It seemed to Aaron that it took him much too long to prepare the tea, and when he returned to the sitting room with the tray, his worst fears had been realized. She was gone. The French doors were now open, and a damp chill blew in off the Sound. Aaron set the tray down on the mantle piece beside the cookies and looked around. The room seemed cheerless now, despite the firelight and chandelier.

Aaron rushed out onto the veranda where the cold wind met him with full force. The yellow chandelier light shone faintly through the French doors and fell upon the brown and broken remains of last summer's geraniums. "Dana?" Aaron's voice trailed off in the wind.

He hurried down the cement staircase and stood on the sea wall looking out over a wide expanse of beach. The tide was at its lowest point, which was still rather high at this time of year, and the surface of the water was discomforted by the wind. A brightly lit ferry approached now very slowly. It resembled an orange caterpillar crossing an oil black road. Aaron wasn't sure, but he might have spotted Dana running down the beach toward the ferry landing. It might have been an illusion. Maybe it was a branch blowing in the wind.

He called to her again without expecting a reply. After Aaron returned to the house, he hurried on through to the front driveway to make certain Dana wasn't in the car before he went back in to the liquor cabinet.

There was still time before ferry departure, so he sat on the brocaded settee nearest the fire and warmed himself while sipping a shot of cognac. By the time the tumbler was empty, all the sentimentality he had felt that day was gone. Also dissipated were his humiliation and dismay at first realizing she had given him the slip. In their place was a healthy trace of anger. That little fly would wind up "pinned and wriggling on the wall" one day, that was for sure.

Leaving the unwashed tea things and shot glass where they lay on the mantle, Aaron locked up the house and returned to his car. As he opened the door, the interior light came on and his spirits lifted. On the floor of the passenger side lay her red backpack stretched awkwardly around a now familiar, large rectangular shape. She must have been terribly frightened of him. Otherwise, she would not have run off and left her sketchpad behind.

BAINBRIDGE ISLAND BEACH ~ EVENING, FEBRUARY 6,1985

Running along the beach, Dana begun to relax a little after her harrowing experience with Mr. Genzforth. It was difficult to tell what the man was up to, but one thing for sure, he was some sort of narc or spy, and he had an unhealthy interest in her. To think, she had started to trust him enough to accept a ride back to the ferry without any of the other kids along. But, there had been no other way to get back to the ferry, short of sticking out her thumb and hitching another ride.

Still, Dana had to admit that it was mostly curiosity that had coaxed her into Genzforth's car. She had hoped that the long ride would induce a trance, and the blue light would come. Then she might have found out what the man was really thinking. She had not intended to fall asleep, but it had been an exhausting day and, with the warmth of the car heater and relaxing to let the blue light come, it had happened very quickly. Dana could recall little of the trip. But there was the lingering memory of a dream.

The dream had been induced, of course, by all the talk lately in Ms. Watson's class about so many women being raped and how they should learn self-defense. Elvira Maxwell had done her project on it and presented to the class earlier in the week, and that had sparked several lengthy discussions. Ms. Watson had promised to bring in an expert to teach some basic self-defense. A lot of the kids were riled up, but Dana had not known she was frightened until she awoke from the dream in Mr. Genzforth's car.

Although she had to admit that, in real life, Mr. Genzforth was not bad looking with his long slender nose and pale skin, he was positively horrid in the dream. His features were all red and swollen. In the dream, he turned the car off the main road onto a side street and parked in a dark, deserted place. Then he suddenly lunged toward Dana like some phantom in a horror film. That was when she woke up to find he had actually turned off the main road onto a dark country road, just as in her dream.

Dana had learned over the years not to make too much of dreams nor to take them too lightly either. But she had been really wary of what might happen when Mr. Genzforth invited her into the big fancy house he claimed belonged to his mother. When the lights came on and shone out through the stained-glass window, it felt like Dana was looking into a giant kaleidoscope.

She wasn't sure what to do. At first she didn't plan to go in, but then she decided it would feel safer standing up in a lighted place than sitting outside in the dark.

The sitting room that greeted her was awesome with its brocaded furniture and big ornate mantelpiece. What really struck her was the row of French doors that formed the back wall of the room. There was no sign of Mr. Genzforth. Maybe he had gone out through the doors. When she crossed the room to investigate, Dana was even more impressed by the obvious escape route that lay before her. A wide veranda lead down several steps onto a lawn, and just below that was the beach. Even in the darkness, it was obvious where total blackness of beach gave way to water that picked up every particle of light from the distant Seattle skyline. Across the expanse of shiny black water, a ferry boat glided slowly toward the terminal. Without allowing time to shake her nerve, Dana reached for the door handle. It was a lever type and opened easily.

Once down on the beach and running, Dana felt more at home. She knew how to run on the beach during the evening low tide. She had been doing this all her life. She had faint memories of running the beach at night with Wella when she was very small. It was important to concentrate so as to avoid tripping over driftwood or slipping on rocks. Such concentration kept her mind off other worries. She glanced back a couple of times to see whether Mr. Genzforth was coming, even though she felt certain he would not follow.

Dana was within sight of the ferry terminal when she heard the distant sound of barking dogs. At first she paid little attention because the sight of car lights moving up the ramp told her the ship was being loaded and would soon leave. The threat of missing the ferry was greater than that of the neighborhood mutts. The barking was almost at her heels, when Dana stopped to pivot around and have a look. The silhouettes of two husky retrievers bore down on her like lumbering black bears, their canine teeth gleaming in the faint light from the ferry terminal. Another little rat of a dog came up from behind them, yelping more ferociously than the others.

Dana bent over to pick up a rock, but instead spotted a stick of driftwood about the size of a generous soup bone. She picked up the stick and waved it into the wind. "Hi, Rover! she called gently, and the dogs all stopped just a few feet away. The smaller dog continued yelping and dancing about, but the two retrievers stood at attention as Dana shouted, "Hi, Rover, fetch!" and tossed the stick away down the beach.

To Dana's immense satisfaction, the diversion worked. The dogs ran off in the opposite direction after the stick, and she proceeded more slowly across the half-mile of beach between herself and the ferry landing. The cars were almost all loaded, and Dana was only a few hundred feet from the landing, when the dogs returned.

Dana took the piece of drift wood from the anxious jaws of the largest retriever. This time she hurled it farther down the beach at an angle, so the stick landed in the water. As soon as the dogs started to run after it, Dana took off running again. She had crossed the remaining expanse of beach and had climbed the stone levy onto the road before the dogs returned again. It wasn't until she reached the ticket gate that Dana noticed that she no longer had her back pack. "Oh, my God, I've lost my back pack!" she screamed. "And my ticket was in it!"

The ticket agent, a young man with gentle eyes, waved her through. "Better hustle," he urged. "They're holding up the boat for you."

Dana sprinted up the ramp as an attendant held the gate ajar. The deck floor departed from the ramp almost as she set foot on it.

Dana felt uncomfortable and exposed inside the large lighted passenger seating area, so she headed for the Women's room. Mr. Genzforth would not go there. Within the safe enclosure of a toilet stall, she could think. She sat down on the stool and closed her eyes to blot out the jungle of graffiti on the wall. If Mr. Genzforth was on the ferry, he would probably visit the coffee shop rather than remain in his car. Her backpack would still be in the car with her social studies project that was due in little more than a week. She would get an A in Ms. Watson's class if she could make any kind of decent presentation on the due date. It would have been such an easy A and probably the only one she would get this quarter. Maybe she could reproduce some of the drawings from memory or go back to some of the same places and do them again. Ms. Watson might give her an extension on the due date if she explained that her work was lost. Ms. Watson, being extremely honest herself, tended to be trusting of others. No, it would be better to find Mr. Genzforth and get back the sketchbook.

Dana left the bathroom and spent the rest of the crossing in search of the formidable Genzforth. She searched the coffee shop and then all the passenger seating areas. She even examined the faces of suited men asleep on benches. She searched the decks outside where a few hearty sea lovers still sat braving the night wind. A few times, Dana noticed someone who looked a little like Genzforth, but it always turned out to be someone very different.

Finally, Dana systematically searched the car deck at both levels. She recalled that Mr. Genzforth drove a silver-gray car that might belong to some sort of big shot. But there were lots of cars like that down there. An attendant eyed her suspiciously when she began peering inside the windows of cars looking for her red backpack.

The whole time she stood on the street corner in front of the ferry terminal waiting for the bus, Dana wondered if the fancy gray car would pull up, and Mr. Genzforth would poke his head out to ask her whether she wanted another ride. He was fond of giving her rides. Dana didn't entirely give up the hope of getting her drawings back until she got on the bus. Mr. Genzforth was the sort who wouldn't be caught dead on Metro. If he wanted to talk to someone riding a bus, he would probably follow it around with his fancy car until they got off. Once Dana had seen a narc do that on television. Maybe Genzforth would be waiting for her when she got off the bus. Even though the thought terrified her, Dana entertained a wistful hope he would be there waiting with the sketchbook.

When Dana got home, the newspaper and mail were still on the front porch. That meant neither Mom nor Dad had been there since morning. Maybe Charlie assumed Dana had gone some place with her parents and would keep his mouth shut about her not being in school that day. Maybe no one would ever know she went to the big demonstration at the Base. Dana went to bed right away. She was snuggled way down under the covers and facing the wall when she heard the front door open and close. She could tell it was Dad because of his gentle unhurried footsteps in the hallway. Mom would have come in pounding her high heels and slamming doors.

It was obvious that something was wrong when Dad came all the way into Dana's room instead of just opening the door to say, "Good night." In fact, he sat down on the edge of the bed as if he meant to tell her a story, something he had not done for years. One of her fondest childhood memories was of lying there in the darkness while Dad told a bedtime story. But something told her this would not be a pleasant story.

"Hi, Dana. You awake?"

"Yeah, Hi Dad. Have a nice day?"

"All right, I guess."

"Is something wrong?"

"I don't know. Is something wrong?"

"I lost the drawings for my social studies project."

"Oh. Can you do them over?"

Dana shrugged and didn't answer. People didn't understand about drawings. People who didn't use drawing to communicate much thought you could do them over at the drop of a hat. They didn't realize all that went into it. They didn't understand it would be as hard as reproducing the research for a term paper. She wished Dad would go away and let her worry in peace, but he just sat there weighing down the side of her bed. Something was on his mind. Maybe Charlie had told him she wasn't in school today.

Finally Dad said "Dana, I had a terrible shock as I was leaving the school building today. Helen Gabriel came up to me and said, 'I saw your daughter on the Channel Five News.'"

Dana rolled over and looked at Dad. He was serious. He looked shaken. "Someone saw me on TV? I've never been on tv in my life! There must be some mistake."

"That's what I said. I told Helen she must have mistaken you for someone else."

"I guess so," agreed Dana. She rolled back over to face the wall again hoping Dad would leave, but instead he reached over and switched on the small reading lamp on the bedstand. Dana felt a tightening in her stomach and chest.

When the light came on Dana found herself still gazing, in a sense, into darkness. For in its place was her big wall poster with a picture of the Milky Way. In about the middle of the upper left hand quadrant was a little arrow labeled, "YOU ARE HERE." The poster helped put things in perspective. What were the problems of a school girl getting in trouble with her parents and teachers in comparison with the size and life span of the universe?

"Dana, I hate to tell you this, but a lot of people saw you on tv. today. Charlie videotaped some of it, and I saw it myself just a few minutes ago over at Theresa's house."

"Really?"

"Yes, really. Dana, did you go all the way over to the Submarine Base by yourself today?"

"No. I went with some other kids from school. I needed to make some drawings of real civil disobedience for my Martin Luther King project. Was I really on tv?"

"Big as life. How did you get all the way over to the Base?"

"On the ferry."

"How did you get from the ferry terminal to the Base?"

"We hitched a ride. There were three other kids in the car with me going over." Ms. Watson would never stoop to telling such self-protective half-truths. She called half-truths, lies.

"Hitchhiking is dangerous for a young girl."

"I know."

"Your Mom'll come unglued when she hears about this."

"Will you tell her?"

"No, but she's sure to find out. Thousands of people saw you."

"Why was I on television? Why me? I was in a big crowd of four thousand people waiting for the nuclear weapons train. There were lots of people who played important parts. I just went there to draw pictures of the people sitting on the tracks and the police officers and the sheriff, things like that. I had to go there. It was the only example of nonviolent civil disobedience anywhere around here, and that's what my project is supposed to be about. Who knows how long it will be before anything like that happens around here again. There were lots of observers and picture takers. Why me?"

"The cameraman must have liked you. He focused on you for a long time. Your Mom'll be pissed. And now you say you've lost the drawings." Dad shook his head and chuckled softly, letting Dana know he didn't really take the matter all that seriously himself.

Dana rolled back over facing Dad and reached up to give him a hug. He chuckled softly again, warmly returning the hug. Maybe he was even a little proud of her going to the demonstration alone.

UNIVERSITY HIGH SCHOOL ~ FEBRUARY 4, 1985

Of all times and places, Dana felt most alien in the halls of University High School between classes. For one thing, she was one of the tallest kids in the school, and it felt like her head was a boat bobbing about on a turbulent tide of hats and hair. Her body beneath served as the keel to be jostled and tormented by waves and currents of other bodies.

One thing for sure, there was no collective consciousness in the hallway. Everyone rushed about in the great sea, never connecting, it seemed, except for maybe a few of the "popular" kids who would stop and bubble effervescently with one another. Dana was glad they didn't stop to talk with her. She felt little enthusiasm for their football games or love affairs.

Dana had started wearing black when she noticed that popular kids were repelled by the color. They thought the black-clothed kids were all junkies or something, which was by no means the case. Some were, of course, but most of them were just kids who, like Dana, didn't feel part of the dominant culture. In fact, some preferred not to be. Black clothing gave them a kind of nameless identity that no one could label or classify. The "wearers-of-black" seldom stopped to talk in the hallways. They usually sat together in the lunchroom, but they were all quiet kids. If they did talk, it was about art, or music, or feelings, or even politics. It was acceptable in their circles to sit in perfect silence for the entire lunch period. They certainly didn't bubble.

The strategy of wearing black had been a good popularity deterrent until today. Apparently, everyone had seen Dana on television the night before. Kids she hardly knew looked up at Dana as if suddenly noticing her for the first time and said, "I saw you on tv last night!" She had been on almost every news broadcast in the Seattle area. Charlie had made a videotape copy of the segment, and he carried the thing around proudly announcing that he planned to show it in social studies class. But at the last moment, Charlie remembered that he was scheduled to make a presentation on his own project before the class and had to run back to get his audiovisuals. In his haste, he then left the tape in his locker. For once, Charlie's absentmindedness had saved rather than spoiled the day.

While Charlie was getting himself organized, Ms. Watson passed the talking-stick around for "check-in." The class of about thirty eleventh-graders sat in a circle of chairs looking nonchalant, many of them affecting an attitude of insolence by slouching, chewing gum, wearing their sweatshirts and baseball caps. But there seemed to be something magical about that talking-stick and its power to keep them quiet. No one spoke when someone else held the stick. All around them on the walls hung posters with pictures of famous people with caption quotes. The largest and most prominent was a silhouette of Susan B. Anthony declaring in bold three-inch letters, "Failure is impossible."

Dana felt anxious as the stick came around to her. She had spent most of the day fretting about the loss of her sketchbook and fearing she would have no project. But the words that came out were, "I feel popular today because I was on tv last night."

Ms. Watson responded with her customary nod of grave appreciation, and the class followed suit. There was seldom any belittling or snickering in Ms. Watson's class. She stressed "positive affirmation" of others by example more than anything else.

They had barely completed the circle when Charlie stood before them with his visual aids hung from the flip-chart stand. Ms. Watson stood up and handed Charlie the talking-stick. He stood beside her appearing totally confident of his full equality with the teacher. They were roughly the same size, extra large, except that Ms. Watson was somewhat pudgier. Still, she looked beautiful with her high, angular cheekbones and broad-based African nose, glowing a copper-brown beneath the prominent whites of her enormous eyes. Ms. Watson had a fantastic wardrobe, and today she wore her blue turquoise blouse and white linen suit.

It had been distressing when Dana had first realized that she was in love with Lucinda Watson. Being in love with a woman meant she was probably a lesbian, which was worse than being an alien. Later, however, Dana had noticed that a lot of kids, many of them girls, hung around after class wanting to talk with Ms. Watson. Nearly everyone was in love with her.

Charlie, in contrast with Ms. Watson, was dressed like old snap shots of his dad from the sixties before he was drafted into the Army. Charlie wore roughly the same kind of beaded headband and long braids. Around his neck hung a cord strung with the claws and teeth of unknown animals. Probably it was the same necklace Charlie's dad wore in the photo.

Aunt Theresa never threw anything away, and she was fond of giving Charlie things that had belonged to his father.

Charlie began his presentation by lifting the talking-stick like a pointer and waving it at the flip-chart pad as he turned back the cover to unveil his first visual aid. "This is a photograph of the planet Earth taken from a space ship," he began. "This view includes the entire continent of North America with a little bit of Central America showing over the curve here."

Dana would have to take his word for it. There were too many white twists and swirls of what must have been clouds and stuff in the way. It might just as well have been a colossal enlargement of one of his marbles.

Fortunately, Charlie had another visual aid. Dramatically, he reached up and pulled down a big piece of clear plastic on which he had drawn a circular map the same size as the Earth photo. The map was divided into many small segments that now appeared to be drawn on the photograph.

"This is a map roughly of how this continent would have been divided thousands of years before the Europeans came here," he proclaimed importantly. "These are roughly the territories occupied by the many various nations, although these peoples never thought to build fences or draw boundary lines. The land belonged to the Great Spirit. People and plants and animals were allowed to use it, as long as they were willing to share."

Dana glanced around the circle. Charlie had grabbed everyone's attention with this opening. Ms. Watson nodded extremely grave appreciation. This was very likely the start of a collective consciousness if only there was time before the bell rang. One thing Dana had learned this year in Ms. Watson's class was to sense the formation of a collective without the blue light coming first. Then she could induce the blue light, simply by concentrating on what was happening in class. It seemed Ms. Watson had a gift for invoking a collective spirit in a group. It happened most when she told stories about her childhood growing up on the south side of Chicago, or about more recent summer travels to foreign lands, but it even happened sometimes when a student had the talking-stick.

There had been plenty of opportunities for Dana to tap into the collective when she liked the subject well enough. If it was a subject she didn't like, say Elvira Maxwell's project on rape, Dana would divert her attention, and do homework for another class or something. As for Charlie's project, it had been inspired during one of his visits with Grandma Redtree, and nothing could be more pleasant or harmless. It would be a great collective experience, maybe not up to the caliber of yesterday's rally, but pleasant enough.

Charlie switched the talking-stick to his left hand, took a large marking pen in his right, and wrote on one of the little spaces the name "Suquammish."

"This is where my ancestors lived, and it is where we live now," he announced proudly. "This city is named 'Seattle' after one of the leaders of our nation." Charlie thrust forth his chest proudly as he spoke. Dana had noticed many personality changes, some of them actual improvements, in the Charlie that had gradually emerged during the long years of his recovery from the accident. One of the less attractive alterations was the loss of his former humility. On the other hand, a major improvement had occurred since they had met Lucinda Watson. Charlie had discovered that, though reading was now arduous, he could obtain plenty of information without having to read. Upon learning of Charlie's left brain damage, Ms. Watson had enrolled him in the books-on-tape program used by blind people, and obtained tape recordings of all Charlie's textbooks. Charlie also got tapes of fantasy novels about wizards and dragons, or anything he wanted. Suddenly, some of the pre-morbid Charlie returned in the form of his interest in books. As far as Kim Lui, Patrick or any of Charlie's dyslexic pals could tell, Charlie was the same. When they saw him sitting in the park, on the bus, or on his front porch with a Walkman, they thought Charlie was listening to hard rock. They hadn't the slightest inkling that he might be doing homework or studying for a test., or just enjoying a novel.

Charlie proceeded with his presentation by labeling a small space on the coast with the name, Makah. "This is the home of the Makah Nation who still live there today. They built many seaworthy canoes and were great whalers and fishermen. Their language, customs and legends live on, as we speak."

Charlie continued in an almost monotonous singsong, rhythm naming almost every space on the diagram, Puyallup, Lakota, Tallalup. As he wrote each name, Charlie told little stories and mentioned important leaders. "This is the Wallowa Valley, land of the Nez Perce. They were great horsemen who bred the beautiful, spotted Appaloosas. Their leader was Joseph, a just man who loved peace. Joseph is remembered and honored among all the world's peoples."

By the time Charlie finished his talk, the collective trance was very deep. He finished by admitting that he had not read one book for his project. Instead, he had taken his Earth photo, map, and tape recorder to a big Eastern Oregon Pow Wow with his grandma. There, he had shown the map about, asking people to indicate where various native people had lived. Then Charlie had listened to the tape repeatedly, studying the map all the way home in the car. That was all he had done for the project other than make an edited tape with which he concluded the presentation. The tape consisted of small excerpts of Native American voices telling stories.

All the while, a wailing chorus of drums and chant haunted the background. When Charlie finished and passed the stick into Ms. Watson's strong left hand, the collective was sustained in eager anticipation of what would clearly happen next, for the teacher's right hand was already poised to switch on her slide projector. "Thank you, Mr. Redtree. That was an inspired presentation. I'm no expert on this subject, but I just wanted to show a few pictures of some native people I've met on my travels since I've been out here in the West."

Ms. Watson tapped the switch and projected a life-sized image before them of a man sitting in a small, outboard motorboat. He was draped in a big, army surplus poncho. Dark friendly eyes smiled out from under the garment's hood into the rain. In the background was a muddy river bank and what appeared to be gray fog settling over a brown, grassy wet land. "This is Robert," began Ms. Watson. "I met this gentleman last New Year's Day when I was hiking with friends on the Nisqually Delta. Robert said he had been sitting in the boat since dawn, and it was nearly noon. He was waiting for a fish to swim into his net."

Ms. Watson flipped the switch to reveal Robert now standing in the boat holding the tiller in one hand and a net in the other. His face wore a startled but pleased expression like that of a baseball player who had, quite by accident hit a home run. The net hung from Robert's hand like a sack bulging with the prize of a large bottom fish. "To our amazement, Robert actually caught this fish while we were standing there watching him. It almost got away, but Robert outsmarted the animal by moving the net around and trapping it in a curve of the bank. Then he used a long pole to scare the thing away from the bank and into his net. "Ms. Watson laughed, enjoying her memory and her laughter rippled contagiously around the circle.

The next slide was of a boy about ten years old. Thick black hair hung down over the collar of a bright red parka. The boy was perched on what appeared to be an abandoned, rusty automobile part, perhaps a fender. A variety of other metal pieces were strewn about the ground in front of the door of a trailer house. The door contained a four-paned window, only three sections of which contained glass. The fourth was covered with a piece of tin. "This is Anthony. I met him last summer on a bicycling trip. I was awfully thirsty so I stopped to ask how far it was to the tribal store for a Pepsi. We got to talking, and Anthony asked how far I had come and things like that. When I told him I was a teacher, he said they needed a teacher at the tribal school and suggested that I apply. He said he hopes he can be a teacher when he grows up."

Ms. Watson went on showing and narrating her summer vacation slides with the class spellbound until the bell rang. Ms. Watson was a master at keeping conglomerates of human brain waves focused on her trip, no matter how trivial the subject. The bell was a cruel sound bringing Dana out of a blissful trance. She left the room and reluctantly returned to the rushing river of human heads. But the euphoric residue remained of the hour with Ms. Watson and with it, fantasies of one day being a teacher herself and working with Ms. Watson in a small tribal school far away in a remote mountain village. The aura lingered throughout most of the afternoon with little snatches of fantasy surfacing above the flow of other thoughts. Occasionally a thought of Ms. Watson would bring with it an unpleasant recollection of the loss of her sketchbook.

Her head was thrust into her jumbled locker when Dana felt an ungentle tug at her arm. She was not surprised when she pulled her head out to find Charlie's face just a few inches from hers. In his dark gentle eyes there was an uncharacteristically intense expression. "Harold Prinder just told me something you won't believe," he said.

"Oh, what?"

"Ms. Watson's getting the axe."

"Oh, come on, Charlie. That can't be. Ms. Watson's the best teacher in the school. She has tenure. They can't fire Lucinda Watson."

"Harold says the school board are a bunch of old fuddy-duddies. They don't like the fact that Ms. Watson spends the whole time showing her vacation slides and talks about sex and stuff like that in class."

"She doesn't. The kids do."

"Ms. Watson lets them. Harold says the school board thinks she encourages that kind of talk, instead of teaching what's expected."

"I'll ask Dad if he's heard anything. It might be just a rumor." Dana felt like a cinch had been clamped around her chest, but it was best not to let on to Charlie. Stress and change were hard on him.

"It's true. Harold Prinder says some of the kids are getting together after school to plan a strike."

"We'll see. I'll ask Dad about it tonight."

• • •

Papers were piled in orderly stacks a foot high, all over Ms. Watson's desk. She didn't look up or even seem to notice Dana walking in and towering above her. Dana didn't want to interrupt, so she just stood and waited in silence until Ms. Watson finally looked up. Her greeting was casual, almost as if she had known Dana was there all the time. "Hi Dana, what's up?" Ms. Watson gestured toward the chair beside her desk. She never talked to anyone from across the desk. Instead she always kept a chair beside the desk for students to meet with her at closer, unobstructed range. According to Ms. Watson, communication was the most important aspect of education, in fact of life in general. To obstruct communication was bad. To facilitate communication was good.

Dana sat down and handed Ms. Watson a small green slip of paper. It was the hall pass that had to be signed excusing her from math. Without a word, Ms. Watson checked the box that said "Excused for instructor consultation," signed it "L. Watson," and handed back the pass.

"Thanks," said Dana. "I need to talk with you about my class project, and I also want to ask about some other things."

Ms. Watson nodded and smiled.

"It's about the rumors. They say you're getting fired. Some of the kids are planning a protest." Harold and Charlie would be pissed if they found out she told about the planned demonstration. They said to be effective, it had to be sudden and unexpected. They wanted Dana involved because they considered her an expert at protests since she had done her social studies project on civil disobedience. But Dana was hesitant to get involved. Mom was hardly speaking to her after last week's television fiasco. Besides, everyone knew her Dad taught for the same school district. Maybe he would get fired, too. Dad, after all, agreed that the school board were a bunch of old fuddy-duddies, and tried to attract as little of their attention as possible.

Ms. Watson smiled amusement as well as reassurance. "Oh, no.

They needn't have a protest. I mean, they can if they want, but it isn't necessary. I've had my differences with the school board, but they could not easily fire me. I have tenure."

"Whew! That's a relief."

"Mom has an absolute phobia about me going to demonstrations and things like that. I feel torn, not knowing what to do. Charlie will be crushed if they have a demonstration and I don't go. What do you think I should do, Ms. Watson?"

Ms. Watson answered without hesitation, "Listen to your inner voice. Be yourself. When you feel torn, that may be because there are two voices. Listen to where they're coming from and obey the one that speaks from the innermost core of your being."

Dana thought for a moment about Ms. Watson's advice, and then smiled. She would attend the demonstration if it materialized. Then she said, "I'm sure glad you're not really being fired. I want to take your World History class next year."

"Oh, I'm sorry, I won't be back next year. You'll probably have Mr. Friedman for World History."

"You mean you're leaving, just like that? You're going to teach somewhere else?"

"No, I'm not going to teach anywhere. I'm going to pursue another career."

"You don't like teaching? But, you're the world's greatest teacher!" Even as she asked the question, Dana knew the answer. Ms. Watson loved her job. She didn't even mind grading papers, which must take most of her waking hours considering how carefully she did it.

Ms. Watson laughed in her jovial, uninhibited way. "It isn't that I don't like teaching. It's just that I have only one life to live, and it's time to try something else for awhile. As for being the world's best teacher, Dana, you're entitled to your opinion, and I'm deeply honored by it, but I don't agree." She laughed again. "You know, I've often wondered what is really meant by the phrase, 'good teacher'. I'm sure no one could ever define it. I think I make a good talk show host maybe, but great teacher? I wouldn't claim such an honor. I've often thought we should just keep the Camcorder going in here all day, and I could go on the air as *The Lucinda Watson Teenage Talk Show*." She reached forward and comfortingly tapped the back of Dana's hand with her thick, dark fingers. "I'm not making fun of your opinion, Dana. Maybe you're right. Maybe my way is the right way to teach, but what really matters is that the Superintendent and Dr. Izaks both think otherwise. They didn't fire me, but they said I should leave or change. Unfortunately, I can't be whatever it is they want me to be."

"What way is that?"

Ms. Watson shrugged. "Oh, like Mr. Friedman, I suppose."

"Mr. Friedman. He's boring."

"He doesn't tear history books apart. He doesn't talk about using condoms when he's supposed to be covering the Black Plague. He concentrates on the concepts he's supposed to teach."

"Don't you?"

"Heavens, no! That's against my philosophy. Each mind has its own hunger to satisfy. I just try to step back and let it happen. As I said, the administration and I have basic philosophical differences."

"Did they give you a warning?"

"Yes, but then I just went in to Izaks' office and told him I'm not signing on for next year because I have a scholarship to Harvard Law School."

"That's great, Ms. Watson. Congratulations!" Dana reached out and offered Ms. Watson a handshake which she accepted vigorously.

Even though she was happy about Ms. Watson being so highly honored and being able to do something she wanted to do, Dana felt a sadness that needed to be dealt with in solitude, so she started to get up and leave. Then she remembered about the sketchbook, blushed, and sat back down. Her main purpose for the meeting was to tell Ms. Watson she lost her original project and to discuss plans for an alternative. The original idea had been to show transparencies of her drawings on an overhead projector while reading excerpts on non-violence, from Thoreau, Gandhi, and Martin Luther King. Her new plan was to show Charlie's video tape, which actually turned out to be a sympathetic news report of the Bangor rally. It would show non-violent, civil disobedience in action. After that, she would read the same excerpts while playing Mom's favorite audio tape of Bette Midler singing *The Rose* softly in the background.

Ms. Watson seemed to read her thoughts, because she said "You came to discuss your project." She gasped as if recalling something. "Speaking of which, I still have your sketches here in my desk. They're wonderful! You do have a gift, Dana." Ms. Watson slid her chair back and bent down to open the bottom right-hand drawer. Then she gently, almost reverently, placed Dana's long lost red canvas day pack atop the piles of paper on her desk.

Dana was dumbfounded but tried to keep her cool. "You have my sketchbook," she gasped.

"Yes," continued Ms. Watson nonchalantly. "I appreciate your leaving them in my mailbox for a sneak preview before your presentation. Sorry, I didn't give them back sooner. But you still have time to make some transparencies. Maybe you can stop by the library before your next class. We're really looking forward to your presentation on Monday. Is there anything else you want to say about the project?"

Dana shook her head mechanically. She was speechless. If only she could tell Ms. Watson the whole story, but where to begin? Finally, she said, "Ms. Watson, I must tell you the truth. Actually, I lost my backpack on my way home from the submarine base last week. I, well, I hitched a ride with a stranger who frightened me, so I ran off and left the backpack in his car."

Ms. Watson stared at Dana in shock. "Did he harm you?"

"No, he didn't do anything, really."

The teacher shrugged. "I thought you knew better than that, after Elvira Maxwell's presentation on rape. Fortunately, this must have been a nice man and quite resourceful to figure out where to return your backpack. You were lucky this time, but I'm sure I needn't tell you to be more careful from now on."

"It was Elvira's presentation, more than him, that scared me."

Dana opened her palm and looked at her hall pass, which was now folded into the shape of a tiny green kite. She often folded paper unconsciously to get rid of nervous energy. "It's almost time for the bell," she said and stood up as if to leave, though not really wanting to. It was comforting to be with Ms. Watson, but there would be no more fantasies about being her teacher's aide in a mountain village school. Ms. Watson would soon be far away pursuing another life.

As she completed that thought, Dana was struck with an inexplicable intuition that Ms. Watson had somehow intercepted it in full, and then, strangely enough, the teacher made direct eye contact with Dana and said, "Drop by anytime during my prep period. I'm always glad to see you, Dana. I feel there's something special between us. I have a hunch we'll be friends for a long time."

At that moment, the bell rang and Dana floated out into the rushing river on a crest of euphoria.

Part Three: WOMANHOOD

SOUTH SEATTLE SUBURBS NEAR AUBURN ~ JUNE 15, 1992

There were no signs or markings anywhere along the suburban complex of bicycle paths, but Dana guessed that the town up ahead and to the left might be her destination. She stopped and peered into the distance, shading her eyes from the mid-afternoon sun with one hand while steadying the handlebars with the other. Then she reached into the pocket of her shorts and pulled out a tattered invoice on the back of which was scrawled a crude map. A cycling enthusiast had made it for her during a chance meeting at the bike shop in Wallingford. The fellow had assured Dana it would be a great trip, said he often whipped down there on training rides in the evenings after work. But it had taken Dana since early morning to get here, what with getting lost a couple of times.

She had tried to ask directions, but there were few pedestrians in this part of town. There were lots of people, but most were not very approachable racing by in automobiles. The few people she found to talk with blinked at her and shrugged almost as if they didn't speak English. When someone did give directions, Dana found herself on entirely the wrong path, headed many miles out of the way. Eventually, Dana had stumbled, quite by accident, upon the right path, and it had been a pretty straight shot ever since, like a bicycle freeway.

A hazy apparition of Mount Rainier appeared in the sky overhead, otherwise, the scenery was not inspiring. The bike path severed a swath of mowed weeds alongside a railroad track. The opposite side was flanked by endless rows of gray concrete warehouses with metal roofs. Why had Charlie come to live in such a dismal place?

There were plenty of alcohol recovery houses in the city. Once inside the town, with its maze of streets and turn-of-the-century cottages, Dana found the atmosphere innocuous enough, but the sight of the Recovery House was appalling. It was obviously a converted, low-rent apartment house, its gray plastic siding cracked and broken away to reveal the cheap, raw lumber underneath. For landscaping, there was nothing but an asphalt parking lot with a few abandoned cars or pickups ready for the scrap heap. Apparently, a few square feet of lawn had once graced the courtyard between the buildings. It had been trodden away, leaving brown clay for flooring, with tufts of grass along the sidewalk's edge. People sat around at rickety wooden picnic tables looking idle and depressed. Most of them smoked cigarettes or drank coca-cola from cans. A young woman wearing jeans and a crocheted shawl looked up and smiled wanly at Dana in greeting.

"I'm looking for a guy named Charlie Redtree," said Dana.

"You have to ask in the office round back."

The reception office contrasted darkly with the sunlit courtyard. There were no windows. The only light came in through the open doorway and shown on the orange, Formica-topped reception counter behind which a wiry little man with shaggy hair bounced about shuffling papers. When Dana asked about Charlie, the man nodded and bounded out through the open door. Dana sat down in the waiting area, which consisted of three folding chairs along the wall.

Despite her eagerness to see Charlie, Dana felt vaguely apprehensive. She had not kept in touch with her cousin after she went away to college. She had written him a letter once, but he didn't answer, and Dana was much too busy to pursue him. Mom had said Charlie got a good job in construction and even belonged to the Union. When he worked, Charlie earned more money than Jim or Pam, but the work wasn't all that steady, especially during the winter months. The last time Dana had seen Charlie was at Aunt Theresa's memorial service. Stoop-shouldered like an old man, Charlie had stood at the foot of the casket. A black band circled the crown of his head, and the hair was pulled severely back into a tight ponytail. He wore a dark wool suit and one tiny, gold earring. A bouquet of red roses hung limply from his hands.

Lots of people had taken turns stepping forward and saying nice things about Theresa, but it was hard to tell whether Charlie was listening. He didn't react to anything. When his turn came at the very end, Charlie stepped forward and with trembling hands, draped his bouquet over the casket. "Bye, Mom," he said. "We'll all miss you, especially me. You were the best Mom... " Charlie broke off as if he were about to cry, and then stepped backwards into his place.

Afterwards Pam and Jim had a get-together for all the relatives who had come over from the islands, and it had created quite a stir when Charlie didn't show up.

News of Charlie had been scarce after that, and mostly bad. He had lost his job in construction after getting in a fight with his boss, and had then taken a job on a fishing boat in Alaska. No one knew what happened with that job, but Pam said Charlie hitchhiked all the way home from Fairbanks along the Al-Can Highway.

Dana stood up when a black silhouette appeared in the doorway. As Charlie pivoted and his face caught some light from the doorway, Dana noticed a solemn intensity in his gaze that was also evident in his hammer-lock embrace of a greeting. It was the kind of unequivocal hug Marlon Brando, as the imperial Godfather, would have given one of his subjects. "Hi, old friend. What's up?" he said, letting go of Dana and wiping away a furtive tear with the hairy back of his hand.

That there had been some sort of change in Charlie was evident. For one thing, he had short, blow-dried hair and wore a sports coat, almost like he had turned preppy. He didn't even offer to take Dana on a tour of the compound. Instead he said, "Let's take a walk. I told my counselor it'd be safe to go off with my teatotaler cousin." Then he charged resolutely in a given direction through the streets of the town. Dana suspected his destination might be a tavern or crack house, but she followed doggedly, even at her peril, as Charlie jaywalked across busy four-lane thoroughfares, ignoring traffic lights. Eventually, he turned off the paved streets onto a path leading down through some alder trees and out along a levy above the river. Below, several children screamed and splashed by on inner tubes as they dodged rocks and driftwood snags. The water looked cold and inviting in its opaque greenness.

So intent was her cousin upon heading for his destination that Dana was hesitant to interrupt him by trying to make conversation, so they walked in silence. Maybe he had a stash hidden in the bushes. Dad warned that Charlie had made many aborted attempts at sobriety, so it was difficult to trust him.

After they had walked about a half-mile along the path, Charlie suddenly dropped onto a steep way-trail leading down the embankment through a tangle of blackberry briars. Before Dana could catch up, her cousin had completely disappeared. Maybe this was where he kept the stuff.

Soon emerging from the tangle of bushes and briars, Dana found herself on a sandbar beside the river. Charlie's clothes, even his new sports jacket, lay upon a rock, piled as haphazardly as dirty laundry.

Barechested, Charlie stood waist-deep in what appeared to be an ideal swimming hole. He seemed intent upon the question of whether to take the plunge and submerge himself fully. "It's pretty cold," he said.

Dana peered across at the apartment houses, duplexes and lawns lining the opposite bank.

"There are lots of people around," she observed.

As if he had taken Dana's remark as a prod or cue, Charlie drifted gently into the current and began to breaststroke across the hole, but the current carried him on down. Crouching down to keep his lower body submerged, he waded back upstream.

Dana took off her shoes and socks and waded carefully into the stream. Sharp rocks bit and gouged at her toes and arches. The water was so cold, that her entire body was completely cooled by the time her knees were submerged. It would have felt good to go skinny-dipping like Charlie, but this swimming hole wasn't private enough.

After several minutes of swashing about, Charlie stood up and walked back up onto the sandbar. "This is a great place to cool off," he mused as he stood casually before her, naked, except for the little streams of water dripping from his stomach and thighs. Dana glanced again at the apartment houses across the way. "You should get dressed, Charlie. Someone will see you."

"That's all right, I'm sober," said Charlie. But he quickly retrieved his boxer shorts from the pile of clothing and put them on. Then he sat down on a log.

"What has sobriety got to do with it?" asked Dana.

"If someone thinks I'm skinny-dipping because I'm drunk or stoned, they're wrong."

"That's great, Charlie, but you still have to conform to basic rules of society — like wearing clothes in public."

Charlie gestured with a downward wave of his hand and shrugged. "Too bad they have so many rules. For instance, here I am without a towel and needing to dry off in the sun before I put on my clothes. Now my shorts are wet." He sat down on the rock and closed his eyes facing the sun.

Dana waded out of the water and stood barefoot on the warm sand, her body casting a long shadow over Charlie. He had spoken very little during their half-hour walk. When Dana asked him anything, Charlie had answered as briefly as possible, so Dana had taken the hint and remained mostly silent herself. Now Charlie sat silently again with his eyes closed. He seemed to be avoiding her.

She sat down cross-legged on the sand and looked at him. "I've come a long way to visit with you, Charlie. Don't you want to talk?"

Charlie opened his eyes and smiled at Dana. It was a warm smile reflecting pure joy and relief. Then he shook his head emphatically. "No," he said, "I don't want to talk. They've done nothing but talk ever since I came here two months ago. Thank God, you're here, my dear old cousin. I'm not real good at talking, but at the Recovery Center they think the only way to communicate is to talk." Charlie's intense, dark eyes narrowed to tiny gleaming slits. "You know a much better way," he said. Then he closed his eyes and faced the sun again.

That was when it dawned on Dana that Charlie wanted her to go into a trance and basically read his mind. It was the first time anyone had ever asked her to do this. In fact, it was the first time anyone had ever accused her of being able to do it. She had furtively read Charlie's mind several times while they were growing up. Thinking back though, he had been a pretty willing subject every time, giving her opportunities on long bike rides or afternoons at the beach on Levin Island. After each of those sessions, there had been a closeness between them even if they had been quarreling or irritable beforehand.

Perhaps if she had thought about it on a conscious level, Dana would have acknowledged Charlie knew what was happening to him, but they had never referred directly to the mind reading, and Charlie had always kept his cool during the sessions, never getting alarmed or excited about it. Sometimes he had joked with other kids about his cousin being a "spook," but he seemed to be bragging, as if he liked her that way. Dana closed her eyes and looked toward the sun as Charlie was doing. All the fatigue she had felt from her long trip faded into a universe of space and time. Sounds of the town with its cars and traffic jams, the calls of children playing in the river, all disappeared, along with her worries, into the great void. Gradually there arose an overwhelming sadness, like a cold, gray dawn within the void, and Dana recognized that feeling as Charlie's grief. She sat with Charlie a long time, with his mental pain closing in around them like shapeless fog, before it began to take on the forms of distinct memories. There were framed photographs of Charlie's dad on his mom's dresser when he was so small that he had to climb up on the stool to look at them. There was Dana with her father, and Charlie's friend Kim Lui with his father, and Charlie feeling like there must be something wrong with him because he had no father. There was Uncle Jim trying, in so many ways, to be a father to him, and Charlie knowing he couldn't be important to Jim the way Dana was. There was the tiny, shabby mobile home Grandma Redtree lived in on the reservation and Grandma Krandle's big farmhouse at Klahowya Cove and Charlie not knowing which of these vastly different worlds he belonged to, if either. There was the bright, articulate little boy that died the day he fell from the viaduct, and the impulsive bungler who took his place. Here the sadness turned to resentment, and Dana felt the return of old guilt feelings.

Dana's response to Charlie's thoughts with her own feelings introduced a new element into the trance. Charlie immediately perceived those feelings and responded in turn with forgiving thoughts. His sadness changed to fond memories of the gangly giant of girl cousin who looked after him, spoiled him to an irritating degree, who took an almost unhealthy interest in him. Then she was gone, quite suddenly "away at college," a condition of those more privileged than Charlie. The sadness returned with frustration. His sweet, generous mother, bald and weak from chemotherapy, and Charlie, hoping against all hope that she would get well, only to have his hopes repeatedly shattered with each progressive exacerbation of the illness. Then there was darkness, nothing but void and sadness.

After an indeterminable amount of time, Dana and Charlie opened their eyes simultaneously and looked at one another. "You've had some tough times, Charlie," said Dana.

Charlie shrugged and began mechanically putting on the rest of his clothes. Most of the way back they talked idly about news of the family. Dana told Charlie about Pam being passed over for a promotion to manager of her department and how Pam and Jim had been quarreling a lot lately about little things, how Grandma Ruth and Uncle Marvin were getting along well on the farm and how Grandpa Ben hated the nursing home.

They stopped at an espresso cart in front of a supermarket, and sat at a park bench, quietly sipping frothy latté's from white paper cups. "How do you plan to stay sober after you get out of treatment, Charlie?" Dana asked quite suddenly, breaking a long silence.

Charlie didn't answer at first, and Dana was afraid she might have offended him. She expected him to respond with some sarcastic version of "It's none of your business." Finally he just said simply, "I'm court ordered to attend A.A. three times a week."

"Will that be enough?"

"No, I've got to stay away from those bums I was hangin' around with. They're a bunch of boozers and crack-heads. That's why I'm moving down here to the suburbs."

"I think you need something else, Charlie."

"Sure, I probably need a lot else, but what else is there? I have to make do like everybody."

"I think you need something to live for," offered Dana.

"Like what?"

"Something meaningful in your life."

At first Charlie looked perplexed like he thought Dana was asking him a riddle and the answer was beyond him. Then suddenly he brightened as if the solution had dawned on him. "Oh you mean like religion or somethin'. I thought about going over to live on the reservation. Maybe become a shaman. I just can't relate to that Christian stuff." Charlie tossed his cup in the trash can and stood up as if to move on. Dana followed, still sipping her coffee as Charlie punched the traffic signal and waited for the light to change.

Coming up behind, she said, "Charlie, I've been thinking you should try to go to college." She had picked up on that wish of Charlie's during the meditation. He had always felt miserable that Dana went to college without him. If Charlie could commit to something, even something difficult, maybe that would help keep him sober. His face lit up almost imperceptibly at the suggestion of college, but he doused the flames quickly. "I ain't college material." he declared emphatically.

"You could do it Charlie. Mom and Dad and I would help you, if you stayed sober."

"How? Why?"

"Because it's what you want. Besides, college would open up more opportunities for you."

"What opportunities?"

"A better job, maybe."

Charlie scoffed. "Lots of guys working in the Alaska canneries have college degrees."

"Are you planning to get back into construction work, Charlie?"

He shrugged. "I don't know if I can get a job. I tried before, but no one would hire me. That's why I ended up on the streets."

"Why didn't you move in with Mom and Dad?"

"They said they wouldn't take me in unless I got sober and got a job. But if I was sober and had a job, I probably wouldn't need them to take me in. I'd rather be on my own anyway."

"Charlie, I think you should live with me and Mom and Dad and go to community college."

"I can't afford that."

"You can't afford not to either. Besides, we would help in every way possible, if you stayed sober."

Charlie looked at her suspiciously out of the corner of his eye. "Now, why would you want to do that? Don't you have better things to do?"

"No, nothing. Nothing could be more important. It would give me a sense of purpose. You see, I need something to live for, too."

"That's good for the next few years. What will either of us live for after that?"

"You'll learn a lot of things in college, Charlie. You might even learn about something to live for. Education is more than preparation for the job market.

"I know," said Charlie. "That's why I envy those who go to college."

"So, I was right. You do want to go."

"Sure, but how are you going to help pay my way through college when you don't have a job yourself."

"I've been offered a job. I just haven't taken it yet."

"What kind of job?"

"Assistant Manager of the Volume Shoe Store next door to the bicycle shop in Wallingford."

"How much does it pay?"

"Six dollars an hour."

"Dana, did you go to college for four years and major in psychology so you could work in a shoe store?"

"No, but it's the only job offer I've had so far. To do anything in psychology, you need at least a Master's Degree. Then you still don't earn a lot."

They had been walking briskly side by side until that moment when Charlie suddenly stopped and whistled through his teeth. "Say, that reminds me — Sullivan House is looking for a new attendant counselor. They want someone with a four-year degree in psychology."

"Yeah, but how many hundred applicants do they have?"

"I don't think they have too many. Sullivan House is a dump, and the job pays six dollars an hour, just like your Volume Shoe Store."

"Yeah, what's Sullivan House, besides a dump, that is?"

"Sullivan is sort of a halfway house for people coming out of the State Mental Hospital. It's in the same compound as the Recovery House right across the courtyard. If you're interested in the job, you ought to pick up an application while you're here. The attendant counselor doesn't do that much, just gives out meds, does paperwork, sits around jawin' with folks. Stuff like that."

"Sure," said Dana. "Sure, I'll apply. Sullivan House couldn't be worse than Volume Shoe Store, and if I get the job, you'll go to college and attend A.A. meetings."

Charlie grabbed Dana and clamped her in another death-grip, loving embrace. "Maybe I've had a rough life otherwise, but I've got one hell of a girl cousin."

SULLIVAN HOUSE ~ JUNE, 1998

Dana drained the last dregs of tepid coffee from her mug and placed it on the desk beside the phone. It was after nine, and Charlie had promised to call from Eastern Washington by now.

Idly, she switched on the computer, even though she didn't expect to get much work done. In less than half an hour she would have to go in and start the meditation group. Meanwhile interruptions by residents would make it difficult to concentrate, as would her own excitement about plans for the weekend. And, although she hated to admit it, Dana was still worried about Charlie having a relapse. It wasn't like him not to call.

Of course, this problem was entirely hers, not Charlie's. Charlie had finished a two-year engineering technology degree in three years, which was better than average these days, what with the overcrowding in community colleges. He had done it pretty much on his own, spending most evenings in the math lab. In fact, Charlie had performed so well that he had been offered an internship, then a full-time paid position at the Hanford Nuclear Reservation. But even that worried Dana. The job was in "Hazardous Waste Handling," and Dana wondered what that really meant. Would Charlie glow in the dark or develop some ugly form of cancer? Still, her cousin seemed fulfilled and happy. For him, it was enough to have a job, any job, where he was treated with respect and could use some of those precious abilities he had worked so hard to salvage from the wreckage of his head injury.

The phone range at nine fifteen, but it was not Charlie. Karen Simeona's voice shrieked into the phone, demanding to know whether Dana had seen the note she left on her desk. Dana had seen the note insisting that Karen be assigned a new roommate. Martha Parks was getting on her nerves, as if that were news.

Dana crooned monotonously into the phone. "No one wants to trade roommates." She hadn't really looked into the matter, but it was safe to assume that no one wanted to room with either Karen Simeona or Martha Parks. They were disagreeable people, or as Dr. Wong would have it, "borderline personalities," one with histrionic and the other agoraphobic qualities. Dana would make sure they both got single rooms eventually, but meanwhile they were both growing in the experience of learning to live with one another.

"So, that means I'm stuck with Martha?" Karen's voice whined like a power drill piercing Dana's inner ear.

"Well, yes, for now, unless you move out, or someone else moves."

"I won't spend another minute in the same room with Martha Parks."

Impassively, as if hypnotized, Dana reached for her appointment book. The only opening that day was at four-thirty and she was supposed to leave at five. Oh well, she seldom left before six or seven anyway. Then after the long bike ride, she would arrive home barely in time to soak in the tub and go to bed. But she was interested in finding out what might happen in another session between Karen and Martha.

It was during last Thursday's meeting that Dana had discovered a new dimension of her abilities. Incredibly, it appeared that from within the depths of a profound trance, she could help other people read minds. As yet, Dana could not comprehend how it worked, but, whereas in prior sessions Karen and Martha had been tight-lipped and strained with one another, this time they had suddenly begun a deep and meaningful dialogue. It had been a rancorous session with Karen squawking and Martha whining in her pathetic way. Yet there had been some remarkable revelations with very little restraint. The meditation portion of the meeting had lasted more than an hour. Upon first entering the blue light, Dana had calmly, nonjudgmentally, watched Karen and Martha's chaotic thoughts raging within the sphere of mental energy. It had been difficult. Then Dana had found herself attending only to the light, as though it were a sunset, with Karen and Martha's thoughts floating on their own, like shapeless clouds. Dana lost consciousness.

When she came out of the trance, Karen was talking very fast, but in soft, sympathetic tones.

"You need to quit hiding under your table all the time, Martha," Karen was saying. "You need to get out and look at the sunshine, open the drapes once in awhile. You've been hiding in the dark since you were a kid."

"I don't like the drapes open. People can see into the room from the street. I wish you didn't insist on opening the drapes all the time, and it's a journal, not a diary."

"Who can see in from the street? We live on the third floor. The giant trolls in your hallucinations aren't real, Martha."

"Yes, they are, and you are one of them."

The meeting had continued in this vain for another half-hour with Dana listening in stunned silence. Here were two psychotic personalities, previously cut off from the rest of society, sharing intimate knowledge of one another's fantasies in a comfortable, offhanded way. Martha never spoke of her hallucinations, Karen must have viewed them firsthand during the trance.

Dana had no idea how long it might have continued, but suddenly the telephone rang, stopping Karen in the middle of a sentence.

"Just ignore the phone," said Dana. "The machine will answer."

But Karen did not finish her sentence. Instead she stared at Dana in apparent shock ,as if Dana and the phone were intruders who had no right to be there, let alone interrupt.

Then Martha intoned, "We've taken up enough of your time, Dana. We really should go." To Dana's added amazement, Martha had turned to Karen, her former arch enemy and said, "We can continue our discussion upstairs." Then they both stood up, and without another word, walked out together.

It had taken a lot of thought for Dana to figure out that Karen and Martha must have shared thoughts during her trance, but there was no other logical explanation, unless Karen read Martha's journals, which were locked and on her person at all times. "What time do you get off work today, Karen?" Dana intoned mechanically. She didn't want to appear too eager to meet with Karen and Martha. That might make them defensive.

"Four."

"Good. Maybe you and Martha could come to my office at four-thirty. We'll have a meditation exercise, and then talk things out."

"Well, all right, we'll try," Karen moaned in her most conciliatory manner. She always sounded barely persuaded when she was actually getting her way.

"Okay. See you then." As she hung up, Dana noted that it was already time for the morning meditation group, and there had been no message from Charlie.

She hurried upstairs to the meeting hall where most of the group was already assembled. The oldest member was a frail-looking woman in her late fifties, but most were young adults of various sizes and physical types. Some sat on couches and chairs, others crouched on cushions or lay flat on their backs on the floor. All wore sweat pants or jogging shorts and running shoes.

The group was well-trained. Several already appeared to be meditating, their eyes closed, breathing slowly and rhythmically as the tape player emitted a soft Gregorian chant. Several of Dana's best character drawings of residents looked down from frames on the otherwise bare, white walls. A semi-abstract sculpture of a vaguely human form stood on a small table in the center of the room. One of the residents had made the statue in art therapy.

Dana took roll mentally before closing the door and settling herself inconspicuously into one of the cushions on the floor. She positioned herself so that the overhead lights cast brightly colored patterns on her closed eyes. It was time now to let go of her own concerns by quietly watching the lights as she had taught the group members to do. When thoughts or emotions arose, they were to watch them in the same manner as they watched the patterns of color on their eyelids without placing value or blame. It had not taken the group long to perfect this technique, which had a calming effect upon them. Soon Dana's mind was absorbed in the collective relaxation trance, and her own relaxation and emptiness of mind enhanced the collective mood.

The tape played several minutes of the relaxing chant, before the music grew more rhythmic and melodic. Dana and the others stood up slowly, one after another, and began jogging or skipping in place. All the while they breathed in slowly, filling their lungs with air and then exhaling very slowly. Meanwhile the tape recorder began emitting affirmations in a soft, female voice along with the music, "Every day in every way, I get better and better," whispered the voice, over and over, in rhythm with music that gradually grew faster and faster.

The music had gradually, almost imperceptibly, transformed itself to classic rock, and everyone was dancing with relaxed joy. With each inhale the collective mind would say, "Every day in every way," and with each exhale, "I get better and better." The fast, steady tempo was maintained for several minutes before it began slowing down again, gradually finding the group at rest on their cushions, couches, and chairs, deep in a group meditative trance.

When the music stopped, the group members gradually opened their eyes. Some of them made eye contact and smiled. Others stood up and hugged one another. Within a few minutes, everyone had left, and Dana still sat alone on the cushion.

Despite her concern about whether Charlie would leave a phone message, Dana was reluctant to leave the meeting hall. Aerobic meditation group was her favorite part of the day, not only because it was as therapeutic for her as for the residents, but because it had secured her place in the mental health field. To all outward appearances, the system was not unlike many popular therapies, but Dana was the only counselor who had developed and implemented an elaborate research study to test its value.

She had worked with four groups of six chronically mentally ill patients who had been on psychotropic medications for several months to years. One group participated in the meditation therapy while still taking medications. One participated while gradually being weaned to placebos. One group continued on medicine with no meditation therapy. One group was weaned to the placebo without the therapy. By all standards of measurement — patient journals, case management reports, frequency of hospitalization — the healthiest patients were the ones with the combined meditation therapy and placebo. Dana's study would have been considered a breakthrough, if others had been able to reproduce it, but so far, no one had. Still, most Sullivan House residents swore by the therapy and looked forward to it eagerly each day. Many even claimed that, besides controlling their depression, hallucinations, moods and symptoms, it kept them from getting colds and other physical ailments. One participant was a diabetic whose internist maintained that his condition had stabilized.

She returned to her office to find a stack of phone messages on her desk. One was from Charlie saying he would call back later.

There was also a message from Mom. Dana had found herself concerned as much lately about Mom as about Charlie. It seemed a bad sign that Mom was not going with Dad on his three-month tour of Europe. Lots of excuses had been given, mostly centering around finances. Mom said she had used up most of her vacation time helping her own mother move to a retirement home, and the rest finding a renter to replace Marvin in the house on Levin Island. Mom also insisted that taking a long leave of absence without pay would threaten her position as Fashion Buyer at Nordstrom for which she had worked so hard all these years. Mom had even railed against Dad spending the money on a vacation when it could have been put to more practical uses, like paying off college loans and contracting for household repairs. But these were excuses. There was a time when Mom would have given anything to go to Europe with Dad.

When Dana tried to return her mother's call, she got a voicemail message saying Pamela Krandle was away from her desk at the moment, but would return the call. Dana couldn't return Charlie's call because he didn't leave a phone number.

The rest of the messages were work related, one resident's mother and two case managers. By the time she had returned those calls and solved everyone's problems, it was lunch time. As usual, Dana bought lunch from the residents' dining hall because the price was right and the food pretty good. She took her tray outside and ate in the courtyard, while admiring the row of potted red geraniums she had arranged along the south face of the building. Afterwards she took a brisk walk, rushing to be back in case Charlie would phone during the lunch hour.

Dana had counseling appointments scheduled back-to-back all afternoon, and Charlie managed to get through at four o'clock. The conversation proved one of the more stressful of the day.

"Hi, Dana. It's Charlie."

"Hello, Charlie. Good to hear your voice. What's up?"

"Hey, Dana. Sorry, I didn't phone this morning. I took the bus out to Hanford and left the cellular in the car. When I got to the nearest pay phone, I called, but you were already gone. I'm awfully sorry."

"That's okay, Charlie. Things like that happen."

"Yeah, shit happens, as they say. Luckily, once in a while something nice happens…"

There was a pause while Dana waited for Charlie to finish the sentence. Maybe there was something he was reluctant to tell her. Maybe he was stoned.

"Is everything all right, Charlie?" He'd better not back out of the cycling trek. They had been planning the trip since Christmas. In April they had paid the sixty-five dollars each for enrollment.

"Yeah, everything's fine, great in fact."

"Good, so what's new? Are we still on for the weekend?"

"What's new? Well, it's high time I told you...I got a new girlfriend."

"Hey, that's great, Charlie!" Dana hastened to respond as enthusiastically as possible, although she didn't have much faith in Charlie's taste in women. Despite the fact that Charlie was quite handsome, he wasn't much of a lady's man, and his previous affairs had been fiascoes. Melissa Start had turned out to be a druggie. She got Charlie into all sorts of trouble, and then ditched him for another guy when she found out about Charlie's disability. It was hard not to be skeptical about Charlie and girls. But, come to think of it, he had not had a serious relationship since he got sober. Everything else with Charlie was better now. Maybe his love attempts would be more successful, too. "Well, uh, that's nice, Charlie. Is this a serious girlfriend?"

"Well, we haven't known each other very long, but we have a really nice relationship. Rosey is real good to me. I'd like you to meet her. She reminds me of you."

"Is she a cyclist?"

"Is she a what?"

"A cyclist?"

"A what?"

"Does she ride a bicycle?"

"Well, yes, of course. Well, I think so. Although right now she doesn't have one. She lives in a small apartment."

"Oh," said Dana, although the causal relationship between living in a small apartment and not owning a bicycle was not immediately obvious to her.

"Over here people don't ride much. Places are so far apart."

"I thought you said there was a bicycle path."

"Sure, but it doesn't go anywhere. I mean, it's just for fun, not for getting you anywhere."

"Oh."

"Does that mean you don't want to meet Rosey — just because she doesn't have a bicycle? Must she have a bicycle to be a nice person?"

"Well, no, Charlie, of course not. I'm sure she's nice. When do you want me to meet her? This weekend?"

"No. You can't meet Rosey this weekend. She's supposed to be a bridesmaid in her sister's wedding Saturday night."

"Oh." Dana didn't readily follow that reasoning either. She had heard that weddings could be time consuming, but if Dana was going to be in town to meet Charlie for the bike trek, couldn't Rosey take a few minutes to get introduced to her boyfriend's cousin?

Charlie, apparently sensing the misunderstanding, hastened to add. "The wedding's in Denver."

"Oh. Well, good. Then she'll be out of town and busy while you're on the trip. She won't miss you that much."

There followed a pause so long that Dana said, "Are you still there, Charlie?"

"Yeah, sure, Dana, but I think, well, maybe you missed the point. I'm going with Rosey to the wedding. She has a real big family, and she wants me to meet everyone."

There was another long pause during which Dana tried to figure out how to feel about all this. She was, of course, angry and disappointed about Charlie canceling out on their plans. On the other hand, there seemed to be something positive about this. The fact that Rosey's sister was having a big, fancy wedding full of relatives was a good sign. None of Charlie's other girlfriends ever had much for families. Another good sign was that Rosey wanted her family to meet Charlie. That must mean she really liked him. Still, this was reminiscent of his irresponsible alcoholic days. "But, Charlie, we had plans this weekend. I already paid our registration for the bike trek."

"That's okay. I called Mike Silvers, the Bike Club President. They have people waiting for cancellations. We can easily sell the tickets."

"That's good, Charlie, but I've been looking forward to this for a long time."

"Say, Dana, maybe you ought to go anyway. There'll be lots of other nice people there. The Okanagon Trails Club are real salt o' the earth. Good folks."

"Sure, Charlie. Maybe I'll go anyway. You have a good time at your wedding in Denver. I'll have a good time in the mountains."

"That's the spirit, Dana. Say, we'll get together later in the summer, maybe go for a hike."

"Good idea. Does Rosey like to hike? You should bring Rosey so I can meet her."

"Sure, Dana. Talk to you later. Gotta go now." Charlie's voice reeked of naive self-satisfaction. He seemed pleased with himself for negotiating the narrow space between the horns of a difficult social dilemma without getting anyone too angry with him.

After hanging up the phone, Dana stared at the surface of her desk for awhile. She hated to admit she felt like a middle-aged mother with a touch of empty nest syndrome. She had expended a lot of emotional energy over the years mothering Charlie. What if it turned out he didn't need her after all? What if he was perfectly capable of looking out for himself, establishing healthy relationships, finding fulfillment on his own? Well what if? What a relief! She would keep her fingers crossed that this Rosey would take good care of Charlie. As for Dana, she would find something else.

Before Dana had time to imagine even one possible candidate for that mysterious "something else," Karen's shrill voice shattered her mind space. "Where's Martha?" Karen demanded, dropping her bulk into the most comfortable armchair beside Dana's desk. The chair complained in small squeaks but miraculously held together.

"I don't know," said Dana. "I left her a message on her voicemail."

"Martha never checks her voicemail."

"She should be here any minute," soothed Dana. "Martha didn't have to work today."

"Martha hardly ever has to work. She might as well be laid off for all she works."

"Dr. Wong says Martha should only work part-time. She can't take the stress of a full-time job yet."

"That's baloney. Martha's just lazy. She wants to stay on Social Security."

Dana shrugged nonchalantly. "I guess it's Martha's choice not to work full-time — if she doesn't mind being poor."

"That's easy for you to say. She doesn't have access to your fridge."

"Karen, please do me a favor and wait for Martha to get here before you start complaining about her."

Karen agreed, but even so continued squawking pretty much in the same vein until Martha appeared in the doorway, a small dark sparrow of a person with a narrow face and bulging eyes. Dana greeted Martha cheerfully, and invited her to sit in the other comfortable chair directly facing Karen. Martha skittered softly into the room and perched on the edge of the chair, affixing a glossy stare upon something invisible on the floor. Martha had once confided in Dana that appearing to be mentally absent while physically present was a good defense. She said the world was full of mean and angry people, but they would only attack present, and therefore vulnerable, people.

As usual, Karen and Martha avoided greeting one another, but when Dana introduced the session with the words, "We will begin with a meditation," the two women flashed split-second, almost simultaneous glances at one another before the lids fell like curtains over their eyes.

Dana put on a tape of soft chamber music and gently instructed them to focus on the present moment, attending to whatever was happening within the space of their current experience — including thoughts, feelings, and sensations. She urged them not to judge or control, but simply to watch, even if the thoughts seemed to be coming from outside themselves, perhaps from the mind of the other. So saying, Dana watched the darkness and light before her own mind's eye, until it entered the blue light and was suspended there, sustaining a collective trance.

Somewhere out there within the space of the trance, Karen's and Martha's brain waves moved about, but Dana paid little heed to specific details. Instead she focused solely on the blue light as she had done in the previous session. Only this time she remained conscious enough to stop the meditation when the flow of energy was at its height.

Dana signaled the end of the meditation by turning off the tape. With that, the two women opened their eyes simultaneously. They were looking at one another now very intently with sympathy and concern. It was the same look that had first clued Dana that they might have gained access to one another's thoughts. Martha spoke first. Despite her meeker persona, Martha was tougher than Karen. After all, she had lived on the streets of Seattle more than half her life.

Dana had first seen Martha two years before beside the bike path under the freeway. She lay on a bench, wrapped in a tattered sleeping bag, using what looked like a small notebook and backpack for a pillow. She had been there for several consecutive mornings. A crudely painted cardboard sign beside her read, "I'll work for food."

Dana had not stopped the first time, but when the same crippled sparrow of a creature called out to her on the following morning, Dana stopped and silently placed her business card into the woman's hand. The large, birdlike eyes blinked once and then opened wide in amazement.

Dana had hurried on then without saying a word. The card would speak for itself, both by informing the woman that Dana was no guileless passerby to be taken advantage of, and by providing the address and phone number of a good residential treatment program. Dana had not really expected to see the woman again and had been amazed when many months later, the haunting aquiline face passed her in the courtyard between Sullivan House and the Recovery Center.

Even though her eyes spoke understanding and concern as she gazed into Karen's, Martha's retained the armor of her words. "You're such a self-centered little bitch," she twittered.

"Remember the rule," warned Dana. "Name-calling isn't allowed."

"I share everything I have with you, Karen, and you hoard everything for yourself."

"Bull shit! You have nothing besides that dumb diary and you keep that locked up. Meanwhile, you consume two-thirds of everything I buy. I'm damned well supporting you, and you won't get a full-time job. You want to sponge off everyone else instead. They should have thrown you out of here long ago."

"I only borrow a few drops of shampoo now and then. Then I offer you things in return. Like last week, I gave you half my pizza."

"We've been over this before. I know you were totally neglected in childhood. I know you were sexually abused by your father. Big deal! Who wasn't sexually abused? That doesn't give you license to clean me out. I shouldn't have to lock up my shampoo like you do your diary."

Martha looked solemnly at Karen. The large eyes glistened now with the hint of rising tears. "Have you ever noticed that your food takes up the entire refrigerator, and that your gallon bottles of shampoo, conditioner, lotion and God knows what else completely cover the surfaces of everything? Even if I could afford to buy supplies, there wouldn't be room for them."

Although the conversation seemed to be headed nowhere, Dana tried to resist any temptation to take the helm. Mostly Dana just listened for signs of how much Karen and Martha knew about one another that they could only have gleaned by direct access to private thoughts. There were innuendos, such as Karen's remark to Martha, "You think I'm your mother. You think I'm going to lock you in a dark closet and make you stay there all day." She didn't get that from Martha's diary or from Martha's mouth. Martha kept her past under lock and key.

"Karen, how do you know Martha's mother locked her in the closet?" asked Dana.

There was a profound silence while Karen gaped at Dana in bewilderment. "Didn't she say so? Awhile ago? Where were you?"

"Did you say that, Martha?" asked Dana.

"No. Karen read my mind again," said Martha nonchalantly.

"Are you sure?" Dana asked.

"Positive."

"Does that surprise you?"

"I guess so. Not really — it seems pretty natural at the time. Now that you mention it, I guess it seems odd."

"Does it upset you?"

Martha looked surprise. "No, not really. Karen and I don't like putting up with each other's habits, but at least she understands me. It's nice to be understood."

Karen and Martha seemed to enjoy the session so much that Dana almost had to be rude to get rid of them by a quarter to six. To further encourage their departure, she put on her bicycle helmet. But they didn't leave until she took her bicycle shoes out of the desk drawer and started changing her shoes. "Let's meet same time next week," called Dana to their retreating backs. When she went to close the window of her office before leaving, Dana saw the pair still conversing in chirps and shrieks from one of the picnic tables in the courtyard. They saw her and waved. "Don't forget — same time next week!" Dana called out.

Dana was about to walk out the door, when she remembered to check E-mail and turn off her computer. There was a letter from Mom. "I've tried several times to reach you by phone today. I have to work late tonight, then I'll be going out with friends. I won't be home until very late. Also, I read in the paper this morning that Dr. Holt, your old psychotherapist, died at the age of 97. There was a nice article about her in *The Seattle Times.*"

Dana turned off the computer and locked her office, then hurried out to her bicycle. She wasn't sure how to feel about Dr. Holt's death. Dana hadn't seen — or even thought much about — the therapist for a long time. Her loneliness was compounded by the realization that the only person who really understood her was gone.

She stopped at the corner mini-mart and bought *The Seattle Times.* Then she sat on the curb beside her bicycle and looked up the obituary. "...Dr. Diana Holt is survived by her many loved ones of the Eastside Women's Hiking Club. Her estate is bequeathed to the Club to continue their trail maintenance projects in the Cascade and Olympic wilderness areas. At the request of the deceased, her ashes will be tossed into the crater of Mount Rainier."

Tears streamed down Dana's cheeks as she folded up the newspaper and tucked it into her bicycle bag. Dr. Holt had known the dark secrets of Dana's mind, but Dana's knowledge of Dr. Holt's life had been limited. Dana would never have guessed that Diana had no family other than her hiking pals, and that the main focus of her life, not to mention her death, was trail maintenance. Maybe she should look up the Eastside Women's Hiking Club, and possibly attend the funeral.

EMMONS GLACIER TRAIL, MOUNT RAINIER ~ AUGUST, 1998

A light fog made the climb feel like a dream, with no connection to anything except the ever-present moment. Dana was in the center of one rope team between Rhona, the climb leader, and her friend, Monica. The slope was steeper than a normal staircase, and very slick. With each step, she placed her boot carefully into Rhona's footprint, then set her ice axe firmly and tested for security before moving the other foot. It was hard to believe that this was only the second day. It seemed as though she had been doing this forever, all of her energy having been expended way back in another eternity. The blue light had come for the first time that morning and had remained with her during lunch. It remained as she leaped across each of the yawning, gaping crevasses that appeared to salivate in its eagerness to devour anyone who might slip in. The thinness of the air helped Dana sustain the light through such experiences.

Dana's shoulders ached from the weight of the pack and she questioned her sanity in joining the Eastside Hiking Club on this climb up Mount Rainier. She should have had sense enough to abandon the idea of attending Dr. Holt's funeral when she found out what was on the program.

Dana had attended a club meeting for the purpose of signing up, only to learn that there was a prerequisite. Prior to this climb, she had to devote every weekend of the entire summer to taking a climbing course. From that, she had learned enough about camping on snow to know that she did not relish the experience. The bottom of the tent would get wet, and her long body would extend out over the end of her insulated pad. The foot of her sleeping bag would then soak up water like a wad of cotton. But Dana felt more comfortable with this group than in the climbing course. Their pace was slower for one thing. Best of all, Rhona Lind had a two-way radio sticking out of her pack, and every so often would converse with Anna, a forest ranger down below.

The first night they camped on a reasonably flat snowfield surrounded by darkness, running water, and the distant rumble of falling ice. Shivering in her polypropylene shirt and windbreaker, Dana held the flashlight while Rhona and Monica swiftly assembled a tidy igloo-shaped tent. Rhona was still wearing a sleeveless tank top. Her well-toned arm muscles rippled beneath smooth, tanned skin. "Are you sure this tent is large enough for the three of us?" Dana worried aloud. The club had insisted she needn't bring her own.

Rhona glanced up at Dana's flashlight long enough for it to catch the clarity of her smile and went on working. "Between us, Monica and I raised three kids in this tent."

Dana had concluded from such remarks that Rhona had to be at least forty-five, even though she could easily have passed for twenty-five. "Where are your kids now?"

"Off doing their own thing," said Monica, whose white curly hair and deep smile lines revealed her age. Dana held the flashlight while Monica, squatting on the snow, boiled water on the camp stove and poured it into the cups and bowls proffered by the others. The club's simple cooking ritual was completed by each climber stirring up her own hot beverage and instant soup. Dana's bowels were overstimulated by the altitude; after each meal she had to stumble off and deposit her excrement in one of the small plastic sacks provided for that purpose by the Ranger. Nothing could be left on the mountain — except Diana's ashes, which had been sterilized.

Dana's blue light remained through the fog of that second day while several climbers took turns setting up belays to cross a snow bridge over a horrendous crevasse. To one side was a deep well that glowed with its own turquoise light. There was no gauging its depth, but it might have been a visceral duct leading to the stomach of the glacial monster.

Dana took her turn setting up belay. She carefully stabbed her axe handle into the snow and wound the rope around it and her boot in a figure eight, creating a safety hold for Rhona, who crossed the bridge as casually as if it had been a stretch of city sidewalk. Next, Monica set the belay for Dana, who looked calmly at the snow bridge. Then, from within the transcendent state of blue light, she stepped forward.

In a split second of terror, the light dissolved. The snow bridge was collapsing, and she was falling. In the brief duration of a scream, Dana resigned herself to the likelihood of death. Then she stopped falling — the belay had worked. Dana was dangling from a delicate thread held by the boot of one unseen grandmotherly person above her. She was not dead, not yet. She looked up into the steady blue eyes gazing down at her over the edge. Rhona spoke slowly and calmly like a teacher instructing a child. "Monica has you on belay, and Christina's setting up another belay at the other end of the rope. It's caught on something. Can you get it loose?"

Dana was in a state of shock, but being asked a question had a rousing, soothing effect on her. In fact, she was flattered that Rhona assumed she could function at all, under such circumstances.

Dana felt around feebly for the rope. It extended from the round metal fastener at her chest, up and over her shoulder, then down the back of her boot. Below that, the rope was caught on the prongs of her crampons.

Dana loosened the rope from her crampons and let it slide between her legs. Someone above immediately pulled it tight. She felt a little more secure now, with the two belays, one at either end, holding on to her by the crotch, as if she were sitting in a swing. She waited, wondering what would happen next. How did they plan to get her out?

Rhona's face appeared again over the edge. "Hurry, Dana. Can you kick steps in the ice?"

Oh! That was it. They expected her to get herself out. Dana kicked and flailed furiously about for awhile, but there was nothing but air as far as her legs could reach in any direction. Rhona, although she couldn't see it from her vantage point, was standing on a thick, curved cornice with a cavern underneath. How could Dana climb such a thing? It was extremely slick and there was nothing to grab hold of.

Then she noticed the ice axe still dangling from her wrist by a thin leather strap. She grabbed the axe and carved a small hand-hold at chest level and a toehold as far down as she could reach. Using these, she was able to raise herself a little higher while someone pulled up the slack on the rope. Working more rapidly, Dana carved herself a ladder of small round toe-holds, and, using the ice axe as a cane, she climbed, clumsy as a crippled troll, up over the breast of snow.

Rhona's body was trembling as she gave Dana a hand up, and hugged her tightly. Dana's heart was pounding fast. She sucked in air, realizing that she had hardly breathed during the ordeal.

While the others waited wide eyed on the opposite side, Rhona, Monica, and Dana stepped carefully to where there was a narrower place to set up belay and jump across.

Dana's long legs cleared it easily, but Monica fell forward. Then she curled up like a baby possum, moaning and rubbing her ankle. "I think it's sprained," she said.

Rhona radioed to the forest ranger. "We have an injury," she said. "Monica hurt her ankle. Looks bad...swelling a little. She's limping."

"You think she can make it back?" Anna's voice snapped, crackled and popped out of the radio.

"No. The snow bridge collapsed. "We had to jump. She wouldn't make it back across. Is there some way she can be rescued?"

"Can she make it to the top?"

Rhona looked questioningly at Monica who nodded uncertainly. "She can make it up, but not back down."

"Good. She'll be medivacced by helicopter."

The rest of their push to the summit was scarcely bearable. Dana felt she had not an ounce of energy left, and it took more than that just to put one foot in front of the other. This was the notorious weakening effect of high altitude. Some of the women had diarrhea, so they had to stop frequently. This all might have been tolerable under trance conditions within the blue light, but after her terrible fright, the light did not return.

By the time they reached the summit and crater's edge, Monica could barely walk. Dana helped her down a little into the crater, out of the relentless wind. There was a cloud cover, so there wasn't any view. They would be lucky to see the wands with the little red flags, which Rhona had left to help them find their way back.

"What is the view like on a clear day?" Dana wondered out loud.

"Like from an airplane," said Monica.

"Speaking of air travel, I thought they were supposed to send a helicopter for Monica," said Dana.

"It's on its way," said Rhona. "I talked to Anna a few minutes ago."

"Who's going to pay for the helicopter? Surely medical evacuation services aren't provided by the Park Service," fretted Monica.

Rhona smiled sheepishly as her chapped, frozen lips would allow. "The chopper is paid for already. It's for a VIP and a newspaper reporter."

While Rhona was speaking, the sound of the chopper's engine could be heard in the distance, groaning closer. It wasn't an entirely welcome sound. Dana rather resented coming all this way at such peril, only to have civilization follow. But when the helicopter shape loomed out of the fog, screaming in high pitched rhythms, the other women cheered.

Monica sighed. "Lucinda Watson's in there, isn't she?" Her eyes glowed with a transcendent smile.

The other women cheered. "Good heavens! She made it! She's really here!"

Dana helped Monica up to a wide, flat spot on the crater's edge to watch the helicopter land. The other women were still cheering as the majestic black woman stepped out elegantly onto the snow. A long, dark overcoat hung down over the tops of her boots. Her hair was in a hundred miniature braids, her neck wrapped in a red plaid muffler.

Dana stared in shock. This was the same Lucinda Watson who had taught Contemporary World Problems at her high school. Dana had not laid eyes on the woman since, but Lucinda had kept her promise to keep in touch; each year she sent a Christmas newsletter describing her many exploits. The letters had been signed "Love, Lucy," which must be what Ms. Watson's friends called her. Dana had faithfully responded to each letter with a handwritten letter about the latest developments in her own life and in Charlie's.

The newspaper reporter, a tall thin man wearing an overcoat and no hat or gloves, stepped out and started taking pictures. The helicopter pilot handed Lucy a thermos and a stack of plastic thermal cups.

They all cheered even louder as Lucy filled the cups and passed around hot chocolate. In the process, she shook each of their hands and said, "Congratulations on reaching the summit. Have a safe trip down." Dana felt as if she were in a time warp, and she was on a field trip with her World Problems class, except Ms. Watson didn't seem to recognize her.

ALIEN CHILD

Everyone gulped the chocolate quickly and handed back the cups.
Rhona produced the bag of gray dust she had carried all the way
in her backpack. "It's time to bid our final farewells to our beloved
friend, Diana Holt. I've asked Lucy to offer a brief eulogy."
Lucy strode to the center of the circle. The ends of her muffler and
all her black braids danced wildly in the wind. "I promised to make
this very short, because I know you need to get down off this heap of
ice before dark," she began. "My God, it's a privilege to be here! I can
hardly believe I'm standing here at this moment.... It's even more of a
privilege to say goodbye to my dear friend and counselor, Diana Holt,
whose memory will always be alive in our hearts." Lucy nodded to
Rhona. Rhona flung the plastic bag, with obvious force, in the direction of the crater. The ashes flew out like gusts of gray smoke in all
directions, but mostly in the wind's direction — away from the crater.
Dana blinked, and wiped some of Diana's remains out of her eyes.
"Now, Monica will recite a short poem," said Rhona.
Monica closed her eyes. At first Dana thought that was to help
her recall the words, but then she noticed that everyone else's eyes
were closed as if in prayer. With her eyes still closed, Monica spoke
slowly. "*Mountain*, by Diana Holt. The Mountain fills the sky. It's
presence is the air. Climbing on the mountain is living in a prayer. The
Great Mother Mountain engulfs my soul. As I reach her holy summit,
I am finally made Whole." She opened her eyes. All the women em-
braced one another in a group hug.
"That was a nice recitation, both simple and profound," Dana
told Monica, as she helped her toward the helicopter.
While Dana supported Monica by one arm, Lucinda Watson approached and took hold of the other. Dana felt the urge to cry out,
but it jammed up in her throat. Lucy still didn't recognize her.
Monica climbed aboard, leaving small empty space between Dana's
face and Lucy's. The great whites of Lucy's eyes and her African nose
were close enough to kiss. "Do you remember me, Ms. Watson? I'm
Dana Krandle. I was in your Contemporary World Problems class in
the eleventh grade."
Lucy gawked at Dana for a moment. Then tears rose in her eyes as
she wrapped both heavily-coated arms around her. "Good God!
Imagine! Can this be true? I wanted so much to see you while I was
here in the Northwest, and here you are!" Dana felt torn. There wasn't
time to stand around and visit. Could such a rare opportunity not
really be one? "Will you be in the area long? I thought you were in
Eastern Europe." Lucy's last Christmas letter had come from there.
She was trying out a new conflict resolution system on some nation-
alist warring factions there.

"Yes, I've been in Albania also, but I'm speaking at the International Workers' Rights Conference in Portland next week. I hope you're planning to come. I'd love to see you." Lucy gave Dana another hug and climbed into the helicopter. The door closed behind her, and she waved through the window as the chopper disappeared behind a curtain of fog.

INTERNATIONAL WORKERS' RIGHTS CONFERENCE, PORTLAND ~ JULY, 1998

Dana stood beside Martha Parks at the fringes of the crowd that overflowed from the hotel conference room into the lobby. Dana had left early that morning in Mom's old Beetle. She had hoped to get a good seat, maybe even a chance to meet with Lucy before her speech. But the generator light had come on, necessitating a stop in Chehalis for a new voltage regulator. As she started back up the freeway ramp, Dana was confronted by a familiar, sparrowlike creature hoisting a makeshift "Portland" sign out into the thoroughfare. Clutched to her chest was the padlocked notebook she called her "journal."

Martha Parks seemed overjoyed when she recognized Dana. She slung her large pack deftly over the headrest onto the back seat and slunk down comfortably next to Dana, still hugging the journal.

"It's dangerous to hitchhike," scolded Dana.

"I know. I've been doing it all my life."

"What will you do in Portland?"

"I'm thinkin' of moving there."

"Really? Why?"

Dana could feel Martha's eyes dart in her direction. "Karen doesn't want me, and no one will trade rooms."

"Do you have a place to live in Portland?"

"Maybe. That's what I'm going to find out."

"Maybe?"

"Yeah. Friend of mine has a subsidized apartment. She's on welfare. I can babysit and share expenses."

Dana figured Martha might be hungry, so she stopped and bought them lunch. They sat in a Taco Bell parking lot eating large burritos from paper wrappers.

Martha asked, "What you gonna do in Portland?."

"Attend the International Workers' Rights Conference. A friend of mine's the keynote speaker."

"No kiddin'? That's cool. What's he gonna talk about?"

"She's giving a speech on international law. That's her specialty."

"Cool. How come you know such an elitist person?"

"Ms. Watson isn't elitist, at least she's not a snob. Otherwise, they wouldn't want her at a workers' rights conference. She taught me social studies in high school. We've kept in touch all these years."

Martha fell silent for a moment. Then she laughed, "I guess anybody with a job is elitist by my standards, let alone people like teachers and law professors. I never kept in touch with any of my teachers. They were probably glad to forget me. I was a troublemaker in school."

"If you had had Ms. Watson for a teacher, it might have been different. She cared about the students, found out where they were coming from at any given moment, and taught from there. She cast a spell on the whole class. No one was left out."

"Did she keep in touch with everybody all these years?"

Dana shrugged and laughed. "Maybe. I'll bet Lucinda Watson's Christmas letter has a circulation the size of People Magazine."

"Totally amazing! This lady must be something else! Think I'll tag along to hear the speech, if it's okay with you."

"Sure, that would be fine." Dana wasn't excited about spending the day with a client, but it would be good to expose Martha to a perspective different from her usual street culture.

By the time they arrived, there wasn't much hope of even getting in to see Lucy, let alone of sitting down. Fortunately, an excellent public address system broadcasted the proceedings from the microphones on stage to the entire building complex. Dana was taller than most and could see over the incredibly diverse throng of mostly women from all parts of the world. Some appeared to be lesbian couples; they stood in pairs and shared intimate looks and body language.

During her college years, Dana had taken part in several lesbian discussion groups in an effort to explore her own sexual identity. Dana had concluded that the gender of another individual had little to do with whether she loved them. Maybe she was a freak in this way too, but Dana had experienced few sexual feelings of any kind in her life so far. Her capacity for familial love and loyalty were intense, perhaps stronger than in others, but she had not yet "fallen in love," at least not as that act was portrayed in movies and literature. She had had strong feelings — Mom called it a "crush" — for Ms. Watson in high school, and there had been a similar attachment to Dr. Holt. She had harbored some romantic feelings recently for the heroic mountain climber, Rhona Lind, but there had been no mating desires that she could identify. Surely she would "fall in love" one day, but the gender of that unknown person was up for grabs. If it happened to be a woman, Mom might have to be protected from reality.

According to the program handout, they were just in time. Lucy was scheduled after the Holy Spirit Gospel Choir, which now swelled

the roof with a jazz rendition of "Amazing Grace." Dana felt spiritu-
ally and physically absorbed into the crowd which had closed in around
her. Martha was nowhere in sight.

Lucinda Watson was introduced by the president of the Portland
Women's Jobs With Justice League. "Lucinda Watson has spent her
life studying international law. She now works in the field of international conflict resolution. Ms. Watson has published widely on that
subject. Recent international treaty agreements have been authored
by corporations and have been the workers' enemy. Lucinda Watson,
however, sees international law as, potentially, the friend of working
people, provided it is enforced, and provided it is law — by and for
the people."

The woman's voice had an alarming high pitch, reminiscent of the
"depleted battery" signal on Pam's laptop computer, but that minor
annoyance served only to enhance Lucy's stronger voice, its melodious timbre second only to the Holy Spirit Gospel Choir.

This was truly the voice of a great person, and listening for traces
of her old favorite teacher, Dana was not disappointed. Lucy did not
make the slightest pretense of boring them with talk about international law, global economics, or conflict resolution techniques, the
subjects she was supposed to cover. In fact, she carried no notes and
apparently had not even prepared a formal speech any more than she
had ever planned her classes at University High School. She stood
before several thousand people, and tuning into their need to relieve
the stress of an over booked event, began telling the story of how she
had been arrested while trying to organize a child labor strike in
Manila. Soon everyone was laughing and having fun.

As Dana began to relax and feel herself drawn in, she became
aware of a powerful collective energy taking hold of the audience.
She must be careful not to let the blue light come. It would be so easy
to get into the mood and enhance it. If she did that, this large crowd
might willingly follow Lucinda Watson to the ends of the Earth.

That thought frightened Dana so much that she turned to leave,
but the crowd had closed in, leaving no escape route. A solid wall of
bodies, perhaps a hundred feet thick, stood between her and the hotel
exit. On the other hand, when she turned again to face into the Conference Hall, she found the crowd in front had given way, leaving a
path into it. What's more, she felt a suction of psychic energy pulling
her down that path like a bit of debris into a vacuum cleaner.

Once inside the hall, Dana recognized Rhona Lind and Monica
seated at the end of a row near the back. They were holding hands.
The obvious had not occurred to Dana, even though she had spent
two consecutive, very cold nights in the same tiny tent with them. To

Dana's amazement, one empty folding chair waited, as if reserved for her, directly behind Rhona. Although there were hundreds of other people standing around, no one had taken the empty chair. Perhaps they were far too enthralled with the speaker, a dark mountain of a woman who stood center stage before the microphone. She was robed in a bright African-style print with appliqued splashes of orange, yellow and red satin. Her hair was still arranged in the same braided style she had worn on the mountain top less than one week before, but now it was crowned with a great African turban that matched her robe. In high school, Dana had been impressed with Lucy's presence, enhanced as it had always been with a variety of tasteful clothing, but this outfit verged on the ostentatious.

Dana leaned forward and buried her head in her hands. It was hard not to succumb to the collective adoration of the powerfully entertaining Lucinda Watson, even if you could not see her, but the visual was too much.

There didn't appear to be anything controversial about Lucy's opening themes. "Every little kid is important!" she cried out. "Every human being on this Earth is precious! Listen. Just listen!" She sang these simple admonitions like nursery rhymes, into the microphone. Then she described violent street gang members in her hometown of Chicago and homeless children she had spoken with in Manila and Bombay. She really had her audience by that time.

In the second half-hour, Lucy began to decry the concentration of a majority of the Earth's resources into the hands of very few while the vast majority of its children endured hunger and homelessness. "The corporations that control the Earth's resources are international, and are not accountable to any government or body of laws. By the terms of what they call "trade agreements," these organizations have established an unelected form of world government of, by, and for wealthy elites, with no accountability to the people. Global corporations have more rights than most national governments. The United Nations Charter must be revised and given lion's teeth to protect the lamb. The United Nations must be transformed into a representative government truly responsive to people's needs. These corporations own everything. They own our food sources, the air we breathe, the water we drink. They even own our DNA, the stuff from which we are made. They control our information sources, the media, in which they distract us with trivial sex scandals and encourage us to quarrel with one another, instead of focusing our attention on a real enemy — them. Manipulated by this media, the Earth's peoples grovel for the few remaining crumbs of her resources, crumbs insufficient to feed their families. We quarrel, make war with, and blame one another. It's a stealthy process. Big companies come in promising jobs and prosperity. They buy up all the land, the mineral rights, the water rights. Property values skyrocket. The local currency becomes worthless. Local governments borrow from the International Monetary Fund to pay for infrastructure to attract and support this so called expansion, and pass the debt on to the people. The local economy is devastated. Nobody can afford anything, let alone an acre of land to grow food. In the wake of all this destruction, what is left? Poverty, crime, sex slavery, children imprisoned in factories. But the wealthy profiteers live far away in their gated mansions and do not see the people suffering.

"Our only hope, I believe is in international law, in a carefully crafted international constitution, a new kind of law created of, by and for the people. Now, I'm not talking about laws created by the corporations like these so-called "trade agreements" we have in place. I'm talking about an international representative government responding not to corporate need, but to the people's need. We need government that protects the rights of workers and ensures the safety of every local environment around the world. You may wonder whether this can be done. I believe it can. I have spent many years studying the law and the process of formulating laws. If carefully planned — with the peoples' help, with your help it can be done. We can do it."

Dana began to feel faint as the audience applauded hysterically. In fact, she was surrounded by a tremendous collective energy force so strong that it was difficult to concentrate on what was being said or to resist the absorption of her own brain waves into the collective. Eventually, she succumbed to the blue light and the realization that all these people were already wrapped in a collective blanket of love for Lucinda Watson. She offered them hope that the world could be dramatically changed and that universal justice could prevail. Why not hope with them? Why not love with them? What had she, Dana Krandle, to lose? The trivial concerns of her life meant very little by comparison.

Dana was not certain at what point Lucy brought up "World Walk." In fact it was difficult to grasp what the phrase meant, but it was some type of movement. Thousands of homeless people, street children, low-income workers, and people from all walks of life would organize walks from various parts of the world to arrive in Bern, Switzerland for some kind of international meeting early in the next millennium. People began passing out literature, filling out forms, their purposeful movements executed as if in a cheerful hypnotic dance. Dana heard one young woman remark that she would join the Walk because she had nothing to lose. "I've been down-sized and out-sourced so often, why not try something different?"

"Why not try something different?" This sentiment certainly applied to Dana's own life at that moment, and it dawned on her that she had finally "fallen in love." She gazed into the blue light, watching that love swell the wave of collective energy.

SUBURBS WEST OF ST. LOUIS ~
DECEMBER, NEAR THE END OF THE SECOND MILLENNIUM

As far as the eye could see, a band of what looked like refugees in heavy jackets and wool stocking caps trudged up the gravel shoulder of the road to where it disappeared over a hill and into the fog. A softly harmonized chorus of carols was heard from behind. Up front, ephemeral puffs of steam rose above random heads. Clucks of peaceful chatter drifted back. Dana marched beside Martha Parks near the end of the line. She had not seen Rhona or Monica since lunch. They would be way up front carrying the huge WORLD WALK banner.

Martha and Dana were guiding one of the official World Walk battery-powered supply carts. Built by a custom wheelchair manufacturer in Seattle, the cart bounced easily over bumps, moaning softly like a meditation mantra that had kept Dana going during long boring treks over the plains and rolling hills of Kansas and Missouri.

Dana eyed the white sky overhead. Maybe it would snow for the rally and there would be a bonfire when they got to St. Louis. They had been promised hot showers afterward at a local high school where they would lodge in a gymnasium during their stay. Better accommodations were important now that the weather was cold. The walkers were in good physical condition from so many months of hiking, but it would be disastrous if people started getting sick.

Word was out that Lucinda Watson had flown in to speak at the rally and was planning to stay with them at the school rather than rent a hotel room, which she could well afford. Small gestures like this were needed to sustain the walkers' enthusiasm through the winter. Their numbers had increased during summer, with people cheerfully bathing in mountain streams and sleeping in parks under portable awnings, but there had been a rash of dropping out lately.

Dana had come to feel so much loyalty to the Walk, that its survival was now her primary concern in life. In fact, she felt less urgency about the passing of Lucy's laws than for the sustenance of World Walk. Although she would not admit it to anyone, Dana didn't have that much faith in any set of laws being able to deliver on its promise to end corporate dominance of the world's economies. But her admiration was boundless for the faith of these people.

A lot of the Walkers on this branch of the march were what the world thought of as "drop-outs," not because they were derelict or inadequate in any way, but because the economy did not need their labor. They were among the masses of the unemployed, "expendable" in an overpopulated world, the casualties of downsizing and welfare reform. In St. Louis, they would meet another branch of the Walk that had come up from Latin America. Many of those were factory workers, union organizers, and leaders of small local rebellions. Some had been rescued by Lucinda Watson when their lives were in danger. The movement was diverse and fairly large, but its impact was limited. The corporations still controlled the media — which controlled the masses. A large and violent element, primarily low-income working people, had become convinced that Lucy's laws threatened national sovereignty, therefore threatening their small share of the crumbs that trickled down to them as privileged white Americans. On many occasions, the walkers had been assaulted — beer bottles, fireworks, and other debris had been thrown at them from car windows. Twice, gunfire had rung out menacingly, overhead. A counter demonstration was expected at the rally in St. Louis.

They had been walking up a barely perceptible incline for some time when Dana looked out over a sprawling suburb with the St. Louis skyline in the distance. "There's the Arch!" exclaimed Dana.

"Big deal!" said Martha. She walked a little farther in silence and grumbled, "What good is it? What's it for?"

"It symbolizes this city's position as the gateway to the west. Lots of people migrated through here toward the West."

"Baloney! That Arch was a pork barrel project. Too bad they didn't fix the streets, make small business grants, do something useful."

Dana shrugged. Martha had a point. They had been passing a lot of crumbling sidewalks and boarded up buildings. She didn't say anything for awhile, but as they moved closer, watching the Arch gradually increase in size, she began to feel curiously uplifted. Finally she said, "I know what it's for. It's their mountain. They needed a mountain." Dana had been homesick for mountains now for several weeks.

"Maybe so," agreed Martha, "But that thing's a damned poor excuse for a mountain."

Dana might not have registered for the Walk if she had known Martha Parks was going. It wasn't that she disliked Martha, but she would not have knowingly gone anywhere with a former client. A lot of soul searching had gone into the decision to take on this project. She had needed to get away, not just from her tedious, stressful job. She had needed to break the pattern of so-called "co-dependency" (in the popular twelve-step terminology) that had ruled her life since childhood. Although intensely aggravated by Charlie's accident, the tendency went back farther than her earliest memories and was tied up somehow with recurrent early childhood nightmares and the sudden disappearance of Wella De Gornia. After Wella left, Dana had begun to feel responsible for everyone in the family, especially Mom who always seemed riddled with anxiety. Dana had taken refuge from the burden by hiding behind her own feelings of inadequacy. If she could not pass algebra, how could she be expected to take care of anyone else?

The moment of truth had occurred on the Saturday after the International Workers' Rights Conference in Portland. She was kneeling on her front porch in front of her bicycle, trying to put the chain back on the derailleur. Her fingers were black with grease, and she was about to reach for a roll of paper towels when it rolled away slightly out of reach. At that very moment, the front door opened and nudged the paper towel roll into more rapid motion, sending it down the front stoop and spilling a long, white runner along the sidewalk.

Mom's black patent leather pumps then occupied the spot where the roll had been. "Oh, I'm sorry," she said. Mom clumped down the steps, retrieved the towels, and wound them back on the spool.

"You look nice, Mom," observed Dana, as she tore off a generous, double thickness of paper towels and began wiping her fingers.

Mom sat down on one of the deck chairs that faced out into the street. Her perfume filled the surrounding air the way the big old lilac bush near Sullivan House did in the springtime. Dana wondered if the same man would pick Mom up this time, but she would not bring up the subject. Instead she said, "Have you heard from Dad?"

Mom didn't answer at first. Finally she said, "Yes, Dana, and I think you should read the letter. He won't be coming back to live with us."

"Is he staying in Spain?"

"Oh, no. I'm sure he can't afford that. He says he's going to take an early retirement and live in the San Juans."

Dana nodded slowly. It made sense. Mom and Dad had not been close lately. They had all been living in different worlds in response to demands of different inner needs, different jobs, different lives. Dad had always wanted to go back to the San Juans, and now he was needed there to take care of Grandma Ruth. Dana felt her chest tighten. Her world was crumbling away.

The man pulled up in his efficient-looking, black foreign car. He climbed out and walked up the sidewalk to the bottom of the stoop. He was tall and handsome in an impeccable gray suit. He had a healthy mane of thick white hair and was the image of a man better matched

to her glamorous mother than was her short, gentle, balding father.
"This is Ken Harrison," said Mom. "Ken, this is my daughter,
Dana."

Ken Harrison reached out a large, tan hand.

Dana unfolded to her full height, and towered over him from the
top step. The roll of paper towels fell from her hand and rolled down
onto the walk again. Dana knew that her fingers were still smeared
with grease, but she bent way over and shook his hand anyway.

While Pam was gone with the man, Dana finally got around to
cleaning out her backpack. Seated on the edge of her bed, she sorted
through all the papers, discarding most of the free literature from the
International Workers' Rights Conference. When she found the glossy
World Walk brochure, she paused. The cover photo was of Lucinda
Watson, conversing with several dark-skinned people in ragtag attire,
who obviously symbolized the world's poor and downtrodden. The
photo was double-exposed over a globe, with black, tattered shoe
prints walking across the page. The words, "World Walk" were
roughly brush-stroked in bright red letters over the entire design.

Dana took the brochure over to her desk, sat down, and turned
on the lamp. As she read the brochure, a sense of relief filled her soul.
The phrases sounded so comforting: "...prevention and peaceful so
lutions to conflicts," "...budgets based on diverting military expendi-
tures to meeting human needs," "...promotion of democracy and
popular participation for the achievement of economic and social justice." It was unlikely that such lofty ideals could ever be achieved by
any means, let alone a code of international law, but it was difficult to
fault the effort. At any rate, what better excuse could there be to cash
in a job and a way of life that no longer held her interest? Besides, she
was angry with Mom and Charlie for not really needing her after all.

Before she rose from her desk that evening, Dana had written Lucy
an honest letter. "Although I don't understand your project, it interests me," she wrote. "I have been bored with my job and discouraged
with my life lately. I haven't seen much of the world; I would like to
do some-thing with a group of people, like the recent mountain climbing expedition where I ran into you again after so many years. I have
no savings yet to support myself while on the Walk, but I could save
my money for the next several months, until the Walk is ready to
leave Seattle."

To Dana's amazement, there was a lengthy E-mail from Lucinda
Watson on her computer when she got to work the following Mon-
day. Lucy had scolded Dana for not contacting her while she was in
Portland. Thus began an exchange of computer mail, during which
Lucy informed Dana about a job opportunity with World Walk. Some-

one had been hired to keep a journal of the walk, and there was still an opening for an illustrator. Dana had not thought much of her chances of getting the job. She had never taken a single college-level art course. Nevertheless, she constructed a portfolio with sketches of people she had met at work, or along the streets and bicycle paths. Amazingly enough, her work had been selected over scores of others and described as "a powerful political statement." Dana would not have been so amazed at her work being selected had she known that Martha Parks was the journalist. Professionalism was not the standard of selection.

All registered walkers got free meals as well as lodgings, such as they were. The job, such as it was, paid an additional two hundred dollars per month for personal expenses. Dana and Martha were among the few being paid to participate in World Walk. Most were on retirement pensions or social security. Many of the walkers had no spending money at all. Worn shoes and clothing were replaced at clothing banks in the cities they passed through.

The presence of Martha turned out to be a comfort. Although Martha was a bit of a whiner and was usually depressed, she knew a lot about living on the road and on the streets. Dana's many drawings of Martha's frail, birdlike face with its large sullen eyes had been published with Martha's journals in newspapers around the world. Actually, their styles fit together very well.

As they marched closer to the inner city, Dana surveyed the sur-roundings with an eye to what she would draw. The houses were Georgian style red brick, very old and in disrepair. The frozen pave-ment was littered with broken wine bottles, wrappings, and faded newspapers. Much of the sidewalk had disintegrated and was pressed like gravel into the dirt. Many stores and houses were boarded up.

Once Martha nodded in the direction of a damaged facade. "Gang war, no doubt," she said, "Or police attack."

Dana had to admit that the wall had been pounded by something powerful and systematic. "That's from a semiautomatic weapon," Martha explained. No wonder there were so few people out and about. Now and then a small child would stare at them from a porch or an old man would walk out of an alley and nod or wave. But the streets were notably empty. "Where are all the people?" Dana asked Martha. "Where do they live and shop with everything boarded up?"

"In the suburbs, I presume," said Martha. Although there had been even fewer people walking in the suburban streets, the houses and stores were in better repair and there were lots of cars.

After they entered the downtown area, they found buildings in better condition. Many older buildings had been restored, their bricks scrubbed clean, and there were new skyscrapers decorated with multicolored Christmas lights. Gradually, sounds distinguishable as music and cheering emerged from the roaring sea of traffic noise.

As Dana and Martha waited at the last traffic light to cross the freeway overpass into the waterfront park rally sight, the air suddenly filled with snowflakes through which music rang like a chorus of rhythmic bells. The Arch soared above them into the fog, its summit barely visible.

Directly below the Arch was a covered platform stage. Large wooden instruments like giant xylophones were being played by several people dressed in bright clothing of many interwoven colors.

"Marimbas!" sighed Martha.

There was no bonfire, but torches were stationed at intervals in back of the stage, and bright spotlights shone on the musicians. A huge crowd cheered the walkers as they arrived through a roped-off pathway across the park.

The walkers gathered in front of the stage, which commanded a view of the old courthouse with its big green dome and thick ionic columns, away across the park. On the terrace below, the brown winter grass was rapidly turning white. The counter demonstration, perhaps a hundred strong, had arranged itself across the courthouse steps and between the columns. They carried signs denouncing the walkers as bums and free loaders. Dana pretended not to see them. "Nice scenery," she remarked to Martha.

"They used to sell slaves on the courthouse steps over there," grumbled Martha.

As the crowd grew, so did the air of excitement. A show of police on horseback stood along the base of the courthouse steps while scores of other police officers mulled through the crowd. Dark silhouettes of media helicopters appeared like flying pterodactyls overhead, their engines rumbling and lights glaring, monstrous eyes peering through the falling snow. They would televise an impressive turnout, much larger than the gatherings in Denver or Kansas City.

The southern contingent of World Walk were there too, wearing yellow arm bands to identify themselves. Green bands were passed out to Dana and the other Westerners, along with walking maps and public transit routes to their lodgings.

The south and west contingents began to mingle and introduce themselves like long lost cousins at a family reunion. Dana donned the green arm band, feeling proud to thus identify herself as one of the "in-crowd" who had walked twenty-six hundred miles. Dana wasn't sure how Lucinda Watson and several other women got through the crowd and up onto the stage without being noticed, but suddenly there she was standing before the microphone. The marimba band stopped playing.

Lucy looked enormous in a long, yellow down-filled overcoat and beaded Alaskan mukluks. "Good evening everyone, and welcome to this deep December gathering of World Walk." Lucy's melodious voice was further empowered by electronic amplification, filling the park as well as perhaps the city and river basin beyond. "My heart is filled with gratitude that so many of you have come to greet these brave people who have walked so far to promote their belief in a just world. We have not planned a long ceremony this evening because we knew the weather would be cold, and the walkers have come a long way today. I would like to take the time to introduce every walker and let them tell their fascinating stories of how far they have come and why they joined World Walk, but that would take a long time, and we would all turn to ice statues. I will introduce just a few of them in hopes that we will have a feel for who these people are and what has prompted their decision to walk from all corners of the Earth to gather at the time and place of United Nations Legislative Conference in Bern, Switzerland."

Dana was really getting into Lucy's speech, and at one point she was sure that Lucy had recognized her in the crowd and nodded to her personally. She had even started to feel a warm trance coming on when suddenly she felt a tug at her arm and she looked down into the fluttering, bird-face of Martha Parks, "Come quickly, Dana. Lucy wants to introduce us. Come!"

"Come where?"

"On stage. We're wanted on stage."

This was confusing. The usual rally format included mention of her and Martha's work, but they had never been put on display. Once or twice Martha had been chosen to read the journal entry on how she had come from homelessness and drug addiction to being a dedicated walker and how World Walk have given her life meaning. But Dana was not prepared for anything like that. She followed reluctantly as Martha literally pulled her through the crowd to a small stairway leading onto the stage. The guitarist, Sylvia Brahm, was already waiting there to lead the group in song. Monica was also there, looking ill at ease as were several others. Rhona, serving as rally coordinator, stood on the bottom step with a clipboard, lining people up in the order they would be introduced.

Willie Graham was being introduced. "This gentleman plans and organizes meals for the western contingent of World Walk," proclaimed Lucy. "That is no small feat when most of the work is done by volunteers, and all supplies and foods are transported, not in trucks, but in the small handcarts you see around you in the park." Lucy shook Willie's hand vigorously and pinned a medal on his chest. This was starting to look like one of those phoney staff recognition ceremonies back at Sullivan House.

As Willie turned to leave the stage, Rhona nodded to Dana. It was her turn to go up.

With shaky stilts for legs, Dana climbed the stairs and walked out on the stage. Lucinda Watson was at the microphone praising her work, "...creator of the delightful illustrations which have become the trademark of World Walk." Dana felt exposed. Thousands of people were watching. But when she stepped under the spotlight, a barrier of invisibility was instantly created within its circle. Gone were the crowd and the cold winter night and the city decorated for Christmas. Dana was alone with Ms. Watson on some mysterious plane of existence where there was nothing but a large, white, blinding light, creating warmth and intimacy between two divergent souls. Ms. Watson did not pin a medal or a ribbon on Dana. Instead, Lucy wrapped her great, down-padded arms around Dana in a magnanimous hug and whispered, "God, it's good to see you, child," with that hint of dialect that occasionally crept into her speech. Dana felt as if she had been hugged by a feather bed. The crowd cheered, hooted, and whistled as if at a rock concert. Dana floated from the stage on a cloud of euphoria.

When Sylvia Brahm began to lead Christmas carols, Dana stuffed her mittens into the pockets of her wool parka, leaned gently into her knees and closed her eyes. The feeling inside her grew warmer, even as the snowflakes licked her cheeks like cold, soft tongues. Then Dana let the blue light come as she always did at rallies, knowing that her own enjoyment of the feeling would enhance the collective mood and increase the popularity of World Walk.

The crowd was singing "Oh come, oh come, Emmanuel, ransom captive Israel," when Dana felt a strong negative force invading the edges of the collective. At the same time, angry rhythmic chants rose above the gentle chorus. The opposition was getting noisier. Dana opened her eyes and the blue light vanished. The opposition were waving their signs and shouting. Police officers from all directions were moving toward them. Others appeared to be dragging someone away. A similar event had occurred at the rally in Denver, and later they had learned that the police had confiscated a semiautomatic rifle from someone in the crowd.

Dana was relieved when Lucinda Watson came to the microphone and brought the proceedings gracefully to a close. "Again, on behalf of World Walk, I am grateful to the people of this beautiful city for their warm welcome. We also wish to thank those who disagree with our views for coming to express their feelings. We welcome opposition in a spirit of nonviolent discourse. Thank you and good night."

As the crowd began to disperse, Dana looked around for Martha who, at first, was nowhere in sight. The cart they had been pushing together was not in sight either. It was easy to lose people in a crowd. Dana walked over to the stage where several walkers had gathered. She was relieved to find Martha with Rhona and Monica They were discussing whether to visit the department stores, which were open for Christmas shopping, or to have something hot to drink at one of the river-boat restaurants before heading for the school.

Martha whined, "It doesn't matter where we go, but I think we better get moving or get out of the cold. I'm starting to feel numb."

Dana was just opening her lips to say she wanted to tag along wherever they happened to be going when she noticed someone just a few feet away staring at her intently. It was a tall man about the age of her father, peering from behind the fur-lined hood of an expensive parka. The top of his head and shoulders were powdered with snow. Dana returned his look with a glare, but the man did not break his gaze. He just continued to make bold eye contact. "You're Dana Krandle," he said. "I know you."

Dana thought there was something vaguely familiar about him, but she could not say she knew this man. As for his knowing her name, that was understandable. She had been introduced only a few moments before over a powerful public address system. "I don't recall that we've met."

"Oh, yes, we have met, but it was too long ago. You've forgotten. You were in high school."

"I remember most of high school, but I don't remember you." Martha and the others were walking away now gingerly across the snow-covered park toward the traffic light. Sylvia Brahm had tucked her guitar under the tarp and was helping Martha push the cart awkwardly before them.

Even as she conversed with the stranger, Dana followed close enough behind her friends to communicate to the man that she was not alone. The man followed, staying within easy conversing distance and continuing to stare at Dana's face as if it were a Mardi Gras mask. "Good!" exclaimed the man. "If you remember most of your high school days, you will recall that you went to a rally much like this. You took a ferry part way, then hitched a ride."

The group had come to a traffic light. Teeth chattering from the cold, they began to discuss plans again.

"Let's have coffee at that hotel over there, then head on to the school. I'm cold," complained Martha. Several others agreed.

Still clinging to the edge of the group, Dana assured the man, "I don't hitchhike."

"You did at least once," insisted the man. "You left your daypack in my car. I returned it to the school."

Impossible! Could this be the same man? Why did he still recognize her after so many years? Dana glowered at him. "Yes, what was your name?"

"Genzforth. Aaron Genzforth."

"Yes. Mr. Genzforth. I've always wanted to thank you for returning my sketchbook. It was my social studies project. How did you remember my name for such a long time?"

The man laughed. "It was not our first meeting. I have known your family ever since you were small and lived in the San Juans."

His statement made Dana feel a little more relaxed, until she noticed that the group had gone on across while the light was green, and now it was red again. She was left behind with Mr. Genzforth. This was an incredible déjà vu. The whole experience was recreating itself in precise detail.

When the light changed again, Mr. Genzforth hurried on across, apparently trying to catch up with the group. Maybe he wanted things to be different this time. Maybe he didn't want her to be afraid and run away from him. Dana crossed the street where Mr. Genzforth watched curiously as Martha Parks chained the supply cart to a bicycle rack under an awning. "Aren't you afraid something will be stolen?" he inquired.

Martha shrugged. "Perhaps. So far, that hasn't happened."

Dana followed them into the hotel lobby where the others stood around the coat rack, brushing snow off their shoulders and stamping it from their shoes. A dining room with white tablecloths was visible through a wide doorway, and the luxurious aroma of fresh ground coffee eclipsed the smell of cold they had brought in with them. The comfort of an artificially-heated building seemed almost unreal after so many hours of walking outdoors and standing in the snow.

Dana took off her parka, and Mr. Genzforth insisted upon taking it from her and hanging it on a hanger in the outmoded fashion of the "older generation."

"How did you know my family in the San Juans? Did you live there?"

"No. It's a long story."

"How long would it take?"

Mr. Genzforth shrugged. He glanced at his watch. "If you have coffee with me at a separate table, I could tell you the story and whatever else you want to know." Dana thought about that a moment. This was after all a safe public place and this man's story might prove interesting, even if not entirely true. Perhaps Mr. Genzforth was some kind of government agent, or maybe he was just a traveling salesman. At any rate, she wanted to know. She lead him into the dining room and sat with him at a table within view, though perhaps not convenient hearing distance, of her friends. Martha Parks nodded sagely in her direction as though she assumed Dana was having a rendezvous with an old lover. It was humiliating to have anyone think she would take up with such an elderly person.

"How did you know my family in the San Juans, Mr. Genzforth?" Dana demanded almost at the volume of a yell. The man responded with a pinched expression of embarrassment. Then he spoke very low, almost in a whisper. "You can call me Aaron."

"Sure, sorry, Aaron." Maybe she should give him a little space. Maybe he didn't need to be prodded.

"Thanks," he said, and then looked away, as if trying to remember. "Let's see, the first time I met you was when you were about four years old. You lived on a small, family-farm island, a rustic sort of hippie place."

"Levin Island." Maybe this guy was on the level.

"Yes, Levin Island."

"You visited us? I don't remember."

"Do you remember much that happened to you at age four?"

"Not much. A friend of ours died and willed Levin Island to my mother when I was four."

"Do you remember that your uncle was wanted by the law?"

Although Dana had maintained an almost unnaturally high volume throughout their dialogue, Aaron's voice had grown progressively softer until it was now almost inaudible.

"Which uncle?" demanded Dana in a virtual shout, which prompted the waitress to rush over and fill their cups. "So sorry about the delay," she sputtered. "I'll be back to take your order right away."

"That's all right. We're in no hurry," Dana reassured her.

"Marvin Krandle," mumbled Aaron, after the waitress had scurried away.

Dana laughed. "I didn't know it, but I'm certainly not surprised. Uncle Marvin is a nonconformist and has some kind of personality disorder, but he's a dear all the same. How did you know he was in trouble with the law?"

"I was assigned to his case."

"Oh, I see. You're the law."

"Of sorts."

"Of what sort?"

"I'm a federal investigator."

"No kidding. Was Uncle Marvin's trouble that serious? Was he a dealer or something?" This time Dana spoke in a whisper.

"Oh, no. Nothing like that, at least not that I know of. He went AWOL from the Marines, though, among other things."

Dana laughed again. "Oh yes. I knew that. It's one of our family legends. Grandpa Ben never forgave him. Oh, I get it! You must have been one of the guys who came looking for Uncle Marvin."

"Yes, that's it! You already know my story, at least part of it."

"Of course. I grew up on it. How many families have such a good family legend?" Aaron was bringing back memories so fond and familiar that they almost hurt here in this alien place so far from home.

There was a long pause during which Aaron gazed at Dana with a tense expression as if there was more he was hesitant to talk about. Finally he whispered almost in the breath of a sigh. "There's another part of the story no one has ever heard before."

"Why not?"

"I've never told anyone. I'm the only one who knows."

Dana leaned forward across the table until her face was only a few inches from Aaron's. This was becoming positively intriguing. "Why not?"

"I never told anyone for fear they would think I'm crazy."

"No kidding!" said Dana. She had once known that feeling well, though it was now old and almost forgotten. She reached over and gently touched Aaron's hand where it rested on the table beside his still untasted coffee. "If you tell me, I won't think you're crazy."

Aaron looked cautiously into Dana's eyes as though he were trying to read her mind. Then he said, "I suppose you won't. I've always wanted to speak with you about this because I thought you were the only one who might believe me."

Dana was on the edge of her seat. It had been a long, exciting day. She was tired, but she had energy left for this. "Please tell me. I won't tell anyone. I promise." She crossed her heart.

"All right then. You remember Wella De Gornia?"

Dana shrugged. "Maybe I remember her. Maybe I only remember dreams of her or what I've been told about her, but I've never been allowed to forget her. My family thinks she was some kind of saint or goddess or something."

Aaron smiled. "In that case you really should believe my story. By all accounts she's dead, is that not right?"

Dana nodded. "By all reputable accounts."

"But I believe she may not be dead. I saw her rise into the sky while her sailboat was sinking in the Strait of Juan De Fuca."

"Rise into the sky? How?"

Aaron waved his hand downward to signal Dana that her voice was getting too loud again. "I have no believable explanation of how she did it, but I have this memory. Perhaps it was an optical illusion or dream, but it's such a vivid image that it has not faded from my mind in thirty years."

"Incredible!"

"Yes, and I'm going to tell you something just as incredible." By now Aaron was barely opening his mouth to speak, releasing his words reluctantly like small reptiles between his teeth.

The waitress had finally returned and was waiting to take their order. "I'll have a croissant," said Dana, without looking at the waitress or breaking eye contact with Aaron.

"I'll just have coffee," said Aaron, maintaining eye contact with Dana until the waitress had moved on. Then he said, "When you were only four years old, you gave me a drawing of the very same event, or dream, or whatever it was."

Dana gasped as another memory surfaced. "My dad told me that when I was little I used to have a lot of strange dreams that would sometimes come true. They say that's fairly common with dreams, but I don't recall any of them now. You still have the drawing after all these years?"

"Oh, yes. Who would part with such a thing? When you go back to Seattle, I'll show it to you."

The mention of Seattle prompted Dana to take a sip of her coffee. Somehow coffee was not as delicious anywhere else. Would she ever get back to Seattle? A chill went through her with a sudden inexplicable fear that she would never see home again. She shrugged off Aaron's invitation as if it were a joke. "I probably won't be going there for a long time, if ever."

"Oh? Why not? Where are you going?"

"To Switzerland. Haven't you heard? We have a charter flight booked from LaGuardia to Paris on June 11."

Aaron laughed and shook his head as if in disbelief. "This World Walk stuff is crazy. Why do you do it?"

"I like it. I like to walk. I'd rather be walking than sitting behind a desk."

"Earning a living like the rest of us. I'll bet your family doesn't approve of this nonsense."

"I'm grown now. I do what I want. I've paid my dues to the family. I paid Cousin Charlie's tuition to junior college. I kept Mom company after Dad left, until she got a boyfriend. Charlie has a girlfriend now. They don't need me to look after them anymore."

"But you need to look after yourself."

"Yes. That's why I'm doing what I want."

"Doing this crazy protest march? You call that taking care of yourself? Sleeping in parks and school buildings, standing outdoors for hours in the snow after trudging through the worst part of town on foot? If that's taking care of yourself..."

"To each his or her own, Mr. Genzforth. Aaron. But it isn't a protest march. We're promoting, not protesting." Dana felt her anger rising. What right did this turkey have to start giving her advice? She would not trade her life for his, that was certain!

Aaron picked up his coffee cup for the first time and drained it all at once. No doubt, it was stone cold by now. His face had reddened, either with embarrassment or anger or both. "Very well," he snapped. "I didn't intend to give you that advice. Perhaps it's dangerous to walk about the world with a bunch of transients, but there are worse things. Those are the things I need to warn you about."

Dana was furious. How could this man have the audacity? She wanted to tell him where to go, but the waitress was refilling their cups, and besides she was curious about his warning, clearly his real agenda for this meeting. So she mechanically lifted her cup for another sip of hot coffee, making intense eye contact with the man, inviting him to continue. "Warn me? About what?"

Aaron took a sip of coffee as if to give himself time to think. Then he said, "There's a rumor out about you. Well, actually it's more than a rumor. We have intelligence that Lucinda Watson plans to give you a sort of promotion."

"A promotion?" Dana laughed. She had never heard of a promotion in World Walk. There were no ranks and few privileges.

"You mean you haven't heard anything about it yet?"

"No."

Aaron leaned toward her. "You'll be hearing soon, no doubt."

"Oh?"

"Yes. If you take the assignment, you'll be going to Switzerland long before June. But I'm advising you not to do it."

"Not to do what?"

"Not to go with Lucinda Watson back to Bern next month."

Dana stared at Aaron, tongue-tied with astonishment for a moment. Then she burst into laughter. "I think that's highly unlikely. Lucy has a lot of things to think about in Bern. What would I do there? Make drawings?"

"Yes. So we're told. Your work is popular. The organizers of your movement want to call more attention to what's going on at the front lines. I suppose they deem it more interesting than walking twenty miles a day. But you must refuse to go."

The idea was absurd, hardly worth considering, but Dana humored the man. "Why shouldn't I go? It would be fun to work in Bern with Lucy. I would like to visit the Alps, maybe learn to ski."

Aaron shook his head. "No!" he said emphatically. "It would not be fun. It would be dangerous. You must not do it."

"Dangerous? Why?"

"Watson's days are numbered. Yours will probably be too, if you ever become personally involved with her."

Now Dana whispered. "Lucy's life is in imminent danger? Why?"

Aaron's whisper was now barely audible, but he spoke condescendingly as if to a small child learning the basic facts of life. "Lots of people don't like her. Don't you know that?"

"Really? Who?"

Aaron sneered. "Only half the world, that's all."

Dana frowned at Aaron. "If you have what you call "intelligence" that someone intends to kill Lucinda Watson, and you represent the law, you must know who wants to kill her. Why don't you protect her. Why don't you tell her?"

A sardonic smile crept across Aaron's face. "I have no doubt that, by telling you, I'm telling her indirectly, but that isn't my concern. If she wants to run around making enemies, that's her business. My interest, however, is in protecting you, not her."

"Why me?"

"As I said, I have known you and your family for many years..."

Aaron broke off mid-sentence. Dana had noticed her friends were leaving and had stood up. "I have to leave. I must go with the others." She wanted to hear more. Obviously, Mr. Genzforth had only revealed the bare surface of his "intelligence." But she would not be left alone in a strange city with him after dark. She hurried after Martha, who was already in the lobby putting on her jacket.

BERN, SWITZERLAND ~ EARLY IN THE THIRD MILLENNIUM

Lucy set her coffee cup on the bedstand and moved her newspaper closer to the lamp. She might not have noticed the front page photo of the bears, if it had not been for the long slender face of Dana Krandle peering over a group of onlookers in the background. It was hardly a coincidence. Dana spent a lot of time at those silly Bear Pits. During her daily walk around the old city, Lucy had noticed Dana standing there, wearing that mysterious far-off look, like she was half asleep or in a trance. That was what Lucy recalled most about Dana Krandle from her high school days, the long face looking half-asleep. Then suddenly she would prove her attentiveness by popping up with some insightful comment or producing one of her fantastic graphic illustrations of the day's topic. Although she would not have admitted it then, Lucy had been enthralled with Dana Krandle's mysterious ways. It had been difficult not to give her special attention. It had been hard not to search for opportunities to get to know her better. That was why she had invited Dana and her friend, Martha Parks, to Bern. But Dana had been somewhat aloof since her arrival, in that daze which, apparently, made it possible for her to draw. Dana and Martha had gone right to work producing numerous drawings and journals and, for some reason, their presence seemed to have a consensus-building effect on the handful of angry people in the courtroom.

In fact, the first breakthrough had occurred on their first day at the conference hall. Zanter's kettle drum voice had pounded something out right in the middle of a heavy discussion. A soft, female British accent translated into Lucy's head phones. "Archaeological findings have proven that the Maruvian people have lived in the Seran Valley for thousands of years. Our ancient monastic ruins still crown the hilltops." No sound, not even the rustle of feet or the drawing of a breath, could be heard. The silence had startled Lucy, resembling as it did the stillness in nature just before a hawk struck its prey. Both U.N. guards flanking the conference table had come to attention and placed their hands on their rifles.

The computer's response, which flashed on the big screen in Maruvian, German, English, and several other languages, was entirely predictable.

"WHAT NEEDS ARE MET BY — THE MARUVIAN PEOPLE LIVED IN THE SERAN VALLEY THOUSANDS OF YEARS? OUR MONASTERIES STILL CROWN THE HILL TOPS."

The collective groan was broadcast globally over C-Span. Every eye, not to mention the tv cameras, focused on Zanter with disgust, as if to say, "Haven't you got the point yet, dodo bird? How long must it take?" Zanter reddened as much with embarrassment as with anger. He hated this game, but his resistance was breaking down. He had to play if he ever intended to get out of here, let alone be president of a new republic one day. "The Maruvian people need the Redon River waters to irrigate the Poaro wheat fields," he mumbled.

Whereupon the wiry little body of the Teri Cross shot out of his seat, "Not to mention your thirst for the oil flowing underneath.

Everyone knows you intend to sell our people's land to the Winco Corporation."

"WHAT NEEDS ARE MET BY — NOT TO MENTION THE OIL FLOWING UNDERNEATH ?" then flashed on the screen.

A group sigh rose to the high ceiling of the conference hall. Teri's brow creased thickly beneath his crown of white hair. He looked around helplessly. "My people need to keep the land and grow domestic crops to feed our people," he mumbled, and his remark was recorded on the screen. Those were the first two distinct needs statements on either side of the screen, one for the Thoringian and one for the Maruvian side. That was the beginning.

Since then they had been on a roll. The computer had recorded dozens of needs statements that would eventually form the basis of compromise negotiations. After weeks of phony power proclamations, the log jam had broken.

MARUVIAN PEOPLE NEED TEACHERS AND SCHOOLS AND THE OPPORTUNITY TO COMPETE FOR BETTER JOBS.

THORINGIAN PEOPLE NEED ASSURANCE THAT THEIR HOMES AND LIVES WILL BE SAFE FROM THREAT AND INVASION.

MARUVIAN AND THORINGIAN PEOPLE NEED TO KNOW THE INSTITUTIONS OF GOVERNMENT WILL BE THERE TO PROTECT THEM AND WILL HAVE THEIR INTERESTS AT HEART.

The list was getting pretty long. Soon the second phase of talks would begin and the computer would collect statements of compromise, potentially satisfying needs of both peoples. In the third phase, Winco Corporation's performance in the region would be reviewed in terms of the people's needs, to determine if its charter should be revoked.

It was amazing how this process had speeded up since Dana Krandle and Martha Parks had arrived. Lucy had always suspected Dana of having a cohesive effect upon her Contemporary World Problems Class but she had passed the suspicion off as preposterous, there being no plausible explanation. All the girl ever did was sit and stare into space and then draw pictures.

Lucy would have liked to receive a little more publicity as a result of the progress that had been made in the peace negotiations. But with the killing stopped in Maruvia, the news media took less interest. After all, the major leaders had been captured and brought to Bern along with a good many farmers, shopkeepers, and other average citizens. The principle players — Teri Cross, Phillip Zanter, and Timothy Smith of Winco — were given the choice of cooperating with Lucy's computer game plan or going on trial for crimes against international law. Meanwhile, a few hundred thousand heavily-armed peacekeeping troops were stationed in Maruvia.

In any case, Lucy did not expect to read much in The Bern *Morgen*, which was predictably boring, concentrating upon squabbles over local building codes and taxes. The lead article always featured some amusing human interest story such as the one this morning about the bears.

The bears had lived for centuries in the famous Bear Pits below the old city. Lucy had often watched as they performed pirouettes, somersaults and other acrobatics for the reward of a carrot tossed from the sidewalk up above. The bears were nothing new. But this morning's article concerned a puzzling development. After several centuries of performing individual stunts, the bears had recently started acting in unison. Two, three, or even four bears would execute a particular feat together, reminiscent of a chorus line at the Folies Bergéres. Lucy made a mental note to stop by the Bear Pits this morning and see if Dana was standing there in her usual spot. For some reason, that image worried Lucy. She even found herself suspecting that Dana's quiet presence there had something to do with the bears' novel antics.

It was a trivial thing for Lucy to worry about. Ever since the age of twelve, about the time that her best childhood friend, Vanessa Stewart, was run over by a car and killed before her very eyes, something had clicked in Lucy's brain, causing her to lose all fear. What was the point of living for security? Safety was an illusion. What was the point to any life that made no mark upon the world? At the age of twelve, Lucy had testified in the trial of the man who ran over Vanessa. He was a well-known drug dealer in the neighborhood. The attorneys in the case had been young African American women, great role models for Lucy, often quoting mysterious phrases called "statutes." Their knowledge of law had been a source of mysterious power.

. . .

Adorned with a large Afro hairdo, wearing a blanket-sized red plaid muffler and a black, double-breasted overcoat, Lucy stepped out of the Hotel Kroeniger and onto the covered walkway, trying not to look in the shop windows full of tantalizing chocolate-covered marzipan bears and blackberry torte. As she came out from under the arcade, Lucy could see light in the arched windows of the ancient sandstone houses across the street. She often found herself wondering who lived in these houses, just as she had wondered about people living in grass shacks in Africa or the jungles of Brazil. She felt vaguely envious. These medieval dwellings had been built with primitive technology by interlacing crude timbers and then piling up stones and clay to fill in the spaces. There was a human dimension to such buildings. Lucy had grown up in Chicago in a government housing project built of structural steel. Its Spartan concrete stairwells were adorned with garish grafitti, their only human touch.

Lucy marched up the street, the tire-like tread of her Gortex walking shoes fearlessly attacking the cobblestones and patches of melting snow. It was still early, so the streets were fairly empty, but the chestnut venders were already out with their flaming braziers. Clouds of blue smoke hung in the air above the street, tempting Lucy's nostrils. She felt ravenous already even though she had just eaten her ration of two large slices of bread, low fat margarine, jam made of Nutrasweet, and coffee. Lucy was endemically overweight, perpetually dieting, and always hungry. She eyed the chestnuts so covetously that the vender, a stout woman wearing a large apron, took pity on her, and served up a free sample on a paper napkin.

Lucy cradled the chestnut in her gloved palm and leaned against a nearby fountain. She blew furiously at the precious morsel, encouraging it to cool as she looked at the fountain statuary. It depicted a blindfolded woman brandishing a sword over a scattering of mangled human bodies, mostly male. A lump of snow clung to the statue's shoulder, melting in a scarcely perceptible trickle down her bare breast. Lucy slowly chewed the chestnut, savoring its rich, nutty flavor as she studied the statue wondering what it meant. Neither European culture nor its climate was her strong suit, but snow-melt so early in the morning must be a sign of spring. Maybe warmer weather might help thaw hostilities between the Maruvian and Thoringian leaders.

It was almost seven o'clock when Lucy passed under the famous Bern clock tower. She pivoted as she came out the other side to look back at the little parade of toy bears and medieval characters marching across the clock's ornately carved facade. The clock toned seven long, resonant notes, introducing the hour with fanfare worthy of a high ranking official. Lucy rewarded the performance with an amused smile, but she noted that even these charming little puppets brandished swords and weapons.

As she crossed the stone bridge over the Aare river, Lucy observed that, despite the early hour, several people had already gathered near the Bear Pits. Dana stood at the edge of the group, leaning her weight against the stone wall of the pit. Her eyes were half-closed. Other people were applauding and cheering as they tossed bits of food into the pits. Lucy placed a coin in one of the street vending machines to buy a package of carrots to feed the bears. Then she squeezed into the narrow space between Dana and a chubby policemen who praised the performance profusely in loud, guttural German.

At first, it was difficult to determine what all the hullabaloo was about. One large brown bear stood in the center of the circular pit urinating into the a drain hole. Two others chewed on bits of carrot held clumsily in their paws.

Something told Lucy not to interrupt. After a silent pause, during which suspense as thick as molasses held the audience spellbound, the two bears finished eating their carrots and stood side by side for a moment looking up wistfully as if listening to some whispered command. Finally, they bent forward together simultaneously in identical, deep courtly bows. Lucy applauded with the others and then turned slightly to look at Dana out of the corner of her eye. The young woman was standing so close that the sleeve of Lucy's black overcoat touched her parka.

Dana did not applaud. Instead she remained perfectly still, her thick lids drooped like cowling over her eyes. Lucy had begun to wonder what would happen if she just walked away without saying anything. But at that moment, Dana's eyes opened and acknowledged Lucy with a radiant smile. The look on her face was not unlike the proud expression of a mother whose baby had just learned to walk. The child had always smiled that way when Lucy thought she had caught her sleeping in class. "These bears are such fun! They love to think together," said Dana.

Yes, that was the same sort of thing she used to say, reassuring Lucy that she had been, somehow, attentive and intensely involved.

Lucy said, "Yes, but they've been here for centuries, and they're likely to be here after work." She tugged at the sleeve of Dana's overcoat and glanced at her wristwatch. "The meeting starts at eight, and we have to get back across town." Then noting Dana's smile of gentle derision, she added, "I know it would only take you five minutes at World Walk pace, but if you're going to walk with me at my pace, that will take a little longer.

"You're pretty fast," Dana reassured Lucy as they slushed out into the street through the melting snow.

"You would make a good walker. In fact, you'd be a pro after the first thousand or so miles."

"If I can get an agreement signed here in time, I should ask for a short sabbatical. Then we could all go back and join the final phases. I like to walk."

"Yes, I've noticed that you walk a lot, but I've been wondering...it's not my place to give advice, but it concerns me to see you about in the streets, alone."

Lucy laughed and walked faster. Didn't the girl know Lucinda Watson had walked alone into a Guatemalan rebel camp? Bern had about the world's lowest crime rate. Besides, Lord knows she needed the exercise. She glanced at her watch again. The sight of the imposing gray stone government buildings crowning the hill seemed a long, hard climb away. "In case you haven't noticed, Dana," observed Lucy in a slightly sarcastic tone, "cars are not allowed in these streets. You have to be mobile to get around here, or take a train, which wouldn't be much safer."

"Oh, no. I've checked into it. There's an electric automobile charter for government officials and people with disabilities."

"I'm not disabled."

"You're an official. You would qualify."

"The Mayor of Bern walks to work, so do all the members of Parliament."

"You're a higher official than any of those, and besides, you're more vulnerable."

"Good Heavens, Dana, I thought you knew me better than that. I'm about as vulnerable as a tank, and as for being a high government official, I've never been accused of that before."

At that moment they were passing one of Bern's most perplexing fountains, gaily painted as all the others. This statuary depicted a giant hungrily gobbling handfuls of children. Lucy stopped to look at it and to appreciate the view beyond. The sun, now fully risen, shone faintly through a layer of clouds. It fell upon a high church tower and the glistening windows of a modern high-rise apartment complex that rose in striking contrast above the warm sandstone buildings and archways of the old city.

"European culture seems terribly barbaric," complained Dana, who was still frowning at the fountain.

Lucy smiled. Dana Krandle had grown up to be quite a mother hen, but it was still nice to be with her. "Maybe it's human nature that's barbaric," she offered, sloshing on up the street.

Dana followed in long, easy strides that barely disturbed the soft patches of snow. "I hope it isn't human nature that's barbaric. There will be no hope for us."

Lucy shrugged. "Maybe we could change. Maybe we could evolve."

"Or mutate." Dana giggled anxiously. They walked on in silence for awhile, but as Lucy puffed and Dana trotted beside her up the hill, Dana reverted to her mother hen role. "If you don't want to take the electric car maybe you should hire a bodyguard."

"Oh come on, Dana. I can't afford a bodyguard. All my extra funds go to World Walk and other causes. Besides, I don't want a bodyguard."

"Then let me go along when you walk in the streets."

Lucy thought about that for a moment. Then she reached over and took Dana's arm as though it belonged to a tall gentleman escorting her on a date. "That's a good idea. You can be my official bodyguard, but you have to understand my needs. I don't like being overprotected and I've long since lost interest in zoos. I can't stand to watch those stupid bears for more than a few minutes at a time."

Dana looked at Lucy fondly, making long, loving eye contact as she had often done as a teenage girl in Contemporary World Problems class. Then pointedly quoting some of Lucy's current favorite jargon, she said, "Surely we can negotiate an agreement that will meet both our needs."

Dana continued to hold Lucy's arm as they trudged up the wide concrete steps into the U.N. Building and down the long corridor to the conference hall. When they entered the amphitheater, Dana gave Lucy's forearm a gentle squeeze and let go, then seated herself in the very last row next to Martha Parks who was already writing away in her journal. Before long, Dana appeared to fall asleep. Later she made an incredible drawing that included not only people who spoke but graphic symbols of the ideas they expressed.

The hall was nearly full of citizen delegates, some in red satin knickers, the Thoringian national dress, others in conservative gray or black European suits. Teri Cross was already slumped over the round-table up front, looking as tense and bored as a terrier on a leash. His black Thoringian tribal robe was trimmed in green satin braid; the sleeves hung loosely over his arms and shoulders.

Lucy sat down at the keyboard facing the delegates, with her back to the giant computer screen. She turned on the computer and typed in "Zanter / Cross."

Two long columns of needs statements instantly appeared. "The screen is nearly full," she observed cheerfully.

"This is very tedious," grumbled Teri. "The needs of my people are limitless. Surely there must be a better way."

Lucy smiled patiently. "Indeed there must be. But this seems the best we have for now."

Lucy had developed the computer system so that the conflict resolution process would not depend on personalities. Experience had taught her that agreements made between personalities often fell apart as soon as those persons died or left office.

Teri brightened when a young woman appeared from behind the screen with a tray of steaming cups. It was the Maruvian custom to drink hot milk in the morning.

While Teri was sipping his milk, Phillip Zanter arrived, flanked by uniformed guards. Phillip glowered at them with his ferocious bulldog expression. He wore a silk suit with wide lapels that made him look like a Mafia boss. Lucy swallowed hard. It was the start of another day.

After Phillip seated himself importantly in his wide conference chair, Lucy bowed her head. "First a moment of silence, while we ask for guidance." She closed her eyes and waited. She waited a long time. No matter how long she waited, everyone would keep their eyes closed for the duration. In the beginning, Zanter and Cross had been hesitant to close their eyes, until they realized the U.N. guards were not about to let anything happen to anyone on their watch. For the last few days, both of them had kept their eyes closed long after Lucy announced an end to the silence. Once, she had tapped Phillip on the shoulder to make certain he had not fallen asleep while he was supposed to be praying. It was curious. Maybe the popularity of prayer and meditation was due to the fact that it provided overburdened people with a short recess, a time for the mind to do nothing. Recreational endeavors, such as fishing and hiking, did much the same thing.

Phillip opened the meeting by standing up and pounding his fist on the table, his silk-sleeved arms flashing up and down in the focused light. "My people need to preserve their way of life. My people need this badly. Ms. Watson, why won't your stupid computer screen register this legitimate need?"

Lucy shrugged. "No one needs to preserve their way of life. What is a way of life? There must be something more specific about your way of life that your people need." A group groan rose from behind.

Teri Cross' body stiffened. "Your people want to preserve the privileges awarded them by the colonial power for your cooperation in the conquest of our lands. But now my people are in charge of the military. Your privileges no longer go unchallenged."

Lucy was tempted to point out that they had been over these issues already.

Phillip Zanter rose. His voice bellowed across the amphitheater. "Our peoples need a strong central leadership, a one-party system. A multi-party system feeds tribal factionalism, which leads to war. We are not Ireland, Ms. Watson. We are not Guatemala. You are trying to fit us in the wrong mold."

A young soldier came down from the second row and stood before the microphone. "My name is Andrew Mir. I would like to restate Mr. Zanter's thoughts in a way that the computer might acknowledge them. "The Maruvian people need to feel safe. We need our homes and our jobs to be safe so we can take care of our families."

The computer flashed Andrew's words on the screen. Phillip sat down and dropped his head into his hands. There was a long silence after that, and although no one spoke, Lucy began to feel sympathetic toward him. Then gradually the feeling changed, widened in a sense. She was not alone. Others felt that way too. How did she know that? No one had said a word about it.

Eventually an elderly woman approached the microphone. "Mr. Zanter worked hard for our country. He ruled for several years, built roads, provided buses and bicycles so people could travel. I had electricity in my store. Then came the coup. Then came the killing. Mr. Zanter tried to do a good job of ruling the country. Some people were jealous of his power. They wanted his power. That's why we had the killing. My people need to share power."

"THE THORINGIAN AND THE MARUVIAN PEOPLE NEED TO SHARE POWER," wrote the computer.

At that moment Lucy became aware of the feeling again. It was a group cohesion. They were all starting to solidify into one body like the cast of a play. How did she know that? No one had said anything about it. It was something you just knew, something you felt.

BERN CLOCK TOWER ~ SAME DAY

It was after six and already getting dark when Lucy and Dana passed under the clock tower. Street lamps were on and many windows of the town were lit. The smell of European cooking, of onions frying in grease, emanated from homes and restaurants. Lucy felt euphoric. The day had been successful. The computer had registered many more needs statements. Phase Two would begin in the morning. "I'll take you to dinner, Dana. We need to celebrate."

"I'm supposed to meet Martha at the Zum Rose. It's down in the next block. We'd be honored to have you join us."

"Yes, but it's my treat."

They found Martha Parks in front of the restaurant perched on one foot and wrinkling her nose at the menu board.

"Don't worry," Dana reassured her. "Lucy's going to pay."

"Really?" Martha didn't seem convinced.

"The prices aren't too bad here anyway," Dana took Martha's arm and ushered her into the restaurant.

A waitress wearing a dirndl, the traditional Swiss dress, led them to a small party room near the back by the kitchen. It was intimate and cozy with large exposed beams. A shelf displayed flowery porcelain goblets and platters against white, rough textured walls. There were three empty tables in the room, but no other guests. Lucy would have preferred to be alone with Dana, but she was also curious about Martha. Inside her gloomy little facade was someone who observed the world meticulously and wrote very well.

Dana and Martha removed their jackets unceremoniously by slipping their arms out of the sleeves and letting them fall naturally onto the backs of their chairs while Lucy laboriously shed the armor of her big overcoat and muffler, draping them over the antique oak hall tree.

The waitress handed Lucy the wine list and swished out through the swinging doors. It must have been obvious who was the "official" in this party.

Lucy examined the list carefully. "My favorite is Beaujolais," she said and looked questioningly at Dana.

Dana blushed. "I'm allergic to alcohol and Martha's in recovery." Both younger women laughed heartily as if it were a great joke on Lucy.

When the waitress came back, Lucy said, "I know you two don't drink, but do you mind if I have a glass anyway?"

"Not at all. Feel free," urged Dana.

Martha pumped her head up and down enthusiastically. Then she said. "I can have wine, so long as we order only one glass and don't buy the whole bottle."

Dana glanced warily at Martha. "Are you sure?"

"Quite sure." Lucy detected a serrated edge in Martha's tone, an irritation with Dana's mothering.

While taking her first sip of wine, Lucy said, "I know drinking is out of style these days, but I've always wondered how people celebrate without alcohol."

Dana shrugged. "I like coffee. How do you celebrate with alcohol?"

"What are we celebrating?" Martha had not gotten the point.

"The conclusion of 'Phase One'..." said Dana.

"The beginning of 'Phase Two'..." continued Lucy.

"I don't understand this 'Phase One and Two' stuff," grumbled Martha.

"You have to read Lucy's book on conflict resolution," said Dana.

Martha said, "I read most of the other one. I'm sorry to say I didn't understand much of it. Can you sort of summarize the main point, Lucy?"

"My first published work was on international law. I don't expect everyone to enjoy it, but I'm proposing substantial changes to the United Nations Charter. They would provide proportional representation by population and give the U.N. greater power. It would be a true government.

"I understood that part, but I couldn't figure out why it would be any better. I mean, how could a government so remote and far away in Switzerland or some place like that be any help to working people in Seattle, let alone Honduras or some of these poorer countries?"

"We would all send elected representatives to the world government," offered Dana, "the same way we send our congressmen to Washington."

Martha's eyes popped open very wide. "Hah! How much help are those jokers?"

Lucy smiled sadly and shook her head. "Not much, because local economies are no longer under local control. They are controlled by international corporations. There is no international regulatory authority for financial markets that is not controlled by wealth. There is not enough international cooperation for the taxation of capital. Big companies control the purse strings of the world, so, in effect, they control everything."

Martha shrugged and sunk into her chair. "I'm a poor person. I've been jobless and homeless a good part of my life. What makes you think I would understand that kind of stuff?"

Dana said, "Martha, you should read Lucy's second book, the one about conflict resolution. It's more interesting. You could have worked things out better with Karen Simeona if you had read it."

Martha smiled mischievously. "We didn't need a book. We had you."

Dana gave Martha a threatening glance as if she had said something wrong.

Martha took perhaps her third sip of wine and looked defiantly back at Dana. "Dana is good at conflict resolution. She puts people into a trance and helps them read each others' minds."

Lucy laughed nervously. Martha was joking of course, but Dana looked embarrassed.

"Now quit that, Martha!" There was a dull edge of warning in Dana's voice.

Martha took another sip of wine and giggled.

"You shouldn't drink even one glass," said Dana. Lucy said, "Don't worry. I won't buy her anymore."

"Good!" said Dana.

The waitress interrupted with an elaborate ritual. First, she set the table with shiny, white plates and cloth napkins. Then she brought a porcelain bowl of delicious-smelling stew which she placed on a chafing dish in the center. She then lit the flame and shuffled out.

Lucy served up large helpings for Martha and Dana, then gave herself a modest portion. Soon everyone was eating contentedly.

"This is great stuff!" Martha exclaimed, licking sauce from her lips.

While Martha was fully engrossed in her food, Lucy took the opportunity to make fond eye contact with Dana.

"This is wonderful, Lucy," said Dana. "Thank you so much for the opportunity to be here with you in this beautiful place."

Lucy wanted to hug Dana. Her gratitude was so ingenuous. "Thank you for celebrating with me," she said. "It's no fun to party alone."

"It's a privilege to recognize your victories, Ms.Watson...Lucy. To think you were once just a school teacher like so many others, but you have done such rare things with your life. Now you're famous."

Although she enjoyed the praise, Lucy found herself growing a little irritated with the direction it was taking. "It isn't fame I want. I hope you understand that, Dana. I only want to promote the charter revisions."

"Oh yes, I understand that. Everyone knows that, Ms. Watson... Lucy. I know you'll succeed. For one thing, you'll soon have an agreement for Maruvia. That will bring you a lot of credibility when the big discussions start in April." Dana reached across the table for Lucy's hand and wrung it vigorously, the long slender fingers wrapping themselves comfortably around Lucy's warm palm.

"Hah! But that's a joke. Lucy could not have done any of it without you, Dana," Martha's voice cut in with a sardonic edge as she set her empty glass down with an air of finality.

"Time to take Martha home and put her to bed," said Dana.

"Baloney!" exclaimed Martha. "I'm not drunk. One glass of wine wouldn't intoxicate even the most susceptible alcoholic. You just want to stop me from letting out your big secret, Dana."

Dana gave Lucy an anguished look. "I'm afraid she is drunk, no matter what she says. We should not let her have wine."

"Martha is an adult. We're not responsible for her," Lucy objected.

"You can't keep your secret forever, Dana," persisted Martha. "I, for one, know about you. If I do, others must, too. But don't worry. They don't burn witches anymore. There's no Spanish Inquisition. You should be proud of what you are. It's a great gift. Go for it, Dana. Tell Lucy. Lucy won't condemn you. Lucy's the nicest lady in the world. She loves you, Dana. Tell her!"

Dana glared at Martha. "Cool it, Martha. You're drunk."

Martha's upper lip quivered. "Okay, I'll cool it. But I was only trying to help." She slipped her arms into her jacket and stood up as if to leave. Lucy took hold of Martha's hand. "Please don't go. That's not how we resolve conflicts. How can we expect whole nations to resolve conflicts peacefully if we can't do it on a personal level in our own lives? Please stay. Let's talk about this."

Martha looked into Lucy's eyes. "I want to talk about it. I've been wanting to for months, but I was too chicken 'til you gave me a glass of wine. But Dana didn't have any wine. She's still scared. She wants me to shut up and go away." Just the same, Martha slumped back into her chair, snuggling into her jacket like a turtle in its shell. It was a pose Dana had drawn many times. Thanks to Dana, Martha Parks was now famous for her ability to look miserable.

Lucy looked at Dana who returned her gaze with a trapped expression. "I think we should make an appointment to discuss this some other time," said Dana.

Lucy asked, "What's wrong with now? I think we should seize the moment." She was curious about what this was all about.

"I want time to think. I don't know how to explain."

Lucy said, "Dana, if you have kept a secret for many months or years, your mind has rehearsed a million times how to tell it. It wants out badly."

"It gets out often, though not in words. That's how Martha knows. Maybe there are no words to really explain it."

"How does Martha know?"

"She has experienced it. So have you, Lucy, lots of times in peripheral ways, only you didn't know what was happening."

Lucy felt a vague sense of dread. Maybe she had experienced this mysterious "witchcraft" without fully realizing it. Maybe this strange quality they were so reluctant to discuss was what attracted her to Dana in the first place. This very morning, Lucy had found herself pondering the mystery of Dana Krandle, as Dana leaned over the Bear Pits in some sort of trance. "So, all right, Dana," she said. "I have experienced this mystery and I didn't know what it was. Now I want you to tell me as best you can."

"If we do a meditation exercise, I can show you," Dana offered hopefully.

"Perhaps," agreed Lucy. Then she turned on Dana with her sternest schoolteacher expression.

"But before you play with my mind again, Miss Krandle, I want you to tell me in plain American English what you are about to do."

Dana looked helpless, then resigned. "I'll try," she said, "but you may not understand."

Martha brightened and came to attention, popping her head out of the shell.

"My brain is freaky," continued Dana. "Most people's thought impulses stay inside their heads, as do mine, most of the time. But sometimes when I get real relaxed, in a trance, so to speak, my brain creates a powerful energy field way out into the space all around it. It picks up the thought impulses from other people's brains and allows thought impulses to blend."

"You mean you read other peoples' minds? How dare you?"

"No. I mean, very seldom. Sometimes they read each other's minds when I'm in this trance, because the energy field allows them to do it, but it takes too much concentration for me to maintain the trance. It would be too distracting to get caught up in people's thoughts. I can read peoples' minds if they participate, if they get themselves into a trance. I've done that with my cousin Charlie several times. He likes it."

Lucy could barely contain her indignation. Imagine snooping on other peoples' thoughts! Was nothing private? Was nothing sacred? "How wide is this energy field you speak of?"

Dana smiled as if she found Lucy's question naive. "I don't think it has size. It can vary in strength."

"How strong is it?"

Dana shrugged. "It depends."

"On what?"

Dana looked bewildered. "As I said, it varies. That's like asking how strong is a mood or a heat wave."

Lucy felt her lips curling into a grimace. "Let's put it this way. As far as you know, how close do people have to be in order for you to read their minds?"

Dana smiled that way again and shrugged. "I've never thought about it."

"Really? I can't believe that. Why not?"

"I guess because the person I've wanted to help this way has, in every case, been sitting right next to me."

"Help? How on earth does it help to have your mind read?"

Dana looked puzzled, but Martha chimed in. "It helps you feel understood."

Dana nodded enthusiastically. "That's why people like it. It's the only way to be really understood by another human being."

Lucy's blood was beginning to boil. "So you go around reading people's minds to help them feel understood?"

Dana flashed Lucy her sweetest, most ingenuous smile. "I've done it a few times, but it's not the way I like to use my ability."

"Oh?"

"No. What I like doing best is enhancing the spirit of a group, say like in a class or audience. Rallies are best."

"Why rallies?"

"There's more of a mood, a group spirit.

"How do you, as you say, enhance the mood? How do you accomplish such a feat?"

Dana shrugged. "It's pretty easy. I get in my trance, sense the powerful group spirit, and feel into it, enjoying it fully. That increases it."

"That's why you, Lucy, have so many followers," interjected Martha.

"Nonsense!" objected Dana.

"Not nonsense at all," said Martha. "People don't even understand Lucy's ideas. They just like her personality, and you enhance the spirit of World Walk gatherings, and everybody gets into it."

Lucy was horrified. "That's immoral!"

Dana shook her head emphatically. "No, it isn't immoral. If you were immoral, my support of you would also be immoral, as would anyone's, but you're on the up and up. Your motives are pure and your ideas are solid. The benevolence of your aims excludes no one. You want the best for every person in every corner of the Earth. What could be immoral about helping you?"

"I'll tell you what could be immoral about it. I don't want your kind of help. That's what. I don't approve of voodoo or magic. I don't believe in such things." How dare this child be so presumptuous?

Tears rose in Dana's eyes. "Please believe me, Ms. Watson. This is not voodoo. This is not magic. This is me! I was born this way. You only think it's magic because it's unfamiliar. In the world of my ancestors, I'm sure it's fairly ordinary."

"What world is that?" Lucy had always assumed Dana was your average Anglo kid from Seattle, but come to think of it, her features were rather...exotic.

Dana dropped her face into her hands and wept. "I wish I knew. I would go there if I could."

Martha reached over and began stroking Dana's hair. "I'm sorry, Dana. I didn't think Lucy would be angry. I'm really sorry." Then she turned on Lucy a menacing glare. "I really overestimated you, Lucinda Watson. I thought you would be kind. I mean, that you really believe in your theories, all this nonviolent conflict resolution stuff you preach. The only reason your system works at all is because it helps people slowly and tediously break down the barriers between their minds. Once those barriers are down, people realize they are basically all alike. They are no different from one another. In fact, they are one another, one and the same. I am you and you are me, Lucy. We are one."

Lucy fidgeted uncomfortably. This smacked of a sermon. She could almost hear the congregation responding with "Yessir!" and "Praise the Lord!" But this was not the time or place for a sermon, and the role of preacher did not become this miserable little prune of a recovering drug addict. "Maybe so," she said, "but I'll take the slow and tedious way."

Martha shrugged. "Suit yourself. But your movement will fall apart without Dana. There are too many strikes against you."

"Like what?"

"Too many groups that don't like you."

"Like who?" demanded Dana.

"Oh, come on, surely you must know about the militia groups that hate Lucy. They think she's trying to overthrow the United States government. And then there are the rich people who think she wants to tell them how to run the world, to play fair, share the wealth. Before Dana came along, they controlled public opinion. There wasn't a darn thing anyone could do about it, not on a measly World Walk budget."

"And now who controls public opinion?" Dana wanted to know. Dana had been gaping at Martha in amazement. Martha slumped back into her jacket.

"The rich people still, but we're starting to scratch the surface. It'll make a difference if Lucy gains agreement between Teri Cross and What's-His-Name by April, when the main conference talks begin."

"Zanter. Phillip Zanter," said Lucy.

"Yes. Mr. Zanter. You won't be able to do that without Dana's — what she calls her — energy field. I'm sorry, Lucy. Your system is good, but it needs Dana's help to be effective."

Lucy looked sharply at Dana waiting for her to disagree, but she just sat there looking sadly down at her long fingers twisted together on the white tablecloth, like massacred bodies on a shroud.

"Is that true, Dana?" Lucy demanded. "Do you agree with that?"

"Yes, I believe it's true." She spoke with reluctant resignation. The fire of Lucy's anger was suddenly doused by a chill of the same or some other emotion. She pushed back her chair and felt the full bulk of her body rising like a geologic fault above the table. "We'll go back to the hotel now and have a meeting. None of us will sleep until we have reached a resolution."

THREE WEEKS LATER EN ROUTE TO HOCHWALD

Dana focused on the hum of the electric train engine. She needed that sound to maintain her concentration and retain the blue light. Otherwise grief would take over, or panic. If the blue light disappeared, the negative energy field could close in before she knew it.

She had escaped for the moment, but it would come again, as it had repeatedly since the rally in St. Louis.

A couple of times the grief had almost taken over, and Dana had felt herself crumpling into a dysfunctional heap. Lucy was surely dead already. Her energy field was gone, blinked out like a tv set.

Martha's field was there, but quite weak. It would be Dana's fault if Martha died alone and friendless in a hospital in Bern. Martha would not have come to Europe without Dana. Dana had warned Martha about the danger, but instead of laying low, Martha had joined Dana in acting as security guard for Lucy.

If only Dana could visit Martha and comfort her, but she dared not go near any of her friends right now. The mountains were calling. Maybe she would find a good hiding place there.

Dana had been intrigued to hear of Alpine villages that could only be approached by train, or perhaps on foot in summer. Surely, no one would look for her there. They would expect to find her in Cleveland with World Walk, where Rhona and Monica were now conducting a mass vigil. But Dana must stay away from airports and rallies. The negative energy would be there, waiting.

Dana had tried to ignore, to deny, the negative energy. She had all but laughed at Mr. Genzforth's warning. But her peripheral consciousness had known he was right. Its power had been felt at the rally in St. Louis. Its nameless presence had walked the streets of Bern, lodged in the tall buildings on the hillside looking down over the city. It had watched as Lucy, Dana, and Martha strolled openly and cheerfully about the city enjoying the shops and restaurants. Dana had tried to warn Lucy, of course, but Lucinda Watson was not susceptible to fear. "If I die, my work will go on," Lucy had stated during one of their evening meals at the Zum Rose.

"Who will do the work?" asked Martha.

"Perhaps you will."

"And Dana?" grinned Martha.

"No, not Dana. Her drawings may help, but not her voodoo mind reading. I forbid it!"

Lucy had been adamant about that, forbidding Dana to attend any more of the conferences. Dana had agreed to stay away from the meetings on the condition that Lucy take one of the electric cars or walk with someone else. Whereupon Martha had volunteered to walk with Lucy.

Dana had felt like a prisoner each morning, as she watched from the window as Lucy and Martha emerged from under the arcade and strode up the street, an unlikely couple, sparrow and peacock, walking side by side.

After they were out of sight, Dana would turn on the television
and watch live coverage of the conference which was being broadcast
by satellite to the far corners of the Earth. This had gone on for a
couple of days before she noticed a pair of virtual reality goggles on a
shelf with the VCR. Perhaps she should try them. She had used the
technology in a movie theater once without much satisfaction. It had
been a lonely experience, as she lost her awareness of the rest of the
audience. This was different. In this case, the rest of the audience was
inside the conference room with the tv camera moving among them.
With the goggles on, Dana had felt like a bird flying about the room
unnoticed, zeroing in on people's faces, touching them, feeling them,
seeing the world from their eyes.

Eventually the blue light had come, and with it the startling perception of a large collective consciousness, greater by far than the one
she had experienced inside the conference room itself. This collective
included much of the television audience as well. The experience had
been awesome, even addicting, as she became aware that through
television contact, her own enjoyment of group feelings could enhance a collective mood that stretched to the far corners of the Earth.

The days had gone by very fast. Sometimes she felt guilty about
going against Lucy's command, but was powerless over the compelling urge of her mind to use its abilities.

After each daily round of meetings Dana would meet Lucy and
Martha for dinner at the Zum Rose. Lucy had been ecstatic about the
progress of the negotiations, her computer screen filling quickly with
statements of compromise, satisfying the needs of both the Maruvian
and Thoringian peoples. She was especially pleased about it all happening with no help from Dana, or so she thought. This time Martha,
although she probably knew, had managed to keep quiet.

Dana had been on her way to the Zum Rose early that evening to
wait for Lucy and Martha. It was to be a celebration, because the
official Maruvian Agreement had been drawn up that afternoon. She
had not been thinking about the negative energy field, but it had
suddenly swooped down on her like the shadow of a great bird as she
stepped out from under the clock tower. Something was wrong!
The terrible sound of several dozen European police sirens rang out
from the distance, a chorus of high and low alternating tones like an
enormous bugle corps tuning up. Dana ran toward the sound, her
heart pounding.

The street leading up the hill to the U.N. building was clogged
with police vans. A policeman got out, shouted something indistin-
guishable at Dana in German and waved her away. Dana noticed the
scarcity of pedestrians as she hurried back through the streets toward

the Hotel Kroeniger. She caught bits of conversation about sniper fire and assassinations as people rushed away.

By the time she reached the door of her hotel room, Dana's entire body was trembling. She could barely steady her hands enough to place her identification card into the slot and unlock the door. Once inside, she turned on the television and huddled down on her bed under the eiderdown. Her body shook uncontrollably, as if she had contracted malaria.

Dana watched through her tears the same news videos repeated again and again, clips of several people carried on stretchers down the steps of the U.N. building. She recognized only two of them. There was the unmistakable wounded-sparrow look of Martha; Lucy retained her air of regal dignity even in this most ignominious pose, with tubes and wires protruding from her exquisitely carved lips and oval nostrils.

A brief interview with the Bern Chief of Police was also repeated over and over. He would not offer any theories about a possible motive for the attack. But a variety of commentators presented a range of conjectures. Some believed Maruvian or Thoringian factions were disgruntled about the agreement. Others said this was a random act of someone criminally insane. Various black-market weapons trade cartels were blamed, as were several European left-wing terrorist organizations. No one, not even Rhona Lind or the World Walk leadership, admitted to suspicions of a powerful multinational corporate connection. But Dana remembered Martha's simplistic warning about rich people. She also thought about Aaron Genzforth.

At first, Dana had planned to stay in the hotel room and avoid the streets, but she soon felt trapped. The negative energy field had begun to close in. There might be better hiding places in the mountains.

Dana deliberately left her suitcase unpacked, and did not check out of the hotel. She stuffed all her remaining Swiss francs into a small daypack with a few essential items of clothing. Even though she would not be a convincing tourist with her eyes swollen from crying, Dana tried to act as though sight-seeing or winter sports was on her agenda as she headed for the station. The garishly-lit railway station was like a big fish bowl in the center of the old city. Along the inner walls, schedules of trains flashed on and off in bright orange letters. Within minutes, Dana had boarded a train for Interlaken.

Once there, she bought a tourist guidebook about ski trains to mountain villages, and, to be less conspicuous, she also bought skis and boots. She paid for everything with local currency. She would avoid using her credit card as long as possible, for fear of announcing her whereabouts to international computer networks.

She arrived in Hochwald in the early morning. Lights were still on in the windows of a dozen or more hotels. The village was more like a dream than a town, nestled in the breasts of a glaciated gorge with white peaks looming into the gray dawn. The train stopped near a steep-roofed building with scalloped gables and shuttered windows. Three balloon-cheeked men in lederhosen and woolen stockings stood out front, puffing into alphorns larger than themselves.

Dana paid for three nights' lodging with the rest of her cash. Instead of showing her credit card, she relinquished her passport. The fat, jovial proprietor didn't even open the passport. He scrawled something on a slip of carbon paper, handed Dana the original, and stuffed the copy into her passport, which he stashed in a small safe behind the desk without keying anything into his computer. This seemed to be a good hiding place.

Once inside her room, Dana began to have misgivings. After stashing the awkward burden of her skis against the wall beside the window, she looked out through a lace curtain onto the balcony which connected her room with several others. It commanded a fine view of the ski lift and glacier. The lift was so close that she could almost make eye contact with people waiting in line for their early morning run. This was rather public for a hiding place.

A quick survey of the interior was no more reassuring. One end of the room adjoined a small, white tile bathroom with an ordinary European style toilet and bidet. These facilities appeared to be shared with another room because there was an additional locked door on the other side. She considered asking for a more private location but thought the request might attract too much attention.

Lowering the outer window blind might also attract attention because it was the European custom to keep them open during the day. So Dana made do with merely closing the innermost layer of curtains. She could still see through them a little.

Beside the antique oak bedstead was a stand with a small lamp and phone. There was also an upholstered chair and a big oak wardrobe with a stenciled border of vines and flowers. At the foot of the bed, was an entertainment center complete with television, video game player, VR goggles, remote control, stereo, the works.

Dana took off all but her long underwear and turned on the television. Ignoring the wardrobe, Dana draped her clothes and pack over the chair. Then she removed a large croissant from her daypack, and nestled into the cloud of feather bed. Even though she had not eaten since the evening before, Dana was not particularly hungry. She nibbled dutifully at the stale morsel. She might need her strength.

The news channel was still replaying the same ugly footage of the previous day's events outside the government buildings in Bern. A reporter gave an update on the death toll and injuries. In addition to Lucy, two Maruvian women had died, tribeswomen who had been sponsored by the United Nations to attend the conference. The blue light came upon Dana while their stories were being told, and she found herself nodding off into a half-sleep, comforted by the light.

Even though she was exhausted from being up all night, Dana didn't completely lose consciousness. Her mind became enmeshed in a dream melange of hospitals, ambulances, and death. In one dream, her own body was placed on an autopsy table, and a latex-gloved hand made an incision carefully cutting her face in half from her Adam's apple, up over the chin and across her forehead. Her brain was then carefully removed and placed into a jar of clear liquid for preservation.

When she awoke, the blue light was still with her. But now somewhere within the light, Dana sensed that the negative energy field had returned. She opened her eyes and looked out through the white lace curtains at the vague line of skiers waiting to board the lift. She was a sitting duck here.

Her new skis stood guard where she had propped them against the wall. If she knew how to ski well, she could get away to a better hiding place. According to the guidebook, that lift took skiers high into the mountains, and they could ski to distant valleys where there were more hotels and ski huts. But she would not have enough francs to pay for all that. She would have to use the credit card. It was too much to hope that ski huts way up in the mountains didn't have computers. Dana was shocked to realize that she was entertaining serious thoughts of going up there. Was she crazy? Maybe the grief was making her suicidal. Or had Lucy's fearless spirit left her dead body and come to inhabit Dana? Not so. Dana was scared. Scared of what? Some nebulous energy field? Lucy wouldn't be caught dead with such a fear. Lucy would at least try the skis.

In front of the hotel was a long bench where Dana sat while mustering the courage to put on the skis. She had only been on skis a few times as a child and couldn't remember much about the rudimentary instructions she had received. For a long time she just stared at the long slender boards lying on the ground in front of her. Then she remembered about the negative energy field. The blue light was gone now so she could not tell whether the field was increasing, but she was certainly a target sitting still on this bench.

She stood up, placed her right toe in the clip and resolutely snapped her heel into the binding. Then using the poles for balance, she did likewise with the other foot and pushed gently forward, remembering to bend at the knees. A toddler whisked by, followed deftly by its grandmother. Dana felt like an infant giant learning to walk, as she inched toward one of the beginner towropes and grabbed hold.

Dana hesitated at the top of the slope, which was a gentle forty-degree angle and barely a hundred feet long. Remembering the first basic lesson from childhood, Dana bent deeply at the knees, spread her heels to make a snowplow and coasted uneventfully down. When she teetered slightly, Dana bent down even lower to catch her balance. That was easy, and she was soon engrossed in the practice of snowplows and turns. After she had negotiated the beginner slope several times, Dana began to eye a slightly steeper one that fell gently away and then disappeared into some trees farther down the valley. She couldn't see the bottom, but she knew the only way back was by train from another village. There was no telling what lay between. Still, the hiding was bound to be better down there. If worse came to worse, she could abandon the skis and glissade. But first she would have to go back to the hotel and get her daypack.

It had started to snow lightly when Dana came out of the hotel again wearing her small backpack. Big, soft flakes stuck to the skis tucked under her arm and to the cobblestone walkway that had been shoveled clean that morning. Someone was sitting on the bench in front of the hotel putting on skis. Snow fell on the his dark blue parka as the person's face turned toward Dana, revealing its long slender nose and sagging jowls.

Aaron Genzforth. Every muscle in her body tightened as she recognized him. The man stood up looking very much as he had at the rally in St. Louis. He wore the same parka dusted just as it had been with flakes of freshly fallen snow. Dana hesitated for a mere fraction of a second. Then she dropped her skis, and within a split second, snapped her boots into the bindings.

When she reached the top of the rope tow, Aaron had already latched on and was starting up. He could not have been more obvious about pursuing her. The negative presence she had sensed all along must have been his.

Pushing off with her poles to start down the slope, Dana glanced back over her shoulder. He was still following. Dana bent deeply at the knees, compressing her body like an accordion down to half its height, and tucked her poles in behind the way she had seen experts do on television. She was headed frightfully fast down the beginner slope, poised to go into a snowplow any second, if necessary. With luck, he would be a worse skier even than she and would not try to follow.

Without pausing at the bottom of the beginner run, Dana sighted the lower slope with the grove of trees. The fear that had previously tightened her muscles, now became a driving force, charging them with energy. Knees bent, body crouched very low, she started down. But as the trees sped toward her, it occurred to Dana that she wasn't sure how to avoid colliding with one of them just ahead. At the last possible moment, she blinked and leaned into her right knee and to her amazement, she slid like a pro around the obstacle. In like manner, leaning jauntily first right, then left, again and again, she managed to avoid all the trees and to come out beyond the woodlet. By now she had picked up speed and was tearing across the vacant landscape. She thought she heard someone calling, but when she glanced back over her shoulder, Dana found the slope deserted. It crossed her mind to wonder why this part of the run was so unpopular, and that was when the realization dawned. She was approaching a precipice.

Dana's entire body turned itself into a wrenching snowplow. Her skis crossed, forming an X in the air as she was hurled over the edge of a cornice which dispersed like a cloud beneath her. In that same instant, Dana became aware of the distance she was falling. There was a crushing impact with the loss of both skis as her entire body plunged into a bath of snow. Instinctively, Dana began flailing, lashing her arms and legs frantically as her body slid several feet and then stopped. Her next sensation was the extreme pain in her right leg, and the cold. She could see light shining from above as from the mouth of a cave, but she could not move a muscle. She was at least partially buried, but with some relief, found that she could still breath. It seemed she had finally completed the fall that had been aborted several years before on the slopes of Mount Rainier. It was as though she had been predestined for an icy grave.

Dana began to meditate on her imminent death and to reassure herself that hypothermia was not reputed to be a bad way to go. She was alarmingly cold. The blue light would come soon and her mind with its powerful energy field, would move into the light, losing consciousness of the pain and cold. Soon, her body would grow numb and she would fall asleep, never to awaken into a world of cruel realities where good people are killed in senseless acts of violence. Maybe she had put on the skis out of a subconscious wish to die.

But then she heard voices coming from somewhere, all around, from above. Soon there were busy, frantic sounds of scraping and crunching. Unlike the Eastside Hiking Club, who had simply waited above for Dana to rescue herself, unseen people were allowing her to lie passively in the snow while they dug her out.

They spoke in a flow of babble, German perhaps, in some unfamiliar dialect, but their tones were unequivocally reassuring.

Dana was profoundly grateful when a black, gloved hand wiped a lump of ice out of her eyes and then dried her cheeks with something soft and warm. But she shuddered from the pain when someone touched her right knee. After that they touched her ever so carefully. They wrapped a splint and gauze bandage around the leg before lifting her carefully onto a sled and covering her with a blanket. Dana found herself admiring their skillful movements and reassuring ways. This must be an official rescue patrol because they all wore sleek black ski uniforms. Each of their chests was decorated with the Swiss flag, a large red square with a white cross in the center. The scene would have been complete if they had been accompanied by a St. Bernard dog.

When she awoke, Dana's leg was fully cast and her arms were wrapped in bandages. She was lying on the bed in her hotel room. The outer blind on the window was closed, the only light coming from the small lamp on the bedstand. She wore the extra-long sweatshirt that doubled as her nightgown, but she had no recollection of having put it on. The pain was still intense but not as bad as before.

An incredibly tall, elderly woman came in, unbandaged Dana's arms and gently massaged her wrists which ached badly from sprain or frost bite or both. Although they ached, Dana felt sure the arms were not broken. The leg was another matter.

The woman looked at Dana with gray, wing-shaped eyes that seemed to reflect a quiet wisdom. She wore black ski clothing like the rescue patrol, only without the Swiss flag or ski cap. Her wavy, white pixie haircut formed a fluffy border around her very wrinkled face. "How are you?" inquired the woman cordially. She spoke with a thick, exotic accent.

"I'm not sure how I am," said Dana, "except that I hurt all over." She glanced in the direction of the bathroom.

"I'll get you a bedpan. You must not get up. You must stay still." That was obvious. It hurt to even think of moving, but she was not sure how to use a bedpan, especially without moving. What an idiot she was to get herself into this predicament! The woman left and returned very soon with a shiny stainless steel receptacle resembling a cross between a wash basin and a toilet seat. She set the bed pan beside Dana on the edge of the bed. "Would you like some help?"

Dana thought about that a moment and shook her head. Then she carefully raised the upper part of her body into a sitting position, relieved to find she was able to do this, even with excruciating pain. Next she made deliberate eye contact with the woman, as if asking her telepathically to leave the room.

The woman left, but came back immediately after Dana finished, as if she had been listening at the door as Dana struggled, moaning every so often from pain, when she accidently moved her leg. The woman took the pan into the bathroom and could be heard emptying and washing it out. When she came back, she set the ugly thing on the chair beside the bed.

The woman left again and returned with a tray of food. Rolls, coffee, and margarine comprised the entire menu, suggesting that it must be morning; otherwise Dana would not have known the time of day. Her watch was gone, perhaps stored with the rest of her clothes somewhere, maybe in the wardrobe.

Dana devoured the breakfast quickly, surprised that she was able to feel hungry again. Maybe that was because the weight of responsibility she felt for Lucy's death and Martha's injuries was lighter, now that she had paid for it by getting hurt herself.

When the woman came back again with a pitcher of ice water, Dana said, "Ich moechte fahrsehen, bitte."

The woman smiled graciously and turned on the television. "News?" she asked.

"Yah, news!" Dana shook her head enthusiastically. The woman handed Dana the remote control and the VR goggles. Then she started to leave, but Dana said, "You seem to know English very well."

"Yes," the woman assured her, "I studied for many years."

"That's good, because I have a question. I was wondering if I will have enough francs to pay for all this."

The woman smiled. "It is all paid for, and more."

"Amazing! Is the Swiss medical care system so benevolent?"

The woman blushed. "The Swiss government does not pay. It is a gift from someone. Your friend."

Dana was astounded. "Who? Why?"

The woman shrugged. "I assure you, the bill is paid, no matter how long you have to stay. Your friend made out several generous vouchers to cover everything.

"My friend..."

The woman nodded and smiled ingenuously.

Dana gasped. Aaron Genzforth. He had been following her down the beginner slope when she saw him last. He must have been the one who called the rescue patrol. It was mortifying to think that this person of whom she was so frightened had actually saved her life. Dana glanced about the small dimly lit room. "How long do I have to stay?"

"I cannot say. It is for Doctor Baucke to tell you that. She will come again soon up from Lichtengarten." She gestured toward the phone on the bedstand. "In the mean time if you need anything, phone the hotel meister and ask for Mina. He will let me know." She reached for the wall switch to open the outer blind. "I presume you prefer natural light?"

"Yah. Danke schön. Thank you, Mina. It was so nice to meet you." The woman left without locking the door, and the busy ski lift was still faintly visible through the lace curtains. It was hard not to feel exposed. Dana thought of trying to get up and close the blind, but that was not possible. Her struggle with the bedpan had proven that.

Despite her feeling of insecurity, Dana put on the goggles and was quickly drawn into the all-day news coverage. The news channel had become an addiction during her last few days in Bern. She felt ashamed of this, having never been a tv junkie — even in childhood — disapproving the habit in Charlie and other friends. The media had become especially compelling, now that there were frequent reports of her own friends.

The first familiar face to appear live that morning was Phillip Zanter. He was shown boarding a taxi in front of his hotel in Bern. The reporter proclaimed confidently that with the agreement signed, this former war criminal was free to go where he wished. Zanter's round, puffy face smiled broadly into the camera and faded out, to be replaced by a replay of the previous day's interview of him seated at a desk in one of the Bern government buildings.

"Will you be returning soon to your homeland and assume the leadership of your country?" the female reporter asked in an officious British accent.

"Perhaps. But first there must be an election in accordance with our agreement. Even so, I will share power with my friend, Teri Cross."

"Word has it you will stop over in America. Will you meet with the President?"

"If she has time for me. I will meet with whomever I can. As you know, Mr. Cross and I were not paid any money by the United States for making this agreement, as were so many others. I will meet with several non-government organizations and ask them to invest in our people."

"Are you planning to tour the United States?"

Phillip laughed. "I cannot afford the luxury of a vacation. I have been gone from home too long already."

"How long will you stay?"

"Perhaps a week, two at most. After meetings in New York and in the Capitol, I will go to Chicago and attend the funeral of my good friend, Lucinda Watson. As you know, that patient facilitator of our discussions was killed in crossfire yesterday. She was a great woman and I must go to honor her."

Dana smiled through her pain. She knew Mr. Zanter had been

torn between love and hate for Lucy. Now that she was gone, love had apparently won, at least so far as the public was concerned.

There followed several unrelated reports, interspersed with commercials depicting all sorts of extreme flights of fantasy. The blue light came while Dana was watching an automobile commercial. The car was being driven to the accompaniment of a Beethoven symphony over the swirling brush strokes of an abstract painting. It was not the first time that a tv commercial had brought on a trance. It had happened in Bern, once she had learned to tune out references to the products, and focus on the mood enhanced by music and special effects.

While Dana's mind was still suspended in the blue light, there was another repeat of the ugly scene with Lucy being carried down the steps of the government building on a stretcher, and the whole tragic story was summarized again. Live coverage of a huge World Walk rally in a Pittsburgh Stadium was broadcast next. A picture of the bust of Lucinda Watson, enlarged three stories high, formed the backdrop for the stage. Standing on a speaker's platform in front of the picture, Rhona Lind looked small enough to be a pin on Lucy's lapel, but her voice rang out loudly over the sound system.

"We have come together to remember our beloved sister, Lucinda Watson." Dana reached for the VR goggles and slipped them over her eyes just as the camera zeroed in on Rhona's face, picking up the luster in her large blue eyes. A shiny tear trickled down Rhona's cheek.

Wiping the tear away with her bare hand, Rhona continued, "Lucy, as she was known to us all, lead a selfless life committed to a promise she made to the working people of the world and to their children. She wanted every one of them to have decent shelter, health care, education, opportunity, hope. Lucy had a vision of how words of law could bring that about. I, too, am convinced that Lucy's laws — if adopted — will change the world's priorities at all levels, placing the world's economic institutions under democratic control of the people affected by them."

Dana felt a surge of love and acquiescence filling every crevice of her mind. At the same time, she felt that emotion broadcasting itself out into a vast energy field, whose size and proportions she could not estimate. Through the virtual reality of television, her thought waves were being broadcast everywhere on the planet. She fell into the vast collective mind again, filling it with her hope and joy as Rhona continued her eulogy.

"My friends, Lucinda Watson had not only a great mind, but also a great heart, and she has left the world a legacy that cannot be taken away. She has also left us with a lot of unfinished business. We must dedicate, not just a moment or two, but rather our entire lives, to finishing what Lucy started. We will take the first very important steps within the next few months. During that time, we, the people of World Walk, will continue our trek from all corners of the Earth to meet in Bern, Switzerland for the International Law Conference. We will insist that the essential elements of Lucy's laws be considered — and adopted — by the Council of Nations, and incorporated into the proposed revision of their new charter."

Dana sensed Rhona's enthusiasm rising to a crescendo as she added, "Everyone is invited to join us on the final phase of our journey. Take leave of your jobs if the work is useless and unfulfilling, if the work is in sweatshops that provide no retirement benefits or security for your future. Please join us and demand laws that protect the rights of all workers, laws that demand protection of the environments in which we live as a world community. You need only bring a small pack with change of clothing and your wish for a better world. My friends, this is an opportunity of a lifetime, no, of many lifetimes. We invite you to share this great moment in history. My friends, how would it have felt to promote and witness the signing of the Magna Carta. My friends, this summer in Bern, Switzerland, we will witness an event more important to humankind than any previous moment. I invite you to be part of this. Come, walk with us. Walk, walk, walk..."

"Walk...walk...walk," Dana could feel the electrochemical impulses in her brain picking up the word and echoing it like a litany into the collective. Rhona Lind faded out with the program theme music, and another commercial came on depicting a computer chip portrayed as a UFO flying around an office to the accompaniment of high-pitched laser music. The blue light vanished, and Dana turned off the television using the remote control device still cradled in the palm of her hand. She felt emotionally and mentally drained and incredibly sleepy.

While sleeping, Dana had a fully cognizant dream, recurrent since childhood, of a bald giant with a large head and skinny long neck. The giant was so tall that he stood in front of the building looking in her second story window. This frightened Dana into wakefulness only to find that there did appear to be someone looking in at her through the lace curtains. There was a knock at the door and without waiting to either be invited, or spurned, Aaron Genzforth came in, and closed the door behind him. At first Dana was frightened, but Aaron seemed so ingenuous and congenial, he almost won her over. "I'm sorry to intrude, but I wanted to know how you were doing. It scared me when you went over that enormous ski jump." He started to make himself at home by sitting in the chair, but noticed that it was filled with the bedpan.

"You chased me over that cliff!" Dana snapped at him. Through the tears starting to well up in her eyes, Dana watched Aaron stop prancing about in search of a place to sit. Finding none, he sat down on top of the bedpan.

"That's garbage! I wasn't chasing you. I was trying to catch up so I could talk to you. It isn't my fault you ran away. Am I so frightening that you have to ski over a cliff to avoid me?"

Dana gazed frankly at Aaron. He looked like an elderly buzzard perched there on the bedpan, his Adam's Apple bulging slightly as he spoke. If only there would be time to find out what he was really up to, but she would not be able to get him into a trance or read his mind. He would be most uncooperative if she tried that. This man's secrets were well-guarded. His stock in trade was not communication, but rather the lack of it. She threw out more accusations. "You're spying on me. You've been doing it all my life. I'll bet it was you who killed Lucinda Watson, the nicest person in the world."

"What? Where do you get these ideas? I may not share your idolatry of Watson, but I did not kill her."

"You know who did kill her, or why she was killed, but you have not told the police."

Aaron rubbed his wrinkled talons together nervously.

"That's nonsense. Besides, even if the killer were named and caught, we would all know that some unknown someone else was really behind it. There will be unresolved conspiracy theories until the end of time. That's how it goes with assassinations. As for why she was killed — Lucinda Watson was a rabble-rouser who wanted to rule the world. If people like her were not so ridiculous, they would be extremely dangerous."

"Lucy didn't want to rule the world. That's absurd."

"Maybe not single-handedly, but she was after world government, another big layer of bureaucracy to interrupt the affairs of business. Lucinda Watson wanted the world to ride a dinosaur into the third millennium."

"Well, she's gone now," Dana said sadly. There was no use in arguing with him. Anyway, she was lost when discussions got too political.

"Maybe so, but her menace isn't," persisted Aaron. "Lucinda Watson's assassination has stirred up a riot of sympathy with her ideas. This World Walk thing is mushrooming out of proportion."

Dana grinned. If he only knew it was she, Dana Krandle, who was feeding the mushroom.

"World Walk can do no harm. They are well-intentioned, good people."

"Well-intentioned people are the worst kind, and I assure you there'll be trouble when they get to Europe. All the cities they'll be traveling through are stepping up security. There are going to be a lot of those rabble-rousers, the likes of which the world hasn't seen since the sixties."

Dana thought about that. She couldn't remember the sixties, but they were legendary in her family history. Mom had told the story over and over of how terrified she had been watching the Chicago riots on television while rocking Dana to sleep on Levin Island. Dana often wondered whether those years had precipitated Mom's dislike of politics. Dad had always seemed a bit nostalgic about the sixties, despite all the misery he had been through with Uncle Marvin. "It won't be like the sixties," Dana said.

Aaron stroked his narrow beak of a nose with his long talon. "That brings up the subject I wanted to talk about yesterday when you ran away from me again. I wanted to tell you that for the rest of your stay in Europe you will be under heavy surveillance."

"Surveillance? Why? I haven't committed any crimes."

"Of course not. It's for your safety. There will always be someone watching...you can't possibly get into trouble."

Dana was furious. "You have no business having me followed! What business is it of yours where I go?"

Aaron looked at Dana with a touch of fondness for a long moment. Then he said, "In a few years, I'll be retired. Then I suppose it won't be any of my business any longer. I hope by then the mystery will be solved, but I doubt it. I'll probably go to my grave not knowing."

"Not knowing? You already know more about me than I know myself. What more do you want to know?"

This time there was an even longer pause as Aaron stared at Dana with deep, piercing eyes.

"Where you really came from. Who your parents really were."

Dana thought about that a moment. Then she shuddered inside as a rush of subconscious knowledge was released to her consciousness. She and Aaron had been wondering all these years about the same thing. She flashed him a wide grin in case he preferred to think she was joking. "I think I am an alien. I think I am from outer space. For some cruel unknown reason my mother came and left me here with a bunch of strangers, primitive barbarians probably, to her way of thinking."

Aaron looked at her with a mixture of shock and curiosity. Then he asked in a mildly sardonic tone, "Would you like to prove it?"

"No, of course not! I would much rather prove otherwise. I would hate to prove that I'm an alien."

He gazed at Dana intently. "And that is where we differ," he said.

"I want very much to prove that you're an alien. What's more, I think it likely that the aliens are not so cruel, and that they may want to give you the opportunity to reunite with them. When they do, I would like to meet them."

"Why?"

"To obtain proof of them."

"What good would come of that?

"I have spent my life collecting reams of paper filled with useless information, to say nothing of rams of computer capacity full of equally useless data. Later I came to realize that most of the time I was pursuing some imaginary enemy born of some group fear or other. But if I could prove human contact with aliens, that would be something noteworthy."

Dana smiled sadly. The man was pathetic, really. "Aaron, it seems a terrible waste for you to spend the government's money following me around. No aliens have ever contacted me in person directly and I'm sure they never will."

Aaron's left eyebrow raised almost imperceptibly. "Have they contacted you some other way?"

"Yes...but no, not really."

"What do you mean, yes-but-no-not-really?"

"They contacted me once or twice in my mind, telepathically, so to speak. That doesn't count. Maybe it was a dream. A dream is hardly proof. Everyone has weird dreams."

Aaron looked at her intently with one eyebrow raised very high. "So, you admit then that you are capable of mental telepathy."

"Sure. Everyone is to some extent."

Aaron shook his head emphatically. "No, not the way you are. Your way is different, very different."

Dana felt a chill go through her. How did he know that? She had never told anyone but Dr. Holt, and more recently, Martha and Lucy. Yet Martha and Charlie knew without being told. They had figured it out on their own. She had used her abilities perhaps too freely and openly at Sullivan House. Lots of people knew, at some level of consciousness. The knowledge was practically in the public domain; Aaron Genzforth would not have let it escape his thorough inquiry. The man was infuriating. "It's none of your business. You have no right to spy on me or keep me under surveillance. Even if you suspect me of being an alien, I am a United States citizen. I have a right to privacy. If you ever enter my quarters again uninvited, I'll call the police."

After Aaron left, Dana phoned the desk and complained that her door had been left open. The man apologized and promised that it would not happen again. Maybe a lock would not be enough to keep

Mr. Genzforth out, but there was no need to encourage him.

Dana lay on her back, fuming about the encounter with Aaron Genzforth. It was intolerable to be so helpless. She was a virtual prisoner. Dana was still fretting when her elderly caretaker came in again. This time, besides a covered bowl of soup, the woman brought a pair of crutches and propped them against the chair. "Doctor Baucke says it's all right for you to try these, but I must help you at first." Perhaps it wouldn't be much more difficult than the bedpan. Dana was grateful. She knew crutches were not all that easy to master, but she saw them as one step toward regaining her freedom. The woman handed her the television remote control device and locked the door on her way out. For a long time, Dana lay there meditating on the slender plastic rectangle in her hand. If Aaron Genzforth had known everything about her telepathic abilities, he would surely have confiscated this. She smiled through her pain and clicked back on the news.

HOCHWALD ~ TWO WEEKS LATER

Dana awoke from the same dream again. This was at least the third night in a row. She knew recurring dreams were important, so before opening her eyes, she played the sequel over in her mind to solidify it in memory. The dream was set in a small room where a group of perhaps two dozen people, mostly women, sat in a circle around what seemed to be a glass cylinder extending from floor to ceiling. The women wore long robes of bright interwoven colors. Dana didn't recognize any of their faces in particular, but a couple of them looked vaguely familiar. Their eyes were closed and they seemed to be concentrating on one group thought, perhaps a single word repeated over and over. Dana listened in her mind to the word which gradually became distinguishable as the subvocalized sound of her own name, "Dana." With that realization, she was filled with a sense of warmth.

A familiar-looking elderly woman stood up and dropped her robe to the floor, revealing a black, form-fitting garment underneath. The woman looked very familiar now, but Dana could not quite place her.

The woman took a giant step toward the cylinder, which created a kind of suction that pulled her into itself. The cylinder closed with the woman clearly visible inside, then descended swiftly as if falling into a well. Dana opened her eyes to find Mina seated in the chair beside the bed. Dana took hold of the crutch that was leaning beside the bed and pulled herself up to a sitting position facing the older woman. "I just dreamt about you, Mina."

The woman bestowed on Dana a smile of quiet wisdom. "What did the dream tell you about me?"

Dana felt a rush of excitement. This was the moment she had been waiting for, for a lifetime. "Perhaps...you are from the aliens? Are you from my real mother, Wella De Gornia?"

Mina stood up solemnly, removed the crutch from Dana's hand and leaned it against the bed. She took both Dana's hands in hers, leaned forward and touched Dana's forehead with her own. Then she sat down in the chair again. "I am so glad that you are ready to receive my message, Dana. I have been wanting so much to tell you."

"You have a message from my mother?"

"Yes, your mother sends her love, but I have much more to speak with you about. I am Shulmina of Severelia. I am in charge of the research project that involved your mother, Wella De Gornia, and you. We have concluded that this project is in jeopardy and we must abandon it. You would be well advised to return with us to Gallata, which is your rightful home."

"But why? You are speaking of an alien world. How do I even know I could live there? It would be strange. This planet is my home."

"The choice will be entirely yours, but you need to know the full implications either way. That's what I've come to tell you about."

"Implications?"

"Yes, I want to describe them in full, but you must be ready. Perhaps you should complete your morning bathroom ritual while I get you some coffee."

Dana was almost too excited to function, but she did feel the need to relieve herself, so she pulled herself up haphazardly on the crutches and stumped toward the bathroom, hoping Shulmina would not disappear like an apparition while she was gone. When she came out of the bathroom, Dana was relieved to find breakfast waiting on the bedstand and Mina seated in the chair. Dana sat down on the edge of the bed. "You were telling me about the implications," she said.

Shulmina said, "The most important thing you need to know is that Aaron Genzforth knows virtually everything about you. He has x-rays of your skull and samples of your brain chemicals. He has also figured out what you've been doing here with your television set and VR goggles."

"So what? He has always known, but he's harmless. He has never done anything about it."

"Oh, but he has, and very recently. He has connections with the those who paid for the killing of your friend, Lucy. He has told them what you're doing and has convinced them of who you are. They will keep you under surveillance and, at the right moment, make you their prisoner, perhaps for life. The only reason you have not been killed is that they wish to study you, in effort to learn more about us."

"Who are these people?"

"Let it suffice to say, they are Earth humans whose power would be diminished by Lucy's version of the new United Nations Charter. You see, Dana, although Aaron Genzforth has always been interested in you, he has not been able to credibly interest anyone else, until recently."

"Those are serious implications," said Dana. "Now tell me, what would be the implications of going with you to this place you call Gallata?"

"The journey will be very long, but most of the time you will sleep. During the few waking hours, and partly through subliminal messages during sleep, you will learn about Gallatan customs. You will be with other Gallatans who are much like you. They have a completely different way of communicating than Earth humans.

"How do they communicate?"

"Your way."

"My way?"

"They join together as a group and focus their minds on a single image. That is, they meditate together and enter a common trance. Their minds are capable of broadcasting and blending thought waves."

"Incredible." To think there really were other people like herself!

"But you would have to learn the protocols," warned Shulmina.

"Protocols?"

"For instance, everyone has to be in the mood and agree to the trance. It can't be one-sided."

"I know," agreed Dana. "It's horrible if it's one-sided. Uh, is that all they do on Gallata?"

Shulmina laughed, "Of course not, otherwise it's like Earth in some ways, but there is a lot less violence because people share thoughts and come to realize that their disagreements were merely misunderstandings, that all mental energy in the universe is of one substance."

Dana took her first bite of roll but found she was too excited to chew, so she took a sip of the rapidly-cooling coffee. Then she asked, "What else do they do — I mean on Gallata?"

"Ordinary things. Gallatans have their own cultures, as do people on every other planet. But you should also know that Gallata is a rural place made up of small islands."

"Like the San Juans?"

"Rather like the San Juans. That's why we chose an island for you. Unfortunately, you were taken away from there after only a few years. It would have been much better for our research — and for you — to have stayed there your entire life. The hope was that you would have children there to inherit your abilities, so that we could carry on the study for several generations.

Mention of the San Juan Islands caused Dana think about her family. Charlie had written that they were worried about her. She had made arrangements to meet with Charlie and her World Walk friends in Bern, as soon as the leg was healed enough to travel, but that was before.... Now it seemed as if she had already boarded a spaceship, destination as yet unknown.

BASEL AIRPORT ~ ONE MONTH LATER

Charlie felt a little more at ease once he had settled into the back seat of the chauffeured electric car headed for Bern. Still, everything seemed unreal, like a visit to Disney World. The car was like a weird little plastic spaceship. Gazing through its bubble of a window and down into a ravine, he could see a group of cottages with honeycomb window panes and red tile roofs. The scenery reminded him of a fairy-tale book Grandma Ruth used to read to him when he was little. There were the same whitewashed farm buildings and pastures as perfect as mowed lawns. Everything was aglow with the warmth of springtime.

Charlie was out of his element in Europe. He had known that from the moment he stepped from the jet liner into the river of human babble that carried him like flotsam up a ramp and into the terminal. Hardly anyone was speaking English, and the only other language Charlie knew was a bit of Suquammish he had learned from Grandma Redtree. If it hadn't been for picture symbols on all the doors and everything, he might not have figured out which was the men's room. Even then, he thought he was mistaken because there was an old woman sitting just inside the door. He blushed and started to leave, but then he saw a man standing there peeing into a hole in the floor.

Charlie had found it pretty hard to pee in front of the woman. Then when he started to leave, she shoved her palm in his face and blasted him with a full volley of nasty-sounding gibberish. Even though he didn't recognize a single word, Charlie got the message. He reached in his pocket and pulled out a dollar, but the woman kept jabbing him with the same grumpy gobbledygook over and over, real insistent-like. That was when Charlie remembered he had the wrong kind of money. Jim had told him there would be an exchange machine at the airport where he could get some Swiss money, and that he should to do that first thing. He really had meant *first*, even before going to the bathroom.

The airport was a madhouse with all sizes, shapes, and colors of people rushing about. Jostled by the crowd, Charlie bumped into one of the security guards, posted regular as pillars along the walls. Heavily armed with assault rifle and bullet belts, the big stump of a fellow might as well have been a pillar, for the little reaction he gave.

Charlie finally found a woman at the information booth who spoke English. She eyed Charlie with cold disdain and assured him all trains for Bern were booked for the next several days. In a sarcastic tone, she said lots of people were walking to Bern. That was when Charlie realized with some embarrassment that the woman thought he was going there for World Walk. Instead, he had strict orders from the father of one walker to bring his daughter home as quickly as possible.

"How far is it?" he asked. Jim had said it was about fifty miles.

"Eighty kilometers."

"That's too far to walk. Is there another way?"

"You could take local transit for short segments, and thumb rides in between."

Charlie grimaced.

"You can buy a bicycle in town."

Charlie considered that idea thoughtfully. But first he would have to find the town, then the store, and then the way to Bern. Besides he didn't have any panniers and wasn't about to pedal all that way with his backpack on. "Can I get a cab?"

The woman laughed. "You could hire one of the electric cars, but there will be a wait. The cars are in use by government officials attending the conference."

It had been a very long wait — since early evening the previous day. Charlie looked at his big, black plastic wristwatch which he had set by the clock in the terminal. It was nine o'clock. He would probably be in Bern around lunchtime. He reached in his coat pocket for the most recent letter from Dana. It was written on a small piece of lined paper that now looked the worse for wear, folded and refolded with a tourist map of Bern. A circle, drawn on the map with the same pen, designated the spot where Charlie was to meet Dana.

The letter read: "Dear Charlie, I'm glad you'll be coming to Bern. Rhona says her contingent will arrive the first week of April, so I'll join them there. Maybe you should show up around the second week when things get going. There's a market square behind the government buildings, and that's where all the action will be. Some of us will camp there so it won't be that hard to find us. Just ask for me by name. I'm well-known. I'm so looking forward to seeing you again. You're the best friend I have in the world, after all..."

Charlie folded the letter again and put it back in his pocket. Then he closed his eyes trying to really feel the pain in his heart. In AA they said to let yourself feel emotional pain, not deny it.

After he got laid off and Rosey left, and there was no Dana around, he had to attend about five AA meetings a week to keep sober. It had meant so much when he got the first letter from Dana inviting him to Europe. He felt so bad that she was injured and all alone way up in the mountains. He still couldn't figure out what might have possessed her to go skiing up there all by herself.

Charlie would not have taken this trip if it hadn't been for Jim insisting and buying his plane ticket. Grandma Redtree had tried to persuade him to get a job at the submarine base. But Jim said Europe was great and Charlie deserved a vacation, and with Charlie's experience in handling hazardous material, there would be jobs waiting when he got back. Jim had practically twisted Charlie's arm, because he didn't want his little girl over there all alone with a broken leg. Jim had given Charlie specific orders to bring Dana home. In fact, Charlie knew that if he came back without Dana, he'd be in big trouble.

The electric car driver was a wiry little fellow with large ears and bulging eyes peering out through thick glasses. He seemed to belong in the car, like a robot manufactured along with it. But he didn't seem to speak English very well so Charlie showed him the circle drawn on the map. The man shook his head. "No cars allowed, only government officials."

"Does that mean I can't go there?"

The man chuckled softly. "You can go there if you want. I would not want to these days. But you must walk. The streets are very crowded." He pointed to another spot on the map. "I take you here. Then you walk uphill."

Charlie took a pen from his breast pocket and drew a circle around the spot where he was to be let off. Then he carefully traced a line along the most direct route connecting the two circles. It was a curved line that might designate a street or road leading up a hill.

When the electric car approached the old quarter of Bern, Charlie began to understand why there might be a limit to how much farther a vehicle could travel. The streets were not much wider than bike paths, and they were clogged with pedestrians. Charlie had never seen such a variety of nationalities in one place. Some of them wore various native costumes like dirndls, robes, and leather knee pants, but there were also a good many silk business suits and everything else, not to mention a good many panhandlers in rags.

Charlie's stress level shot way up when he got out of the car. There were so many people in the streets he could hardly breathe, let alone move. No one seemed to notice him, bent as they all were upon getting through the crowd. He felt invisible.

Instinctively, Charlie moved toward the edge of the street and leaned against a stone wall. He closed his eyes, as though by making the scene disappear, he could remove himself from it. From the darkness behind his closed eyelids, Charlie recalled one summer night on his hitchhiking trip back from Alaska. He had stood all alone beside the Al-Can Highway in a vast wilderness, trying to comprehend the immeasurable distance between himself and another human being, trying to realize the gulf between himself and that one faint star overhead. Charlie needed to go back to that place now. Before opening his eyes, he focused himself by rubbing the wall he was leaning against. Its texture was rough. At waist height, something even rougher bulged out of the wall, helping to shore up his backpack. It was a timber, very large and crude. Charlie stretched his hand across the timber from the nail edge of his thumb to the tip of his index finger. Roughened by hard work, his hand felt like an extension of the wood.

Opening his eyes, he gazed up at the building and noted that its walls were not quite vertical, they leaned a little to the left. The old house reminded him of a faded, gray photo in the Suquammish Museum back home. That was the only surviving photograph of a longhouse built in the ancient way of the tribe. There was a homey imperfection about both buildings. Charlie took a deep breath and felt a little better.

As he shifted his weight from the wall of the house onto his feet and stepped out into the crush of pedestrian traffic, a tiny, birdlike face with large dark eyes appeared just below his and a voice warbled forth in astonishingly clear American English, "Excuse me, sir, would you happen to be Mr. Redtree, Dana Krandle's cousin from Seattle?"

Charlie was too astonished to speak at first. Finally he mumbled, "Yeah, sure. How'd you know who I am?"

He examined the woman curiously. Thin strands of dark hair were pulled back tightly across tiny ear lobes from which hung big gold loops. She wore blue jeans and a soft, gray knit tunic. The big eyes looked up at him as if out of a deep well of sadness and smiled. "Dana said you were coming. She asked us to keep watch for you. I'm Martha Parks," she added in an almost boastful tone, as if she thought her name so famous everyone would recognize it.

"Oh? Do you know where I can find Dana?"

"She was in the square when I left, watching them set up for the rally, but she didn't plan to stay. She was going to watch the rally on tv in the lobby of the Kroeniger Hotel. They have one there so guests can follow conference events without having to brave the crowds."

Charlie thought that was a good idea. He also thought it strange that Dana would leave a live event to watch it on tv. She had always preferred crowds to television. "Where's that?" he asked.

"Where's what?"

"The Kroeniger."

The woman pointed one skinny hand back down the street in the direction from which Charlie had come in the electric car. With the other hand, she reached out and pulled on Charlie's forearm. "I'll take you there."

If he had not followed willingly, Charlie might have been dragged through the thicket of moving bodies. Whenever she bumped into anyone, Martha would mutter, "Enshuldigen, bitte" and Charlie would grunt in polite agreement.

. . .

Charlie spotted Dana the instant he stepped inside the hotel lobby. Though disconcerting, the sight of her was unmistakable. From across the room, her face and limbs looked gray and disproportionately elongated as she sat slouched in a chair. Streams of slightly unkempt hair rained down over the shoulders of her black parka. A metal crutch angled up from the floor and rested across the arm of the chair. Something about her posture, perhaps the way her head tilted forward, suggested that she was in a trance. Charlie figured she wore VR goggles to disguise that fact. It wasn't like her to care much for television.

Martha whispered, "I'm going to leave you here, Mr. Redtree. She doesn't like to be interrupted while she has the goggles on, so I don't want to be the one. But I know how she's been looking forward to your coming. I would go ahead if I were you. Anyway, I need to get back up the hill. I'm on the program with a reading, toward the end of the rally. See you later."

She flitted out leaving Charlie to take stock of his situation. Some of the anxiety was gone now. Dana was found, miraculously it seemed, from amidst the overwhelming crowds.

Even though it was by most standards a busy place with people moving about, the hotel lobby was a haven of peace compared to the streets outside. People spoke more softly, moved more slowly and enjoyed a relatively generous share of space. Charlie walked gently across the room, took off his backpack and leaned it against an upholstered armchair just a few inches away from Dana. Both chairs faced a small television screen, so Charlie sat down as if he, too, had come in to watch.

The tv camera panned a huge audience and then focused on the face of a woman who stood on a raised platform before a microphone. He couldn't hear the words because the volume was muted. Apparently he was supposed to use the pair of headphones hanging over the arm of the chair. So much for his pretense of watching. Charlie wasn't interested enough to put them on. He didn't understand much about World Walk, and what he did understand frightened him. He had heard they were promoting world government, and Charlie didn't comprehend the need for tribal councils and city governments, let alone world ones. He didn't understand why poor people should give a damn about what big governments were doing. Still he knew World Walk couldn't be too bad. Otherwise Dana wouldn't have anything to do with it.

Charlie had even heard some of the Suquammish people were into this stuff. Grandma Redtree said to keep his eyes open for Dolores White Eagle, a tribal council woman who was supposed to be here. As if to oblige this thought, the camera panned the audience again. There were lots of dark round faces that might have been Dolores. Fat chance of running into someone he knew in this mob. Then he recalled his improbable luck at being found by Dana's friend, Martha. He shuddered to think of how it would feel to be at the rally site looking for Dana and she wasn't even there.

He looked over at Dana again. Even though her eyes were covered by the goggles, he could recognize that far-off look. No doubt she was in a trance prompted by the event; she was really getting off on it in her own strange way. He hated to interrupt her, but he was starting to feel bored. Besides, two men seated over near the door seemed to be watching him. Each time he glanced in their direction, Charlie found them staring back. At first, he began to wonder if he looked odd or something, but then it crossed his mind that the two looked remarkably like him. They must be Americans, because there was a distinct melting pot look about them. Both men wore khaki trousers and turtleneck shirts — like his own — and they represented such a varied gene pool that it would be impossible to determine their nationalities. The tall one with dark, wavy hair could have been anything, but the one with orange hair was surely at least half Anglo. At any rate, their mothers should have taught them not to stare. Charlie glared at them pointedly and looked away, but they didn't take the hint, and that was when he noticed other people giving him sideways glances, as if wondering what he was about.

The desk clerk, a young woman about Charlie's age, made direct eye contact with him several times, as if trying to tell him something. Maybe he should try to check in. He would need some place to spend the night. But before doing anything like that, he should talk to Dana. She might have other plans for him.

He reached over and gently tapped the long slender hand resting on the arm of her chair and spoke very softly, "Dana. It's me, Charlie."

At first there was no reaction, almost as if she were a mannikin or statue sitting there in the chair wearing VR goggles. Charlie waited a respectful amount of time and then reached over and ever so gently tried again. "Dana, it's me, Charlie," he whispered, tapping her hand.

This time the hand jerked up and yanked off the goggles. A radiant smile recalled the face from its distant trance. The long, slender fingers reached over, wrapped themselves around Charlie's large rough palm, and shook it vigorously. "It's great to see you, Charlie. I'm so glad you arrived safely. How did you find me?"

Charlie shook his head. "Beats me! Somehow this friend of yours found me in the street and brought me right to you — a nice little lady with big eyes."

"Martha."

"Yeah. That's her name. Can't figure how she found me."

"Martha's been looking for you. I told her to keep an eye out."

"How did she know what I look like?"

"I still have the drawing I made a couple summers ago, the one of you and Uncle Marvin sitting on the dock at Klahowya Cove. It must really look like you."

Charlie recalled the drawing. He had thought his face scary, like a photo he had once seen of an eagle ready to strike its prey. "Baloney! It does not look like me!"

"Martha recognized you. That's proof. But let's not sit around here and argue. Let's go sightseeing. There's lots to see. How long will you stay?"

Charlie shrugged. "Until the money runs out, I guess. But I was thinking it would be nice to go up to Scandinavia and look around there. I don't like it here. Too many people. Wouldn't you like to come up there with me?"

Dana shook her head emphatically. "I'm staying here until after the conference."

"That's eight weeks. My money won't last that long."

"It would if you joined World Walk. There's free food, and we camp out, instead of staying in hotels."

Charlie looked around the quiet lobby. The two men were still in the corner watching him. He felt uncomfortable. "If I'm going to stay in Bern," he said, "I'd rather get a room upstairs. I don't like it out there. The streets are so crowded — too many people." He hated to have Dana think him a party pooper, as usual, but he couldn't scare up much enthusiasm for the streets again. A body could barely move.

"Oh, come on Charlie! Don't be a stick-in-the-mud. I want to show you the Bear Pits, the fountains, the rose gardens, the clock tower...we'll go up to the square and I'll introduce you to my friends."

Charlie felt queasy about all this. It was nice to see Dana again, but, as usual, he wasn't up for her program. Maybe he should head on up to Scandinavia by himself and leave her here to do her own thing. Then he remembered what he came for. He was supposed to talk Dana into going home. The family were worried about her. They had invested their hopes, not to mention a few bucks, in him.

"Sure, Dana, sounds like fun. Let's go."

It was nearly dusk when Charlie followed Dana up the hill toward the government buildings. Even though she was using a crutch for support and had been walking all day, Dana still seemed graceful and lively. Charlie had begun to feel an old intimacy with her even though she acted sort of remote, like she might still be half in the trance, not really present.

The street was not nearly so crowded now. Perhaps this would be a good time to ask about the two men. The same ones he had noticed in the hotel lobby had shown up from time to time throughout the afternoon, always keeping a respectful distance but definitely following them.

Their presence felt eerie, like the time a cougar followed him on a hiking trip in the mountains. Most of the time he didn't see it, but every so often, there it would be, standing on a stump or a rock, eyeing him coolly. Only instead of one four-legged animal, this was a pair of two-legged creatures, who showed up sometimes together, sometimes separately. They weren't even being subtle about following, but, so far, Dana had given no indication that she noticed or cared. In fact, she was, at that moment, looking right past them as she babbled on like a tour guide. "When we get to the square up ahead, I'll introduce you to some of the famous walkers. I especially want you to meet Sabrina, a woman from Brazil who won the Nobel Peace Prize a few years back, and, of course, Rhona Lind. She led that climb I made up Mount Rainier."

"Are there any men in the group?"

"Why, yes. In fact, there's a guy who claims to be Nez Perce. His name is John Winter. You might have met him before. He used to go to those big gatherings you went to with Grandma Redtree. He's into native spirituality and things you like."

Charlie shook his head and wrinkled his nose. "I don't recall that name," he said, "but are you going to introduce me to the two guys who've been following us around all day?"

With that, Dana tossed her head back and released a long, feminine half-laugh, half-giggle. "I would like to, but I'm afraid I don't know them."

"Then why are they following you?"

Dana laughed again. "I presume they were hired."

"By whom? Why?"

She shrugged all too indifferently. "The government perhaps."

"Why?"

Dana didn't answer for a moment, and when she did, there was more than a trace of bitterness in her tone. "For my protection, I've been told."

Charlie thought about that for a moment. Then he said, "If every walker has two government bodyguards, no wonder there are so many people packed in this little one-horse town!"

Dana giggled with delight and trudged on up the hill so fast it was hard to keep up. Puffing slightly, he asked, "Do many of the walkers have this high level of government protection?"

"We all do, that is, at night in the camp." She seemed to be evading his question.

"I mean, do many of them have thugs following them around all over the place like spies?"

"No, not as far as I know."

"Why us, then?"

With that Dana suddenly stopped walking, reached both arms around Charlie in a clumsy hug. "To tell you the truth, I'm not really sure who those guys are. I'm sure glad you're here now to protect me. I've thought of asking them what they're about, but I'm too chicken. Would you do it for me?"

Charlie squirmed. "Not on your life, Dana, I don't like this place. I want you to come home with me. I think we should turn around and head back to the airport right now. We could take the next flight back to Seattle."

She laughed nervously. "What good would that do?"

"You'd get away from this scary place."

She shook her head and started to walk again. "It isn't this town that's scary. It isn't even the country or the continent. It's this world." With that she seemed to drift off into her half-trance again.

Charlie hastened to call her back. "You'll be safe back home."

"What makes you say that?"

"The family is there. They'll all help if you're in some kind of a mess. Those two guys won't follow you there."

"Don't I wish."

"Why would they follow you at home?"

"Why wouldn't they? It's no different than here. Besides, there's nothing to do at home. My life is here."

Charlie took hold of Dana's arm and stopped her from walking. "That reminds me of something important I was supposed to tell you.

Your dad has an idea about a job for you. You could start a halfway house or group home in the farmhouse on Levin Island."

Dana smiled. If Charlie had not known her better, he would have thought she was making fun of him. "It would have to be a group home. Levin Island isn't half-way to anything," she said.

Charlie got the joke. He grinned. "But it's a nice place," he said. "And I'm sure those two guys wouldn't follow you there."

"Why not? They could enroll in my treatment program; it might cure them of whatever's ailing them."

Dana was still laughing as they came in view of the market square, the sight of which made Charlie wish more than ever to turn around and head for the airport. Although he had never seen a real refugee camp, Charlie thought this must surely be one, what with armed guards stationed every few feet around the perimeter. Otherwise the scene reminded him of Native American festive gatherings he had been to back in the States. The place was crawling with activity. People walked around talking or gathered in circles to play instruments, dance, or sing. Some were putting up tents. A big poncho was laid out in front of one of the larger tents, and several women were sitting on it munching whole-meal sandwiches that looked like giant burritos.

It was getting pretty dark. A few dozen lampposts were hung with colorful banners and signs in several languages. In the center of the square was a huge awning where people seemed to be lining up for the sandwiches, each wrapped in its own thin layer of transparent bio-wrap. Charlie was glad Dana had already taken him to the Zum Rose so he wouldn't have to call this dinner.

Charlie followed Dana through the intricate maze of bodies and tents. She nodded and greeted people as she stopped to introduce him to almost everyone. They all responded with what seemed to be warm welcomes in a variety of languages. Everyone was extremely nice. It was incredible that people who had been camping out and walking around the world for months on end could be in such good spirits. A lot of them shook his hand, and a few insisted on hugging him.

His head was spinning by the time they reached the food serving table under the awning. There in the dim light, Charlie recognized the woman giving out sandwiches. "Charlie tells me you've already met," Dana told Martha. "Thanks for keeping an eye out for him."

"My pleasure. The tent's up now, in case you want to turn in, Charlie."

Charlie grunted agreeably. He wasn't sure how long it had been since he had taken off his backpack and stretched out in a horizontal position. He had caught a few winks on the plane, in the airport, in the electric car, wherever he could. He wasn't about to turn down the offer of any sleeping arrangements even though he would have preferred a nice clean bed at the Hotel Kroeniger.

"Sure," said Dana. "We'll go ahead and turn in."

"I'll join you soon," said Martha. "It's almost curfew anyway."

Their tent was way off in the far corner of the square, but Dana led Charlie directly to it through the maze of others just as though she had memorized its exact address. The tiny makeshift dwelling was waist-high, ice blue in color, and shaped like an igloo. One of the armed guards stood directly behind it, eyeing them coldly. If Charlie were not so tired, sleep would have been out of the question. "Where are our two henchmen?" Charlie asked Dana as he crawled through the entrance feeling the unforgiving cobblestones beneath his knees. Still on hands and knees, Charlie could make out in the near darkness, three sleeping bags laid out on pads. They really intended for him to sleep in this tiny space with two women and a guard posted outside.

"They don't follow me after curfew if I'm in the market place. No one can leave here after nine o'clock." Dana's voice filtered nonchalantly down through the roof of the tent.

"Which sleeping bag is mine?"

"The red one." It was a big red mummy bag. Charlie took off all but his T-shirt and shorts, stuffing each item of clothing into his backpack which he tucked under the mummy head for a pillow.

Dana crawled in through the opening and crouched on one of the other sleeping bags, watching him fondly. Still wearing her rain parka, she lay down on top of the bag without getting into it. From an all too slight distance came the sound of a live chorus singing some kind of folk song about one world with everyone living in peace. It was a soft, gentle song that might have made a good lullaby, but Charlie felt agitated now through his fatigue, and could not sleep.

He was still awake, twisting uncomfortably in his mummy bag when Martha crawled in. "You guys still awake?" she whispered.

"How the hell do you sleep in a place like this?" Charlie grumbled. The singers had drawn closer. It sounded like they were suspended above the tent.

"You get used to it," said Martha. "I think Dana is already asleep. I could sleep through a war, if I was tired enough."

It was already too dark to see what she was doing, but Charlie could feel her movement and hear her sleeping bag zipping and unzipping very close. "Good night, Charlie," she said aloud. After all, it wouldn't have made much sense to whisper what with the competition. "Oh, by the way, remind me to sign you up for the Walk in the morning. You're supposed to be on the register before you sleep in the encampment."

"But what if I don't want to be on the register? I don't even know if I agree with this World Walk stuff. I don't understand it really."

"Oh? Why not?" Martha's voice chirped at him in darkness. The singing outside had mercifully stopped, but distant chatter and intermittent laughter could still be heard.

Charlie propped his head up on his elbow. "Oh, I don't know. I think if you want to improve the world, you should start at home in your own backyard. Be community-minded. I don't get the point of running around the world trying to drum up bigger and better systems of international law. What's that got to do with people's everyday lives?"

Suddenly Martha's face was right in front of Charlie's. Her big round eyes seemed to glow in the dark. "Everything. World law has everything to do with people's everyday lives."

"Really? How so?"

Martha was sitting up yoga style on the sleeping bag. Her silhouette in the darkness resembled a small penguin in a soap ad with its upper body leaning slightly forward ready to take a dive. There was a clean, lemony smell about her. Charlie wondered how people stayed clean here. He had not yet seen a tap, let alone a tub or shower.

"Well, for instance," Martha was saying, "Multinational corporations are allowed to exploit child labor, pollute, and do all sorts of evil things that impact people's lives. Lucy's laws would require them to behave more responsibly. You should read her books."

"Really?" Charlie was doubtful.

"Yes, and Lucy's laws would reform international banking practices so they would have to support people's projects that are sustainable and really help poor people out of poverty all over the world. That would make a difference, not only in your neighborhood, but in thousands of villages and towns everywhere."

"Oh, I see," said Charlie. He didn't really see, but he was getting a headache. He rolled over into the opposite direction facing away from Martha, closed his eyes and looked into the darkness, but he could still feel Martha looking down at him. "Nevertheless," he said, "we want Dana to come home."

"Home? Where's that?"

"Somewhere in the northwest corner of the United States."

"So why is that home and not some other place? What's so special about it?"

"Nothing. Its so damp and chilly that moss grows on your bone marrow, but it's home."

"That's home to you. How do you know it's home to Dana? Maybe home is something or someplace else to her."

"You could be right," said Charlie. It was a useful phrase to weasel out of an argument. He had learned it in assertiveness training. Everything else about the class was long forgotten, even the teacher's name.

BERN SWITZERLAND ~ MAY 2000

The street lights were already on when Charlie came out of the public shower. There was a pink glow in the sky above the buildings across the street. He glanced at his watch and hurried toward the Bear Pits. That was where Dana liked to wait while he took his evening shower. He had been scared to leave her alone lately, what with her acting so distant and off in her own world. A couple of times, when he had been nagging her about going home, she had even brought up those old fantasies she used to talk about in high school, about being half-alien. Last night after curfew she even made a big "to-do" about telling him goodbye, and asking him to take her message of love to Pam and Jim, and say she was sorry for leaving. Charlie didn't know what to make of that. She had never talked about suicide before. God forbid Dana should end up a basket case like some of her old clients at Sullivan House. What was wrong with her anyway? She wasn't into drugs or anything. As he neared the Bear Pits, Charlie was relieved to see Dana still leaning over the railing with her weight on her elbows. Her backpack and crutch were propped against the bear pit wall. She looked half asleep, in a trance, no doubt.

Then, to his shock and dismay, Charlie noticed several armed guards standing opposite the pit staring at Dana and pointing their rifles. How could she look so relaxed under these circumstances? Her two inevitable baby-sitters were there too, the darker one seated in a doorway across the street and the redhead standing only a few feet away. All the tourists were gone now, except for the guy with the camera. He must live at the Bear Pits. The same guy had been there everyday when they came and when they left. He must be doing a study on the bears. Maybe he had an obsession for them, worse than Dana's. At the moment he was photographing several bears as they stood in line, gazing up at Dana. Charlie approached quietly and touched her arm. "Hey, Dana! Let's go! It's almost curfew."

Dana came to, as if from a dream, turned her head, and looked at him almost as though she didn't recognize him right away. Then she smiled absently and, Charlie thought, downright sadly. A chill went through him. "I'm sorry, but I won't be going back with you tonight," she said. There was an alarming finality in her tone. Charlie grabbed her wrist. "Are you kidding? I'm not going anywhere without you." She straightened to her full height and looked affectionately down

277

at him. Then she placed her other hand gently over his and led Charlie to a concrete park bench a few feet away. After they were seated, she squeezed his hand and said, "Charlie, I love you. You've always been a brother to me. That's why I wanted to spend some time with you before it was too late. But now I have to leave. Otherwise those guards over there with the guns might take me prisoner."

"Oh, come on, Dana! Why? You haven't done anything."

"They'll say it's the curfew, but that will only be an excuse."

"Why then?"

"Someone is afraid of me...of what I've done for World Walk."

"What have you done? Drawn a few pictures?"

She smiled and shook her head. "Of course not. It's what I've done with my mind."

Charlie stared at her, making eye contact. He didn't believe she was an alien, but she could do strange, magical things with her mind. "Dana, you shouldn't have done that! It's not right!"

She solemnly returned his gaze. "If World Walk were to succeed, it would have been worth it all." Suddenly she reached both arms around Charlie and hugged him as she had been prone to do lately. He realized she was crying. He could feel her body convulsing with little sobs, and her cheek was wet where it brushed his. This was disconcerting; now he needed to comfort her, when he most needed consoling himself. He was relieved when she pulled away and seemed to recover. "I'm sorry it has to be this way, Charlie. I wanted to communicate with you. I tried telling you. I even attempted to let you read my thoughts, but you weren't receptive this time. It's no surprise. All this is outside the realm of Earth human experience."

She stood up very deliberately, walked back over to the Bear Pit, and picked up her crutch. Even in her stretch pants and rain coat, she looked regal, like a shaman standing there, so tall, but lopsided, with her long dark hair streaming over the shoulder that was supported by the crutch. "I have to warn you now. I'll be leaving shortly."

"Leaving? Where? How?" The questions echoed in the confusion of his mind. Maybe he asked them aloud, maybe not. He could barely hear his own thinking, because of another sound, a hum, sort of like a meditation mantra, was coming from somewhere over his head or, perhaps, inside his head. He looked up and saw a light like a ray of sun reflected in a mirror. It was coming nearer. Now it was suspended above the three-story building across the street. The light vanished, and in its place, descending slowly toward them, was something out of a dream, something that could not be real, a transparent cylinder, barely visible, moving with no apparent navigational system.

The guards had just noticed it; the man with the camera was already trying to take its picture. The cameraman edged closer to the object, which was now suspended a few feet above the sidewalk, just an arm's reach from the Bear Pit. One of the guards was shouting "Watch out!" while another ran over and stood between the man and the object, maintaining a careful distance. The thing produced such a terrifying suction force that Charlie could feel from the concrete bench. Charlie was so frightened and distracted by the guards racing about and shouting, that he had forgotten about Dana for a moment. Suddenly, there she stood, right in front of the cylinder, well within the force of its powerful inhalation.

"Dana, get away!" he yelled. As she turned to face him, Charlie started to lunge for her like an awkward quarterback, but her facial expression stopped him. The jaw was firmly set, the eyes glazed with determination. Very deliberately, she backed up one step toward the cylinder, and within the slightest fraction of an instant, was inside, looking out, like a doll in a glass case. No! He wasn't ready for this; it must be a nightmare from which he would soon awaken! Charlie groped for the offensive vessel as it rose with immeasurable speed above his head.

One of the guards fired his rifle, but the shot rebounded from the object with a terrible "gong!" and shattered a window and a geranium pot on the third story of a building across the street. The other guards opened fire in rapid succession, turning the city street into a war zone. Staggering in shock and horror, Charlie fell backward and toppled over the bench onto the sidewalk. When he looked up again, there was no trace of the cylinder. Dana was gone, She had vanished, as if in a magic show, only she was not hiding in the wings waiting to take a bow. She was gone. Only her backpack remained, propped against the wall of the Bear Pit.

When the guards stopped shooting, Charlie walked over and picked up the backpack. Then he sat down and hugged it to his chest like a teddy bear.

BERN POLICE HEADQUARTERS ~ EARLY NEXT MORNING

It was ridiculous to suspect Charlie Redtree of having anything to do with the sudden disappearance of Dana Krandle from the streets of Bern. Even so, Aaron commended the police for locking him up. What else could they do? Aside from their own personnel and Aaron's, there was no one around, except for the bears, and the latter would make poor suspects. At any rate, Aaron was grateful to have Mr. Redtree in jail for the night. He wouldn't have to be rounded up for questioning, and Aaron intended to speak personally with everyone present at the scene. Aside from this round of testimony and the photographs, he had everything ready. All his files on the Krandle case were in the safe in his hotel room, a lifetime of careful research, meticulously organized, with photographs of everything from Dana's skull to her final ascent into the heavens.

The front page of major morning newspapers would resemble supermarket tabloids. Aaron wouldn't have to offer interpretations; the public would draw its own conclusions. Some would suspect Aaron of perpetrating an elaborate hoax, but that would not matter. His facts would never be disproved. The Bern Police gave Aaron a small interrogation room with a table and chairs to interview Charlie and the others. The walls were unadorned and without windows.

There was a defiant look on Charlie's face when the guard brought him in. He offered no resistance, though he was not handcuffed or restrained in any way. "This is Aaron Genzforth, an agent of your government. He wants to ask you a few questions," said the guard, in a kindly tone.

"Sure." Charlie grunted, then cleared his throat. Despite his proud demeanor, the poor fellow was clearly devastated. He slumped in his chair, drawn into himself. Aaron turned on his recorder and placed it on the table in front of Charlie. "Just to let you know, Charlie, this interview will be recorded."

Charlie eyed the machine suspiciously. "Don't I get a lawyer?"

"You don't need a lawyer. You aren't a suspect in this case. You're just being held for questioning. You witnessed an event last night in which a woman disappeared. The public will want an explanation."

"You can say that again! So do I!" exclaimed Charlie.

"So tell me, Mr. Redtree, what, from your perspective, happened last night at the Bear Pits?

Charlie made eye contact with Aaron momentarily, checking him out. "Well, it was freaky. It went by so fast, I'm not real sure I could get it right."

"That's okay. Do the best you can."

"Let's see. I went there to meet my cousin, Dana Krandle. She always liked to wait for me there while I was in the shower house. Believe it or not, she only showers once a week. The rest of the time, she and Martha wash with baby wipes." He glanced at the recording machine. "Who's going to hear this?"

"It's only for the investigators, but it is probably better not to digress too much."

"Sure. Well, Dana started talking again about how she was half alien, and how she'd be going back to the planet she came from. She used to talk that way when we were in high school. It was crazy, I thought, but I guess it wasn't, because last night she gave me a big hug and told me goodbye, and then a big, almost invisible thing — God, I don't know what it was — came down out of the sky and sucked her up. So I guess it was true. She's gone."

"All right, she's gone. Where do you think she is?"

"She's on her way to a place called Gallata."

"How do you know the name of the place? Did she tell you before she left?"

"No. She told me after she left."

"How?"

"She spoke to me in my head. She's telepathic. Believe it or not, Mr. Genzforth, if you get yourself in the right frame of mind — a trance, so to speak — Dana can read minds, things like that."

"How does she do that?"

"I don't know for sure, but I think she can broadcast brain waves somehow. I always thought she had a weird mind. Must be because she's part alien. Otherwise she always seemed pretty normal. A little thoughtless at times, but a fairly nice person."

"All right, tell me, Charlie, if Dana was, is, your cousin, how could she be an alien?"

"Now that's a damned good question. You're probably touching on some well-kept family secrets. But I think she must be adopted. My guess is her real mom was a lady named Wella De Gornia, and that lady must have been the alien. But it's all conjecture. I don't know much about this. You'd have to ask the Krandles."

He stopped suddenly and gasped, sucking in a big gulp of air. "They'd kill me if they knew I told you this. You won't tell them, will you? Besides, I don't know how much of it's true."

Aaron smiled. "It's okay, Charlie. We appreciate your telling everything you've guessed or heard about this case. It might help to get Dana back."

Charlie made ingenuous eye contact with Aaron. "You won't get her back, well, that is, not unless the aliens decide to bring her. I don't think they will."

"Why not?"

"Well, look at it this way, Mr. Genzforth. They must have been around here for some time keeping an eye on Dana, and they never let anyone know who or where they were. If these aliens were planning to reveal themselves, they would have done it already."

"Ah, that makes sense. You're pretty good at figuring these things out, Mr. Redtree. I was wondering if you'd mind giving your opinion on something."

"What's that?"

"Why won't the aliens reveal themselves?"

Charlie grinned. "That's obvious," he said. "Don't you go to science fiction movies?"

"No."

"Well, surely you must have heard some of the jokes. When the little green man comes up to the earthling, what's the first thing he says?"

Aaron thought a moment. "Take me to your leader."

Despite his sorrow, Charlie laughed. "You got it!"

"So?"

"So, who would you take him to?"

"My leader."

"Who? Which leader?"

Aaron thought another moment. "My boss, Wendel Morris, I suppose."

"Oh, come on. The little green man doesn't want to talk to the leader of the U.S. Investigative Services. He wants to talk to the leader of the world, and we don't have one. All we have is a bunch of maniacs grabbing territory from one another. It's always been that way. We earthlings don't have a civilization. We have a free-for-all, a demolition derby!"

Aaron turned off the recorder. "This is an interesting discussion, but we've gone pretty far afield from the investigation. You'll be released shortly after our talk. What do you plan to do then?"

"Go back up to the market square, and register for World Walk. I plan to become active in the movement."

"Really? I thought you just came here to visit Dana and take her home. Why are you joining World Walk?"

"They're promoting world government."

"Are you in favor of that?"

Charlie shrugged. "I don't know but, I promised my Uncle Jim to bring back his daughter, and the only way that will ever happen is if the aliens bring her back. When we get a world government, they'll probably be more willing to deal with us. Besides, there's a cute gal up there named Martha Parks who kind of likes me."

Aaron felt himself cringe. "If you ask me, the World Walk thing is total nonsense. It's all based on the premise that people will one day quit fighting and share with one another. It'll never happen."

"You could be right," said Charlie. "For instance we're having an argument now, and we're not likely to come to an agreement, are we?"

"No."

"But, let's suppose you could get inside my brain and I could get inside yours, and each of us could see the world from where the other guy sits, what would happen then?"

Aaron picked up his recorder and slipped it into his breast pocket. "I don't know. That's impossible anyway, so why discuss it?"

Charlie shook his head. "Dana could do it."

"But we can't. We don't have her brain chemistry."

"No. But Martha says Lucinda Watson developed a system that teaches groups of people, step-by-step, how to see the world from each other's view point. That's how she got the Maruvian Agreement."

"Bull shit! Dana's psychic mob control got Lucinda the Maruvian Agreement."

"Martha says Lucy did this kind of thing even before Dana came along."

Aaron laughed. "That's debatable."

"Maybe," said Charlie. "But, in any case, there's no stopping World Walk now, because of what Dana did to the collective consciousness. Their brain waves are all interconnected. It's contagious, and it's spreading."

"An insidious brain epidemic," snarled Aaron.

"You could be right."

ABOUT THE AUTHOR

A life-long activist for peace and justice, MONA LEE was born and raised in St. Louis, Missouri. She majored in English at St. Louis University and later earned a Master's Degree in counseling psychology from the University of Oregon. She has worked as a counselor in the United States and in Germany. Mona Lee lives in Seattle, Washington, where she works as a vocational counselor for people with disabilities. She is also involved in neighborhood community planning.